Praise for Katie MacAlister's
Aisling Grey, Guardian, Novels

Light My Fire

"Crazy paranormal high jinks, delightful characters, and simmering romance." —*Booklist*

"Once again Katie MacAlister knocks one out of the box with the third book in the Aisling Grey series. *Light My Fire* . . . takes you on a nonstop thrill ride full of sarcastic wit, verve, and action right to the end. Clear your day, because you will not put this book down until it is finished." —*A Romance Review*

"I simply adore Aisling. . . . Get on over to the bookstore and pick up your copy of *Light My Fire* today. You don't want to miss it." —*Romance Reviews Today*

Fire Me Up

"[A] wickedly witty, wildly inventive, and fiendishly fun adventure in the paranormal world." —*Booklist*

"MacAlister's ability to combine adventure, thrills, passion, and outlandish humor is fast making her a superstar. Unstoppable fun!" —*Romantic Times BOOKclub*

You Slay Me

"Smart, sexy, and laugh-out loud funny!" —Christine Feehan

"Graced with MacAlister's signature sharp wit and fabulously fun characters . . . wickedly sensual and irresistibly amusing." —*Booklist*

And praise for *Even Vampires Get the Blues*

"Cheerful mayhem and offbeat characters enliven another MacAlister gem. Witty banter that sparkles with humor and a plot that zips along make even the most outlandish situation seem perfectly reasonable. MacAlister is a rare talent." —*Romantic Times* (4½ Stars)

Other books by Katie MacAlister

Men in Kilts
The Corset Diaries
Hard Day's Knight
Blow Me Down
Even Vampires Get the Blues
The Last of the Red-Hot Vampires

Aisling Grey, Guardian

You Slay Me
Fire Me Up
Light My Fire

Katie MacAlister

Holy Smokes

An Aisling Grey, Guardian, Novel

A SIGNET BOOK

I'd like to thank the three men who kept me happy, amused, and relatively sane during the writing of this book: my friends Brian Murphy and Vance Briceland, and my husband, Michael.

SIGNET
Published by New American Library, a division of
Penguin Group (USA) Inc., 375 Hudson Street,
New York, New York 10014, USA
Penguin Group (Canada), 90 Eglinton Avenue East, Suite 700, Toronto,
Ontario M4P 2Y3, Canada (a division of Pearson Penguin Canada Inc.)
Penguin Books Ltd., 80 Strand, London WC2R 0RL, England
Penguin Ireland, 25 St. Stephen's Green, Dublin 2,
Ireland (a division of Penguin Books Ltd.)
Penguin Group (Australia), 250 Camberwell Road, Camberwell, Victoria 3124,
Australia (a division of Pearson Australia Group Pty. Ltd.)
Penguin Books India Pvt. Ltd., 11 Community Centre, Panchsheel Park,
New Delhi - 110 017, India
Penguin Group (NZ), 67 Apollo Drive, Rosedale, North Shore 0632,
New Zealand (a division of Pearson New Zealand Ltd.)
Penguin Books (South Africa) (Pty.) Ltd., 24 Sturdee Avenue,
Rosebank, Johannesburg 2196, South Africa

Penguin Books Ltd., Registered Offices: 80 Strand, London WC2R 0RL, England

First published by Signet, an imprint of New American Library, a division of Penguin
Group (USA) Inc.

First Printing, November 2007
10 9 8 7 6 5 4 3 2 1

Copyright © Marthe Arends, 2007
All rights reserved

REGISTERED TRADEMARK—MARCA REGISTRADA

Printed in the United States of America

PUBLISHER'S NOTE
This is a work of fiction. Names, characters, places, and incidents either are the product of the author's imagination or are used fictitiously, and any resemblance to actual persons, living or dead, business establishments, events, or locales is entirely coincidental.

The publisher does not have any control over and does not assume any responsibility for author or third-party Web sites or their content.

1

" 'I'm gettin' married in the morning! Ding-dong, the bells are gonna riiiiiiiing!' "

"Will you stop that!" I whapped Jim on its furry black shoulder, sending a quick glance across the small room to make sure no one had heard my demon in doggy form singing. "So help me god, Jim, if you let *anyone* catch you talking—"

"What was that, dear?" Paula, my stepmother, turned from where she was chatting to the others. "Where can he be? Did you need something? Oh, Aisling, no, sweetheart, a bride doesn't sit on her wedding day. Lean against the wall if you're tired. Does your dog need to go out to do its business? David, can you take the dog out? Although why you insist on having a dog as part of the ceremony . . . dog hair is impossible to clean up, everyone knows that. Oh, where can he be? It's half-past already!"

My stepfather, the personification of the absentminded professor stereotype, wandered over wearing his usual befuddled expression as Paula muttered to herself while brushing black dog hairs off my lovely gold and green lace dress.

"What dog?" he asked, clearly overlooking the gigantic black Newfoundland standing next to me.

I smiled fondly and patted him on the arm. "It's OK, Dad,

Jim doesn't need to go walkies. And I'm fine, too. We're both fine. In fact, I'm so fine, why don't you all go out with the others so you can at least enjoy yourselves? I'll just lean against the wall here and take a quick nap while I wait for Drake to show up."

"We couldn't leave you alone," Paula said on a horrified gasp. "That wouldn't be fitting at all . . . goodness, what would people *say*? And dresses wrinkle so badly nowadays. Girls these days just take everything so casually, not at all like it was in my day . . . where can he *be*? David? Where is he?"

"Who?" my stepdad asked, looking as confused as ever.

"The groom, of course. Drake. It's very bad luck for a groom to not show up for a wedding. Not that he's going to jilt you, my dear, heaven knows I'm sure that's the furthest thing from his mind. I wonder if he was in a car accident? People drive so fast here, and on the wrong side of the road, although I'm sure to them it's the right side, but still, they go so *fast*! Drake could be lying dead on the side of the road, and we wouldn't know it . . ."

Long experience with my stepmother had me shooting a look of utter desperation over her head to where my uncle stood in the corner, legs braced wide, arms crossed over his chest, a cigar clamped tightly between his teeth in blatant disregard both of the smoking laws and of the fact that we were in one of the oldest churches in London.

Uncle Damian, as ever, accurately read the plea in my glance and marched over to where my stepmother fussed around plucking and tweaking my dress.

"That's enough, Paula," he said in his usual gruff voice. "You go tend the guests. They'll be wondering what the delay is. And take your husband with you."

She looked toward the door leading out of the vestry to

the church proper, clearly torn between a desire to do her duty and remain at my side until my groom showed up, and the need to be social. "Well . . . I'm sure they are wondering what's taking so long . . ."

"I'll watch Aisling," Uncle Damian reassured her as he gave her a none-too-gentle shove toward the door. "David, escort your wife. Tell everyone that there's a slight delay, but the wedding will get going soon."

"I can't imagine what they're thinking . . . this wedding isn't at all what I would have arranged, although it's very nice, dear, with lovely flowers, and the bouquet is exquisite, but I would have made sure that people arrived on time . . ." As she left, she bumped into the rector scheduled to perform the ceremony, scattering apologies and vague half-finished sentences behind her.

"Go sit out in the first row, Dad," I said, giving my step-father another smile I felt far from feeling. "I'll be out there shortly."

"I'm sure Draco isn't dead," he said, patting my hand. "He probably just can't get his tie done. I had a devil of a time with mine. Your mother had to do it for me."

He toddled out of the room after Paula. I was tempted to send Jim along to make sure he arrived at the pew where my close family members were to sit, knowing full well he was capable of wandering off to who-knew-where, but Jim was currently in a giddy mood due to an extended weekend spent in Paris visiting Amelie, who owned the elderly Welsh corgi upon which Jim had a massive crush.

The rector spoke in undertones to Uncle Damian, shoot-ing me a sympathetic glance that contained more pity than reassurance before hurrying off to resume the watch for Drake.

"I don't hold with men jilting women at the altar," Uncle

Damian said abruptly, giving me a gimlet eye. A little jingling noise came from his pocket. He pulled out a cell phone, looked at the number, and said something about having to take the call.

"And I thought Drake's mom was bad," Jim said in a low voice.

I glanced over to my uncle, but he was across the room, grunting into the phone and barking orders to some poor underling.

"Your family takes the cake, though. Why didn't you tell me your uncle was Ernest Hemingway?"

I whapped Jim again. "Don't be facetious. He's not even remotely like Ernest Hemingway."

Jim cocked a furry eyebrow.

"Well . . . all right, there's a slight similarity. Very slight. Uncle Damian isn't a boozer and doesn't like to shoot innocent animals, although he was in the army and makes dark references to wanting to shoot a few of his superior officers. And I can't help my family—as far as that goes, Paula has been very good for Dad. He was lost when my mom died, and since I was only fourteen at the time, Paula was a godsend to us both. She drives me nuts sometimes with her ditziness and her endless chatter, but she's always been fond of me, and she takes care of Dad so I don't have to." I eyed the clock sitting on the rector's desk, trying to quell the butterflies that were threatening to twist my stomach into a knot. "I don't suppose it would do me any good to ask if you know where my errant groom is?"

Jim shook its head. "I'm a demon, not a seer. I told you we shouldn't have left home last night."

"I didn't really have a choice. Uncle Damian is a bit like a steamroller in that opposition just gets flattened before him, and my argument that his silly notion about brides having to spend the night separated from the groom was outdated and unrealistic didn't stand a chance. Besides, the hotel was pretty nice."

"That's not what I meant, and you know it," Jim answered, making a face.

I sighed and fretted with the lace on my wrist. "I know, but I'm doing the very best I can to hang on to my sanity. It hasn't been an easy month, you know, what with Fiat disappearing, and the red dragons continuing their war on us, and having to organize this wedding. I'd have gone stark raving mad if it hadn't been for Traci."

The moment the name left my lips, I realized what I'd done. I slapped a hand over my mouth but it was too late—the air in front of us shimmered for a second before collecting itself into the form of a middle-aged man of nondescript features.

"You summoned me, my lord?" the demon asked, its expression the usual one of mild annoyance.

I glanced hurriedly over to my uncle, praying he hadn't noticed the sudden materialization, but the determined way he snapped a good-bye into the phone before jamming it into his pocket and marching purposefully toward us pretty much killed that particular hope.

"Well, now you've done it," Jim said in a cheerful little voice. "Uncle Damian at twelve o'clock!"

"Jim!" I shouted, wrapping both my hands around its muzzle.

Uncle Damian's firm step hesitated for a second as he looked at Jim.

"Sowwy," was my demon's muffled reply from beneath my hands.

"I think you have some explaining to do, Aisling," Uncle

Damian said in his no-nonsense voice as he stopped in front of me, his steely eyes taking in all three of us.

I felt like I was ten again and had been caught using my uncle's Cuban cigars as miniature canoes in the toilet.

"Um," I said, trying to kick-start my brain into thinking up a brilliant explanation that would completely bypass the truth.

"My lord, would you like me to deal with this mortal?" Traci asked, a note of weary resignation in its voice.

"My *lord*?" Uncle Damian asked, a puzzled frown pulling down his bushy black eyebrows. "Who is this man? How did he just appear out of nothing? And just what the hell is going on with that monstrous dog of yours?"

I looked at Jim. Jim looked back at me and winked. A familiar black, warm presence nudged my awareness. *You can show him the true extent of your powers. You will have his respect for what you have become.*

"Shut up!" I snarled through gritted teeth, hurriedly adding, "Not you, Uncle Damian. I was talking to . . . er . . ."

"She hears voices in her head," Jim said succinctly. When I glared at it, it shrugged. "He'd already heard me talk. I think you're going to have to tell him what's going on."

"Which I wouldn't have to do if you'd kept your lips zipped like I asked!"

"Asked, but not ordered," Jim pointed out, trying hard to adopt an angelic air.

"A mistake I won't make again. No, Traci, thank you, I don't need you. I didn't intend to summon you. Er . . . how's everything in Paris?"

The demon's lips thinned. "Unpleasant."

"Good. I'll talk to you in a couple of days, as we planned. Bye-bye."

Traci opened its mouth to no doubt continue its protest at being put in charge of the European Otherworld, but I didn't have time to listen to its complaints, not today, not on what was supposed to be the happiest day of my life. I waved my hand at Traci, and the demon disappeared.

Uncle Damian's eyes narrowed. "What the devil is going on, Aisling? I want an answer, and I want it right now."

2

"Right, you want to know what's going on? I'll tell you what's going on." I took a deep breath, dreading what was to come.

"Uh-oh," Jim said, backing away from me. "You may want to get a little distance between you and Ash, Uncle Damian. When she freaks out, stuff happens."

"I'm not going to freak out. Not yet, anyway." I had hoped to keep the truth from my uncle, but I'd had a feeling all along that he wasn't going to buy the story Drake and I had concocted. I fixed him with a determined eye and said, "I'm a demon lord, a prince of Abaddon, which is more or less Hell. I didn't want the job, and I'm going to be trying like the dickens to get out of it without causing some massive rift whereby people from Abaddon can come into our world and wreak . . . well, hell. Jim is not a dog, not really. It's a demon I inadvertently summoned, although it's not really bad, it's kind of a former angel-like being who got sent to Abaddon and was kicked out of another demon lord's legion. And Drake is the leader of a dragon sept. I'm also a Guardian, which as you've seen, is kind of a demon wrangler. Got all that? Good. Now can we move on to the part of the day where I have a nervous breakdown because Drake hasn't shown up to marry me?"

I had expected questions, lots and lots of questions, and sadly, I wasn't mistaken.

"Demon?" Uncle Damian asked, looking at Jim.

"Yes. Sixth class, which is the least obnoxious of all demons."

"Hey! Standing right here!" Jim said.

We both ignored it.

"Demon lord?" my uncle asked, eyeing me from toes to nose.

"Yeah. It's kind of a long story, but I'm not bad either, because I'm really a Guardian, and those are the good guys."

"The demon lord stuff is just a hobby," Jim added from the safety of the other side of the room.

"Not . . . helping," I said through gritted teeth, waggling my eyebrows at it to let it know I was a few seconds away from commanding it to silence.

"Dragon?" Uncle Damian looked thoughtful as he glanced toward the door.

"Uh . . . yeah. Drake is a wyvern, actually. That's the leader of one of the dragon septs. He's a green dragon. He's very powerful, and very well respected," I added, knowing my uncle was big on respect amongst one's peers.

The explosion I was half expecting never came. Nor did the lecture, or the demand that I leave the church that instant and return home to Oregon with him. Instead, he continued to look thoughtful for a minute, then abruptly nodded his head. "Got it. Where's Drake?"

I gawked at him. I outright gawked, never a pretty expression, but there are times when nothing but a gawk will do. "You're not going to rant and rave and demand I leave Drake and Jim and everything? You're not going to tell me what I just said is impossible, and I must be insane? You're going to *believe* me?"

"Of course I believe you. You haven't given me a reason not to." He gave me a long, level look. "I've seen many things before that I've thought were impossible, so I've learned not to make judgments."

"But . . ." I waved my hands around. "It took me weeks to finally get to the point where I believed everything. *Weeks!*"

"You always were more rigid in your thinking than I thought wise," he pointed out.

"And you don't mind that I'm a Guardian? And marrying a dragon?"

He shrugged. "I assume by now you know what you're doing with your life. If you didn't want to be mixed up with all this demons and dragons strangeness, you'd leave."

"Well . . . yeah. I would." I was mollified that he respected my life decisions, but still surprised he accepted it all so easily. "Wait a minute—you threatened to disown me as a niece when I got married the first time. Why are you being so tolerant and understanding now?"

"Drake isn't that mealymouthed twit you married when you were eighteen. He's a man." Uncle Damian frowned again. "At least he looks like one."

"All the dragons use human forms—it's much easier than stomping around with wings and a tail and such," I said absently. "I agree that Drake is miles above my first husband, but I'm a little surprised you've taken to him so quickly. You were only in the house for half an hour before you dragged me away to the hotel."

"A smart person knows how to size up potential competition in less than a minute," he answered, giving me another level look. "And since I see you're going to ask, no, I don't consider him competition, now that I know the truth about him. I had suspicions when you said he dealt with imports and exports, but this changes the situation."

"Well . . . good."

"Besides, you love him. It's written all over your face when you look at him, and since I could see he's just as in love with you, I decided not to interfere."

I knew my uncle would like Drake when he had gotten to know him, but I hadn't expected him to accept the fact that we were getting married quite so quickly or easily. I couldn't help but smile just a little at the faint note of disapproval in my uncle's voice when speaking of love. "Yeah, we're crazy about each other. I'm glad you're go with Drake and me. I guess that leaves me free to have that nervous breakdown now, huh?"

"Don't be ridiculous. No niece of mine has ever been a weakling, and you're not going to start being one now. What about a cell phone? I'm assuming Drake has one?"

Jim came back over to me and leaned on me, wordlessly begging for attention. I mopped up his chops with his drool bib, adroitly whisking out a fresh one from the bag I'd brought into the room with me, tying it around its neck.

"Yes, he has one, although he's not answering. I . . . er . . . tried calling him when you thought I was going to the bathroom." I made a nervous gesture with my hands. "I didn't want anyone to know I was checking up on him. But now I'm just getting worried. Drake wouldn't back out of the wedding. If he's not here, it's because something has happened to him, and . . . well, one of the other dragon septs is at war with us, and it's possible they've done something to him. Or Fiat has. He's another wyvern, a particularly nasty one who has caused trouble for us more than once."

"Don't forget Gabriel," Jim offered helpfully.

"Gabriel is another wyvern," I told my uncle. "He's . . . I

dunno about him. But I don't think this is something he'd do."

"Could be Bael," Jim said. "That's the head demon lord, the premiere prince of Abaddon, and the guy who got Aisling to kill another demon lord so she could take his place."

"It sounds as if you've been having an interesting time here," my uncle said slowly.

Jim grinned. "You could write books about it."

"Hardly," I said, pulling its drool bib tighter before rustling through the bag for my cell phone. "I'll try Drake again. Maybe he's just stuck in traffic?"

The distant noise of London seeped in through the high windows as I punched the speed-dial number, listening through seven rings before Drake's voice clicked on. *"I am away from the phone. Please leave a message following the tone."*

"No answer," I said, my stomach now one giant leaden ball. Tears welled behind my eyelids as, deep within me, I knew something was wrong.

"Aw, Ash," Jim said as I blinked rapidly, trying to dispel the tears before they were visible to others. The demon leaned its big head against me, offering comfort in the only way it could. "Drake's been around the block a few times. He's been at war with Chuan Ren before, and he didn't succumb. He's probably just beating the crap out of a few red dragons before heading to the church."

"I know. I'd feel if he was . . ." My hands fluttered around in a wordless expression of the unthinkable. "Besides, brides are allowed to cry on their wedding day."

"You're not a normal bride," Uncle Damian said abruptly, shoving a box of tissues at me. I took a couple, dabbing at my eyes, wanting like crazy to give in to the emotions of the moment, but knowing it wasn't wise.

You don't have to give in to it, a smooth, dark voice spoke into my head. *Why submit when you can dominate? You have the power, Aisling Grey. Use it to ensure your mate's safety.*

"Shut up!" I snarled, dabbing viciously at the tears that spilled over my eyelashes.

"The voices?" Uncle Damian asked Jim while giving me a wary look.

"It's the dark power. It talks to her."

"Dark power?"

"You don't want to know," I said, sniffling as I tried to keep the tears from ruining the makeup job my stepmother had spent so much time on to ensure I was presentable. My eyes were awash, an uncomfortable feeling. I tried to fix the problem but ended up just making things worse. "Oh, hell. I think I just lost one of my contacts. No one move!"

I squatted, careful not to brush my dress against the floor, feeling around for the contact lens. Jim snuffled around as well.

"Found it. Whew." I stood up with the contact on one finger, smiling weakly as I reached for my bag.

A horrified gasp had me freezing on the spot, the bottle of lens cleaner in my hand as my uncle lifted my chin to look closer at me. "What the hell happened to your eye? And . . . is that blood?"

I wadded up the tissues I'd been using to wipe the tears. "It's only temporary. I think. I . . . oh, it's a long story, too long to tell here. The end result is that I've been proscribed, and one of the side effects of proscription is that your eyes change, and you cry blood."

"Proscribed? Isn't that another word for damned?"

"I thought so, too, although I gather it's just one step on

the road to damnation. There's supposed to be a way to get
out of it, but so far we haven't had any luck trying to figure
out how to reverse the process. Physically, it's no big deal,
although the white eyes look a bit freaky, so I've been wearing tinted contacts so people don't get the willies around me
until we figure out how to get the proscription lifted."

It took him a moment to process all that, but process he
did. He nodded his head and issued a curt, "Smart."

"We thought so." I cleaned the contact, using my purse
mirror to pop it back into place. I had just dabbed away the
last traces of blood when the door opened.

". . . and I said it wasn't smart to do the planning all by
herself, when I was at her disposal. But you know how girls
are these days, Reverend Miller . . . headstrong, always so
headstrong, and particularly so with Aisling. Oh, my dear,
where *is* he?" Paula took my hands in hers, giving my fingers a little squeeze. "It's an hour past time, and Reverend
Miller says there is a christening in a half an hour!"

"I'm very sorry to have to rush you," the rector said, a
look of genuine distress on his face. "It's the McKenzie
triplets, you see. Mr. McKenzie is the drummer in that extreme rock band, the one that bites off the heads of chocolate bats. They are here now, ready to set up for the press,
and . . . well, I'm truly sorry, but Mr. McKenzie is most in-
sistent that the baptism go forward."

"Of course," I said, making a quick decision. "I'm just
sorry we've delayed you this long. Please tell him we'll be
out of your hair in a few minutes. Jim, heel. *Silently.*"

My demon shot me a look that acknowledged it recognized an order when it heard one, although I knew I'd pay
for that later.

"Oh, Aisling, this is terrible, just terrible. Damian, where
is he? Isn't there something we can do?"

I left my stepmother wringing her hands and wailing to Uncle Damian as I marched out to the front of the church. I took a deep breath; the church was heavy with the usual scents of wax and wood polish, topped off with a heady note from the white roses that dotted each pew. The conversations from approximately three hundred people died as everyone looked with expectation at me. I smiled nervously, picking out a few familiar faces in the crowd. Only a handful of my family had come to London for the wedding—my stepparents, uncle, and twin cousins who were on their way back to the US after a year spent working at a commune in Italy. A few of the dragons were known to me, but most were there just as a courtesy to Drake.

"Oy! Get a move on!" called someone at the back of the church, where a crowd of people with elaborate hair and Gothic clothing milled, clearly the rock star and his party.

"Sorry. Hi, everyone. We . . . er . . . we have a bit of a problem, and I'm afraid I'm going to have to cancel the wedding today. Drake has been unavoidably detained, and the church is needed for a celebrity christening. I want to thank you all for coming today, and say how sorry I am that things didn't get off the ground, but we'll try to do this again . . . er . . ." I glanced to my left, where the rector stood. "Do you have time tomorrow?"

He thought for a moment. "I could give you an hour in the afternoon. Shall we say three?"

"Yes, thank you. Three o'clock tomorrow, everyone. I will completely understand if you can't make it, but those of you who can are welcome to attend."

The hum of conversation started up the second I stopped, my cousins immediately swarming me with questions and platitudes. I told them I'd explain later, shooing them on their way as another familiar figure stopped in front of me.

"*Mon amie,* you look very charming in that dress. But what is the matter with Drake?"

"Rene, it's good to see you." I smiled as he hugged me. "Where's your wife?"

His eyes smiled right along with the rest of him. "Ah, she suffers from the allergies of the nose, do you remember? It is an infection of sinus she has now, and it is giving her much grief. She is much distraught at having to miss your wedding, but it looks as if that is a moot point, no?"

"I'm sorry she's sick. And yeah, things have kind of fallen apart. You haven't . . . er . . . *heard* anything about Drake, have you?"

Rene's smile faded a little. "It does not work that way, you know?"

"I know. I just thought since you were evidently assigned to me and all, you might know what's up with Drake. I mean, this does have an impact on my future, so I thought it would fall under the whole fate thing."

"I'm a daimon, Aisling, not a soothsayer. That simply means I am to present myself to you when you need a helping hand. I cannot see into the future any more than you can."

"I'm sorry. I shouldn't have asked, but I'm a bit worried about Drake, what with Chuan Ren still out for blood."

He patted my hands. "I understand, but Drake, he is a dragon most formidable, no? He will not be harmed easily."

"I know, but . . . Oh, I'm just being emotional."

He did the hand pat again. "We shall go look for him, and that will ease your concerns."

"I guess. Don't tell me you've managed to round up another taxi?"

"Not this time." He chuckled. "I have borrowed the car of

my cousin Felix. I will wait outside for you to finish with your family."

"Thanks, Rene."

A couple of the green dragons came up and asked if there was anything they could do. I thanked them, apologized for the delay, and accepted their promise to pass along any word of Drake, after which they left quietly. It took a good ten minutes for my family to help the wedding planners pick up all the decorations, leaving me exhausted, sick with worry about Drake, and still stinging from the blistering the rock star gave me as he yanked down my bundles of white roses and satin ribbons.

"Have you ever wished you could hit a rewind button and start the day over?" I asked Paula as we trudged down the steps to the street, Uncle Damian having gone off to make sure the wedding planner people were simply storing the decorations and not throwing them out.

"Goodness, no! I don't use those remote controls. They have so many confusing buttons. David knows how to use them. Don't you, dear? How they expect people to remember what everything does is just beyond me. You shouldn't have to be a rocket scientist to turn on *Wheel of Fortune.*"

I stopped at the bottom of the stairs, my heart lightening at the sight of the woman there. "Nora!"

Jim rushed to where my former mentor stood, her familiar warm brown eyes shining behind bright red glasses. I knew she didn't want to have anything to do with me since I'd been proscribed, but I couldn't keep from excusing myself and running over to her, enveloping the smaller woman in a big hug. "I'm so glad you came. I knew you said you weren't able to, but . . . oh, Nora, I'm so glad to see you again. How are you? Pál said you found a new flat and were all settled in, but . . . well . . ."

"I shouldn't be here," she said softly, not meeting my eyes as she gently disengaged herself from my embrace. Jim, ordered to silence, rubbed its head on her leg. She patted the top of its furry head absently. "There would be all sorts of trouble if the Guild found out I'd come, but I thought I would just sit at the back. You look well."

I bit my lip to keep the tears from forming again. Nora had been driven away from teaching me by the proscription, fearing a continued close association would lead to her powers being tainted by me. I'd known that couldn't happen— the dark power was very clear it was me it wanted—but I respected her decision to leave, even though it had felt like I was losing my best friend.

"We're OK. Did the Guild reinstate you?"

"Yes."

"Good." People streamed by us on the sidewalk, traffic doing likewise on the busy street. It was incredibly awkward standing there with her. I could tell by the way she wouldn't meet my eyes that she was just as uncomfortable as I was. "Oh, for heaven's sake, this is ridiculous. Paula, tell Rene I'll be right there. I just want to have a word with my friend."

I grabbed Nora's arm to keep her from escaping and pulled her after me around to the side of the church, into a small yard area where the garbage cans were stored off the street. "Sorry, but there's so much I want to say to you, so much that's happened in the last month, but Drake told me not to stand around on the street in case Chuan Ren's men were lurking about. Can we get together a little later? Maybe have a coffee or something? I'd really love to have a long talk with you."

She took a step back, still looking at her hands. "I'm sorry, Aisling, that wouldn't be prudent for either of us."

I swallowed down a painful lump, nodding despite the

fact that I wanted to yell and scream and generally have a good old-fashioned hissy fit. I was a professional, dammit. I might be proscribed, but I was a Guardian, and a wyvern's mate, and a demon lord. And although it broke my heart to lose Nora as a friend, I'd do what it took to go on.

"I understand. It was nice seeing you. I miss talking to you."

"As I do you." She glanced up, meeting my gaze for a moment. I was shocked to see the sadness in her eyes. "I should be on my way. I just wanted to wish you well and offer my congrat—"

A wave of rust-colored bodies exploded from nowhere, most likely the alley that ran alongside the church, but wherever they came from, they had the element of surprise on their side.

"Good god, what the—Jim! Help!"

The small foxlike creatures leaped straight for me, knocking me back against the stone wall of the church. Jim, obeying my command, snarled silently and lunged at the nearest creature. "What the hell . . . what are these?" I yelled, frantically drawing a protection ward in front of me with one hand while trying to beat off the fox things with the other.

Nora didn't hesitate, immediately going into full Guardian mode as she drew wards, her hands dancing in the air as she sent creature after creature back to Abaddon. "They are huli jing."

Whatever they were, they had sharp little needle teeth that tore at the flesh of my hands as I flung them off me. My hands were slick with blood as Jim snatched as many as it could, shaking its head to snap their necks.

"Huli jing, huli jing. Let's see, those are . . ." I dug

through the information in my mind, trying to sort out the bit of information I needed. "Chinese fox spirits!"

"They are susceptible to fire," Nora yelled as she waved a hand and chanted a quick spell that summoned up a fireball which wiped out a half dozen of the little spirits.

Automatically, I reached for Drake's fire, but it wasn't there.

Use me, the dark voice spoke into my head.

I ground my teeth and ignored it, flashing another binding ward on the nearest demon. The huli jing weren't large, about the size of a large squirrel, but their bites hurt. "Dammit! Ow! Jim—thank you."

Use me to end this.

"Over my dead body," I swore under my breath.

Your death would serve no purpose. You must use your full powers, Aisling Grey. Show the world what you are capable of. Use me now.

Jim snarled and lunged as three huli jing went for my throat.

Inside me, the dark voice was teasing a response from me, an almost overwhelming need to use it. I knew how powerful it could be—just channeling it made me feel invincible, righteous, an instrument of justice.

You can do anything with me, Aisling Grey. You could rule Abaddon, rule the Otherworld. Your heart's desire is within your grasp—all you need do is reach out and take it.

I grunted as a small herd of huli jing slammed into me, my hands flashing as I drew wards to protect myself. They glowed golden in the air for a moment before dissolving to nothing.

You could destroy them all with just a wave of your hand. Use me.

"Fire, Aisling, use the dragon fire," Nora ordered, releasing another fireball as another wave of huli jing descended upon us.

"No!" I screamed, trying to shut the voice out of my mind, but it was useless. A person I could keep from my awareness, but not the dark voice, not while I was proscribed.

Nora shot me a quick, startled look before lifting both hands in the air, bringing them down with a thunderclap that sent Jim and me flying backwards into the wall, the deafening noise making my ears ring.

"What . . . good god, what did you do?" I asked a few seconds later, as soon as my wits returned. I used Jim to haul myself to my feet, looking around with astonishment to note that all the fox creatures had disappeared.

"I banished them. Are you bleeding?" She spoke the last word as if it was inconceivable.

I touched the spot on my head that had collided with the edge of the large square garbage bin, not surprised to see that my fingers came away red. "Yeah, but it's OK, I'm not hurt badly. Just a little cut."

A group of people charged around the corner to the alley, a couple of strangers and my family all asking questions about the loud noise.

"It's nothing. Just . . . er . . . I accidentally slammed a brick into the garbage bin," I yelled down to them, pointing at the large square object. "Sorry to startle everyone."

Rene stepped forward, his eyes moving from the cut on my face, to my dress, to Nora. He nodded and said something to my stepparents before herding them back toward the street. Uncle Damian was thankfully nowhere to be seen.

"You shouldn't be hurt at all, not from a banishing," Nora said with a frown. "Aisling, I know we are no longer mentor and pupil, and thus you do not owe me any explanations, but why did you refuse to use fire to destroy the demons when I asked? Destroying them that way would have caused much less notice than using a group banishment."

My lovely lace dress was filthy with blood and muck from the alley, torn in several places where the huli jing had attacked, and pretty much destroyed as a wearable garment. I sighed and yanked off one chunk of it that had been torn, using it to mop up the blood that was streaming down my face from the cut on my head. "I didn't refuse. I can't use Drake's fire anymore. Not since that night."

Her eyes went to mine, her lips thinning. "The proscription?"

"No. Fiat and his damned meddling. I can't use Drake's fire anymore because I'm no longer his mate," I answered, limping over to pick up my sandal. The heel on it was broken. I put it on regardless. "I'm afraid the only power I have is my own."

Not true. You have me. I will make you strong again.

I gritted my teeth.

"Big bad talking to you again?" Jim asked.

"Yes."

"Big bad?" Nora asked, looking slightly startled.

"The dark power talks to Ash. She gets testy when it does."

Her eyes widened behind the lenses of her glasses. "It . . . it *talks* to you?"

"Um . . . maybe. Sometimes. Not all the time, just now and again."

She backed up a couple of steps, a look of horror on her face. "Aisling—that is not normal. The dark power is not a living being. It cannot speak."

She does not know anything about me. She has no idea of what abilities you have with me, of what future you could write, the voice said. I closed my eyes for a moment, suddenly exhausted, overwhelmed with the events of the day and the constant battle I fought to keep from using the dark power. I swayed slightly as part of my mind urged me to give in to the hypnotic lure the voice held out in front of me. I wasn't a bad person; I wasn't evil. Couldn't I change the power from bad to good?

You can do anything you want.

Jim touched its cold, wet nose on the back of my hand, bringing me back to reality. "Aisling?"

I opened my eyes and straightened up, squaring my shoulders. "I'm OK. Get my purse, will you?" I limped over to Nora and bit my lip. I wanted to hug her, to thank her for saving me. "Nora, I don't know what to say. Thank you for everything."

You can save yourself, you know. You've done so in the past. You are not weak.

"And thank you for coming to the wedding. I just wish there had actually been a wedding for you to see."

You do not have to subordinate yourself to her. She has little compared to you.

"Lastly, thank you for being my friend, even though I know things are difficult right now."

It doesn't have to be that way. You can change your life to whatever you want. Right the wrongs, Aisling Grey. Be what you were meant to be.

"Aisling . . ." Nora took a step forward, one hand extended as if she was going to take mine, but she stopped, her eyes filled with pity. "I'm so sorry. I blame myself for this. If I'd had the time to warn you . . . but hindsight will do no good now. I must be off. The Guild will not be happy to know I was here in the first place, and I mustn't linger. My best wishes to you and Drake."

Hot, painful tears started up again behind my eyes as a wave of self-pity washed over me. Dammit, it wasn't fair!

Make it right. Fix it.

"I won't give in to you," I said softly, dragging my mind from the knowledge that the voice was right—using it, I could do anything. "I am a Guardian. I protect people. I am not an instrument of vengeance. I'm *good*, dammit!"

"Yes, you are," Nora said softly, reaching for me again, her hand stopping a hairsbreadth from mine. "And that is why you are able to withstand the dark power. Keep fighting, Aisling. Don't let it win. Don't take the easy road. Be what you were meant to be."

That's all I ask, the voice cooed. *Be what you were meant to be.*

3

"Well, lookie what the cat dragged in," Jim quipped as the door to Drake's study was thrown open with enough force to make the pictures rattle on the wall. "Hmm. No blood, no signs of a fight . . . not good, man, not good at all. You should at least have made it look like you guys had been roughed up. You might have scored some sympathy points that way, but looking like you stepped off the cover of *GQ* isn't going to win you any friends."

"Be quiet, annoying one," I said, my heart doing its usual somersault at the sight of the dragon of my dreams.

Drake stormed into the room, his jaw tight, his eyes blazing. The pupils were narrow elongated vertical slits set in emerald that glittered a warning to all that the man behind the eyes was more than he seemed.

"Your eyes are all dragony. I take it— Oh, hello. I'm sorry, it was a false alarm. He just came home. Thank you for checking the emergency ward." I clicked off the phone, sliding off the top of the desk to face the furious man in front of me. "I take it that there was a problem?"

Drake's eyes narrowed as he eyed the bandage on my forehead. "You look like hell."

"Oh, man. This is so not going to end well," Jim said, putting a paw over its eyes.

"Out!" I ordered, pointing to the door. In the hallway beyond, Pál and István, Drake's two red-headed bodyguards, were visible talking to Uncle Damian. "Yes, that's an order. Go afflict yourself on someone else."

"What happened?" Drake asked, touching the bandage.

I leaned into him, wrapping my arms around his waist, breathing deeply to absorb that wonderful spicy Drake scent that simultaneously made me feel safe, and want to rip off all his clothing and have my way with him. "Oddly enough, I was about to ask you the same thing."

"You answer first. I have not been injured. What happened to you?"

"Demon attack. Nora was there and banished them. I hit my head on a garbage can, that's all. Oh, the wedding is rescheduled for tomorrow at three. Your turn—where were you?"

Drake pushed me back off him, his hands quickly running over my body, obviously in an attempt to check for injuries.

"That would be a whole lot more fun if we were both naked, but since we aren't, and since you haven't answered my question, you can stop now," I told him, slapping at his hands as he felt my rib cage.

His frown was a thing of beauty to behold—beautiful in its fierceness, that is. No one could frown quite like Drake. I think it was a combination of that square jaw, the long, thin nose, the black hair sweeping back . . . or maybe it was his eyes, those fascinating green eyes that were never quite human, the slightly elongated pupils giving his eyes an exotic, foreign appearance that always fascinated me.

"Have you seen a doctor?" he asked, his hands ignoring mine to settle on my belly.

"No, there was no need to. It's just a small cut on my head."

"The baby could be hurt. I will call a doctor." He leaned over to grab the phone.

I snatched it up before he could get it. "The baby is not hurt. *If* there is a baby, and we're not sure there is, so please stop with the overprotective stuff."

"The pregnancy tests came back positive," he answered, trying to pry my fingers off the phone.

"Two did. The other two said I wasn't pregnant." I curled my fingers tighter around the phone. Drake had always been a protective sort of guy, but he'd gone into overdrive with the possibility of a baby.

"It's been three months. We know. You're pregnant," he answered, his frown growing darker as he realized he couldn't get the phone from me without hurting my hand.

"It's been two and a half months, and the doctor said the demon lord stuff was messing up the test results. We're just going to have to wait and see what the ultrasound shows."

"You will have that now rather than wait until your appointment next week," Drake ordered in his bossy voice.

I smiled. Dear god, how I loved him, annoying ways and all. "All right."

"I know you had the appointment arranged for after our trip to Paris . . . all right?" His brow cleared. I giggled at his look of surprise.

"Yeah, I was a bit stressed when I made that appointment. I think it's going to be better for us both if we know for certain sooner rather than later. I'll try to get them to move it up to this week, OK?"

"Now," he said, trying to tug the phone from my hand.

"After the wedding," I answered, my grip and intentions resolute.

He pursed his lips. I licked them.

"Immediately afterwards."

I thought for a few seconds. The reception was scheduled to follow the wedding, but since the hotel ballroom was booked for earlier today and not tomorrow, our chances of having that were nil. I sighed. "It's not a horribly romantic way to end a wedding, but I'll try to get the appointment for tomorrow afternoon."

"I think it's romantic," Drake answered, desire making his eyes go molten as he pulled me up against his body. "We have made a child together. I greatly enjoyed the creative process."

"Well, put that way, I suppose it is . . . go on, say it. You haven't yet today, and you know the rule—I have to hear it once a day until you can say it without making a big drama over it."

Drake sighed an exaggerated, much-put-upon sigh, although I noticed his hands were busy groping my butt. He growled low in his throat, a sound that never failed to make my toes curl with delight. "What if I were to breathe fire on you instead, *kincsem*?"

"How about you do both?"

His lips touched mine, teasing, tasting, sending me into a near frenzy of desire as I opened myself up to his dragon fire. His kiss was as fiery hot as the dragon fire that surrounded us, burning around our bodies in a spiral of flame that would have set off the smoke detectors if Drake hadn't had this room specially fireproofed.

Drake's tongue got all bossy with mine, as it was wont to do, something I tolerated with extreme pleasure. As kisses went, it was at the top of the scale, his body moving seductively against mine to the point where I was considering how long it would take to engage in wild, sweaty bunny sex on the floor of the study. But there was something missing from the kiss, something that I'd taken for granted until it was gone, something that I hadn't realized I would miss so much when it was denied to me.

I couldn't share his dragon fire. He could heat me up from the outside with it, as he was now, but it was the sharing of his fire that had bound us so intimately, the fire doing more than just giving me energy—it had woven itself into my being, an element that was part Drake, part me, one that was unique to us. Without it, I felt . . . unfinished.

I kissed him with all the passion I had. He tasted as he always did—hot and spicy, like he'd been drinking dragon's blood, a potent spiced wine that was favored by the dragons, and which could be fatal to mortals. Reluctantly, I pulled away from him, my heart aching for all that we'd lost. "Why did you have enough time to have a drink, but not to marry me?"

"István had a flask with him," Drake murmured against my neck, his lips branding a hot trail of fire over to the spot behind my ear that made my legs go weak. "The police gave it back to him when they released us, and we had a pull on it in the car on the way home."

I pulled back so I could look at him. "Police? You were arrested? Why?"

The passion in his beautiful eyes faded to a hard glint that made me shiver . . . and not with excitement. "Chuan Ren."

"Goddamn it! She had you arrested?" I grabbed the lapels on Drake's tuxedo, realized what I was doing, and smoothed out the wrinkles. "Why is she still doing this? I thought you took care of her silly legal wranglings when you went to Budapest last week."

"I stopped her attacks on the holdings of the sept members in Europe, yes. But somehow, she managed to manipulate a judge here and had warrants issued for the arrest of Pál, István, and myself on trumped-up charges of terrorism."

"Terrorism? *You*? That bitch!" I stormed around the room, so frustrated I wanted to scream.

Why be frustrated? If you use me, you can—

"Shut up!" I bellowed as I stomped past the desk.

Drake cocked an eyebrow but knew I wasn't addressing him.

"Sweetie, I know you're doing everything you can, but you have to stop this war with the red dragons. If Chuan Ren has the sort of power to get you arrested on your wedding day, then who knows what else she can do! I'm sure those huli jing were sent by her today—they're Chinese fox spirits, and I can't think of anyone else I've pissed off enough lately to set demonic beings after me."

"You were on the street?" Drake asked, frowning.

"Not for long. Nora was at the wedding—what was supposed to be the wedding—and I couldn't let the opportunity to talk with her slip away, so I dragged her around to the back of the church, out of sight of the street. I don't know how the huli jing found us, but that is really a moot point. We can't continue to live our lives in perpetual fear that the red dragons are going to attack us at any moment! We've got to stop the war once and for all! We can't let it go on as long as the last war you had with them—that was, what, thirty years or something?"

"Forty-three."

I put my hands on my hips. "This last month has been hell, what with the assassination attempts, you having to fly out to Budapest every couple of days, and all the other crap Chuan Ren is throwing at us. It has to stop, Drake."

Drake sat on the edge of his desk, his eyes distraught.

Immediately, I was filled with remorse for railing at him when he was doing his best to end the war between the septs.

"Oh, sweetie, I'm sorry," I said, rushing over to stand between his legs, wrapping my arms around him. "I know you're doing everything you can, and I'm not blaming you one little bit. You've worked miracles these last couple of weeks, keeping Chuan Ren from destroying the sept businesses and homes and such. And everyone is grateful for the guards you've sent—Tamas from Germany said earlier today that they'd caught two red dragons trying to set fire to their house, and they would have been goners if the guards weren't there. So I'm not holding you responsible at all for the fact that Chuan Ren is a lunatic who will do anything to destroy us— it's just . . . if I am pregnant . . . I just don't want . . .".

"I know, *kincsem.* I do not want a child growing up in the middle of a war, either," he said, holding me tight as I gave in to the emotions of the day and had a little cry on his shoulder. "If it is within my power to stop the war, I will do so."

"Our power," I said, my voice muffled against the cloth of his tux as I hiccuped the end of my tears. "We will stop it. We work together now, remember?"

He kissed the top of my head and said nothing. I smiled into his shoulder, relishing both the feeling of protection he offered and the maddening frustration that was inevitable whenever he tried to keep me from becoming involved in something dangerous.

"Oh, crap," I said, pulling away from him. "Your suit—I just ruined it."

Drake looked at the sodden, bloody shoulder of his tuxedo. "It does not matter. I have others."

"I hope so. Did I tell you the wedding was rescheduled for tomorrow?"

"Yes. Kiss me."

"You are the bossiest dragon I know," I said, leaning into him again.

Behind me, the door clicked open. Jim's voice said, "Nope, they're still at it."

Drake nibbled my lip for a moment before I pulled away and turned to glare at the demon in the doorway. "I thought I ordered you out."

"You did. You didn't say I couldn't come back," it pointed out with a waggle of its doggy eyebrows. "You guys gettin' busy, or should I tell Stephano you'll see him?"

"Stephano?" I asked, surprised to hear the name. "Fiat's Stephano?"

"You know any other blue dragons named Stephano?" Jim asked, moving away from the door as I started toward it. Drake caught my arm and held me back until he could go out the door first. I whumped him on the back as I followed.

Drake stopped in the doorway, his eyes narrowed, his arms crossed. "What do you want here?"

Stephano, one of the blue wyvern's elite guards, gave Drake a stiff nod. "Fiat sent me to notify his mate of a conclave called for Wednesday. Her attendance is mandatory." He made a little bow to me, then turned and would have left the house if Pál and István hadn't been standing in front of the door that led out to the street.

"Hang on a minute," I said, pushing past Drake. He caught my arm and held me close to his body. "I was thinking about this earlier, when I read the history of the green dragons. I know Fiat set up one of the green dragons to take a fall so I'd end up being his mate instead of Drake's—"

"You are my mate," Drake growled. "Nothing Fiat can do will change that."

I kissed the tip of his nose. "You're so cute when you're stubborn. It's one of your many charms, and although normally it drives me up the wall, sometimes it's just downright adorable. Where was I? Oh, the mate thing." I turned back to Stephano. "I know that Fiat used the *lusus naturae* challenge on the green dragon he set up as temporary wyvern, but he didn't follow the rules of the challenge to win. He used a gun, and that wasn't in the terms of the challenge. Thus, he didn't really win, which means I'm back to being the green-dragon mate, and as far as I'm concerned, Fiat can stick his conclave where the sun don't shine."

Silence filled the hall. I looked from Stephano, to Pál and István, finally to Drake, all of whom were standing with odd looks on their faces.

"What?" I asked.

Jim shook its head. "Just when you were getting a clue, too."

"What's wrong in my reasoning?" I asked Drake.

"A challenge for *lusus naturae* is different from a challenge for control of the sept," he answered, giving me a reassuring squeeze. "The latter must follow the terms of the challenge specifically. The former . . ." He shrugged. "There is a mortal saying that all is fair in love and war. I'm afraid that would apply to a *lusus naturae* challenge, as well."

"Well, hell," I said, grinding my teeth just a little as I looked at Stephano. "What time is this conclave thing?"

"Noon." Stephano named a well-known hotel that was relatively close. "I will tell Fiat you will attend?"

"Are you good on that time?" I asked Drake.

Stephano interrupted before he could answer. "The green wyvern will not be allowed to attend."

"Sorry, I don't go anywhere without Drake."

His gaze moved warily between Drake and me. "No dragon outside the sept is allowed at a conclave. It is not done."

"Is that kosher?" I asked Drake.

His jaw tightened as he nodded. "Unfortunately, it is a law most septs adhere to—only members of the sept are allowed to attend formal meetings."

"Well, the answer is simple then. I just won't go." I turned back to Stephano. "Please pass along my regrets to Fiat, and tell him it was a good try, but I wasn't born yesterday. If he wants me at a meeting, he'll have to make it a less formal function so that I can bring Drake."

The blue dragon smiled. For some reason it wasn't a reassuring gesture. "Fiat assumed you would refuse, and instructed me to tell the green wyvern that if you do not attend the conclave, he will consider that an act of war and will reciprocate as necessary."

Drake stepped forward, his hands fisted, clearly bent on telling Stephano what Fiat could do with his threat.

"Wait a minute," I said quickly, moving between the two men. "This is stupid. The green dragons don't have anything to do with my decision to not go to the conclave. Fiat can't war with them because I don't want to hang around with him."

Stephano's smile changed to a smirk. "You live with the green wyvern. You bear his child. You are treated as a member of the sept. If you do not attend, it will clearly be due to influence by the sept, and thus Fiat will be within his rights to reclaim his mate by force."

I bit my lip as Drake said something to Pál and István in their native Hungarian. The two men closed ranks on Stephano, whose smirk, I was momentarily gratified to notice, took on a strained cast.

"Now, just wait a second, guys. Nothing is going to be served by beating the crap out of the messenger. Let's think this out."

"You will not go to the conclave," Drake told me. "I will not allow you to go there unprotected."

I nodded. "I have no intention of putting myself in Fiat's control, but at the same time, I'm not going to allow another war to be declared. We have enough on our hands with the red dragons. There has to be another way around the situation."

You are so foolish. You could end the situation so very easily.

"Argh!" I yelled, startling everyone in the hall.

"Ash," Jim said.

"I'm sorry. It was the voice. Man, I'm sick and tired of it yammering at me day and night. What I'd give to shut it up . . ."

Everyone was looking at me oddly again. I cleared my throat and reminded myself that professional Guardians didn't rant in front of others about the evil voices in their heads. "Sorry."

Jim sighed and said, "You're not thinking."

I looked at it. It cocked its head. As a demon, Jim was bound by some silly rule that said it couldn't come right out and tell me something helpful unless I asked for specific information, but it could—and often did—hint when I was missing something obvious.

Obvious like . . . "Oh! Brilliant! Jim, you get two dog cookies when you go to bed tonight. Stephano, you said I couldn't bring a member of the green sept, correct?"

"No other sept may attend a conclave."

"Gotcha. The answer is simple, then." I turned my smile onto Drake.

He frowned.

"It is?" Pál asked, looking confused.

"Yup. I'm a prince of Abaddon, remember?"

"It's not something we could easily forget," Drake said dryly.

"Yeah, well, as a big, bad demon lord, I have scads and scads of demons under my control. If Fiat won't let me bring a green dragon bodyguard, I'll simply call up my demon legions and bring them instead. There's nothing in the sept laws that says a mate can't bring demons, is there?"

Stephano's mouth opened and closed a couple of times before he finally answered. "No."

"Good. Problem solved."

"Er . . ." Jim said.

"It's not?"

Drake took my hands in his, his thumbs gently brushing over the backs of my hands. "*Kincsem,* it would not be wise for you to summon your legions."

"Why not?" I looked deep into his eyes. Regret was in there, as well as something extremely distasteful . . . pity.

Do not listen to him. You have struck a perfect solution.

I closed my eyes for a moment, swamped with sadness. "You mean I'd have to use the dark power to summon the legions."

"Yes."

"But I don't use it to summon Jim or Tr—the steward," I said, careful not to say Traci's name out loud. For some reason we had yet to figure out, I had the demon on auto-call, and just saying its name summoned it to me.

"They are your personal servants. Legions are different."

"All right then," I said, nodding as I turned back to

Stephano. "If Fiat wants to play hardball, I'll play hardball. You can tell his royal majesty that I will attend his con-clave—with a non–green dragon bodyguard sufficient to en-sure my safety and general well-being."

"Hoo boy, this ought to be good," Jim said, its eyes light-ing up as it realized what I was saying.

Drake rubbed his chin and looked thoughtful for a mo-ment, then nodded. "That will do."

Pál and István exchanged glances before István asked, "Who will be bodyguard?"

"Aisling's going for blood," Jim said, snickering. "I can't wait to see what Uncle Damian makes of Fiat. You think I could place a bet on who's left after the dust settles?"

Stephano's smile faded completely. I leaned into Drake and breathed in his dragon essence, allowing it to seep deep within me, content in his arms.

"Don't worry, sweetie. Everything is going to be all right. You'll see—Uncle Damian can be a badass when he wants."

4

Cold air suddenly swirled around me, causing my bare nipples to harden painfully. Startled, I jumped, and was grabbing for the towel when a familiar voice said, "There you are. I wondered where you were hiding."

I let the towel drop and smiled as Drake stood in the doorway of the sauna, quickly removing his clothing. "You're letting out all the steam," I pointed out.

The look he gave me could have melted asbestos. "I assure you that you'll have as much steam as you can stand. If you don't mind me joining you, that is?"

"That 'Occupied' sign on the door to the sauna doesn't apply to you. Although . . . how did you know Paula and Dad weren't the ones in here?"

He laid the last of his clothing on the bench outside of the sauna, closing the door behind him. His emerald-eyed gaze took its time moving along my body, making me shiver a little with its intensity.

"They just went to bed. Paula said you were going to take a late night swim," he answered, dumping a ladleful of water on the hot coals. Steam boiled up around him, obscuring the sight of his body for a moment.

"Yeah, well, there's nothing like a relaxing steam after a nice dip." I lay back on the bench, my breath catching in my throat at the sight of his sleek muscles moving as he picked up the towel that had fallen on the floor. "So, I was thinking about you."

"Good things, I hope?" he asked, his eyes glittering brightly as he watched me.

I stretched a little in order to arch my back in a shameless display. "I was thinking about how you shift for a second into dragon form when you have an orgasm. It got me musing over what it must be like to be an animal in human form."

Drake had started for me, but at my words paused and cocked an expressive eyebrow. "I am most decidedly *not* an animal, *kincsem.*"

"Sorry, I didn't mean it like that. I know you're a man. But sometimes I have a hard time remembering that there are other emotions that you must be feeling than those experienced by the average joe."

His other eyebrow rose. "I am not a man, either. I am a dragon. I have simply adopted this form as one which is both comfortable and practical."

"You're certainly not getting any complaints from me about it. But I wondered . . ." I allowed my gaze to wander over his impressive expanse of flesh. "Perhaps if you got in touch with your inner dragon, you might be able to shift at other times?"

"It is common for dragons who stay in one form for a long period of time to lose their ability to shift into their traditional form," he said quietly. "You seem to be under the impression that we are at our most dragon when we are in the latter form—which is not true. We are dragons no matter what our appearance."

"I'm not disputing that at all. I wonder, though, just *how* dragon are you?"

He was on me in a heartbeat, his body warmed and slickened by the steam. "You question my dragonhood?"

"I want to know if there are deep, primal instincts driving you that I have yet to see," I answered, gasping when he took the tip of my breast in his mouth, bathing it in fire.

"I assure you that I have many primal needs," he answered. "Needs which only you can fulfill."

"Good. I thought we'd explore your dragon side tonight. Just to see if it has any effect on the whole shifting thing," I said, squirming underneath him.

"I am more than happy for you to explore any side of me you like," he answered, nuzzling my other breast.

I allowed my hands to play along his sides, sweeping down to dig my fingers into the heavy muscles of his behind. "You want me, don't you?"

"Do you need to ask?" He wiggled just a little. He was quite obviously aroused, his body slick against mine.

"Not really. " I nibbled his neck, then bit him on the shoulder. "I want you, too, in case you didn't notice."

His hand, which had been busily stroking a path up my thigh to parts northern, paused. "I noticed," he said, plunging a finger inside me.

I damn near came off the bench at that. "Let's try a little experiment . . . oh, god, yes. Do that again!"

His fingers flexed. My eyes crossed, but through the haze of steam that filled the sauna, I could see a quizzical look on his handsome face. "What did you have in mind?"

It took some effort to remove myself from the paradise of his hands and mouth and body, but I wiggled out from under him and snatched up a towel, saying as I did so, "Dragons like to hunt things, don't they?"

"That depends what the prey is," he answered, blowing a ring of fire at me.

The towel, not one that had been specially treated to inhibit fire, burst into flames. I dropped it and picked up another one.

"How about me?"

He stood up slowly, his eyes lit with a strange look. "Run," he said.

"What?"

"You wish to see the predator in me, do you not? Very well. Run."

My mouth opened to tell him that there was no way in Abaddon I could outrun him, but at a low growl deep in his chest, I turned on my heel and ran.

My heart was beating wildly, adrenaline spiking through me as I ran across the room, hesitating for a moment as I tried to decide where to go. Drake emerged from the sauna, his head lowered slightly, an intense look on his face as he stalked toward me.

"Do you know what it is to hunt, *kincsem*? It is a feral drive, one of the most primal urges in dragons, the need to find and possess. It heightens my senses until I can hear your heart pounding, hear the rasp of every breath you take. Your scent lies heavy in the air, sinking deep into my blood, teasing me, tormenting me until all I can think of is possessing you."

I gasped and backed away, too caught up in the moment to think straight.

"Do you really wish to unleash the beast within me?" he asked, continuing to prowl toward me, the muscles of his body moving in a beautiful ballet of power and grace. "Do you think you can handle the feral side of a dragon, *kincsem*?"

Cold stone touched my back, stopping me from escaping. I knew just how a mouse felt when it was dropped into a snake's cage. I tried to answer, but all that came out was an

unintelligible squeak. I was caught between intense arousal
and a base need to escape, unsure of which emotion to act
upon. My body and heart told me Drake would never harm
me, but the primitive part of my brain was demanding I get
away from the big, scary beast that wanted to eat me.

He was a hairsbreadth away from me now, the look in his
eyes a mixture of passion and something I didn't recognize,
something so frightening it sent my brain into a screaming
fit. "Do you really wish to face my true being?"

I was poised to run, the flight instinct in me swamping
other emotions, but just as I was about to flee, Drake lifted
his hand. Instead of the expected fingers, a curved blue claw
touched the mark he'd branded into my flesh.

"Oh, dear god, yes!" I cried, flinging myself on him,
wrapping my legs around his hips as his hands . . . claws . . .
whatever they were dug into my butt and hoisted me high. I
kissed him with every ounce of love I had, offering myself
as a sacrifice to tame the wild dragon, my mouth welcoming
the intrusion of his tongue even as he thrust hard into my
body.

Our lovemaking was fast as he claimed and I surrendered.
Flames licked along my skin as he pressed me into the wall,
his body moving in a rhythm that sent me soaring. I bit his
neck, sobbing incoherently into his shoulder, my hands mim-
icking his claws as I raked them along his back. There was
no gentleness between us, no soft, teasing touches—this was
mating, pure and simple. I had unleashed Drake's tightly held
primal emotions, triggering his need to dominate.

But I was a wyvern's mate. I answered every hard thrust
with little movements of my own, somewhat hindered by
our unorthodox position, but using my hands and mouth to
show him he wasn't the only one who could go wild. As a
familiar tension built inside me, I clutched his butt and urged

him on faster, crying out his name when I was swept over the edge.

A fireball exploded around us as Drake's shout of exultation changed to an animal roar of triumph. The throat I had pressed my face against changed, elongated, the hot, sweaty skin morphing for a fraction of a second into greenish yellow scales.

I collapsed against him, my heart and soul singing, my brain completely unable to cope with anything else at that moment but the depth of my feelings for the man who had so completely filled my life.

Consciousness returned with a warm, enveloping air that caressed my bare flesh. I opened my eyes to find myself lying on the bench in the sauna, and Drake splashing water on the rocks. He looked down at where I lay, a smug little smile curling the edges of his mouth.

"You're just lucky I'm a wyvern's mate," I told his smile, holding out my arms for him. "If I'd still been mortal, I doubt I could have survived that. When can we do it again?"

He sank down upon me with a hot look, and even hotter kisses.

When I toddled down the stairs to the front hallway the next morning, no one was around except Jim, lying on the floor in a pool of sunlight reading a newspaper featuring bare-breasted women.

"There you are. I wondered if you were going to get up anytime before noon," Jim said, flipping a page.

"I've been up for a couple of hours, Mr. Smarty Demon, trying to find a hotel with a decent-sized room we can use for a reception. Man, I have a headache. Where is everyone? Is Uncle Damian here yet? And Rene? Have you seen

Drake? Did Paula go out shopping, or is she going to come with us to find a new dress?"

"For a prince of Abaddon, you sure don't seem to know much," Jim answered, not bothering to look up from the newspaper. "Hoo baby! Look at those hooters! You gotta love the English newspapers!"

"Answer my question, oh ye of the smart-aleck mouth."

Jim heaved a profound sigh. "Depends on who you mean. Yes. No. Yes, but he left. No, she and the absentminded professor went for their morning walk, and finally, yes. Anything more you'd like to know? The square root of fifteen million? Why the sky is blue? How many demons can dance on the head of a pin?"

"Left?" I asked, focusing on the most important tidbit of information. "Drake left? Where did he go? We only have a couple of hours before the wedding."

"Dunno. He just said Uncle Damian and Rene were going to be your guards this morning, and took off with Pál and István."

Uncle Damian loomed up in the doorway, fixing me with a gimlet eye. "There you are."

"Good morning. Do you happen to know where Drake has gone off to?"

"He didn't say, and I didn't ask. Come in here. I want to talk to you." He did an about-face back into the living room.

"Uh-oh. Someone's in trouble," Jim said, standing up and stretching.

"Hardly that," I said, although I had to admit my uncle's forebidding frown was not something I took lightly.

"I'm going to see if Suzanne needs any help with breakfast," Jim said, strolling toward the back regions of the house where the kitchen was.

"Just remember that she works for Drake and me, not

you. If you try to bribe her into hiding the fact that you filched an additional breakfast, she'll tell me!"

"Who is Suzanne?" Uncle Damian asked as I closed the door behind me.

"A green dragon who is our cook and general dogsbody, no reference to Jim intended. She's István's girlfriend. You probably saw her last night."

"Ah. Short girl. Dark hair." He nodded.

"That's her. She's a doll; I don't know what we'd do without her. Is this going to take long? I'm afraid I don't have a lot of time," I said, glancing with fondness at a small table in the corner of the room. Drake and I had enjoyed many steamy moments by means of that particular piece of furniture. Just thinking about some of the times had my pulse pounding. "I've had a horrible time trying to find a room for the reception, and there's still the shopping to be done. Are you sure Drake didn't say where he was going?"

"Yes."

"Dammit. I suppose I could call him—" I had started reaching for the phone when Uncle Damian stopped me with a few words.

"He says you're pregnant."

I sighed and sat down on the arm of the couch, clicking off the phone. "*Possibly* pregnant. We're not sure, although I do have an ultrasound scheduled for this afternoon. I'm sorry if you're shocked that it's possible I'm pregnant before we got married, but—"

Scorn curled his lip. "Do you seriously believe I care about that?"

"Well . . . I know Paula will be full of lectures for weeks when she finds out."

"I am not your stepmother. But I *am* evidently now your

bodyguard. What's this business of you going over to another group of dragons?"

"Drake told you about that, huh? It would take hours to explain it, so I'll just give you the quick and dirty version—two other wyverns pulled a nasty on us last month, with the end result that I am temporarily considered the blue wyvern's mate. And since we're already at war with one sept, I'd like to avoid any similar confrontation with the blue dragons, hence the need for me to have a bodyguard when I attend their meeting tomorrow. If you're not up to the job—"

Uncle Damian made an impatient noise. "As if a little job like protecting you from some dragons is going to challenge me. I just want to know the lay of the land so I can make some plans."

I gave him the name of the hotel and added that I would bring in a couple of other people to help. "I'll have Jim and Rene, and possibly my demon steward, and in a pinch, Dad."

"I doubt he would be of much use," Uncle Damian replied, not quite rolling his eyes, but I could tell he wanted to.

"There's more to him than you see," I answered, reaching for the phone again.

"Hrmph."

Uncle Damian was busily making security plans by the time Drake answered his cell phone.

"When do you want to leave?" Uncle Damian asked as he was about to exit the room.

"Oh, hi, sweetie, hang on a sec. As soon as Paula gets back and Rene shows up, OK?" He nodded and left. I returned my attention to the phone. "Sorry about that. My escort was inquiring what time I wanted to leave to buy a new dress. And speaking of the dress I will wear to marry an incredibly sexy green-eyed dragon who didn't wake me up in a manner guaranteed to keep a smile on my face all day, where are you?"

Drake's voice had an oddly strained note to it. "A situation has come up, and we're investigating it. I will be at the church on time, if that's what you're worried about."

"A situation? More Chuan Ren?"

"No. This has nothing to do with the war. I do not have time to explain to you now, *kincsem*."

"You know, a lesser woman would demand to know what it is you're up to, but I am one with serenity and trust you entirely, despite the fact that yesterday you stood me up in front of everyone I ever knew."

Drake snorted.

"Love you. Kisses and hugs. Smoochies galore. Licks, nibbles, and assorted gropages."

I could almost hear Drake's eyes rolling. He disliked overt shows of affection in public, which just made me say the most outrageous things to him in private. "Good-bye, Aisling."

"Wait a second, buster. Come on, you have to say it."

"No, I don't."

"Yes, you do. The rules say you have to say it once a day, and you haven't said it at all today."

"Pál and István are here," he answered, clearly trying to muster a hint of outrage even though he knew I wasn't going to buy it. "That negates the rules."

"They're big boys, I'm willing to bet they won't keel over if they hear their leader tell his fiancée that he loves her. Say it!"

"Our train just arrived at the station. I can't say it now. I must go, *kincsem*."

"Train? You're on a train somewhere?" Now, that got my attention. Drake puttering around town taking care of business was one thing, but what could be so important that it forced him to leave town a few hours before our wedding? "Sweetie, what's going on?"

"I'll explain the situation to you at a later time. Heed your uncle's warnings and do as he says."

He clicked off before I could ask where he had gone to.

"How did they get Abaddon into a small Kensington shop?" Jim asked, scrunching itself down so as not to get whapped in the face by flying beaded satin.

"Don't be silly. This is London, not Hell."

Three giggling young women hurried past us with hot-pink bridesmaid dresses that lay limp in their arms like some sort of gigantic, horribly mutated jellyfish, trailing tendrils of ruffled lace and ribbons.

Jim cocked an eyebrow.

"Well, all right, there are similarities, but it is not Abaddon. And hush. Someone is going to hear you if you keep talking."

Jim shot me a look that I ignored as Paula bustled over with her arms full of tulle, glitter-bespecked white satin, and marabou feathers. "Now, this one is absolutely lovely, dear, and would look fabulous on you. It glitters! I know you said you didn't want white, but just look at it! Oh, if only they had dresses like this when I was young!"

I tried to avoid looking at the dress full on, lest it burn out my retinas with its glittering hideousness. "It's very nice, Paula, but you know, I'm just not a white wedding dress sort of girl. I mean, I did that once, and we all know how that ended. I wanted something with a bit of color, something different, something—oh, hi. Um. That's a bit too different."

The salesclerk, who had gone into the bridal shop's sister store—specializing in corsets and Goth wear—presented me with an electric blue tulle miniskirt with lime green corset. "It's very popular," the clerk reassured me.

"I'm sure it is, but I'm thinking of something with just a smidgen more tradition, while not being a full-fledged wedding gown. Maybe something in the mother-of-the-bride area?"

Paula looked shocked. "Good heavens, Aisling, what are you thinking! Mother-of-the-bride gown, indeed. No, I'll go find you something. There are plenty of other choices if you don't want white. There's peach, and pale pink, and a lovely mauve I saw in the corner . . ." She dumped the white monstrosity and wandered off to look for another dress.

"Maybe you'd better come and look yourself," the salesgirl said, clearly exasperated.

"Maybe I'd better," I agreed, putting back a sage-colored backless gown and following her into the sister shop. It took a half hour of poking around, but by the time I found a beautiful emerald green crushed-velvet corset, and a champagne-colored heavy satin draped skirt to go with it, I was exhausted, both mentally and physically.

"I'm sorry, I think I'm going to have to sit—" The world spun around me as I handed the salesgirl my credit card, an inky blackness threatening to envelop me. Jim's bark sounded a long way away as I fell toward the blackness, but before it could consume me wholly, a soft voice spoke next to my ear, pulling me back out of the darkness.

"Aisling, do not do that. Come back to us."

I opened my eyes to find a familiar face smiling down at me. Bright gray eyes, skin the color of my favorite latte, cornrowed hair, and dimples that seemed to go on forever. "Gabriel?"

"Good morning."

I glanced around quickly and realized I was on the floor,

cradled against his chest as he propped me up. "What the . . . let go, I'm fine," I said as I got to my feet, my legs more than a little wobbly.

"Dear, do you think it's wise to get up so soon after you've swooned? This nice man caught you before you hit the counter and hurt yourself, but I don't think it's a good idea for you to be standing. You could faint again, or—"

"I'm all right," I interrupted, grasping the counter. The salesclerk who had been ringing up my purchases emerged from the back room with a paper cup of water. I took it, watching Gabriel over the rim as I sipped.

He smiled at me, looking just as friendly as could be, but I knew better.

"Paula, would you be an angel and go to the Starbucks down the road and tell Rene and Uncle Damian that I'm done shopping? By the time you guys get back, I'll feel much better, I'm sure."

She didn't look like she believed me, but muttering something about modern girls and how things were in her day, the ills of fainting, and the poor choice she felt I made on the matter of a wedding gown, she trotted out of the bridal shop and headed down the street a few doors.

I accepted the box containing my new wedding outfit from the salesgirl, reassured her I was fine, and with Jim at my side, allowed Gabriel to carry the box to the door of the shop.

"What are you doing here?" I asked as soon as we were by ourselves. "And don't tell me you were just passing by and happened to look in and see me faint, because that's too much of a coincidence, even for you."

He grinned. "I was looking for you, naturally. I heard that your wedding was canceled."

"And you thought what? You'd just zoom in and scoop

me up?" I shook my head. "I know you silver wyverns have some sort of curse hanging over your heads that prevents mates being born to you, but I am not the answer to the problem. I love Drake. I'm his mate, no matter what Fiat says. And I'm not going to leave him for anyone, so you can just knock that idea right out the window—"

"I gave up the idea of challenging Drake for you as soon as he said you were pregnant," Gabriel interrupted. "I realized then that you had committed yourself wholly to him, and that we had no future. Do not fear on that accord, Aisling. I simply wanted to see you, to explain what happened last month, and to wish you and Drake well. I have always considered you my friend, despite the situation we found ourselves in."

"Uh-huh." I glanced down at my furry demon. "Jim, you can speak so long as no one mortal is around to hear."

"About time, too. Hey, Gabe. Double-cross anyone lately?"

A flicker of annoyance crossed Gabriel's eyes. Normally I'd have squelched such wisecracks from Jim, but after the recent events with Fiat and Gabriel, I figured the latter deserved a little grief. Heaven knew he'd certainly given me a ton.

"I did not double-cross anyone. I admit to a certain lack of control where Fiat was concerned—I honestly thought he was going to threaten you with the poison, not use it on you—but what I did, I did for honorable reasons."

"You betrayed me. You betrayed Drake. You sold yourself to Fiat for what . . . a chance at a mate? I'd hardly call that honorable," I answered, my anger firing up all over again.

He deserves to be punished. Right the wrongs he has done to you.

"Ignore what I'm about to say, Gabriel. I'm not listening

to you, OK? I'm never going to listen to you again. So you can just take your oily little voice and pester someone else, because I'm not going to use you ever again. Got it? Good. Now go away!"

Both of Gabriel's eyebrows rose. "Problems?"

"It's just the dark power trying to convince me to use it again. It never shuts up."

"Ah." He glanced at my eyes. "Contacts?"

"Yeah. It weirds people out if they see my eyes the other way. And that is about the extent of my polite chitchat, Gabriel. My ride will be here any minute, so while I appreciate you showing up just as I was fainting, I don't feel I owe you any big reconciliation scene."

He took my hand. I pulled it away. He tried to take it again. Jim growled.

"Aisling, we have so much to talk about," he said, sighing.

"Yeah, right, like how you're going to try to screw her over again?" Jim asked.

"That is unfair," Gabriel protested. "You are judging me without hearing my side of the situation."

Beyond him, through the window of the shop I could see a familiar blue BMW pull up. "You allowed Fiat to mess with the green dragons. You had a hand in the death of one of their members. You sided with Fiat against us and allowed him to nearly destroy me, and by association, Drake. I don't think there's going to be a whole lot to *your side* of the story that I'm going to find particularly redeeming."

I pushed past him, through the door to the crowded London street, being careful to scan the area for potential red dragon assassins. Uncle Damian was already out on the sidewalk, his head turning slowly as he perused the people around us. Clearly, he took the matter of security just as seriously as did Drake.

"Your continued refusal to grasp the truth will only bring harm to us all," Gabriel said, following me out into the street.

Suddenly angry, I whirled around to face him, inadvertently bumping into a woman who was trying to pass us.

"Oh, sorry. Did I step on you?" I asked, handing her a shopping bag I'd knocked from her arms.

She smiled. "No, I'm fine. You're American, too? Isn't it fabulous here?"

"Yes, it is. If you'll excuse me, there's someone whose head I need to bite off."

The tourist's eyes widened as I marched backed to Gabriel, standing close to him so I could whisper with much vehemence. "How dare you insinuate that I'm responsible for bringing harm to anyone! You are not the victim here, Gabriel—I am."

"Are you so sure?" he asked quietly, all signs of the smile that usually lit his eyes gone.

I hesitated for a moment, wondering why he was pursuing this. Was he working with Fiat again, trying to set us up for some other heinous act? Or had there really been some circumstance that had befallen him that made it appear he had betrayed us?

"Aisling?" Uncle Damian called from where he stood next to the car. Jim had already gotten into the backseat.

"Be there in a second." Drake had been oddly silent on the subject of Gabriel. I'd tried to talk to him about it once or twice since the events at the fencing club, but what with the wedding planning, and Drake's ability to distract me simply by kissing me, we'd never fully discussed what happened.

"Aisling, I am not your enemy. I never was," Gabriel said, making a gesture as if he wanted to take my hand again.

The car behind the double-parked Rene tooted its horn.

I could see by Uncle Damian's agitated reflection in the shopwindow that he was uncomfortable with me standing out on the street. This was clearly not the time or place to debate the subject of past actions. "I'm busy right now, Gabriel. Maybe in a few months when I have forgotten what it was like to almost die of poisoning, I'll be in the mood to talk to you about what happened, but not right now."

"I *saved* you from dying," he called as I started toward Uncle Damian and the car. "And I can save you now, Aisling."

"Save me how?" I asked, putting as much scorn into my voice as was possible.

He took a step toward me, his gray-eyed gaze intense as it searched mine. "I know how you can end the proscription."

Hope lit within me. If I could be pardoned, or forgiven, or whatever the act was that ended the proscription, I would be able to work with Nora again. Not to mention the fact that the dark power would stop trying to seduce me. But the flicker of hope died when I realized that this was quite likely a trick, some sort of trap that Gabriel was using to do god-knew-what.

I lifted my chin and bit back all the nasty things I wanted to say to him. I might not technically be Drake's mate any longer, but he and the sept still treated me as such, and it behooved me to act with dignity when dealing with other dragons. "I will tell Drake of your offer. Good-bye."

I was about to get into the car when the American tourist I'd bumped into suddenly ran toward me calling, "Oh, hey, you dropped something!"

Time slowed to a crawl as I turned to see what it was I'd dropped. Behind me, Uncle Damian stood holding the car door, waiting for me to get in. People streamed around us on the busy sidewalk as the smiling tourist approached me, her hand outstretched.

She uncurled her fingers, revealing a silver symbol that seemed to float in the air above her palm.

I stared at the ward in confusion, not understanding what I was seeing until it was too late.

"Begone," the woman said, and horrible pain ripped through my body as I was yanked through the fabric of existence.

5

Awareness ebbed and flowed around me, the pain gradually wearing off. Slowly, voices filtered through my fogged brain.

"—think we should call it. The old lord never used to regurgitate whenever he visited," a troubled voice said.

"You're right there. And this one has done it before. You remember when she banished the old one?" a second voice said.

Every part of my body ached, including my teeth and hair. Even my eyebrows hurt.

"That was a horrible mess to clean up, let me tell you," the second person continued. "I was all for destroying the room, but Traci said it wasn't cost-efficient and would have a negative impact on the budget. 'But we're demons,' I told it at the time. 'Negative is what we do!'"

"What did it say to that?" the first voice asked.

"It just shrugged and said the lord insisted on a no-negativity policy and a very strict budget, and if I had problems with that, I'd have to take it up with her. Well, you can see what she's like!"

I could feel the speakers eyeballing me. I made an effort to pull myself together, absently noting that something was cold beneath my cheek.

The first voice tsked. "They're just not making demon lords the way they used to, are they?"

"I hope to god they aren't." I opened my eyes and lifted my head to find myself on a familiar gray marble floor. Next to my head were two pairs of shoes. I winced as I tilted my head back to see the speakers. "Hello, Saris. And you're . . ."

"Caron, my lord," the first speaker said, bowing stiffly. "Greetings, Lord Aisling. Traci did not inform us that you would be paying a visit to Abaddon."

I heaved myself off the floor, trying not to retch again as another wave of nausea hit me. "This isn't a planned visit. Someone zapped me here."

"Someone . . . zapped you?" the demon named Saris asked.

"Yeah. Jim, I summon thee." I staggered over to the red velvet fainting couch that I remembered sitting in the room which used to belong to Ariton. My demon doggy appeared with a look of surprise on its face.

"Man, Ash! Your uncle is going bonkers on the streets of London! Hi, Caron. Hey, Saris. Long time no see."

Both demons bowed at the sight of Jim. "Greetings and welcome, Effrijim."

Jim grinned. "I could get used to being your second-in-command."

"Enjoy it while you can, it's not going to last," I said, checking my body for any injuries. "Did you see the tourist?"

"Only about a gazillion of them. Which one in particular did you mean?"

"The one who slam-dunked me here."

"Oh, her. Long curly blond hair, lots of shopping bags?"

"Yeah. What the hell did she do? All I saw was a silver ward, and whammo!"

Jim pursed its lips and glanced toward the open door, where Saris and Caron stood. "Not in front of the emonsday," it said.

"Thanks, guys," I said with what I hoped was a confident, in-control smile. "I won't be needing you any longer. I'm just going to be on my way as soon as I catch my breath."

The two demons looked at each other, then nodded and left. Jim padded over and pushed the door closed. "Jeez, Aisling, you want people to think you're a noob or something?"

"A noob?"

"Newbie. Boob. Idget."

"I get the meaning, thanks." Still a bit shaky, I hauled myself up and looked around the room, trying to decide which was the best place to rip open a passage to get us back to the shop. "And I'd like to point out that if I am a newbie about some things, it's because no one tells me anything. I have to find out stuff the hard way."

"Whatever. The first rule of successful prince-of-Abaddoning is that you never want your legions to know that you don't know what's going on. Word gets around fast here. First thing you know, all the other demon lords will be getting a plan together to get rid of you."

"Like I'd complain about that?" I touched the nearest wall. It didn't feel any different than a normal wall.

"Permanently," it added.

"That's fine by me. I don't want to come back."

"Think long and hard about the words 'get rid of you' because in this case, they could well be literal."

I wrinkled my nose. "Point taken. What did I do that was so wrong?"

"The chick who banished you?" Jim said, clearly expecting me to get some other point.

I stopped hunting for the weak spot in the room and thought about the woman. I'd never seen her before, so Jim must be referring to something about her rather than the person herself.

"She'd drawn a ward," I said slowly.

"Right."

"A banishing ward." A little light dawned in the dusty back corners of my brain. "Oh my god. She was a Guardian!"

"Bingo!"

I stared at Jim in horror, my skin crawling. "A Guardian banished me. Me! But *I'm* a Guardian. Can we banish each other? Oh, crap!"

Jim nodded. "You're not just a Guardian, you're a Guardian Plus! Now with extra 'prince of Abaddon' cleaning power."

I'd like to point out— the dark power's voice started to say.

"I have enough on my plate right now!" I snapped at it.

The voice sulked into silence.

"Yeah, well, you may just have to deal with it," Jim said, moseying over to where I'd been standing. "What were you looking for?"

"I can't believe another Guardian banished me just because I happen to be a prince of Abaddon. There should be some rule about not banishing demon lords who are also Guardians."

Jim cocked an eyebrow. "Like you think this is a normal situation?"

"Normal? I don't even know what's normal anymore," I fumed, marching around the room while wringing my hands. "And now look, I'm wringing my hands. Have you ever known me to be a hand-wringer? I detest the sort of woman who wrings her hands! It signifies weakness, and lack of coherence, and a totally unprofessional attitude!"

"And if we know anything about you, it's that you're a professional, and you're confident," Jim said, nosing a spot on the floor.

"Damn straight I am!" I yelled, forcing my hands apart so they couldn't wring themselves. "Look, they're trying to do it again. It's like my hands are possessed or something! Dear god, it's the dark power. The dark power has taken over my hands and is trying to wring me into insanity!"

"Is this little drama going to take long? 'Cause if it is, I want popcorn and a Diet Coke with extra ice."

"You're not going to like where I put the popcorn and extra ice," I said, ignoring my possessed hands to glare at the demon with much intent.

Jim's eyes widened as it backed away. "You've got that evil, slightly insane look down pat. Have you been practicing? We're talking seriously scary, Ash. Hannibal-Lecter-has-nothing-on-you sort of scary."

"Enough banter from you, buster," I said, trying to pull myself together. "Let's go over this situation again calmly. One: the dark power has taken over my hands."

I have not!

"Not listening! Two: there is a Guardian out there who can banish me at will. Which means that every other Guardian can probably do the same. Lovely. Just what I need—more people trying to do me in."

I slumped down into a chair and thought seriously about crying, but dropped that thought when my hands crept toward each other.

"What were you looking for over here?" Jim asked again.

"I wonder if you can exorcise hands . . . hmm? Oh, where on the wall was that place I sent you through before. Do you remember?"

Jim shook its head. "Why are you looking for that particular spot? It have fond memories for you or something?"

"Hardly. You told me that it was easier to tear the fabric
of existence in a spot where it had previously been rent. And
I know I sent you through it from this room, but I don't remember where, exactly." I glanced at the clock on the man-
tel, leaping to my feet when I saw the time. "Oh my god. *Oh
my god!* Tell me that clock isn't right!"

"That clock isn't right."

Relief made me sag a bit as I dug through my purse looking for my cell phone. "Thank god. I was worried there for
a minute that I'd missed the wedding."

"You have," Jim said complacently, snuffling around behind the fainting couch.

"What? You just told me the clock was wrong!"

"Yuh-uh. And who ordered me to tell her that?"

"Gah!" I screamed, punching a speed-dial number into
the phone. "Talk about your day from hell . . . Jim, look
around and find the weak spot. I'm not going to let something like a deranged Guardian ruin my day."

"Sooo many things I could say to that," Jim said, shaking
its head. "I'll confine myself to pointing out that even if I
found the spot, it wouldn't do you any good."

"It wouldn't? Why not?"

Inside my head, a dark, sinuous voice whistled a peppy
little tune.

I ground my teeth. "Don't tell me—I'd have to use the
dark power in order to push us through."

"Yup."

Smirk.

"Bloody he—Drake!"

"Aisling?" I held the phone away from my ear at the
sound of Drake's roar.

"Hi, sweetie. Um. I guess we're even on the whole jilting-at-the-altar thing, huh?"

"Where are you? Where have you been? Why have you not answered my calls?" Drake growled. "Rene and your uncle said you just disappeared on the street. Have you been harmed?"

"I'm fine. Jim's here with me. I'm in . . . er . . . oh, hell."

"Abaddon," Jim corrected.

I sighed. "I'm in Abaddon. Apparently the woman I bumped into on the street outside the bridal shop wasn't an innocent tourist. She flashed some sort of a ward on me, and whammo! I found myself here. No, I'm not hurt, just a bit shaky, with a horrifying tendency to wring my hands, but we won't go into that little problem now. I'm really, really sorry I missed the wedding. Were people upset? Maybe if I apologize to them, they won't be too pissed with us."

Drake took a long breath and said in a voice that had me flinching, "The only person you need worry about pacifying at this moment is me."

"Well, I'll start the pacifying as soon as I get home. As I remember, the physical extension of this house into our reality is in Islington. I'll call a cab and be home soon."

"You will do nothing of the kind. Do not move from that house until I arrive."

"I am perfectly capable of ordering a cab and getting myself home—"

"Do not argue with me about this, Aisling," he said somewhat snappishly. I wanted to point out that my experience today was no more my fault than him being arrested the day before, but upon consideration of the last few hours he'd probably gone through, I decided the best tactic was to appease.

"All right. We'll wait here. But I'm through with trying to

have a wedding. We're going to find the nearest registry office and get it done that way."

"We will talk about that later. Do not leave the house!"

He hung up after delivering a few more orders, which I
naturally dismissed as not being pertinent to the situation.

"I hate it when Drake goes all bossy," I muttered, glaring
at the room in general.

"Like you're not the queen of ordering people and incredibly handsome Newfies around? Ew. Morning sickness?"
Jim asked as it moved around a damp spot on the floor.

"You know full well I haven't had any morning sickness.
It's one reason why I think Drake is a bit premature with all
the baby talk."

"Your denial of the obvious, while generally amusing,
isn't the issue here, chicky."

"Oh, stop with the baby innuendoes already! Is there anything I can do to keep from being banished to Abaddon by
any passing Guardian?"

"Is there anything that you as a Guardian can do to keep
a demon lord from being banished?" Jim asked.

I pointed a finger at it. "I also hate it when you do that."

"Why?" it asked, tipping its head to the side.

"Argh!"

"Heh heh heh. Hey! What are you doing with those scissors? All right, all right! I'd answer your question if I could,
but I'm not a Guardian. You are, so you should know!"

I set down the scissors, frowning in thought. "It's even
more annoying when you're right."

"Just tryin' to help, babe."

"Uh-huh. As I'm sure you well know, there isn't anything
I can think of that would keep a being of Abaddon from
being banished. I suppose I could ask Nora, but I doubt if
she'd answer any technical questions since it would proba-

bly violate all sorts of Guardian Guild codes. No, there's only one thing for it."

Jim looked worried.

I nodded at it. "Yup. I'm going to have to go back to the Guardians' Guild and ask *them* for some help."

6

Drake was pacing the room when I emerged from freshening up.

"You don't look like a man thrilled to be in the presence of his bride," I said, eyeing the dragon of my dreams for a moment before flinging myself on him. "You look more like a man who is annoyed almost to the point of lecturing the aforementioned bride, which, given the day that the bride in question has had, would not be the wisest move. Oh, Drake!"

"Has she turned on the waterworks again?" Jim asked as it wandered into the room. "Man, I'm going to be glad when her hormones settle back down. We leaving?"

"Yes," Drake told it over my head. "Go out to the car. Rene is there. We'll be a minute."

I sobbed out the story of the day thus far, too far gone in my relief to see Drake to care that I was watering his tux again.

"*Kincsem,* I understand that it was difficult to be banished in that way. I do not understand why you believe your hands are possessed, but I am confident you will fill me in on that aspect of your day. We must leave now, however. I cannot protect this house, and I will not have you at further risk."

I sniffled and accepted the tissues that he had recently started carrying. "I know. And I want to go. I'm just so glad you're here. Sometimes things get so overwhelming, and only when you're around do I feel better."

Drake tipped my chin up, his eyes sparkling with a brilliant emerald light. "That has to be one of the nicest things you've said to me. You have made yourself necessary to me, as well."

I balled up my fingers and punched him in the stomach.

He laughed as he rubbed his belly, then pulled me tightly against his chest. "All right, I will say it, but you must make note that this fulfills the requirement for the day."

"Too much talking and not enough kissing," I said as I grabbed his head and pulled it down to me. His kiss was as hot as his dragon fire, scorching more than just my lips. His tongue danced along mine, driving me into squirming against him, wanting what only he could give me.

"Give it," I whispered into his mouth, and quivered to the tips of my toes when he opened his mouth and let his fire sweep through me. It blazed a trail along my veins, burning my blood, carrying me along in an inferno of desire, love, and need.

"I love you more than all the treasures of the world, Aisling. Our love will burn for an eternity until we have taken our last breaths, and even then it will continue to shine as a testament to that which we are together, a beacon of passion for all to see like a glittering star in the darkness of the night sky."

"You sure know how to sweep a girl off her feet," I said, kissing the corners of his delectable mouth as his dragon fire faded away. I felt empty inside without it, as if a part of me was missing, a sadness so profound it made my soul weep. "I love you, too."

"We must leave. I do not like this place."

"I know the feeling."

Jim was yakking to Rene, who was once again double-parked. " . . . she ralphed again, which is *so* morning sickness, don't you think? I mean, how in denial can you . . . oh, hi, Ash."

I pointed to the front seat of the car. Jim grinned and hopped in.

"Where are Pál and István?" I asked, looking around.

"Looking for you," Drake answered, cocking one glossy ebony eyebrow in a way that never failed to make my stomach tighten.

"Didn't you call them after you heard from me?"

Drake waited until we were both in the car, nodding to Rene, who shot out into the afternoon traffic with his usual disregard of other vehicles and pedestrians. "Yes. They are on their way back home now. We feared the red dragons had you, and they broke into Chuan Ren's London house to see if you were being held there."

"Are they OK?" I asked.

Drake looked faintly surprised that I should ask that. "Of course."

"Oh. Good. Hi, Rene. Sorry if I worried you at all earlier today. Did you happen to see the Guardian who nailed me?"

"Nailed you?" He shook his head. "I did not see anyone, unfortunately."

"Damn." I slumped back into the seat of the car as Rene drove, worrying like crazy despite the reassuring presence of Drake beside me.

"You do not have the look of a bride," Rene commented, watching me in the rearview mirror, narrowly missing plowing down a group of schoolgirls crossing the road. "You have the look of one carrying the load of many burdens upon her shoulders."

"Ack!" I yelled, pointing out the front window.

He glanced at the large truck against which we had, by some miracle, escaped smashing ourselves to smithereens. "Pfft. I was nowhere near that lorry."

"Had to be a good two inches of space between us," Jim commented, peering out the window at the truck as its driver screamed and clutched his chest while slamming on his brakes. "You're losing your touch, Rene."

My friend, chauffeur, and fate extraordinaire just grinned and gave his particularly Gallic shrug. "I will do better the next time, *hein*?"

"My money is on you, my man," Jim replied.

"What is it you are worrying about?" Rene asked me. "The wedding, or the red dragons?"

"Neither. Or, them, too. I've got so much going on right now, I can't keep half of it straight," I answered, rubbing my forehead. "There's Gabriel for one."

"Gabriel?" Drake asked. "What does he have to do with your concerns?"

I bit my lip, considering how much I should tell him. "I ran into him today at the bridal shop. He tried to give me a song and dance about doing what he had to do, and that he was innocent, et cetera. Have you talked with him since he betrayed us?"

"No." Drake's pupils elongated, warning me he was not pleased to be discussing the subject.

I'd never let that stop me before and wasn't about to now. "We haven't talked much about what happened that day because of all the other crap going on, and then the wedding planning took up all my time. Maybe we should talk about it now."

"It can wait. What else did he say to you?"

"Huh-uh," I said, shaking my head. "We're not going to play 'I'll ignore your questions but you must answer mine' unless I get to be the ignorer."

I put my hand on his thigh to let him know I meant business, but before I could stop myself, I was stroking his leg, igniting the slumbering coals of desire that were never completely extinguished within me.

Drake's expression changed in a flash from obstinate to interested. My breath caught as I massaged the steely thigh beneath the material of his pants, a little thrill skittering down my back.

"Kincsem," he said, his eyes flashing a warning.

"Yeah, not a good idea right now," I said, pulling my hand back, well aware that I was dangerously close to jumping his bones right there in the car.

"Did I miss something?" Jim asked, swiveling around to peer at us with suspicious eyes. "Was Drake copping a grope?"

"No," I told it with perfect truth. "We were talking about Gabriel."

Jim pursed its lips. "What about him?"

"Well . . . like what's he up to, hunting me down at the bridal shop just to spin me a yarn about him being innocent? Can he be trusted? Is he still working with Fiat?"

Rene's reflection in the mirror looked thoughtful. "Those are good questions. Me, I do not have the answers."

"Welcome to the club," I said, sighing before turning to eye Drake. "I don't suppose you have any insight you'd like to add?"

"About Gabriel? No," he said, rubbing his chin as if in thought. But there was something in his voice, a faint tone of something indefinable that worried me.

"Did you get your business this morning taken care of all right?"

"No. When is your ultrasound appointment?"

I pushed his sleeve back and consulted his watch, gloating to myself for a moment about the wedding present that was wrapped up and waiting for me to give him—a twenty-four-carat gold watch. Knowing the dragon's love of gold, I figured Drake would go gaga over it. "An hour and a half. We have time."

"Perhaps, but it may cut the time too fine. We will go home instead, Rene," Drake said in his usual bossy voice.

"Belay that order, Rene! I'm declaring a mutiny and taking over this ship. We're going to the Guardians' Guild."

The look Drake shot me spoke volumes, and none of them were pleasant reading. "Why is it so important we go there now?"

"I can't be married if my hands are possessed."

The look intensified until I was squirming in the seat.

"Oh, all right, I don't seriously believe my hands are possessed by the dark power, although I wouldn't put it past it to try."

Like I don't have something better to possess?

"However," I said, purposely ignoring the voice in my head, "it worries me greatly that a Guardian can just walk up to me and banish me. I have to find out what's going on, and what I can do to stop it, otherwise . . . well, what's to prevent a Guardian from just waltzing into the church and zapping me in front of everyone? The dragons would understand, but the rest of my family . . . urgh." I shuddered.

"Very well. I will admit that I am not comfortable with the thought of you being vulnerable to other Guardians. As for your family . . ." His lips tightened.

"Yeah, like you have anything to complain about? At

least my stepmother isn't actively trying to have you killed."

"I told you I spoke with my mother about the contract she placed on you. She understands now that to cross you is to cross me. She will not try anything like that again," Drake said with a complacency I was far from feeling. He might trust Catalina, but I sure didn't. "Since we are not going home right away, you should call your stepmother. She was very distressed earlier when you failed to show up for our wedding."

"Don't even think about trying to make me feel guilty about that, Mr. You Jilted Me First," I said as I pulled out my cell phone. "Hi, Suzanne, it's me. Is Paula there? Thanks."

"Are we stopping to get a bite to eat? I'm famished," Jim said, looking wistfully at an Indian restaurant as we drove past it.

"Later, after the— Ack! Rene! Stop doing that! You almost scared the shit out of me!"

"Aisling, dear!" a shocked voice breathed into the phone. "A lady never says that word! Manure or droppings, but never the other!"

"Sorry, but Rene insists on pulling race car driver moves on the streets of London."

Rene's smile flashed in the rearview mirror.

"Where *were* you? Why didn't you go to the church? My dear, the wedding was a *complete* disaster without you!"

I smiled at Drake. "Yeah, I know, a wedding kind of needs a bride. I was unavoidably—"

I was cut off in the middle of my explanation by a lengthy lecture on the proper duties of a bride on her wedding day. It lasted through the better part of our drive across London, luckily petering out just as we arrived at the parking garage adjacent to the Guardians' Guild.

". . . we can try again, but honestly, Aisling, if you aren't going to go to your own wedding, I don't know how you can keep expecting others to show up. As for your hair, dear . . . I know you wanted an upswept style, but if you were to leave your hair down, and if we were to find a flower garland and several spools of ribbon, it might do well to help hide some of that bondage outfit—"

"It's not bondage, Paula. It's a velvet corset, and it's perfectly suitable—"

"You have to allow me to know best about these things," she interrupted. "I'm not naïve, you know. I recognize bondage when I see it. Oh, David, why are you still wearing your tuxedo? You'll get it all wrinkled, dear . . ." Paula's voice drifted off as she hung up the phone.

"I need to use a bush," Jim announced as we all got out of the car, looking meaningfully out the side of the garage to the square located across the street. "Like, right now."

"I'll take it," Rene offered, snapping the leash onto Jim's collar. "We'll meet you inside, yes?"

"Thanks. Right," I said, facing the building. "Time to grit our loins and gird our teeth."

Drake slid me a tolerant look. "There are times when I wonder why of all women, you turned out to be my mate."

"And then you got down on your knees and thanked god that I came around, right?" I answered, pinching his arm.

"Hmm," was his noncommittal reply.

"Right?" I asked, pinching him harder.

He just took my hand in his and escorted me inside. The second my foot hit the tiled floor, alarms went off all over the building. The front lobby, which was manned by a couple of women and two large, burly guys, turned into something out of a Marx Brothers movie as dozens of people suddenly poured into the small room from various back offices. In less time than you could say "prince of Abaddon," the room was filled to capacity with Guardians, all of whom bore expressions that would have better suited the Nuremberg trials.

I mustered up a smile and tried to share it amongst the approximately thirty people jammed into the room around me. "Er . . . hi. I forgot about the demon lord sensor thingie. I'm—"

"We know who you are," a man's voice said from behind the wad of people. Instantly, the crowd parted to reveal a smallish, dapper black man wearing a Savile Row suit and bearing a mildly interested expression. He looked from Drake to me. "The question is, why are you here?"

Jim came bursting through the door, skidding to a stop in front of me. "Did we miss anyth—fires of Abaddon! Did you bring out everyone in the building?"

Rene slipped in through the door behind him, his eyebrows raised as he took in the scene.

"Do you wish for me to handle this situation?" Drake asked me in a low tone.

"No, thank you, sweetie," I said, giving him a smile to show how much I appreciated him allowing me to deal with the situation.

"I want bonus points for this," he murmured, his muscles tight with control as he kept himself quiet next to me.

I turned back to the little man, figuring he had to be someone important if the others were deferring to him. "I'm here to talk to someone about a rogue Guardian who banished me to Abaddon."

The man pursed his lips. "A *rogue* Guardian?"

"Yes. Well . . . technically I suppose she wasn't rogue per se, but I am a Guardian as well, and I—"

"You are *not* a Guardian," the man interrupted.

"I am," I said firmly. "I know that most Guardians aren't demon lords—"

The crowd, as one man, turned to stone.

"Sorry. I know that there are no other Guardians who are demon lords, but there was nothing in the rules that said one can't be, so if you'll check the records, I think you'll find that I am, in fact, a member of the Guardians' Guild, and thus, a Guardian."

"I am aware of the rules, and of your status," the man answered politely. "But you seem to be missing the pertinent issue: a demon lord, as you said, was not excluded from membership when you applied and were accepted. However, proscripted individuals, no matter who or what they are, are not allowed. The moment you became proscribed, Aisling Grey, you ceased being a member of this Guild, and thus are not entitled to any protection or benefits therein."

I looked around at all the faces watching me. Every single one of them was hostile, warily waiting for me to do . . . what?

"Kincsem," Drake said softly, his fingers brushing the back of my neck. "Let me take it from here."

"No. This is my problem, Drake. I can handle it. But thank you for offering," I answered, taking his hand for a moment.

He frowned but nodded, his fingers tightening around mine in a little squeeze of support.

I released his hand and stepped forward, looking again at the people around me, wondering what I'd done to screw up one of the most important things in my life.

You did not use me when you had the chance . . . but all is not yet lost.

My teeth ground at the voice in my head. It was the dark power's fault. It seduced me. It had persuaded me to use it when I had no idea of what it was. It had used me for its own purpose and destroyed part of my life without any qualms whatsoever.

Rage crashed through me, fury at the dark power for using me, which spilled over into anger at the crowd of people who circled me. "You're so quick to judge, so quick to condemn," I ground out, the hot, thick power seeping into me. "Is your world so black and white that you can't see shades of gray any longer?"

"Aisling," Drake said at the same time that Jim, looking worried, whispered, "Ash, that's not a good idea."

I allowed the dark power to fill me, ignoring the smugly satisfied sense of triumph that went with it. "No? What do I have to lose? I'm proscribed already, remember? It doesn't matter to these people, these fellow Guardians sworn to protect people, that I was tricked into the proscription. They don't care to even *try* to understand my position, let alone to find out the least little thing about me. Rather than work with me, help me, let Nora train me, they've done everything they can to keep me from fulfilling my destiny."

Power crackled off of me like black static electricity. Instantly, a good dozen wards were drawn, binding me with invisible chains.

"Do not make matters worse by doing something that will make your path irreversible," Drake warned, stepping close to me.

I laughed as I opened the little door in my head that allowed me to use my Otherworld powers. "They're afraid of me, Drake. Can you feel it? Fear is thick in the air around us."

"Seriously, Drake is right. You really don't want to go there," Jim said, touching its wet nose to the back of my hand.

The dark power seeped into every pore, a blackish blue corona surrounding me, as if I was standing in the middle of a plasma ball. It wasn't the burning power of Drake's fire, but much, much more insidious . . . and stronger.

"I could wipe you all out," I mused out loud, watching with a wicked sort of amusement as the wary expressions turned to fear as the people gathered together in the room realized the truth in my statement. Over their heads, I could see people packing the hallway, all eyes on me. "I could wave one hand, and destroy you all, destroy everyone in this building."

"Aisling, you must not do this."

I ignored Drake, smiling as I allowed a little tendril of power to snap at the nearest person. He leaped backwards, his eyes black with fear.

"Jeez, Ash, you can't—"

"Silence!" I roared, silencing Jim with the wave of a hand. Rene stepped forward, his eyes dark and unreadable.

I shot him a look that knocked him backwards three steps. Drake stood silent next to me, his face an impassive mask, his eyes dragonish as they watched me carefully.

The air flashed bright with the wards that were drawn on me, layer upon layer of binding holding me into place where I stood until I felt as if I was buried beneath tons of concrete. Several of the Guardians glanced at the small man in the business suit. He shook his head, his eyes curious as they watched me.

I flung wide my arms, smashing the wards bound to me, startling the Guardians into cries of surprise.

"No more would you trouble me with your petty policies and intolerance!" I yelled, my voice taking on a timbre I'd never heard. "You would be under my rule, my dominion! And the torment I could bring upon you would encompass a level of suffering unimaginable to your pitiful minds! You would worship me even as I destroyed the very fiber of your beings!"

The building shook as I closed my eyes and imagined the possibilities. Darkness seeped out of me and filled the room, dimming the lights as if a haze of dense black smoke obscured the vision. The people in the room held their collective breaths as the walls seemed to tremble and lean inward, the building itself poised on the verge of imploding.

"Yes," the man in the suit finally said. "I believe that you could do that. But will you?"

Triumph sang in my veins. With one sweep of my hands, I could take charge of my life again. I could eliminate those who opposed me, and right every wrong ever done. I could fulfill the destiny that lay before me like a glittering, tempting smorgasbord of power.

Now you're singing my song!

A slow smile curled my lips as I let my arms drop, releasing the dark power. It ebbed from me slowly, leaving me weak and shaking. The thick blackness of the air dissipated as everyone breathed once again.

Noooo! echoed in my head.

"No," I said, meeting the gaze of the man before me. "You're quite right. I wouldn't."

He nodded and turned, the people in the hallway parting behind him as he left the room. "I believe I will make time in my schedule to speak with you."

"Thank you," I said politely, more than a little amused by the stunned expressions surrounding us. "Oh, sorry, Jim. You can talk."

"Fires of Abaddon, Aisling! You could have given me a heart attack!" Jim sputtered. "Why don't you warn me when you're about to pull something like that?"

"It wouldn't have been nearly as effective if I had," I answered, fondling its ears before turning to Rene. "Are you OK? I didn't mean to scare you, but—"

"You had a point to make, yes," he said, nodding his head as he came forward. He rubbed the back of his neck. "Like Jim, I wish you had warned me of what you were planning, but eh. It is done, yes? And you have driven home the point you wished to make most dramatically."

"You're the daimon," I said softly as we were escorted down the hallway after the man in the suit. "You should know better than anyone what fate has in store for me."

"I do not make the path you follow, only help you find it," he reminded me, taking my hand and pressing a swift kiss to the back of it. "But you get ten out of ten for style."

Double doors at the end of the hallway were thrown open. I shot Drake a quick glance as we were swept through the door into a large, open room dominated by a curved, light oak desk.

"Did I worry you?" I asked him quietly.

"I was concerned that the others in the room did not know you as I did, and thus would not realize that although you might be a demon lord, you do not have it in you to be evil."

I smiled, my heart warmed by the words. The feeling lasted until I saw the nameplate on the doors as they were closed behind us.

"You're Caribbean Battiste, the head of the Guild," I said to the dapper man.

He bowed slightly before sitting behind the big desk. "I have that honor. And you present the Guild with a very difficult situation, Aisling Grey."

"I'm sorry. And I'm sorry about all of that business out there, but I knew I could tell you guys I'm not bad until I'm blue in the face, and you wouldn't believe me."

"So you thought you would prove to us that your intentions are pure?" Caribbean asked, steepling his fingers. "But now that you admit it was all a charade, can we not say that you are simply trying to lull us into a false sense of security, and that the danger you pose remains?"

I held his piercing gaze. "The power I could yield is beyond anything I have as a mere Guardian, or even as a wyvern's mate. That I do not choose to use it has to show my true intentions."

He bowed his head in acknowledgement. "There is that." He glanced at the screen of the laptop sitting on his left side. "I'm afraid that much as I would enjoy conversing with you, I am very limited in time. What do you wish me to do about the Guardian who banished you?"

"Nothing. She's not the problem, nor are any of them—they're only doing their jobs. What I want from you is help."

The tips of his fingers tapped against each other. "What form would this help take?"

I glanced at Drake. He nodded.

"I want to end the proscription. Drake has done what he can to find out information about how to end it, but with no luck. Today, another wyvern mentioned to me that he knew a way possible to do that. If *he* knew that, then the Guardians' Guild must know as well. I'm not a bad person, Mr. Battiste. I was drawn into the situation partly through my own incompetence, but also through trickery and adverse circumstance. I want to be a Guardian again. I want to kick demonic ass, not have them work for me. I want to just be the simple demon lord, wyvern's mate, and Guardian that I used to be."

Jim snorted.

"Simple?" Caribbean asked.

"You know what I mean—demon lord to just one little

demon. But most of all, I want this damned dark power to go away and leave me alone!"

I will never leave. I am as much a part of you as you are a part—

"I want to be me again!" I said loudly, drowning out the voice. "Can you help me? Please?"

"No," he said.

My heart dropped. My hopes, dreams, everything that was anything to me—Drake excepted—crashed, burned, and turned to ash.

Caribbean Battiste pressed a button on his desk and stood up as the doors behind us opened. "But I know someone who can."

7

There were dragons everywhere, green dragons, members of the sept gathered to celebrate our still-unachieved marriage. The nightclub that held the party had been reserved just for us; it was owned by a friend of Drake's, an ilargi (reaper) named Traian, a man with a sweet smile that was at odds with his rather sinister job.

He was acting as bartender for the evening, Drake obviously not wanting to trust the job to anyone else from outside the sept at a dragon gathering. He nodded to me as I drifted down the bar, smiling at everyone as I hunted for the one man who filled my thoughts.

Music pulsed in the background, loud enough to mute the conversation around me, but not so loud that it dominated the scene. I smiled to myself as various dragons exited and entered the doors at the far end of the club, the atmosphere inside completely smoke-free. Drake had no doubt given an order that those members who smoked do so outside.

The main part of the club was given over to the dance floor. Like the rest of the décor, it was black with little twists of silver through it. Along the sides of the dance floor, curved alcoves made inky pools of shadows that made the occupants all but invisible. I shimmied through the crowd of dancers, unintentionally moving to the time of the pulsing music, smiling and nodding at people as they greeted me, but searching the whole time for one person, one man, the one being on this planet to whom I was willing to give everything I had.

Occasional sounds and glimpses of movement from the alcoves alerted me to the occupants, but none of them had the right feel. It wasn't until I had shimmied my way to the end of the club that I saw an emerald glimmer from the last alcove.

I smiled and strolled slowly toward the man waiting there, skirting the small table to stand in front of the dark figure that all but blended into the shadows.

"Enjoying yourself?" I asked, brushing back an errant tendril of ebony hair that had fallen over Drake's forehead.

"Not until this moment," he answered, his voice smoky with desire. It sent a little shimmer of arousal up my back and arms.

"Dance with me?"

He shook his head. There was a candle glowing dimly on the table behind me, throwing just enough light on him for me to see the planes of his face, but his eyes were bright with passion, shining in the darkness like beacons that drew me closer. "We've already done that."

"What do you want to do, then?" I asked, my skin flushing as his gaze roamed over me. I was wearing a dress he had picked out for me, black, slinky, and backless. The neckline plunged down to my waist, the material clinging to my body in a way that seemed almost to caress my flesh.

His face was all hard planes, not a line of softness to be found anywhere from the black slashes of his eyebrows, to his arrogant, aquiline nose, and the stubborn line of his jaw. The expression in his eyes, however, was unmistakable. "Do you have to ask?"

"I suppose not," I answered, taking the hand he held out. He pulled me forward onto his lap so I was sitting astride him, the material of his pants rough against the flesh of my inner thighs. It was a rather risqué position in public, but I trusted that the shadows were deep enough that no one could see us. I let my fingers dance along his skin as I unbuttoned his silky shirt, reveling in the feeling of him. His hands slid up my bare thighs, curling into my hips to pull me closer to him, until we were nestled together in an intimacy that was only hampered by our clothing . . . and the environment.

Drake's mouth burned along my neck as he kissed a path down my chest, nudging aside the clinging material to reveal my breast.

"Sweetie," I said, squirming when he took my nipple in his mouth, laving his tongue over the tip. "Not that I want to stop you, but this is a public place."

"No one can see us," he answered, allowing his dragon fire to lick along my flesh. I arched my back against the sensation, my entire body tightening, as if poised to explode.

"Someone could come back here to talk to you—"

"There is no one else. There is only you and me." His eyes all but burnt my flesh, his pupils narrow little slits against the glittering green.

My fingers curled into the thick muscles of his shoulders as he slid his hands under my dress, quickly snapping the minuscule satin straps of my underwear, his mouth taking possession of my nipple just as his fingers danced along my sensitive flesh. I sucked in my breath, arching my back again as his fire swept over me, his touch driving the tension within me to a breaking point.

Around us, people danced, drank, talked . . . and for all I knew, made love in the darkened alcoves just as Drake was making love to me with his hands and mouth.

"It's too much," I moaned, stopping him just long enough to pull his shirt off, moaning again when I leaned against him, my exposed breasts brushing against the soft hairs on his chest, breathing in the wonderfully spicy dragon scent of him that seemed to sink deep into my bones.

"There is no such thing as too much when it comes to you, *kincsem*," he murmured as I stroked the wonderful muscles in his chest and arms. I wanted to touch him, all of him, with my hands and mouth and body, my passion driven by the desire to give him as much pleasure as his still-dancing fingers were giving me.

I kissed him, urging him with my body and mind to what I wanted most . . . and then he did it. Dragon fire filled me, burning through my heart and soul, lighting my very being on fire until I thought I would explode in a wild conflagration that would destroy us both. The fire poured back from me to him, the cycle complete, filling me with joy so profound it almost drove me to the brink of ecstasy.

"Take me home," I all but sobbed, desperate with my need for him, wanting what we had together, frantic to revel in the fire that was shared between us. "Dear god, take me home right now!"

He wrapped his arms around me, pulling me with him as he fell backwards into pillows that tumbled from our bed to the floor. The material of his pants beneath my thighs melted into steely, hot flesh, flesh that shimmered goldish green for a moment before resolving itself into familiar muscled thighs.

"You shifted," I said on a gasp as his penis nudged my sensitive parts. "For a second you shifted, just like you do when you have an orgasm."

"I'm not that far off," he growled, biting my neck. "I want you, Aisling. I need you. I cannot live without you. You are mine, my treasure, my love, and no one will ever take you away from me."

"Never," I swore, trying to twist to reach him, reach the part of him that I desperately needed burning deep within me.

"No. Not tonight. This night is for you," he growled, his fire licking along my skin. He spun me around, moving so that I was facedown on the blankets, his body covering my back. My breasts, sensitized by his dragon fire, rubbed against the cool of the silk pillows as he parted my legs, entering me just enough to leave my body hanging on the edge of anticipation.

"Drake!" I yelled, pounding the pillows, helpless to pull him into me as I wanted.

"I do not wish to harm you."

"The doctor said it was perfectly safe to do anything that was comfortable, and if you don't finish this in the next few seconds, I'm going to die of sexual frustration, and then you'll have to explain to everyone why I'm dead with a tremendous scowl on my face!"

His growl matched mine as he lunged forward, his fire filling me even as his body did, the combination of the two pushing me into a deep well of rapture that seemed to consume me. The world condensed to the moment, the sound of his body meeting mine, of the growls of pleasure that came from deep within his chest, his breathing as ragged and fast as mine.

"I love you, Aisling." Strong, tanned fingers splayed on the pillows next to my head changed into blue claws, the flesh of his arm shimmering into iridescent scales as fire burst up in a ring around us. I took his fire into me and returned it with a shout of completion that he picked up and continued, our bodies and souls and hearts burning as one for a bright, endless moment that would live in my memory for eternity.

And then I woke up.

"Goddamn it!" I swore, as soon as I realized the space next to me was cold and empty. I punched Drake's pillow, wanting to scream to the heavens. My body still hummed with the aftershocks of the pleasure he'd given me . . . but had it been real? Or just a figment of my disturbed mind? "Damn it! Damn *him*!"

A thump sounded against the door connecting to the opulent bathroom that Jim had claimed as its bedroom.

"What?"

"You OK?" Jim's voice asked, muffled.

"No! Oh . . . hell!"

"Abaddon."

"Hell!" I yelled, and punched Drake's pillow again.

"Can I come in, or are you and Drake gettin' it on?"

"He's not here, the bastard!"

The bathroom door opened, and Jim's face peered into the room, an almost comical expression of wariness on its face. "What happened? You guys were all lovey-dovey last night. I thought Drake was happy about the baby?"

"He is, although he's not happy I refused to let the doctor tell us the gender," I snarled, pulling up the sheet and rubbing my arms as I glanced at the clock. It was just barely morning, my skin still tingling as if in response to Drake's fire. I shook my head at my foolishness—of course our lovemaking hadn't been real. I couldn't share Drake's fire. If the scene melting from a club to our bedroom hadn't been a clue, the fact that I could share his fire should have raised all sorts of red flags in my head. What was worse was that, if he had to resort to a dream rather than making love to me in person, it meant he wasn't here. Sometime during the night while I was sleeping, he'd left me. "God *damn* him!"

"Well, if that's all you're going to say, I might as well go back to bed," Jim said, padding over to give my arm a quick swipe with its tongue. I patted its head, reminding myself that it wasn't fair to take my bad humor out on Jim.

"You didn't happen to hear Drake leave last night? He told me to go to bed because I was tired out after the long day, but if something happened and he had to go take care of a sept member or beat Chuan Ren's head in or something, he would have told me."

Jim cocked its head at something on the floor. "Looks like he decided you and the baby needed your sleep. There's a letter."

I pushed Jim aside to pick up the creamy envelope bearing the sept emblem, ripping it open to read the note inside.

"You've been hanging around sailors too much," Jim said a minute later as the blue streak I was swearing came to an end. "Although I liked the bit about stinky, slimy weasel poop."

"You're right, he says he didn't want to disturb my rest, the bastard," I growled, wrapping a sheet around me as I stormed into the bathroom.

Jim, wisely, stayed where it was.

I emerged a few minutes later wearing my favorite bathrobe, a soft, comfy velvet garment that made me think of Victorian dressing gowns, but which Drake disliked because he said it covered up too much flesh. I buttoned it now with defiance as I marched to the closet that contained my clothes. "He says he had to go help someone in a desperate situation. Who, exactly, he refuses to say. He doesn't know when he's going to be back, but suggests we put off the wedding for a few days. The rotter! How dare he just zoom off and not tell me where he's going, or who he's going to help, or what exactly he's up to!"

"Yeah, how dare he go out and be all heroic and stuff when you want him here slobbering over your big boobs."

I shot the demon a look that warned of retribution. "Leave my boobs out of this. They have nothing to do with this extraordinary lack of trust that Drake is exhibiting by doing this. The rat! I thought we were to the point where we shared everything. He's not supposed to keep secrets from me! Lord knows, he makes me tell him everything!"

"Everything?" Jim asked, raising one doggy eyebrow.

I froze as I thought over a few facts I'd decided to keep to myself. I'd told Drake that I had seen Gabriel, but I hadn't recounted the entire conversation, not wanting Drake to get so annoyed that he went after Gabriel. That could be excused as a desire to keep any more of the dragon septs from warring with us, but the fact that I'd downplayed to him the involvement the dark power had in my life was less easily explained away. He knew it spoke to me, he knew I could easily wield it, but until the previous day's demonstration at the Guardians' Guild, I don't think he fully realized just how much power I had at my fingertips.

Admit it—you love me.

I swore under my breath as I thought over what effect that realization might have had on him. Had he been so disquieted, felt so threatened because I had more impact using the dark power than his own dragon fire that he left me on a flimsy pretense? I ran over the events of the past evening, mentally shaking my head. He'd been quietly pleased when the ultrasound had proven beyond all doubts that the next generation of green dragons was a half-year away. He had treated me with his usual blend of courtesy and arrogance, laying down a series of ridiculous laws ranging from me not being allowed to lift anything heavier than ten pounds to an outright refusal to let me keep the meeting with the blue dragons.

Things were a bit dicey for a short while when I told him what I thought of his silly rules, but by the time he'd escorted me upstairs to our room, we'd come to a compromise whereby he'd stop being unnecessarily protective, and I wouldn't light his hair on fire while he slept.

Then he slipped away during the night without a word and sent me the most erotic dream of my life.

"Damn him," I said, banging my forehead gently on the closet door.

8

"*Cara!*"

I turned at the familiar voice that called down at me, looking with a dispassionate eye at the man who walked toward us.

"That him?" Uncle Damian asked, giving Fiat the same jaded eye.

"Yup."

"Looks like a porn star."

"Do I wanna ask how he knows what a porn star looks like?" Jim asked Rene.

"I do not think so, my friend. Aisling, I have my little companion with me, if there is any trouble with the blue wyvern," Rene said, touching my arm as he patted the breast of his jacket. "Him, I do not trust farther than I can spit."

"How on earth did you get a gun smuggled into England?" I asked, surprised.

He gave his trademark Gallic shrug. "I did not travel by conventional means."

"I don't think I want to know," Uncle Damian muttered, shooting me an odd look.

I smiled and tried to look as normal as possible, which, given that I was standing on the steps of St. Paul's Cathedral, surrounded by my uncle, a daimon, and my demon dog, wasn't very successful. "Oh, Traci!"

The demon steward popped into view in front of me holding a cup of coffee and a croissant. Its startled expression changed to one of resignation that morphed almost instantly to irritation. "My lord Aisling. I wondered when you were going to summon me. The situation is most urgent, I assure you. If you had just warned me ahead of time that you would be summoning me, I would have had the paperwork in my possession—"

"What situation?" I asked, one eye on Fiat as he trotted down the steps of the cathedral, flanked on either side by his two henchmen. "No, never mind, I don't have time for it right now. I have to attend a meeting of the blue dragons, and you're here in the guise of protection. Got it?"

"Er—"

"That guy approaching who looks like he should be on the cover of *GQ*, that's Fiat, the blue wyvern. You're to particularly watch him, OK?"

"Eh—"

"And his cronies." I straightened my shoulders and tried to look a lot calmer and cooler than I felt. "They may all look like Adonises, but they're sneakier than snakes. Don't take your eyes off of them."

Jim squinted at Fiat as he stopped in front of us. "Hey, Fiat. Nice highlights. You use Miss Clairol or another brand?"

I tried to keep from smiling at Jim's irreverent quip. There was no love lost between Fiat and my demon, but I didn't need any more antagonism than was absolutely necessary. "Hush, Jim. Hello, Fiat. Long time no see."

Fiat ran a quick glance around at my companions before taking my hand and kissing it. "*Cara, cara,* do you really think I would harm my own mate? This show of force is unnecessary, I assure you."

"Unnecessary, possibly, but I have no intention of putting myself in your control." I tried to pull my hand back from where he was still holding it, but his grip was deceptively strong.

He smiled. It made my skin crawl. "Do you believe you could be free of that?"

"Let's get something straight right now," I said briskly, jerking my hand out of his. A flash of blue fire lit his eyes for a moment, but it was nothing to my ire at finding myself in this position. "You may have finessed a way for me to act as your mate, but we both know that it's not going to be a relationship that will work out. The green dragons acknowledge me as their wyvern's mate. Drake and I are going to be married in a few days. We love each other, and nothing you can do is going to stop any of that. I accept the fact that I have to attend your sept meetings until such time as you come to your senses, but don't deceive yourself that I am weak and powerless. I may not technically be a Guardian at the moment, but I am a friggin' prince of Abaddon, and you do *not* want to see what happens when I get sufficiently pissed."

"Yeah," Jim said, plopping its big old Newfie butt on my foot in a show of support. "She came close to bringing the Guardians' Guild building down around their ears yesterday."

"I find that rather difficult to believe," Fiat said, eyeing me up and down as if I were a piece of beef.

"Believe it," Rene said, straightening his shoulders and adopting a grim expression. "I was present. I saw the head of the Guild acknowledge her power."

"Such a brave little woman," Fiat answered, clearly

amused. "Threatening the Guardians' Guild all on her own? I am most impressed."

"Aisling is not alone," Uncle Damian said in a low voice that would have sent a lesser man screaming from the scene.

Fiat, however, was not so easily intimidated.

"So I see." His gaze flickered over Uncle Damian before moving to Rene and Traci. "A mortal."

"This is my uncle, Damian Carson. And don't let the mortal bit fool you—Drake has absolute confidence in my uncle's ability to serve as my bodyguard."

Fiat's eyebrows rose a smidgen. "High praise indeed. And here we have . . . a power?"

"Daimon," Rene said, his jaw set firmly.

"A fate. What a very interesting choice of companions." Fiat bowed his head at him before turning back to me. "And two demon minions. Very well, *cara*. Since I have no choice but to accept your foolish desire to be accompanied by a crowd, I will acquiesce. Shall we go? I have a car waiting."

Uncle Damian went into full security mode as we approached the waiting limo, whipping out a small electronic device that he used to examine the car briefly before nodding at me. "It's safe."

"Really, *cara,* you must give me more credit than that," Fiat said in a low voice right next to my ear, his hand cool on my back as I got into the car. A little shiver went down my arms and back as I shrugged his hand off. The blue dragon element was air, which caused them to feel a few degrees cooler than everyone else. "As if I would harm you."

"You don't think shoving a needle in my neck and injecting me with poison is harmful?" I asked, scooting a few inches away when he seated himself next to me. His two bodyguards, just as blond and gorgeous as Fiat himself, took their positions on the seat across from us, while Uncle

Damian, Rene, and Traci were along the side. Jim sat on my feet and covertly drooled on Fiat's expensive shoes.

Fiat reached for my hand. I made a fist and glared at him. He gave an exaggerated sigh instead and let his hand fall. "Why you insist on creating such difficulties is beyond me. The incident with the poison was regrettable, I admit, but alas, necessary."

"That's your interpretation of the word 'necessary,'" I said, starting to get riled up again over the memory of the event a month past.

Oh good. I love it when you get riled.

"*Cara—,*" Fiat started to say.

"No, never mind, it's not important now," I said quickly, trying to squelch the desire to pull on the dark power. "I'm sorry I brought it up. I'd rather focus on the current situation."

Fiat leaned back with casual grace and smiled. Like most of the wyverns, he had a tendency to wear articles of clothing bearing the color of his sept. Currently, he was dressed in an extremely well-cut suit made of midnight blue fabric.

"Is that dragonweave?" I couldn't help but ask, watching with fascination as the material in Fiat's suit seemed to shimmer and change.

"Yes. I shall have some sent to you."

I smiled. "Don't bother. Drake had some made into dresses for me. I just didn't know it came in colors other than green."

"I wouldn't mind a dog collar made in it," Jim said, unobtrusively wiping a tendril of drool on Fiat's pant leg.

Fiat and I both glared at it.

"What?" it asked, blinking its eyes at me in an attempt at innocence.

Rene snickered. Uncle Damian watched Fiat with narrowed eyes. Traci was absorbed in its Palm Pilot, no doubt taking care of some of the business I'd put it in charge of.

"I take it that the meeting today is something important if you've trotted out the good suit?" I asked Fiat.

"You could say that. We will discuss our involvement in the war between the red and green septs."

I stiffened. "Your involvement as in working *with* Chuan Ren?"

"Who can say?" He made an elegant gesture, his eyes half-closed as he watched me. "That is what we meet to decide."

"I think you can guess how my vote is going to go," I answered, smiling as sweetly as I could, which was a minor miracle considering I wanted to throttle Fiat.

Why strain your hands? You could destroy him so much more easily.

"Alas, as my mate, your role is to support me in all things, and thus you do not have a vote of your own."

I ground my teeth just a tiny bit.

"I have every confidence that your support will drive home to the sept just how unswerving is your devotion to me. It will do much to convince them of the rightness of our chosen path."

"You're enjoying this, aren't you?" I asked.

He leaned forward, his sapphire gaze piercing mine. "Oh, yes. Very much so, *cara*."

There was a warning in his voice, a warning I should have taken heed of . . . but hindsight is such an annoying thing.

As dragon events go, the meeting itself started off at a brisk pace. We arrived at the convention center where the gathering was being held.

"Holy cow," I murmured under my breath as Renaldo,

one of Fiat's bodyguards, ushered us into the room where
the meeting was taking place. I was used to the green dragon
sept gatherings with its two hundred or so members. This
room was filled with at least three times that number of
dragons, a vast expanse of ballroom that was covered wall-
to-wall in dragons.

"Merde," Rene whispered under his breath, patting the
spot on his chest where his gun was hidden. "So many?"

"How many members of the blue sept are there?" I asked
Renaldo.

"More than twelve hundred," he answered as we marched
up to a raised dais at one end of the room. Fiat was already
there, surrounded by a group of men. In the center of the
dais was a chair that can only be described as a throne, dark
wood carved into intricate scenes of dragons, embellished
with gold. "Although only half that number is here today.
You sit here when Fiat tells you to."

He turned his back on me. I looked around the platform.
There was a podium with a microphone, the throne, a small
folding chair that was evidently my seat . . . and nothing
else.

"And he talks about me doing things the hard way," I
said, shaking my head and sighing to myself as I strolled off
the platform and over to the first row of chairs. People were
still wandering around, chatting, mingling, and socializing
in general, but the ones nearest me stopped dead and turned
to look as I smiled.

"Hi. You using those? No? Thanks much." I grabbed two
chairs and started hauling them over to the dais.

"Drake will not like that," Rene said as he rushed to take
the chairs from me. "Remember *le bébé*!"

Uncle Damian jumped down and snagged another chair.
Evidently someone said something to Fiat, or he noticed the

shocked silence in my corner of the room, the dragons coming to a halt as they watched my little group carry chairs up to the dais.

"Cara!"

"Chair or floor?" I asked Jim.

It tipped its head to the side. "Oh, chair, don't you think? For maximum effect."

"Cara, what are you doing?" Fiat hurried over to us.

"A demon after my own heart," I said, patting it on its head. I nodded toward another chair. Traci heaved a long-suffering sigh and fetched it. I lifted my chin and smiled at Fiat. "Just arranging for seats for my support team. Set them behind mine, guys, in a nice little row. Excellent. Are we ready to go, Fiat?"

His eyes flashed fury, his hands fisting for a moment before he forced them open. He bowed and gestured toward the chair waiting for me. "As you desire, mate."

The word grated on me coming from his lips, but I knew he knew that, so I kept the smile on my face as I took my place next to him. He stood before the throne, his expression relaxed, but I could feel a sense of keyed-up excitement emanating from him as he waited for everyone to take their seats.

He went through the usual formalities, issuing a greeting in Italian, and going over official sept business that held no interest for me, if Rene's whispered translation was accurate.

It was a bit trying to be formally introduced to the sept as his mate, but I got through it by reminding myself that what could be done, could be undone.

Quite easily, as a matter of fact, but will you do that? Oh no, you insist on being stubborn.

I pushed down the voice, ignoring it as I focused on

Rene's whispers in my ear as he translated Fiat's speech. The members rose and bowed to me when Fiat introduced me, but I had the feeling everyone here knew it was a meaningless gesture.

"You have to wonder what they think of Fiat taking another wyvern's mate as his own," I whispered over my shoulder to Rene.

Renaldo, standing on the other side of Fiat, shot me a glare.

"I do not believe they have much choice in the matter," Rene whispered back. "The blue wyvern seems to rule with very much the hand of iron."

"Wouldn't surprise me to find out he took the position by force," Uncle Damian said softly.

I glanced at him in surprise. "Why do you say that? The blue dragons don't seem to be cowed or afraid of Fiat, just kind of subdued when compared to the green dragons."

"He's got the dictator mentality. Seen it before in men who've forcibly taken over businesses. You watch him—I bet he'll lay down the law to those folks over this war. They won't have a thing to say about it."

"They may not, but I certainly will," I muttered, lapsing into silence at yet another pointed look from Renaldo.

It took another half hour before Fiat stopped speaking, the crowd applauding politely. He turned to me and held out his hand, clearly desiring my presence next to him. I took a deep breath and got up, placing just the tips of my fingers in his hand. I would have ignored it altogether, but I hesitated to embarrass him in that manner with so many sept members watching.

He said something to the crowd, holding up our joined hands. There were several murmurs until a hush fell over them. I glanced back at Rene, who rose and started toward me.

Renaldo intercepted him.

"Rene speaks Italian. He's translating for me," I said quietly to Fiat.

He shook his head at Renaldo, who pushed Rene back into his seat. "You do not need him. I will tell you what is being said. We are to discuss the war now."

Fiat was one of those people who needed his hands to speak, releasing my hand as he addressed the congregation. I covertly rubbed my fingers, trying to get the warmth back into them as he talked. At one point he gestured to someone in the audience, who stood up and said a few words. Fiat smiled, nodded, and spoke some more before turning to me. "You must now state your support of the sept decision, *cara*. I will tell you what to say in Italian. It is not difficult."

I just bet it wasn't. "What exactly has the sept decided?" I asked.

A lazy smile curled his lips. "Naturally, they are distressed by the war and wish to see it brought to a timely end."

"Uh-huh. And that's going to be achieved how? By helping the green dragons beat the snot out of the red ones?"

His smile widened. "The red dragons are stronger, *cara*. They must surely win in time. We will simply ensure that fewer dragons die by helping them bring the war to a swift close."

You know—

I gritted my teeth and blocked out the voice before it could tempt me. "And you expect me to stand here and tell these six hundred dragons that I support that?"

"You have no choice, mate," he answered, his eyes going

cold and hard. "It is your role to support me. To do otherwise would be intolerable."

"Why do you even bother having me speak to them when you know I won't mean a single word?" I asked, frustrated beyond all belief. I hated Fiat at that moment and thought seriously about banishing him . . . except that would get me deeper into trouble than I already was.

What do you have to lose?

"You are my mate. The sept needs to hear you speak."

I took a few deep breaths to calm myself, sick to death of all Fiat's machinations. "Rene?"

Renaldo leaped forward as Rene stood up, obviously intending to stop him. My temper, already frayed, snapped at that point. I spun around and drew a binding ward on Renaldo, stopping him cold.

Uncle Damian and Jim hurried over to stand behind us, Traci following, a wary look on its face.

"You dare?" Fiat hissed, his face tightening. Stephano, the other bodyguard, started toward us. I nailed him to the floor by the same ward.

"I dare. You want me to speak to the sept? Fine, I'll speak, I'll tell them exactly what I think, but Rene is going to translate for me."

I grabbed for the microphone but Fiat caught my arm and jerked me up close to his body. Uncle Damian shouted and would have leaped forward, but I waved him back.

Fiat's eyes burnt into mine, his breath cool on my cheek as he spoke a few inches away from my face. "Do not try it, *cara*. I have not laid my plans so carefully to have you destroy them with a few ill-chosen words."

"Oh, I'll choose my words carefully, I assure you," I told him, fury mingling with an uncomfortable spike of fear.

There was something in Fiat's eyes I hadn't seen before, a conscienceless element that frankly scared me silly.

"You had best do so, if you want to see Drake again," he warned, the intent in his voice crawling along my skin.

"Are you threatening him? You can't do that. It would mean war between the blue and green septs."

His fingers tightened around my upper arm until I thought he would break the bone. "The green dragons would be lost without Drake, as I have so easily proven. If he were dead, they would not fight. Just remember that when you speak to my sept. You hold the fate of your beloved Drake in your hands. Choose your words wisely, *cara*. You will not like the outcome if you do otherwise."

I stared at him, unable to believe what I was seeing and hearing, and yet knowing in my heart he meant what he said. If I told this sept that I did not support Fiat, he'd try to have Drake killed. It wouldn't be an easy feat, but I knew that he wouldn't stop until he'd utterly destroyed Drake.

If he died, so would my heart. I couldn't bear that.

"Aisling?" Rene asked, his eyes going from Fiat to me. "What do you wish me to say?"

Fiat released my arm, standing back, his face a smooth mask. I looked out at all the dragons gathered and wanted to vomit. I had no choice. Fiat after Drake's blood was not an option. If the blue dragons joined forces with the red . . . well, wars had ended before; this one could end as well. I wasn't alone in this battle—I had Drake and friends. We would think of some way to end the war.

"Aisling?" Rene touched my arm.

"You must speak, *cara*. They are waiting."

It went against everything I wanted, everything I felt, everything I knew to be true and right and good, but there was simply no other choice.

There is a way. You choose not to use it. Silly woman.

The dark power nudged me, tempted me, teased me with all the possibilities it had to offer. I fought a little battle within myself to keep from pulling on it, finally turning to Rene and growling through my teeth, "Tell them I support Fiat."

9

"Aisling, are you sure this is wise?"

I paced past where Rene was sitting on the couch, sipping a gin and tonic.

"I don't see that I have a choice. It's either Fiat or us, and I'll be damned if I let him destroy Drake or the sept. In this case, Gabriel is the lesser of two evils."

"I do not know," he said slowly, frowning into his drink. "You said you did not trust him."

"I don't have to trust him to pump him for information," I pointed out.

"This is true. But is there not someone else you can ask for help? What about that man the Guardian mentioned who could help you with the proscription?"

"Dr. Kostich?" A little chill skittered down my back at the memory of my one and only meeting with the man, a few months before in Hungary.

"Yes, that is the one. He is on the committee, no?"

"What committee?" Uncle Damian asked from the depths of one of Drake's deep leather chairs.

"It's the governing body of the Otherworld. And yes, Rene, Dr. Kostich is very powerful and likes to scare the crap out of people when he's annoyed. But he's an archimage, and I doubt if he knows enough about dragon history to help with Fiat—what is it, Suzanne?"

István's girlfriend, a lovely woman who acted as our chef, gave me a wry smile. "It's your stepmother."

"I thought she went shopping?" I asked Uncle Damian. "Didn't you say Paula went out?"

"Yes. I urged her to. I figured you'd rather not sit through another lecture."

I threw him a grateful smile as Jim piped up from where it was lying in front of the gas fireplace. "I thought Ash was going to throw everything to Abaddon in a handbag when Paula hit her with that last one."

"The dark power is nothing to joke about, but I admit, I thought about it for a second or two," I said, shuddering at the mention of the lecture Paula had felt necessary to release upon me when we returned from the blue dragon function. It had started with a demand that I call everyone who had been invited to the wedding with an explanation, and a new date and time of the ceremony, and ended with a general summary of what happens to women who are unable to bring a man to the point of marriage. "What's going on with her now, Suzanne?"

"She can't find her husband. Evidently she parked him at the British Museum, and he's wandered off somewhere."

I sighed and looked at the clock. "Like life isn't complicated enough as is . . . Rene, will you tell Gabriel I'll be back as soon as possible? Hopefully we'll be able to find David quickly—"

"You stay here and have your talk," Uncle Damian said as he got to his feet. "I'm the least important person here— I'll go." His bushy gray eyebrows beetled meaningfully at Rene. "I'm sure you'll be safe enough here, with Rene and that thing."

"Hey! I'm not a thing! I'm an extremely handsome, if cruelly starved, demon," Jim complained, rolling over on its back. "Wanna rub my belly?"

Uncle Damian rolled his eyes and paused in front of me. "I told that man of yours I'd keep you safe while he was gone. He seems to think you're unable to take of yourself. I know better."

I smiled and kissed his cheek. "Thank you for the vote of confidence."

"It seems to me that you've done some foolish things lately, Aisling," he continued, my smile fading at the stern look he bent upon me. "I taught you better. And I expect you to not shame me by doing anything else stupid."

"So much for confidence," Jim said, sniggering slightly.

I sighed. "Pregnant does not mean made of glass, nor does it mean stupid. I'm not going to do anything to endanger myself or the baby. Or anyone else, for that matter."

"See that you don't," he said with another piercing glance, then nodded his head curtly at Rene and left.

"I don't know how I'm going to get through another six and a half months of that sort of behavior," I said, grabbing a couple of tissues from a nearby table, using them to mop up Jim's slobbery flews. "No more belly rubs; you've had enough already. What did you do with your drool bib?"

"Pfft," it answered, standing up and shaking when the doorbell rang. "Looks like your boyfriend is here."

"Boyfriend?" Rene asked, looking surprised.

"Ignore Jim. It was raised by sewer rats." I slapped a polite smile on my face as Suzanne ushered Gabriel into the room.

"Aisling, what a delight it was to receive your message," Gabriel said, taking my hand and kissing the back of it. All the dragons—except the female Chuan Ren—had lovely old-world manners, something that would have seemed pretentious on anyone else, but on them looked perfectly natural.

"Thank you for coming over. I appreciate your willingness to overlook my brusqueness at our last meeting. Do you remember Rene Lesueur?"

Gabriel made a little bow to Rene, who had moved over to stand next to Jim in front of the fireplace. Rene inclined his head, but his normally dancing dark eyes were watchful.

"Hey, Gabe," Jim said, wandering over to snuffle his pants. "He's clean, Ash. No guns or nuclear weapons strapped to his legs."

"Oh, for god's sake . . . go sit over there!" I said, pointing to the fireplace.

Jim grinned and retreated.

"I'm sorry about that. Jim knows better than to examine people without being so ordered."

"It is nothing. I half expected to be frisked coming into the house," Gabriel answered.

"It's not necessary. You know how Drake is about gadgets. He had a millimeter-wave imaging system built into the foyer. It scans everyone who enters for weapons. If you'd been armed, you wouldn't have gotten inside the house," I said, waving him to the couch as I sat at one end.

He sat next to me, his dimples visible. I examined him for a minute, searching his face for any signs of deception. Gabriel was of Australasian and African descent, with brilliant silver eyes, long black hair swept back in cornrows, and a smile that could melt the coldest heart. He exuded a sense of warmth and friendliness that I had trusted until he'd proven he wasn't all that he seemed. His dimples deepened as I sat silent, trying to put into words what I wanted to know without giving away too much of the current situation.

"I won't bite, you know," he said with a distinct twinkle in his eyes. "Unless you ask me to."

"I'm pregnant," I blurted out, my mouth temporarily overriding my brain. "Oh, god. I'm sorry. That came out a lot more abrupt than I meant."

He laughed and took my hand again, giving my fingers a squeeze. "I know. I am very pleased for you. Drake must be ecstatic."

"He is. I just wanted you to know . . . before, last month, before all the nastiness, you made a reference to you and me . . . to *lusus naturae* . . . to us . . . oh hell."

"Abaddon," Jim corrected. I glared. "Sorry. Lips zipped."

"I told you before that the possibility of a pregnancy changed the situation," Gabriel said, his fingers stroking mine. "I don't say that I wouldn't have challenged Drake for you, but not now. I am many things, Aisling, but I do not break up families . . . unless I am driven to do so."

I searched his face again, the hairs on the back of my neck standing on end. "That sounded remarkably like a threat."

"It wasn't meant as one. It was simply a warning that I, too, have limits. As wyvern, I must do everything within my power to protect my sept."

I glanced at Rene. The conversation wasn't going at all along the path I wanted. Rene shrugged. Evidently he didn't understand what it was Gabriel was alluding to, either.

"As it happens, I didn't ask you here to discuss the unfortunate events of last month. You said yesterday that you wanted to help me."

"The proscription," he said, nodding. "I thought you might be interested in that. The history of the silver dragons is not long—you know, perhaps, that my sept was formed when a splinter group left the black dragons?"

"Yeah, Drake told me a little about it. Something about a group of black dragons not being happy with the wyvern?"

Gabriel nodded, his eyes darkening a little. "Baltic. One of the bloodiest and most dangerous dragons ever to rule. When the first silver wyvern pulled our people from the black sept, Baltic cursed us."

"He cursed the wyverns to not have a mate born to them?"

"No. He cursed all members of the sept—no mate is born to any silver dragon. It will stay so until a black dragon is made wyvern, which will never happen, no matter what Baltic hopes."

I stared at Gabriel. "Hopes? Present tense? This Baltic guy is alive?"

"I can't help you with the proscription itself," Gabriel said, looking away as he withdrew his hand. "But I can tell you who helped our member. There is an archimage on the L'au-delà committee—"

"Wait a second," I interrupted, not buying his change of topic. "The dragon who cursed your sept is still alive? Wasn't that whole thing around the Middle Ages?"

"The black dragon sept does not exist," Gabriel said, meeting my gaze with one that was flat and uncompromising. "It destroyed itself centuries ago."

"But dragons don't die so easily. Surely some of the members must have survived."

Gabriel just looked at me, all hints of a smile long since gone. "Your mate was the last member born to the sept. If you wish to know more about their destruction, I suggest you ask him."

"I will." I shook away my mental confusion and refocused on what was important. "I got off topic. I didn't actually want to ask you about the proscription—I've got a referral to Dr. Kostich already, but thanks for mentioning him—what I want to know about is the blue dragons."

Gabriel's eyebrows rose in surprise. "If you don't mind me asking, why? And would not Fiat be the best person to ask for history of his sept?"

"Fiat and I are a bit on the outs," I said with a rueful smile. I chose my words carefully, not wanting to lie outright but wary of giving Gabriel too much information until I knew if he could be trusted. "The blue dragons are going to side with Chuan Ren against Drake. Fiat can't be reasoned with, but perhaps the members of his sept can. I was hoping to get some information about them so I could see what would be the best way to approach them."

"Ah," Gabriel said, nodding. "I will tell you what I know, although I have not interested myself in them overly much."

I bit my tongue to keep from retorting that he could be perfectly chummy with Fiat when it served his interest, instead listening as he ran over the main points in blue dragon history. Most of it was unexceptional, with the usual power struggles of members to become wyvern, and the odd assassination or two.

"Most of the sept was destroyed during the Endless War," Gabriel said, staring into the fire as he dredged through his memory for tidbits.

"Endless War?"

"Yes. It was started by Chuan Ren, but driven in large part by Baltic, who desired to rule all five septs. The resulting war went on for centuries. With his destruction of the bulk of their sept, the blue dragons withdrew from the weyr while they regrouped. They stayed mainly to themselves for the next few centuries, until they reemerged in the late eighteenth century. Did you know that it was a blue dragon who created the recipe for dragon's blood?"

"No, I didn't, although he should get some sort of an award for that. It's the best drink I've ever had."

Gabriel laughed. "Spoken like a true mate. Fiat took over the sept in . . . let me think . . . the early 1920s, I believe." He paused a moment.

"And?" I asked, sensing something in his hesitation.

"There was a bit of an incident when he took over," Gabriel said slowly, an odd look on his face. "Tanistry dictated that his uncle Bastiano be named the next wyvern, but he disappeared somewhat mysteriously, and Fiat came forward to claim the position."

"Fiat took his uncle out of the running, you mean? That wouldn't surprise me."

"No," Gabriel said, shaking his head. "At least, I do not think Fiat had him destroyed. It was said at the time—I was just a young man, you understand, and not yet deep in the politics of the weyr—that Fiat claimed his uncle was insane and had him locked away in a remote village in the Italian Alps."

"Sounds like something Fiat would pull. I assume the uncle wasn't actually insane?"

"I have no idea, but I had never heard he was before that time. As I said, I am not very conversant with the history of the blue dragons, but frankly, what knowledge I do have of them does not lead me to believe that you will stand much of a chance to convince the members to go against their wyvern's will."

"It can't hurt to try," I answered, thinking furiously.

Gabriel remained for another half hour, during which time we chatted lightly about non-dragon topics. He seemed relaxed and open, making it very difficult for me to remain on my guard with him. I had always liked Gabriel—until he betrayed Drake and me—and I wanted to like him again.

But the memory of the prior month was still stark in my mind.

"Thanks for the information," I told him a short while later as I escorted him to the front door, crossing my fingers against the little white lie I was about to tell. "I'm not quite sure what I'll do with it, but it is helpful nonetheless."

Gabriel shot a quick glance over my shoulder to where Jim and Rene stood silent in the doorway to the living room. "It saddens me that you no longer trust me, sweet Aisling."

"Broken trust is hard to overcome," I said slowly. "I'm aware that you may have had a reason I don't know or understand for doing the things that you did, but it's hard for me to just forget them and carry on like nothing happened."

He was silent for a moment. "I have always considered Drake a friend—insomuch as another wyvern can be a friend. I thought the same of you. I regret that my actions seem to you to be a betrayal of that friendship, but you may wish to consider what Fiat would have done if I had refused participation."

A chill knot formed in my stomach and spread slowly outward. After the day's experiences with Fiat, I was in no doubt that his actions would have been just as devastating, if not more, acting on his own. It could well be that Gabriel thought he was tempering Fiat, acting as a buffer and safety net combined in case Fiat went too far in his plan to . . . I shook my head. I still had no idea of what Fiat was up to.

Gabriel sighed. "I'm sorry you do not believe me, Aisling."

"No, it's not that—" I put my hand on his arm to stop him from leaving. "I was shaking my head at myself, not you. Whatever else, I am grateful you were present at that horrible day. I'd be dead or worse if you hadn't saved me, and Drake . . . well, I don't like to think about what would have happened to him. I guess what I'm trying to say is that I'm willing to give our friendship another chance."

He smiled, warmth shining from his eyes as he kissed my hand again. "You have given me much joy, Aisling. I cherish that."

"Fwah. You're not actually buying that big ham's Mary Sunshine act, are you?" Jim asked a minute later after the door closed behind Gabriel.

"You're always pointing out how much there is I don't know," I answered, giving it a pointed look. "Well, maybe Gabriel is right. Maybe he was acting as best he knew how. Maybe he knew it was inevitable that Fiat was going to try to destroy us, and he joined forces with him to keep him from going totally bonkers."

"Yeah, and maybe monkeys will fly out of my butt, but I'm not going to buy any bananas on the chance they will."

"Rene, you're a fate; you must know whether or not Gabriel is telling the truth. I'm sure there's some sort of a rule saying you're not supposed to interfere, but can you at least tell me if he's being honest with me or not?"

Rene donned an inscrutable look. "A daimon is not a mind reader or a seer, *mon ami*. I know no more than you whether or not Gabriel is to be trusted. For that, you must trust your own instincts. Me, I think you're right. I think that perhaps there is more here than we first assumed."

"That's reassuring to hear," I said, marching back into the living room. "Jim, is there any way for me to transport myself and others to another location without using the dark power?"

Jim shook its head. "Not unless you've got Captain Kirk in your pocket."

"Very funny. Right. I guess we're going to have to do this the hard way. Traci, I summon thee."

Traci appeared before us, stark naked, wet, and covered in bubbles.

"Oh, jeez, I'm sorry—I didn't mean to interrupt your bubble bath. Here, take this blanket . . ."

The look the demon gave me as it snatched a small cashmere lap blanket from my hands was one that could have curdled an entire dairy full of milk. "Is it too much to ask that you warn me before summoning?" it snapped.

"Sorry. I didn't know that . . . er . . . demons bathed."

Its eyes opened wide in indignation. "Of course we bathe! I'm a demon, not a barbarian." Traci took a deep breath and visibly calmed itself. "I apologize for the tone of my voice, my lord. I assume you summoned me to discuss the situation in Paris."

"What situation in Paris?"

I thought Jim had a long-suffering look down pat, but Traci's expression put Jim to shame. "The situation about which I have been trying to talk to you for some time. The one concerning the role of Venediger, which you so . . . *graciously* . . . inflicted upon me."

"What about it? I haven't heard anyone complain about the job you're doing, so you're obviously doing something right."

"I am referring to the challenger to the position," Traci all but snapped, clearly at the end of its rope. "I have sent you faxes and e-mails about it, not to mention copious voice mails, but you have not responded!"

"Someone wants to take the position over? Is it someone evil?" I asked with a little stab of guilt at the fact that I'd been avoiding dealing with anything but the most pressing of items.

"Not that I am aware. The challenger is a mage by the name of Jovana."

"Human? Not a demon lord or demonic in any sense of the word?"

"No. Evidently she is well-known in the community as a scholar."

"Oh, well then," I said with a relieved sigh, waving away the worry that someone like Bael was trying to take control of the French Otherworld. "She sounds perfect for the job. Let her win the challenge. I'm glad that's taken care of, because I need you to book me three tickets to—what was the name of that little town in Italy that Gabriel mentioned?"

"But, my lord—"

"Santa Cristina?" Rene answered.

"That's the one. It's in the Tyrol, he said. I want you to book us three tickets on as direct a flight as you can get us, and arrange for a car while you're at it."

Traci fretted as I started out of the room. "My lord, the challenge—"

I paused long enough to give it a firm smile. "I know it's kind of galling to purposely throw a challenge, but believe me, you'll get over it fast enough."

"But what sort of challenge—"

"It doesn't matter. Pick whatever sort of event you like for the challenge," I said, ruthlessly interrupting its bleats. Traci had a tendency to go on and on about trivial matters if you didn't keep a firm hand with it. "Now please get onto finding us those tickets. I want to be out there as soon as we can. I assume you'll want to come, Rene?"

"I wouldn't miss it . . . er . . . what is it exactly we will be doing in Italy?"

"We're going to enact a revolution," I said succinctly, and closed the door softly on the stunned expressions of their faces.

10

"I'm cold."

"Shush. Is that it, Rene?"

A tiny penlight pierced the blackness of the car and shone down on a map. "I think so."

"It's got to be below zero in here. Can we turn on the heat, at least?"

"No. We don't want anyone to hear the car. Was that an owl? A real owl, or a some sort of a signal, do you think?" I asked, peering blindly out into the night. Surrounded as we were by dense forest, there was nothing to see but a whole lot of dark.

Rene's shadow cocked its head. "I did not hear. Aisling, I am beginning to believe that perhaps there are not the guards present that you imagined."

"I can't feel my toes. I can't feel my legs. I can't feel my package," Jim said in a mournful tone. "How'm I ever going to make little demons if my package ices up and drops off, huh? *Huh?*"

"Oh, for heaven's sake! Here, you can have my blanket, although I'd like to point out that you do, in fact, have a thick furry coat, and your genitals are not going to freeze and fall off your body." I wrapped the car blanket that I'd been huddled under around Jim, who recoiled in horror.

"I'm not going to take a blanket away from a pregnant woman! That's like a cardinal sin or something! I'll get double demerits!"

"Oh, stop comp—ack!" I jumped at least a foot off the backseat of the car, where Jim and I had been sitting, at the sudden movement outside the window. "Uncle Damian! You just about gave me a heart attack!"

"You told me to be stealthy," he said gruffly as he slid into the front passenger seat. "You can turn the engine on, Rene. There's no one out here."

"Oh, good, heat at last. I hope one of my legs doesn't snap off before it's thawed out," Jim said, crowding forward to try to get some of the heat as Rene started the car.

"There's no one? Are you sure?" I asked Uncle Damian. He raised an eyebrow.

"Yeah, yeah, I know, you were in the black berets or something during the war," I said, trying to mollify him.

"The term is black ops. Not that I'm admitting to having been involved in anything like that," he said.

"Plausible deniability, we know. But it's been a few years since you were doing anything like that, and if Fiat has dragons guarding his uncle, they could be very tricky."

"Aisling, I said there was no one out there," he answered, his voice as hard as flint.

"Well, hell."

"Abaddon."

I sucked on my lower lip for a moment, thinking hard and fast. "Maybe this isn't the right place."

"It's the right place," Uncle Damian answered.

"You're sure that Bastian Blu lives here?"

"That's what the man said."

I thought a bit more. "He could be lying. I wouldn't put

it past Fiat to have set up a false house so people would think his uncle was here, but really, he was somewhere else."

Uncle Damian sighed, his breath making a little puff of smoke in the cold mountain air. The Italian Alps in winter were lovely, but there was a reason that the tiny town of Santa Cristina was best known as a ski resort. Outside the car, the snow was piled up at least six feet deep. "He didn't lie. I didn't give him the opportunity to do so. I may not have been in the service for twenty-six years, but I have not forgotten how to interrogate an individual or search for enemy patrols. Now let's get going. I can think of other places I'd rather be than sitting here."

Rene turned the wheel and drove us up a long, snowy road, the headlights picking up occasional glimpses of startled deer and nocturnal animals as they hurried out of our path.

"I can't believe Fiat doesn't have anyone guarding his uncle," I mused, pinching my lip.

"Maybe no one cares about him." Jim shrugged. "Fiat's been in control of the sept for a long time. Maybe he doesn't think his uncle is a threat anymore."

I smiled to myself. "He's going to have a big surprise then, isn't he?"

"Maybe. Or maybe it'll be you that gets the surprise," Jim said.

"Bah. Holy cow, is that the villa?" I gawked as the car rounded a wooded curve, the sight of a large square stone villa being highlighted by the car's lights. "That's a heck of a nice place to be exiled to."

As we drove up to the front, I could see that the main part of the villa was shaped like a square block, but an addition on one side gave it a bit more depth. On the far side, standing slightly away from the main building, a four-story stone square tower pulled the eye upward, following the line of the hill behind it. Gothic domed windows and doors gave the place a faintly medieval sense, a feeling that was enhanced by the aged figure who opened one of the double front doors as we stopped before them.

"Hello. Do you speak English?" I asked the elderly man who stood bent and crooked, carrying a large candelabra in one hand.

"Yes," the old man said, gesturing toward the open door with the candles. The flames danced and sputtered in the freezing night air, not doing a whole lot to light up the area around us. The old man squinted at me for a minute. "You are a mate. You are here to see Signor Blu?"

"Yes, we are. My name is Aisling Grey. Er . . . is Mr. Blu up to having visitors?"

The old man blinked rheumy eyes at me. I was startled to see that his pupils were elongated, although it made sense that dragons were taking care of Fiat's uncle. Still, it was rare you saw an elderly one.

"Is he . . . I mean, he's not strapped into anything, right?"

"Strapped into anything?" He looked at me like I was the one who'd been shut away for being insane.

I glanced at the others. They just stood silent, content to let me handle things. Blast them. "We don't want to disturb Mr. Blu if he is . . . unwell."

"The signor has remarkable health." The old guy gestured toward the door. "We do not have many visitors. Enter."

"Thank you. It's a bit cold out tonight," I said, stepping into the villa, trying to keep from gawking at the gorgeous surroundings as the old man hurried us through an open-vaulted entryway. Given that he walked about as fast as an elderly snail, there was plenty of time for appreciating the décor.

I felt a little tingle as I went through the doorway, usually a sign of a protection ward. Jim had no problem passing through it, though, so it couldn't have been a very strong one.

"Stand as far away from anything antique as is possible, don't shed, and try not to drool," I ordered it in a low tone of voice as we were escorted into a small room.

"You're so anal these days. It's just a bit of old furniture. Hey, you think that's a Fabergé egg over there?"

"Move so much as one toenail, and I'll have your ears!" I whispered, praying that I could get through the evening without disaster striking.

"The man, he did not seem to act as if his master was insane," Rene mused as he examined the paintings hanging on the wall. "When you told us of your plan last night, I was not so sure it would work. People are not locked away without reason, *hein*? But now . . . pfft. It is possible."

"It pretty much hinges on whether Fiat was being kind to an ailing relative, or a rat fink who wouldn't hesitate to strong-arm family out of his path to power. Knowing him as I do, I'm willing to bet you that his uncle is as sane as I am."

Three pairs of eyes considered me with what I thought was excessive speculation. Before I could point that out, the door opened and Fiat stepped into the room.

"Oh, shit," I swore under my breath, desperately trying to think of some explanation for being there.

Rene was standing close enough to hear me. *"Merde,"* he corrected.

"Um . . . hi, Fiat," I said with all the wit and vim of a stale pancake. "I expect you'd like to know why we're here, huh?"

Fiat's eyes widened. "An explanation is always pleasant, although I believe greetings are generally conducted first.

Orazio said your name is Aisling Grey? I am Bastiano de Girardin Blu."

My jaw dropped. I couldn't help myself, it dropped a whole inch or so while I stared at the Fiat double and tried to process the information. "You're Fiat's *uncle*?"

"Yes." He nodded, glancing at the others. His voice had a heavier Italian accent than Fiat's, but other than that, it was difficult to tell the two men weren't one and the same. "You are a Guardian. You have a demon with you. You are here to banish me to the Akasha?"

"Am I seeing things, or does he look just like Fiat?" I whispered to Jim.

"There are a few differences. He isn't a snake in the grass, for one," it answered.

Bastiano straightened his shoulders. It was really uncanny how much he looked like Fiat, from the curly blond hair, to the brilliant blue eyes, right down to the same square chin. "I knew this day would come. If you will allow me a few minutes to see to my people, I would be grateful."

"No, I'm sorry—" I said, about to explain the misunderstanding.

"They have been with me since Fiat imprisoned me. They are harmless, but deserve a reward for serving me so well," Bastiano interrupted. "If you wish me to beg you for this concession, I will do so."

"Oh, jeez, no! Mr. Blu, you've got this totally wrong. We're not bad guys," I said, waving my hand toward the three others. "I'm a Guardian, yes, and Jim is a demon, but we're not here to banish you to limbo. We're here to rescue you."

"Rescue me?" Now it was his turn to look stunned. "Do you mean it? No, you cannot. This is a cruel game you play."

"I assure you, we're not playing games. Maybe I'd better start at the beginning . . ."

"You're gonna want to sit down," Jim told the dragon. "Once she gets going, it's hard to stop her."

"Silence, demonic one," I said, smiling at Bastiano. If I thought he looked surprised at the news that we weren't there to banish him, he was downright flabbergasted by the time I was done relating the pertinent events of the last few months.

"You were the mate of the green wyvern—I am glad to know that Drake still has charge of the sept—but now you are Fiat's mate?" he asked.

"In name only. Fiat tricked us into that situation. He's . . . well, you know what he is."

Bastiano nodded. "Cruel," he said.

"Bastard," Jim said with a sniff.

"Evil to the core," said Rene.

"Looks like a porn star," added Uncle Damian. "Don't trust men who look like they make their livings with their dicks."

A slight flush rose on Bastiano's cheeks.

"Present company excluded, naturally," I told him, shooting my uncle a glance. "This is going to sound horribly rude, I just know it, but would you mind me asking how old you are? Because you really do look just like Fiat, and I wondered if you were born around the same time as him?"

He blinked. "I was born in 1442. Fiat was born to my sister in . . . I believe it was 1585? Sometime around then, so yes, I was still young when he was born. As for the similarity of our appearance . . ." His hands made an eloquent gesture of dismissal. "That is a family trait, and not important. What *is* important is the regrettable fact that by your very act of coming here, you have doomed yourself to imprisonment as well."

"Huh?" I asked, trying hard to keep my jaw from dropping a second time.

"Do you think I would stay here if I could leave?" His eyes darkened until they were almost black. "This house is nothing more than a prison, and for us all, there is no way out."

11

"No one . . . argh . . . locks me . . . oooph! . . . into a house without my . . . dammit! That hurt! . . . permission! Look out!"

The confinement wards that were drawn each morning on all exits of the house by one of Fiat's employees were pretty darned good, but not good enough. True, it took me five minutes of struggling to shove Bastian (who told us he preferred the shortened form of his name) through the one on the front door, but in the end, brute force and my own determination won the day.

"That was sure a heck of a lot easier coming in than going out," I said, blowing a strand of hair back from my damp forehead.

Bastian looked a bit worse for wear, but at last he stood on the front steps of the house in which he'd been held a prisoner for eighty-some years, jubilation filling his face as he swung his arms wide and spun in a circle. "I do not believe it! You did it! You have done the impossible!"

"All in a day's work," I said modestly, watching as he executed a little dance of joy. "I've had pretty good luck getting through wards before, so I was almost certain I could get you out of this one, too."

"Hey, Princess Modesty, you want to come flex your

übermuscles for us, too?" Jim called from just inside the doorway.

"Oh, sorry. Yeah, let me give you guys a hand." I entered the house, feeling only a little tingle of the ward until I turned around and tried to leave again.

Bastian babbled happily as over the next forty minutes I shoved Jim, Rene, Uncle Damian, three elderly retainers who had taken care of Bastian and were loyal to him rather than Fiat, and what seemed to be an inordinate amount of luggage out through the confinement ward. By the time we were done, I was exhausted and had a horrible feeling that I looked like I'd been pulled through a hedge backwards a few dozen times.

"The demon says you have a plan," Bastian said a short while later as Rene returned from fetching a taxi. The five of us piled into the car Rene had rented, with Bastian's people taking the taxi. "Now that I am free, you may count on my assistance in whatever manner you deem necessary."

"We're going to fly back to London first," I answered, chewing on my lip and wishing I'd thought more about what we were going to do once we had Bastian. "Fiat is there right now, and it seems as good a place as any to tackle the situation."

Bastian nodded and waited for me to continue.

"Er . . . I haven't quite worked out all the details, but I thought you could go before the blue dragons, tell them how Fiat unjustly imprisoned you so he could be wyvern when he wasn't born to the job, have him removed, and then you can take over and disown me as mate."

The silence that followed my words was almost deafening. "*That* is your plan?" Bastian asked.

I nodded.

"The full extent of it?"

I nodded again, a bit less enthusiastically.

He sighed and sat back against the seat, his eyes closed.

Uncle Damian turned around in the seat to give me a dark look. Jim pursed its lips. Rene's gaze in the rearview mirror was all too readable.

"Well, I'm doing the best I can!" I burst out, pricked by all those looks. "I can't think of everything! It's not like I don't have a gazillion other things on my mind!"

"It's all right," Bastian said, his eyes still shut. "You have done the impossible already, the rest is up to me."

His face was barely visible in the darkness, little flashes of it glowing dimly now and again as the lights from buildings penetrated the car.

"A challenge?" I asked.

"Yes. You said Fiat engineered the situation with you via a challenge . . . very well. I will give him a taste of his own medicine."

I eyed the man next to me. His voice had thus far been lyrical and quite pleasant to listen to, but a note of something indefinable had entered it at the last minute. Was that phrase "the enemy of my enemy is my friend" quite so true as I had hoped? Or had I just unleashed a power a whole lot worse than Fiat?

"Merde," I muttered.

"No word?" Uncle Damian asked six hours later as I rubbed my arms in the cold morning air, our conversation drowned out for a moment by the sound of a plane taking off.

I shook my head, worry making my belly churn. "That's not like him. He didn't even have his voice mail on, and he always has that in case I need him for something. I don't mind saying I'm starting to get really worried. And pissed. Dammit, why didn't he tell me where he was going?"

"He doesn't want you following," Uncle Damian answered as I watched people haul their luggage over to the passenger pickup area.

"Arrogant, foolish, bossy man," I grumbled to myself. "Jim, I summon thee."

Jim popped into view, shaking itself in a manner guaranteed to send dog hair and spittle flying. "Do you have to send me to the Akashic plane every time? Couldn't I, like, go somewhere else? Bahamas? Venice? How about the Mexican Riviera?"

"Hush, someone will hear you. Do you think we did the right thing by letting Bastian go off on his own?" I asked my uncle.

"Possibly. I'll check into the address he gave us to make sure he's not up to anything."

"I just thought it was a bit odd that he didn't want to stay with us, but I guess it makes sense that he must still have friends in the sept who would take him in. Oh, good, here comes Rene with the car."

I picked up my small bag, glancing at my cell phone for a moment, willing Drake to call me and tell me he was OK, but no such miracle happened.

"As usual, it's up to me to make my own miracles," I said, sighing wearily.

"Uh-oh. That's bound to end up with me losing another toe or two," Jim said, backing away from me.

"I said hu—aieeee!"

A short, squat man suddenly burst into being directly in front of us, growling in a voice that had chunks of cement flaking off a wall behind me, "You are summoned."

Before I could protest, the demon grabbed my arm and yanked me through the hole it had created. Uncle Damian threw himself on me just before I was sucked in, the two of us falling together in a heap on a cold stone floor.

I knelt on my hands and knees for a moment while I fought the horrible sensations that accompanied being yanked through the fabric of being, finally raising my head to see which demon lord had summoned me so summarily.

"I should have guessed," I said a moment later as Uncle Damian, looking a bit green about the gills, helped me to my feet.

"You all right?" he asked.

"Yeah. You?"

He nodded, glancing around quickly. "We where I think we are?"

"Yes. Welcome to Abaddon. Jim, I summon thee."

"Fires of Ab—woops." Jim's mouth slammed shut as soon as the figure standing at a window turned toward us.

"Aisling Grey," the man said, looking much as I remembered him. Dark-haired, handsome, with a slight European accent—but it was his eyes that bothered me the most. They were flat, a façade to hide his true thoughts. He raised his eyebrows at Uncle Damian. "And a mortal?"

"This is my Uncle Damian. Uncle, this is Bael, the premier prince of Abaddon, and incidentally the one who tricked me into taking on this position and ending up proscribed."

"I'm evil," Bael said with a shrug. "It's what I do best."

"Does he always . . . er . . . summon you this way?" Uncle Damian asked, watching Bael warily.

"Yes. Annoying, isn't it?"

Uncle Damian appraised the demon lord and answered in a voice that was rich with warning, "I'm not sure I'd use that word just now."

"You have much more circumspection than your niece,

who has decreed this manner of communication by her repeated dismissal of much more civilized attempts at meeting," Bael answered, seating himself in a deep, black leather chair. There was nowhere for us to sit, not that I wanted to make myself comfortable for a cozy little chat with the head honcho of Hell. "You cannot blame me, Aisling Grey, if you drive me to taking extreme measures. And speaking of pleasures waiting to be had at your expense, might I ask when I may expect my homage?"

"Er . . . homage? What homage would that be?"

"Surely you have read the Doctrine by now?" Bael asked, tapping his fingers on a letter opener that appeared to be made of bone.

I wondered if there was ever going to be a time when I wasn't at least five paces behind everyone else, mentally speaking.

Bael sighed and set down the letter opener, waving a hand that instantly summoned a minion. "Nefere, present Aisling Grey with the Doctrine of Unending Conscious."

The demon, short, squat, and reeking of evil, rolled over to me with a peculiar gait. I stood my ground, not recoiling from its presence as I wanted to do, instead watching with increasing horror as it bared its yellow teeth at me in a grotesque parody of a smile, then pulled out a penknife and slashed a sizeable chunk of skin off its arm.

"Oh, my god!" I screamed as it slapped the repulsive blob of skin into my hand. My own flesh crawled as I stared at the monstrosity that lay wetly on my fingers. It wasn't particularly bloody, demons not going in much for blood, but the mere fact that it was someone's skin made me want to run screaming from the room. "What the hell is this?"

"Doctrine," the demon answered.

The blob of flesh continued to hold an unhealthy fascination for me. I couldn't look away from it, just kept staring at it as if I expected it to . . . what, I had no idea. It was just so terrible, I couldn't look away from it.

"The Doctrine of Unending Conscious is the set of laws that govern Abaddon," Bael said in a bored voice. "It is burnt into the flesh of all minions. I would be surprised that any other demon lord had not availed himself of it in order to learn our ways, but your continued flaunting of our traditions no longer surprises me. Read the Doctrine and return to me with the homage."

"There's a whole doctrine on it?" I asked, feeling in my pocket for something into which I could place the chunk of skin. I squinted at it, seeing the faintest spidery writing in its wrinkled folds. "I'm going to have to use a microscope to read it!"

"You want bigger piece?" Nefere asked, pulling up its shirt and flicking open its penknife.

"No!" I yelled as it was about to slash off a piece of skin from its stomach. "This is fine. I'll just use a microscope."

Bael glanced at his desk calendar. "The new moon is in five days. You have until that time to bring me the sacrifices."

I considered the last word he spoke with much foreboding. "This homage is going to involve something truly appalling, isn't it?"

"You are dismissed," he answered without glancing our way.

I wanted badly to tell him that there was no way I'd ever participate in rituals of Abaddon, but luckily, I didn't have the chance. Nefere picked me up with one arm and, before I could do so much as yell for help, tossed me out on the front steps of a redbrick house.

"Hey! Be more careful with her! Aisling is—"

"Jim, silence!" I snarled as I got to my feet, rubbing my

hip where it had hit one of the stone columns that supported a portico. The last thing I needed was for everyone in Abaddon to know I was pregnant.

"Did he hurt you?" Uncle Damian asked, dusting me off. "Should we go to a hospital?"

"No, I'm fine. I more rebounded off the column than hit the ground." Behind us, the door slammed. I looked around, not recognizing the area. The house appeared to be isolated on a few acres of landscaped lawn. A crushed-gravel path led down to a wrought-iron gate. "Anyone have any idea where we are? Jim, you can talk, just keep quiet about the baby, OK?"

"Sorry," it answered, rubbing its head on my hand. "I don't know where we are, but rumor going around the demonic watercooler said that Bael liked to mingle with the mortal world. This must be his place."

We walked slowly down the drive, no one else in sight until we reached the gate. A demon stood there, watching us silently until we stopped before it.

"We are leaving. Unlock the gate," Uncle Damian told it.

The demon sneered, crossing its arms over its sizeable chest. "I don't take orders from mortals."

"How about from a prince of Abaddon?" I snapped, too tired to put up with crap from a demon. "Jim, who is this idiot?"

"Kobal. I heard he got dumped onto sentry duty because his master caught him doing time with a supermodel."

"Better to take a lesser job than to be excommunicated altogether, Effrijim," it snarled at Jim. "That makes, what, two for you? First from the Court, then from Amaymon's legions?"

Jim rolled its eyes. "Yeah, right, like being booted out of Abaddon ruined my day."

"Enough," I interrupted, a headache starting to build. "Open the damned gates. We want to get out of here."

The sneer dropped a notch or two, but the demon stood impassive, its gaze shifting between us. "You have no authority over me, Lord Aisling."

I leaned close to it. "No? Your boss told us to leave. You want us to tell him that you were the one who defied his explicit order?"

Kobal had the gate opened before you could say "demonic blackmail." We stood outside it, glancing up and down a deserted street. There were no other houses to be seen, nothing but pastures and woods on either side, as far as the eye could see.

"I guess we walk," I sighed, suddenly too tired to even contemplate moving one foot in front of another.

"You sit and call Rene to pick us up," Uncle Damian said, pointing at a brick planter.

"I'm sure he'd be happy to, but we don't know where we . . . oh."

Uncle Damian held up his cell phone. I used to tease him about his obsession with the latest electronic gadget, but I had to admit that now was a time when it came in handy. "GPS?"

"Yes," he replied, punching in a few buttons. "We're not far out of London."

My butt was numb from sitting on the hard brick planter by the time Rene toodled out from town and tracked us down thanks to the global positioning device. It didn't take that long to make up my mind, however. By the time we were back home, I'd come to a decision.

"Uh-oh," Jim said as I marched into the house, throwing my purse on a chair and heading straight for Drake's office. "Warning, warning! Danger, Will Robinson!"

"What are you going on about?" I heard Uncle Damian ask from the hall.

"She's got that look on her face. The one that says she's been watching too many William Holden movies again."

"I'm mad as hell, and I'm not going to take this anymore!" I shouted at no one in particular as the three of them followed after me. "Traci, I summon thee."

The demon appeared, its arms curled around something that wasn't there, spinning blithely on one foot until it stumbled to a stop.

"Were you . . . dancing?" I asked, momentarily distracted by the thought of a dancing demon.

It narrowed its eyes and dropped its arms. "Is there anything in the rules that says I can't take dance lessons?"

"No, but why . . . oh, never mind. Here." I pulled out the handkerchief my uncle had given me earlier and dumped the piece of flesh into Traci's hand. "Read this, then report back to me on any loopholes you can find to get out of paying some sort of homage to Bael."

The demon's eyes widened as it stared at the repulsive bit of flesh, prodding it with the tip of one finger. "Is this . . . is this the Doctrine?"

"Yes. Bael says I have to pay homage. He mentioned a sacrifice."

Traci nodded. "Six innocent souls must be paid to the ruling prince."

"Only six? Lovely." I snatched up the phone, punched Drake's cell phone number, listened for a minute as he did not answer, then slammed down the receiver and started out of the room. "Find me a loophole. Put every single demon in my legions onto the problem, but find me a way to get out of it!"

"Where are you going now?" Uncle Damian asked as I ran up the curved stairs to the floor above.

"To bed. If a dream is the only way Drake wants to talk to me, then by god, I'm going to have a dream he'll never forget!"

12

"Come out, come out, wherever you are!"

My voice echoed along the long, dark room as I lazily swam into deeper shadows. This dreamscape was familiar—a stone swimming pool filled with warm, scented water that was one of Drake's favorite places. Columns lined either side of the pool, their shadowy fingers stretching across the surface of the water like inky tendrils. It was impossible to see anything beyond the columns, although I knew that at the far end of the room, a scarlet fainting couch resided. Usually we never made it as far as the couch, Drake preferring to make love in the water, but as I swam slowly down the length of the pool, I searched the shadows for signs of my errant lover.

"I know you're here, sweetie. I can feel your presence. Are you teasing me with your dragon form?"

I waited for a flash of green scales in the dim light or flicker of a tail in my peripheral vision. Nothing moved but the water. I swam on, briefly admiring the white mosaic of a leaping horse on the bottom of the pool.

"You're not in the least bit shy, which means you're teasing me. Normally I'd be up for that, but I've had a day from Abaddon—literally—and I could really use the benefit of your oh-so-sexy self. Why don't you come out here and make mad, passionate dragon love to me, and then we can play hide-and-go-seek in the shadows, hmm?"

There was no answer, no sound from even the darkest depths of the shadows. I paused, treading water as I listened intently. The only sound was of me in the water, and yet I knew Drake was here. I could feel him nearby, feel the heat that always accompanied him, my body reacting to his nearness just as it always did. And yet . . . something wasn't right.

I opened the door in my mind that gave me access to my powers, using my improved vision to look deeper into the shadows surrounding me.

A flash of white caught the corner of my eye. I spun around in the water, watching with openmouthed surprise as a white lion padded out from the blackness to the edge of the pool. The animal simply looked at me for a moment before turning around and fading into the darkness.

"Um . . . OK. Is this some sort of game? Am I supposed to guess the meaning of a white lion?"

A fluttering sound overhead drew my attention to a great bird the size of an eagle that soared over me. It, too, disappeared into the shadows.

"Right. White lion and big eagle. Er . . . nope. Not getting it."

Behind me, a low growl rumbled. I twisted around in the water, backpedaling madly as a huge tiger crouched at the edge of the pool, its muscles bunched as if it was about to spring. Before I could back up more than a few feet, it launched itself into the air. I shrieked and instinctively ducked, but the animal simply dissolved into nothing directly over my head.

"Ten out of ten for style, but I'm going to have to seriously dock you for the frustration factor, not to mention just about scaring the crap out of me," I called out, swimming somewhat shakily to the steps and climbing out of the pool. Before me, one end of the fainting couch lay half-hidden in shadows, a large green cloth draped over one end. It was covered in symbols and what looked to be writing in Hindi, a springing horse in the center bearing some sort of fire on its back. I squinted at it for a moment, then realized it was the same pattern as was on the bottom of the pool. I wrapped the cloth around me, trying to hold on to the tattered edges of my patience. "Enough of the funny animals. When does the sexy, naked dragon show up?"

A man stepped out of the shadows at the far end of the pool, looking around him curiously.

"Gabriel?"

He turned around to face me, confusion written all over his face. "Aisling?"

"What are *you* doing in my dream?" I asked him, clutching the cloth tighter around myself.

"I don't know," he answered, stepping backwards until he disappeared into the shadows. I ran down the length of the pool, but by the time I made it to his end, he was gone.

"I don't think this is funny, Drake!" I yelled, spinning around helplessly. "I don't think this is funny at all!"

"Aisling?"

"I'm not laughing!" I bellowed, my voice echoing down the columns.

"No, but you are yelling. Fires of Abaddon, you're a heavy sleeper."

I opened my eyes to find Jim peering down at me. "Huh? What? Jim?"

"In glorious Technicolor. You OK? You were yelling in your sleep. And not a good sort of 'Drake was boinking your brains out' yell, either."

I pushed my hair out of my face and sat up. "I was dreaming. There was no boinking, not that that is any of your business. What . . . what the heck?"

A small green cloth was clutched in my hand. I spread it out on the bed, staring at it. It was a smaller version of the one I'd had wrapped around myself in the dream. "Where did this come from?"

"Tibet, from the looks of it. You may want to get up and get dressed."

"Tibet?" I said, looking closer at the cloth.

"Yeah, it's a prayer flag, isn't it? What they call a wind horse?"

I traced the figure of the horse in the center of the cloth, noticing with a prickle of gooseflesh that drawn in each corner were four animal symbols—a dragon, lion, tiger, and bird. "What on earth?"

"Ash, I really think you need to get up and get dressed. Traci said we were going to be summoned at three, and it's five after already."

"Oh, god. This is going to be another one of those days where people start talking about stuff like I know what's going on, only I really don't, and I spend the whole time trying to catch up, isn't it?" I asked, pointing a finger at Jim.

"Yup," it answered cheerfully.

I thought of pinning the demon down with questions, but if experience had taught me anything, it was not to question when Jim said to get dressed. I gathered up a bundle of clothing and retired to the bathroom, emerging a few minutes later to find Jim, Traci, and my uncle standing together in my bedroom.

"If you tell me you know what's going on while I'm in the dark, I may well scream," I told Uncle Damian.

"How can you not know what's going on?" he asked, frowning.

I gritted my teeth and fought back the scream, turning instead to the steward. "What's happening?"

The little rat had the nerve to look smug. "It is time for the challenge for the position of Venediger," it answered.

"Ah," I said, enlightenment dawning. "And I am supposed to watch you duke it out with the contender? OK. You guys could have chosen a better time, but I suppose it's petty to quibble about a little lack of sleep."

Traci looked at Jim. Jim looked at Uncle Damian. Uncle Damian frowned even harder.

"What?" I asked, a horrible presentiment stealing over me with an icy chill. "Oh, dear god. You can't possibly mean . . . no."

"You are the one holding the title of Venediger," Traci pointed out, making me close my eyes as I tried to block out the horror of the truth. "I am simply acting on your behalf. Therefore, it falls to you to conduct the actual challenge, not me."

"This is what you were trying to tell me the other day, isn't it?" I asked, swearing at myself.

"It is."

I opened my eyes, glancing with longing at the bed. There was nothing more I wanted at that moment than to crawl back into it, pull the covers over my head, and block out the world. "Right. Lesson learned: don't assume you know what a minion is thinking. What horrible event have you set up for me as the challenge? Dueling pistols? Swords? I really could do without being skewered again. The dragon doctor said the baby wasn't hurt by the last sword someone jammed through me, but I'd like to not risk that again."

Traci's face took on a shocked appearance. "My lord, I would not arrange for you to participate in an event that put you in danger of physical harm."

"Oh," I said, mollified. "Well, thank you. I appreciate that. What form will the challenge take?"

An odd expression stole over the demon's face, one of mingled embarrassment and discomfort. "It was not easy to get the mage Jovana to agree to a form of challenge that would not harm you, my lord."

"Uh-huh. What did you settle on?"

Traci pointed to Jim. "It was Effrijim's idea. I asked it what sorts of skills you had, thinking to use that as a basis for a challenge that you would be comfortable with."

I turned my attention on Jim, starting to get worried.

Nerves shot? Love life got you down? Heinous challenge for superiority on the horizon? Have we got the product for you! Try new and improved Dark Power for the solution to all the pesky problems in your life!

"It wasn't easy, let me tell you," Jim said, meeting my gaze without flinching in the least. "I mean, you could hardly have a challenge based on eating a whole box of chocolate-covered Oreos without once ralphing, could you?"

I made a face at it.

"Or balancing a spoon on the end of your nose."

"Hey now! That's very difficult to do!" I protested.

"Yuh-huh. I did think of the one thing you've gotten really good at of late."

"Castration with just one glance?" I asked sweetly.

"Boinking Drake. But I figured you wouldn't want the mage having her shot at him, in case, you know, she was better at it than you."

I narrowed my eyes at the demon. "You are perilously

close to eunuchdom, dog. What did you tell Traci to use as the challenge?"

"Dragon's Lair."

I blinked a couple of times, hoping against hope it would clear the obvious problem in my hearing. "What?"

"Dragon's Lair. You know, the arcade game? Your uncle says you were addicted to it when you were younger."

"She played it night and day," Uncle Damian said, nodding. "Couldn't get her away from the damned arcade place for a good two years. Had to threaten to send her to one of those cult detox places before she stopped playing."

"I was in college!" I told him. "Everyone played it!"

He raised an eyebrow.

"Yeah, so I figured if you were Miss Dragon's Lair, then you were probably pretty good at it," Jim finished. "So I told Traci to try that."

Traci nodded. "The mage didn't want to accept it as a form of challenge, feeling the more traditional fight to the death was in line with the importance of the position, but when I pointed out to her that you had hundreds of thousands of demons who would avenge you if need be, she decided to withdraw the lethality requirement of the challenge."

"You're getting a raise," I told the steward.

It smiled modestly. "I do my best to serve you in all things, Lord Aisling."

And so it was that a half hour later, I found myself at a familiar machine, my hands caressing the familiar lines of the sleek black plastic as the jaunty little Dragon's Lair tune burbled happily around us.

The mage, Jovana, was a serious-looking woman with a pageboy cut and dark power suit that all but reeked professional. I offered her my hand when we met; she just looked at it as if I was still holding the repulsive bit of demon flesh.

"I do not touch others," she said curtly without the least hint of apology. "It upsets my psyche."

"Ah. Sorry. So, best two out of three high scores wins?"

She nodded, her mouth a thin slash in her white face. "I wish to formally protest the method of this challenge. It does not represent in the least the importance of the position, a position I understand you have not even undertaken to conduct yourself."

"There've been a few things going on in my life lately," I said by way of an explanation.

Her expression was frozen. "I suppose you are aware that the members of the L'au-delà have given me their full support."

"No, but I'm glad to hear it. That bodes well," I answered with cheerful sangfroid.

She looked disconcerted for all of a second; then her haughty expression returned. "When I take over the position, I intend to amend the laws governing Venediger to ensure that no one like you is ever allowed to take control again."

"Sounds good," I said, glancing at my watch. "Would you mind if we hurried things up a bit? There's something really important I have to do, and I'd like to get cracking on it as soon as possible."

The three members of the Parisian Otherworld who accompanied her, acting as witnesses to the challenge, gasped in surprise.

"You would so mock this position?" Jovana asked, her dark eyes blazing. "Do you have so little respect for it?"

I crossed my arms. "The last Venediger tried to have me tossed in jail on murder charges. And kill me. You're going to have to forgive me if I'm not overly enamored with the job."

Fury lashed out from her as she gripped the machine next to mine. "You will rue the day you ever mocked the title Venediger, Aisling Grey."

"Whatever," I said, plopping a coin into my machine.

It didn't take long for me to lose two games.

"It would have been faster if you hadn't won the first round," Jim said in a whisper.

"I lost my head. I forgot for a few minutes what I was doing," I answered.

"Aisling Grey, you have lost the challenge for the position of Venediger of the L'au-delà!" Jovana said in a loud, piercing voice that echoed through the empty arcade. "It is my right and duty to so proclaim myself Venediger!"

"Congrats. Knock yourself out. Thanks for coming along," I turned from Jovana to tell the three witnesses, who were huddled together. The two men and one woman had watched me warily the whole time, as if they expected me to burst out in hellfire and brimstone at any moment.

"Kneel before me, Aisling Grey," Jovana ordered, pointing to the floor in front of her.

"Uh . . . I think I'll pass on the groveling bit. You won fair and square. Congratulations and all that, but I really do have to be going."

"Kneel!" she yelled, pointing.

I slid a glance at Traci. "Do I have to?"

It shrugged. "It is part of the ceremony."

"Great." I sighed heavily, then knelt before Jovana, just wanting to get the whole thing over with.

"Swear your fealty to me," she said, holding out her hand so I could kiss it.

I raised both eyebrows. "Oh, I don't think so."

Anger bristled off her. "You must! Since we did not fight to the death, you must swear fealty to me."

I sighed again. "Traci?"

"My lord, there are precedents. If a defender is not killed by the challenger, it is traditional for the losing party to swear allegiance to the winner so as to avoid any further confrontations in the future."

"You must swear fealty to me," Jovana said in a voice that was beginning to strike me as officious and annoying.

"Well, I can't, OK? I already swore fealty to the green dragons. I can't swear it to you, too."

"You must," she said stubbornly, shaking her hand in front of my face.

"You people really are single-minded," I said, kneeling. "And Drake used to give *me* a hard time about seeing everything in black and white. If it will get you off my back and let me get out of here, I will swear my allegiance to you insofar as it doesn't conflict with my allegiance to the green dragons, the Guardians' Guild, or anything else I'm involved with that doesn't have its origins in Abaddon."

She sputtered a couple of times as I gave the back of her hand a peck and stood up. "That is not a proper oath of fealty!"

"It's as good a one as you're going to get," I said, snapping a leash on Jim's collar. "Right, Uncle Damian, Traci . . . let's go."

"Go where?" Jim asked as we marched out of the arcade.

"You have not heard the last of me!" Jovana yelled after us.

"To find Drake," I answered, waving my hand at her to let her know I heard.

"I don't believe he wants you to follow him," Uncle Damian started to say, but I stopped him with a look.

"That was before."

"Before?" he asked.

"Before he sent a dragon, bird, lion, and tiger into my dreams."

Jim pursed its lips and blew out a whistle as we emerged from the arcade to the cold air of a January morning. "The wind horse."

"Yup." I stopped on the sidewalk, admiring for a moment a tiny glimpse of peachy-red sky between buildings. Above the horizon, the sky deepened into darker blue, then finally indigo, a faint scattering of stars still visible. I wondered if Drake had seen that same sunrise, my heart tightening painfully at the thought. "Gentlemen, I hope you have some warm clothing. I understand Tibet in winter is a bit nippy."

13

"I feel like I've just participated in a *Star Trek* episode," Uncle Damian said.

I shook my head to clear the muzziness, regretting the action when my temple collided with the sharp corner of a shelf next to me. "Ow! *Star Trek*? You mean one of the episodes when the *Enterprise* was being attacked, and everyone was shaken off of their seats?"

"Who am I? Where am I? Do I still have all my toes? And why am I on top of a fridge?" Jim's voice wafted down from above my head. I pushed myself away from the wall I was slouched against and looked over to where the demon was splayed out across the top of an ancient refrigerator.

"No," Uncle Damian answered my question, the word accompanied by the clatter of several metal pots and pans as they were shoved out of a low cupboard. He followed them, uncurling himself awkwardly from the cramped space. "I'm talking about how one of the characters always protested having his atoms beamed around the universe. I think I liked it better when we used an airplane."

"Sorry. There wasn't time to get a flight and take care of visas and everything."

"Hrmph. I'll take my chances with any dragons watching the airport next time, thank you."

"Rene?" I looked around the small room. Faint light was coming in via a dirty window, revealing our landing spot to be an untidy kitchen. "Has anyone seen Rene?"

"I'm here," his voice answered, muffled and somewhat strained. I peered around the room as Jim slid off the top of the refrigerator to land on the floor with an audible "Oof!"

"Here where?"

"Under the bags."

"Oh. You OK?" I asked as I pulled my two leather suitcases off of the mound of luggage that turned out to have a Rene core.

"*Oui.* Although I, too, believe I will make my own way out of Tibet rather than use that portal company again," he answered as I helped him to his feet. I dusted him off before shivering in the chill air of the room.

"How many toes did I have when we left London, does anyone remember?" Jim asked, examining its feet. "I think one is missing."

"Stop fussing about a missing toe. We have more important things to focus on, like finding Drake and saving him from whatever trouble he's in," I answered, straightening my clothing and zipping up my heavy parka.

"Oh, man, I am missing one! I know I had four on this foot! What sort of place was that company you used, demon-haters or something?"

"Budget Teleporters is a perfectly good company. Didn't you listen to their warning about keeping your arms and legs in the portal at all times? And although I admit the landing was a bit rougher than I had imagined it would be, we're all here in one piece, and considering the red dragons are watching every normal portal channel, that means we're one step ahead of the game."

"Does anyone else think it's not going to be such a good

idea to be just a stone's throw from Chuan Ren and all the rest of the red dragons?" Jim grumbled, shaking out its fur and licking a spot on its shoulder.

"You don't have a choice, buster. Uncle Damian and Rene did, and they chose to come with me, so let's keep the mutinous rumbles to a low din," I answered, slinging a bag over my shoulder. I reached for the other piece, but Rene got to it before I did, with a meaningful glance at my mid-section. "And this town is probably more safe than London since no one would expect us to come to Tibet in the first place."

"Uh-huh. Like we're not going to stand out at all?"

I straightened the demon's drool bib with a tweak and strapped on the doggy coat I'd gotten it for the cold. "That's what you think. Zhangmu is one of the towns mountain climbers visit before they hit Mount Everest, so the place is crawling with tourists. Now, stop complaining and lift your feet so I can put your doggy boots on."

"Now that we're here, where are we going?" Uncle Damian asked, collecting the rest of the luggage as I got Jim cold weather–proofed.

I pulled out a small notebook from my pocket. "Gabriel said he'd meet us at the Friendship Bridge. It's a tourist spot about six miles out of town. Rene?"

"I will find a car to rent, yes," he said, giving us a brief salute before pulling on a hat and disappearing out the door.

"And that's another thing," Jim complained, examining itself in the reflection from a cracked mirror. "How come you're trusting Gabriel all of a sudden?"

"I don't really have a choice, do I? Drake is in trouble; he wouldn't have been so cryptic in my dream if he wasn't in trouble. The green dragons are all too busy coping with the attacks orchestrated by Chuan Ren to come on a rescue mission, even if it is for Drake, and I'll be damned if I let Fiat know there's trouble. Bastian is busy trying to reestablish his old contacts, and there's no one at the Guardians' Guild who can help me. Gabriel offered his help, so I took him up on it."

Jim didn't say anything, but the look on its face just ramped up my worry. I turned to my uncle, who was checking over his gear. "What do you think of Gabriel? Is he trustworthy or not?"

"Didn't talk to him long enough to know for certain," he answered. "Never trust anyone you haven't known for a long time, that's my policy."

"You trust Drake," I pointed out. "You haven't known him for more than a week."

"He's different," Uncle Damian said curtly.

I smiled a sad, melancholy smile. "Yeah, he is. Damn his dragon hide. Why couldn't he have told me where he was going? We only have Gabriel's best guess to go on—we could be in the wrong place altogether."

Uncle Damian was saved from having to answer by the arrival of the owner of the kitchen, a short, squat woman who looked startled to see us there.

We made our apologies as best as possible with our limited knowledge of Tibetan, finally resorting to shoving a wad of money in the woman's hand before hauling our things outside. I slipped on the icy stone sidewalk, almost falling, but righted myself before I could bruise anything more than my dignity.

"Holy cow! This place is wild," I said, wrapping my scarf tighter around the lower part of my face as I gazed at the expanse that spread out before me. My breath hung in the thin, cold air, the light from the sunny day almost blinding after emerging from the dim room. Red stone buildings intermingled with white, clinging to the side of a mountain, one long road winding back and forth up its steep slopes. The town was busy enough, even in the dead of winter, a bustling bazaar visible down the street. I turned to look in the other direction, down into a gorge. "It looks like one good earthquake will send the whole place sliding down into the valley there. Oooh, there's Mount Everest! It's so close. And big. Damn, I wish I had my camera."

"This is a rescue mission, not a tourist visit," Uncle Damian said quietly, moving to the narrow street when a twenty-year-old VW van pulled up, Rene at the wheel.

I was silent at that rebuke, although I didn't need to be reminded of our purpose. I missed Drake. It felt like there was an empty spot in my soul that only he could fill, and although we'd been separated occasionally the last month due to business concerns and arranging protection for sept members, he'd always stayed in touch, either by phone or, more rarely, by dream.

By the time we made it out of the town and to the famous Friendship Bridge that connected Nepal to Tibet, spanning the Bhotekoshi River, I sat huddled in my coat, wishing like hell we were back in the London house, snuggled up together in bed while Drake told me stories of his childhood.

"If wishes were horses, beggars would ride," I said to myself, sighing.

"I never understood that saying," Jim said. "If I was a beggar, I'd wish for huge truckloads of money over a horse. And food. Lots and lots of food. Oh, sure, you can eat a horse, but then once it's gone, you've got nothing left."

"What is it talking about?" Uncle Damian asked, giving Jim a look as if a penguin had suddenly appeared on the demon's head.

"Nothing. This looks like it, Rene. I bet that car over there is Gabriel's. Bless him for being so prompt."

"Yeah. Let's just hope it's not a trap, and we won't end up dead or worse out here in the middle of nowhere."

Jim wasn't saying anything I hadn't already considered, but I really did not have a choice.

I'm not even going to point out the obvious.

Gabriel swore I could trust him, and I had to do just that.

Rather than take care of the situation yourself, which would be far too proactive, right? And you call yourself a professional!

If he betrayed me again . . . well, I'd deal with that situation if it arose.

Like you dealt with his first betrayal? And just how effective was that?

I ground my teeth against the ever-persuasive dark power and focused my attention on the man who emerged from the Land Rover parked next to a sign describing the bridge. Luckily, there were no tourists to witness our meeting, huddled against the side of our van as we hurriedly caught up on news.

"You've heard nothing from Drake?" Gabriel asked, his silver eyes shaded by the thick black hat he wore.

I shook my head. "Still not answering. What did you find out from Fiat?"

Gabriel hesitated for a moment, sliding quick glances at his two companions, who were muffled to the eyeballs. I assumed they were his bodyguards, Tipene and Maata, and waved at them. They both nodded at me. "He said he had not heard anything from Chuan Ren for three days, but he didn't believe that would be the case if they had captured Drake. I must say that I agree with him on that, Aisling. If Chuan Ren had Drake in her power, she would use him to destroy the sept . . . and you. You have heard nothing from the red dragons?"

"Not a peep." Beneath my scarf, I chewed at my chilly lip. "It's possible that someone else is holding him captive. A red dragon would turn him over immediately to Chuan Ren, but maybe someone else, someone who has a vendetta against him, found him doing whatever mysterious thing he was doing out here and nabbed him."

"That is possible," Gabriel allowed.

There was something in his voice, an undertone that sounded strained to my ears. I turned my attention to him, searching his eyes for a sign of betrayal. There was none there, but he looked away after a few seconds, as if he was uncomfortable with close examination.

"What are you keeping back?" I asked him.

He was silent for a few minutes.

"Gabriel, please, if you know something about where Drake could be, you've got to tell me." I put my hands on his, giving them a squeeze. "He's everything to me. I love him with every tiny little atom of my being. Please, help me find him. Please."

Gabriel watched me for another minute, clearly unwilling to tell me what he knew. I considered asking my uncle to get the truth out of him, but I doubted if even Uncle Damian, wise in the ways of covert operations and the like, could handle a wyvern and his two bodyguards.

For a moment, for a brief moment that seemed to stretch to eternity, I considered using the dark power to get what I wanted from Gabriel.

Oh, goody.

Gabriel must have seen my inner struggle. "Many years ago, before I was wyvern, I heard the wyvern at the time speaking of a secret aerie in the south of Tibet that had been

forgotten by most dragons. Only a few knew of its existence; even fewer knew of its location. When you said
Drake was held captive in Tibet, my first thought was that
Chuan Ren had found the aerie. That is why I had you meet
me here. But Fiat's comments made me think twice. Now I
do not know what to think."

"Do you know where this place is?" I asked, hope filling me.

It took him another long pause, but he nodded. "I am one
of probably five dragons in existence who know. But to take
anyone there from outside the sept is absolutely forbidden,
Aisling."

I lifted my chin and let him see my intentions. "I will do
whatever I have to do to find Drake, Gabriel."

He nodded, an unhappy look on his face. "I have no
doubt you would destroy yourself in the attempt to rescue
him, which is why I am going to go against my oath as
wyvern and take you there." He glanced at Maata and
Tipene, saying something to them in a language I didn't understand.

They sent him identical outraged looks, one of them
snapping something back which caused him to smile. "I
told them that I would not risk them being in trouble with
the weyr for helping me break our laws. Maata threatened
to break my kneecaps if I tried to leave her behind."

I grinned at Maata. "A woman after my own heart.
Thank you all. You can be sure that none of us will ever
mention any of this—"

Gabriel held up a hand to stop me. "For you I will break
the laws of my own sept. But I cannot allow anyone else to
come with you."

"But you know Rene! And my uncle is very trustworthy—"

"I'm sorry, it is not possible," he said, his voice apologetic, but firm.

"Aisling does not go anywhere without protection," Uncle Damian said, speaking up for the first time.

"We are her bodyguards," Rene added.

"What he said. Although I think my left leg is frozen," Jim said, shaking its back leg. "How do you tell if you've got frostbite?"

"About this, I cannot yield," Gabriel said, his eyes steady on mine.

I hesitated, wanting to trust him. But I was putting myself completely in his power, giving him the opportunity to do god-knew-what with me.

Gabriel waited, clearly understanding my dilemma, but not trying to reassure me. I knew instinctively that Gabriel wouldn't physically harm me, so I didn't fear for the well-being of myself or the baby. The only thing he might do was betray me to Fiat or Chuan Ren, and if that happened . . . well, there was a way out of that problem.

So nice you remembered me.

"Aisling, I told Drake I'd protect you, and I'm going to," Uncle Damian said grimly in my ear. "You're not going off with that man without me to watch over you."

It came down to a decision of Drake or me. And when put like that, there was nothing to decide.

I took my uncle's gloved hands in mine, smiling up at him. "Thank you, Uncle Damian. I know this is going to be hard for you, but I'm going to ask you to stay here. I have to find Drake, do you understand? I *have* to find him. And if this is the only way I can do it, then that's the way it'll be."

"I can't allow—"

I shook my head. "I'm a big girl. I've got powers of my

own, you know. I'm not completely helpless, and I'll have Jim with me."

"Oh, yippee," the demon said, looking anything but thrilled.

"No," Uncle Damian said, his face expressionless. "The subject is not open for any further discussion."

I argued for another couple of minutes, but it did no good.

"This is ridiculous," I stormed, stomping my way around to the far side of the car. "I'm freezing out here. At least we can be warm while I try to reason with you."

Rene slid back into the front seat as I opened the back door. Across from me, Uncle Damian did the same. I waited until both men were in the car, their doors closed, before I slammed mine shut and drew the most powerful ward I knew on the car.

"Fires of Abaddon!" Jim said, its eyes widening. "You didn't just—"

My uncle realized what I'd done almost immediately. He tried to open the door, banging his fists on the window when he realized the ward wouldn't let him out of the car.

"We'll be back as soon as we can," I yelled close to the window, my voice faint over the howl of the wind. "Go back to town. We'll meet you back at the hotel. The ward should wear off by the time you get there. And don't worry about me; I'll be OK."

"Yeah, she'll be OK. I'll be minus several more toes due to frostbite, but Aisling will be perfectly fine," Jim yelled as well.

"Not helping," I told it.

Uncle Damian pounded some more and yelled a few choice words I decided I'd rather not acknowledge. I gave

Rene a thumbs-up and hurried over to where Gabriel stood waiting.

My uncle was going to be furious at my actions, but we'd just have to live with that. There were more important things at stake right now . . . like finding Drake.

14

"Your uncle is going to be sooo pissed," Jim said a few minutes later, as we were ensconced in Gabriel's Land Rover.

"He'll get over it. I think. I hope," I said, rubbing my forehead with an icy glove. "Oh, god, no, you're right, he's going to be livid. But what choice did I have?"

"This is not going to be an easy trip," Gabriel warned as the car bounced over a rough, snowy track that was apparently used by sheep or goats or some nimble animal that didn't have a problem with horrible terrain. "We will have to climb part of the way ourselves. There is no road to the aerie. I will do the best I can to take the easiest route, but you should be warned there is not much I can do to ease your path."

Jim opened its mouth to make a no doubt snarky comment, but I forestalled it by saying simply, "We'll be OK."

Seven hours later, as I crumpled into a small, Aisling-shaped icy blob of exhaustion, those words came back to haunt me.

"Define OK," Jim gasped, collapsing beside me. " 'Cause where I'm standing . . . lying . . . OK is pretty much synonymous for nearly dead."

"We're here," Gabriel said, crawling over to where I lay,

his voice thin and reedy with exertion. "The aerie is a short distance away. Are you all right?"

"Yeah, we're fine. Just a little light-headed."

"I'll get the oxygen," he answered, going back to where Tipene and Maata were lying alongside a rocky outcropping. I rolled over and cast an eye down the side of the mountain we'd just climbed, my eyes crossing at the nearly vertical expanse of snow, ice, and rock. Winds whipped through us with needlelike icy blades, making me shiver despite the arctic-class garments we'd bought on Gabriel's advice.

I breathed deeply from one of the oxygen tubes Tipene had hauled up, feeling better almost immediately.

"Jim?" I asked.

"Hit me," it said, its eyes closed.

"I'd have thought that being immortal and all meant we wouldn't be prone to altitude sickness," I said a short while later as I accepted Gabriel's hand to get to my feet.

He shot me an amused look. "You would not be here now if you were not immortal. It would have been impossible to climb as high as this without acclimatization. That is one other reason we could not bring your uncle."

"Oh. Well, then. Shall we?"

Gabriel nodded, unhooking the ropes that had connected us. "We won't need these now. The aerie should be just around the curve. It is built into the solid rock of the mountain."

I had no idea what to expect from a secret dragon aerie hidden on the side of the Himalayas, but the forbidding stone building set deep into a natural overhang sure fit the image.

"That's one hell of an aerie," I said as we picked our way along a faint rocky path.

"It is, isn't it? I've only seen it once before. It's hidden from aerial view by the rock overhead, and as you can see, it was built to blend into the background. Unless you knew to look for it, it would be all but invisible. We will approach from the side."

We followed Gabriel silently as he led us along what seemed to be a nonexistent path that wound through twisted snow-covered rock. The light was starting to fail, leaving the terrain difficult to make out in the long shadows, but eventually we crept our way up to the side of the building.

I stared at it, wondering if I was walking into a trap . . . or about to save the man who was everything to me. "What now?"

"You stay here with Maata. Tipene and I will see if there are guards," Gabriel announced.

I nodded, wanting to go along with him, but knowing it was wiser to let him scout out the area. A few minutes later he returned, minus his hat.

"It is clear. Hurry, the light is going, and it looks as if a storm will be coming in soon."

"You OK?" I asked as he flexed his hand.

He flashed me a fast grin. "It has been a long time since I had the opportunity of taking down another dragon with my fists."

"Another dragon? Red?"

He shook his head and motioned me to be silent. We followed after him as he led us alongside the stone building, back into the shallow cave formed by the overhang to where a door's outline could dimly be seen. Two bodies were stacked alongside the building, out of the weather. I paused at the sight of them, raising an inquiring eyebrow at Gabriel.

"If they're not red dragons, what sept do they belong to?" I whispered.

"None," he answered, taking me by surprise.

"What—"

"Shhh," he warned, carefully opening the stone door. He and Tipene slipped through the opening. I waited for his wave before continuing, Maata following Jim and me.

We were in a hallway, the walls and floor made of the same stone, evidently quarried right out of the side of the mountain itself. The light was dim, one bulb hanging behind us at the junction, another ahead some sixty feet or so.

"Which way?" I asked Gabriel in a whisper.

He hesitated, turning first one way, then the other. Tipene said something, nodding to the end closest. Gabriel shook his head, pointing to the left. "We have removed the guards for this door, so you should be safe here. We will scout ahead, to the left."

I shivered despite being out of the atrocious weather, but nodded to let him know I understood. The three of them slipped into the shadows and disappeared around the corner, silent as ghosts. There was no noise in the building, no sounds of human occupation, no noises of any sort, just a faint little hum of electrical lights from the bulbs. It was cold inside as well, not as cold as outside, but still cold enough that my breath hung in the air before my face.

"I'm not going to have any toes left by the time this little caper is over," Jim moaned softly to itself as it shook off a doggy bootie to examine its paw. "Oh, man, I think gangrene has set in! My toes are black!"

"That's your fur, you idiot," I said, kneeling to feel its feet. They were cold, but not icy blocks of lifeless flesh. "Thank god for immortality. Your feet are fine. So are mine, for that matter. I'm cold, but not deathly cold. This place sure does give me the willies, though."

"Definitely creepsville," Jim agreed, padding down to the end of the hallway.

"Do you see them?" I asked in a soft whisper that I knew Jim would hear.

"Nope."

I crept down after it and peered carefully around the corner. The aerie was evidently build around a U shape, the hollow part being made up of a large open area that was dominated at one end by an absolutely gigantic fireplace, the kind big enough to roast a whole ox in one go.

There was no sign of life in the area, not so much as one single dragon lounging around on the thick, dark medieval-looking wood furniture.

"Where'd they go?" I asked Jim.

It shrugged.

"Hell."

"Abaddon."

"Will you stop correcting me! I know the difference!"

"Oh yeah? Is the Underworld contained in Hell or Abaddon?" it asked with a particularly annoying cock of its eyebrow.

I glared. "Don't mess with me. There are pregnancy hormones flooding my body right this very minute, and you never know when they might cause me to spontaneously banish the nearest demon to the Akasha."

Jim looked thoughtful. "Point taken."

"Good. Now skinny along there and peek around the corner to see if you can see signs of Gabriel or the others. Or anyone else for that matter. But don't get caught!"

"Stealth Newfie on duty!" it answered, saluting me before shuffling soundlessly down the hallway toward the large open area.

I held my breath as I clung to the rough-hewn stone corner, listening intently for sounds that Jim—or the others—had been found, but before I could begin to seriously worry, Jim returned.

"No one there. No Gabriel, no Maata, no Tipene . . . no one."

A little chill skittered down my spine. "Are they just out scouting the area, or have they set us up?" I wondered aloud.

"Dunno. I'd think if this was a setup, though, you'd have been caught by now."

"Good point." I thought for a moment, then turned to look down the right side of the passageway. "Which means that either they've been caught, or they're looking around. Either way, we're running out of time. Someone is bound to notice those guards aren't around, which means we need to get moving. Come on. We'll try this way."

"Uh, Ash? You sure you want to do this? Gabriel said to stay put."

"And what happens if they don't come back? I'd rather not just sit around helpless, thank you," I whispered, making my way as silently as possible down the corridor.

"There is that."

We came to another corner, leading along the flat bottom side of the U shape. Just as I was gathering up my nerve to peek around the corner, a man strolled around it, stopping to stare at us with as much surprise as we stared at him.

He blinked dark but unmistakably dragon eyes for a moment, his reflexes just a hair too slow. By the time his hand reached inside his jacket for a gun, I'd drawn silencing and binding wards on him.

"Oh, man. Now we're really in for it," Jim whispered, giving the dragon a worried eye as we slipped around both him and the corner. The hallway that stretched before us was almost identical to the one we'd just left, with the exception of four doors, two on either side. "How long are the wards going to hold?"

"Long enough," I muttered, praying they would do just that. "We're going to have to see what's in these rooms. You know of any way to do that without opening the doors?"

Jim sighed. "I'm not the Guardian, now, am I?"

I smiled, patting the demon on its furry head. I was starting to get wise to its ways. Whenever it mentioned Guardianhood, I knew I had whatever skill was needed . . . the trouble was figuring out *which* skill that was. I ran over my mental list of my abilities, but didn't find one that screamed "can see through doors." It had to be the trusty old standby. I opened the mental door in my mind and looked at the nearest metal door with my enhanced vision, seeing nothing but a dense bit of metal. The door farther along the passage was the same—just a door. But when I turned to look at the door to my right, a ward flared to life for a second, the intricate knot that made up the ward glowing silver in the air before dissolving to nothing.

"If this door has been warded, there has to be something behind it that's pretty important," I said, bending down to examine the ward, which had been drawn around the door handle.

"Makes sense to me. What are you going to do about it?"

"I wish I knew how to unmake them like that girl we met last month."

"The charmer? Yeah. Handy skill, that."

I eyed the door and considered my options. I just didn't have any left. "Gotta be brute force."

"Oh, man," Jim said as I gripped the doorknob. "This ain't gonna be pretty."

And it wasn't. By the time I managed to wrestle the door open and shove us both through the ward guarding it, Jim had lost two booties, and my scarf had mysteriously disappeared. We looked around the small room that faced us, but there was nothing there but another dim light hanging overhead, a broken wooden table lurking drunkenly in the corner, and yet another metal door.

"Crap," I swore to myself as I faced the rather substantial padlock that hung heavily from the door. "OK. Nothing for it. Stand back, Jim."

The demon retreated to the doorway we'd just come through as I took off my gloves, rubbing my hands while I focused on pulling power from the room. It wasn't much, and it wasn't nearly as powerful as Drake's fire—

Or mine.

—but it was enough to concentrate into a small ball of energy, which when hurtled into the lock, shattered it completely.

"Nice going. Let's hope you didn't just release a herd of maniacs who are going to leap out and chop you up into little bitty Guardian pieces," Jim said cheerfully as I carefully opened the door and peered inside.

The smells hit me first, unwholesome odors that made me want to gag. But riding the stench was a scent that was totally different, one that made tears prick in my eyes as I flung the door open, throwing myself into the dark maw.

"Aisling!" Jim called as I lurched toward an ebony shape in the darkness.

"Drake!" I said at the same time, flinging myself on the shadow.

"Aisling?"

The black shape on the floor grunted as I flung myself on it, kissing every bit of him I could reach.

"What are you doing—*kincsem*, stop. That was my

eyeball. What are you doing here? How did you find this place?"

Beneath me, Drake struggled to sit up.

"It was your clever dream, you brilliant man. Although I have to say, you could have just walked up and told me where you were rather than doing that symbolism thing. Oh, dear god, are you all right?" Faint little fingers of light from the room behind us stretched across a floor that appeared to be made of dirt and rock, covered in matted straw. "You feel all right? Does anything hurt on you? Are Pál and István here, too?"

"Yes, they're here," Drake answered, and beyond him, two pale faces hove into view. "We're not hurt. What dream are you talking about? What symbolism?"

"The dream you sent me." I swallowed back a painful lump of tears, unable to keep from patting Drake to reassure myself that he was all right. "Thank god we guessed right. Gabriel brought us here, but he's disappeared."

"Gabriel?" Drake's eyes widened for a moment, the look of shock quickly fading to something that looked horribly like fear. "*Kincsem*, get up. We must get out of here, right now."

"Oh, god. Don't tell me—he's behind this, isn't he?" I said, scrambling to my feet, my heart dropping to my stomach.

"No. István, take Aisling. Pál, help me."

"Help you with what? Are you hurt? And if Gabriel isn't the one behind you being kidnapped, who is?"

"The time for questions is later," István told me, limping toward me, his face dirty and bruised. He grabbed my arm and started pulling me after him toward the door.

I couldn't argue with that reasoning, but I am nothing if

not consistent—I argued. "Drake, what the hell is going on—and who's that?"

An unfamiliar man emerged from the shadows, held up on either side by Drake and Pál, dirty, dark-haired and dark-eyed from what I could tell, but in far worse shape, his cheekbones pronounced, a gaunt, almost emaciated appearance to his face.

"His name is Konstantin," Drake answered, using one hand to shove me toward the door at which István waited. "We do not have time for this. We must get out before Gabriel finds us."

"I just hope you explain why you're so afraid of Gabriel if he's not the one who kidnapped you," I told him as I followed István out the door. All three of them—four if you counted the fourth dragon named Konstantin—looked worse for wear, but I could see that other than some bruises and a layer of filth that would wash off, they were apparently unharmed. I wondered what Gabriel's plan was in holding them, swearing at myself for being so foolish as to fall for his lies a second time.

Drake looked curiously at the door I'd blasted open, narrowing his eyes when faced with the outer door, the one with the powerful wards.

"This is going to hurt a bit," I said, gathering my strength.

His lips thinned at the sight of the half-opened door. "There is no other way. Do what you must."

It took me five minutes to get everyone through the ward. I wanted to leave the man named Konstantin for the last, but Drake insisted he go second, after István.

"He's in pretty bad shape now," I grunted, shoving Jim through the ward. "If I can weaken the ward a little by sending more people through it, it might be easier on him."

"Do it now," Drake ordered. "At all costs, Kostya must be freed."

"I'm sorry, this isn't going to be pleasant," I told the man as I put both hands on his back. I swung open my mental door and gathered together as much power as I could rally from the stone walls and floors, trying to shield the frail dragon as I shoved him through the ward.

He collapsed on the other side, but István was ready for him. Drake and Pál went through with just as much difficulty, both of them pale with the strain as I forced my way through the ward.

"That way," I said, pointing a shaky hand to the left to indicate the way I'd initially come. "Jim, show them—oh, hell."

"Abaddon," it said, leaping on the dragon that rounded the corner. It was the man I'd bound and silenced, his yell echoing down the stone corridor as Drake grabbed his neck and slammed him against the rough wall.

The dragon slid to the floor in a crumpled heap. I said nothing as Drake held out his hand for me, skirting the unconscious dragon carefully.

I pulled back, however, at the door leading to the outside. "This is the way we came in, but Drake, we really need to talk for a minute."

"We don't have time," he answered, opening the door. A blast of icy air whirled in through it. I put both hands on the door and closed it again.

"Your friend there isn't dressed for a romp outside in the blizzard," I said quietly. "Neither are you three. You might possibly survive, although I don't know how even a dragon can tolerate exposure to such cold, but he won't. He's in bad shape now, and the climb down is going to be hairy."

Drake hesitated.

"Sweetie, I know we don't have time for a lengthy conversation, but you have to answer me one question—is Gabriel responsible for kidnapping you or not?"

"Not," he answered, gesturing toward the crumpled body of the man at the far end of the hallway. "István, get his things. We'll put them on Kostya."

"If Gabriel isn't our enemy, then we've got to find him. He can help us get down off the side of this mountain."

"No," he repeated, his jaw set with a familiar stubborn cast.

"Dammit, Drake! You just said he's not our enemy!"

"I said he wasn't responsible for kidnapping us—and he isn't. But he is just about the deadliest enemy Kostya has, and above all else, Gabriel must not know of his existence."

My mouth hung open a moment in surprise, but before I could ask what was going on, a piercing scream rent the air, dying off in a horrible gargle that hinted of a more permanent end than that of the dragon lying unconscious at the end of the hall. A man's voice shouted, another answered, followed quickly by the sound of running feet.

Drake sprang to action, jerking a heavy nylon parka onto the man he called Kostya, turning to open the door. But before he could shove the other dragon through it, Gabriel and his bodyguards burst around the corner, running for their lives toward us. He yelled something and waved his arm, skidding to a halt as the injured dragon turned to face him.

"Kostya Fekete," Gabriel said, his voice filled with shock. "You live."

"As you see," the other dragon answered, stumbling forward as if to meet Gabriel, falling heavily with a pained grunt.

Drake bent to help him just as I did the same.

"Fekete?" I asked as we hauled him to his feet. "That means black, doesn't it? This is a black dragon?"

Gabriel gave a sharp bark of laughter that held absolutely zero percent humor. Another shout echoed down the hallway. He glanced over his shoulder, then looked back at Kostya. "I believe I've had enough of your hospitality. We are leaving."

"As are we," Drake said grimly, taking Kostya's arm. "Aisling, stay close to me."

"What's going on here?" I asked, confused. "What do you mean *his* hospitality? The aerie belongs to Kostya? Who exactly is this guy? Someone you know?"

"You could say that," Drake answered, opening the door. Snow and wind swirled through it, hitting me with enough force to steal my breath. "He's my brother."

15

"I will be all right. Thank you."

I set down on the nightstand a carafe of water, bottle of aspirin, and bowl of ice. "Don't mention it. I'll have Suzanne send you up another bowl of soup in a few hours, after we know you can keep the first one down."

"It will stay down," the dragon said with a stubborn set of his jaw.

"My dear, do you not think a doctor is called for in this situation? Drake's brother looks very ill, and although I'd never scoff at the healing power of homemade soup, I fear that even the most nourishing of meals won't help him."

"He'll be fine, Paula. A doctor looked him over while he was in Tibet." It was a lie, but only a slight one. Gabriel wasn't a doctor per se, but he was a healer extraordinaire, and he'd reluctantly given Kostya a clean bill of health.

"Oh, a doctor checked him over?" My stepmother bustled around the room, being what she termed useful, although in reality she was more of a hindrance than a help. "A real one? Not one of those suspicious faith healers who pretend to pull organs out of your stomach when all the while they are really using sleight of hand with chicken livers and the like? I saw a show on those men, Aisling, and they are not to be trusted in the least. Perhaps we should call a reputable doctor to have a look at him now."

"It wasn't a faith healer, I promise. Why don't we leave Kostya alone to get some sleep?"

"I suppose that would be best," she said, fluffing up his pillow for the last time before heading to the door, trailing gauzy scarves and advice as she left. "It's all very mysterious how he just appeared, though . . ."

I waited until she'd drifted down the hallway to the stairs before giving the man in the bed a little smile. "You'll have to forgive her. She means well, but she can be a bit much sometimes."

"She is mortal," he said with a shrug, as if that explained everything.

"Yes, she is, and I dread trying to explain dragons and the Otherworld to her, so if you could keep the fire-breathing to a minimum, I'd be greatly appreciative. Is there anything else you'd like?"

"No."

I picked up the tray and went to the door. "Try to get some sleep. I'm sure you'll feel better afterwards."

Before I could close the door, his voice called out my name. "Aisling?"

I paused and looked back.

As seen by electric light, Konstantin Fekete—a name I was gravely informed was never used, the man in question preferring the diminutive Kostya instead—looked a far cry from the filthy, unkempt creature who crawled out of the back of the aerie prison. The long face, reddish brown hair that swept back from a high forehead, and ebony eyes were unfamiliar to me, but the jaw and chin were all Drake. Kostya shifted slightly in bed, winced as his still-healing wounds pulled, and gave me a smile filled with irony. "You are angry at Drake."

"That's neither here nor there, but yes, I am."

"You do him an injustice. His loyalty was given to me centuries before he met you."

I thought about that for a moment, nodded, and left the room, quietly closing the door behind me.

Drake stood directly opposite, leaning against the wall in apparent negligence, but I knew better. His dragon fire was barely contained, indicating his emotions were running very high at the moment. "Would you prefer to yell at me now, or can it wait until later?"

"I'm not going to yell at you," I said serenely, and headed down the hallway to the stairs.

"You're not?"

"No. There is nothing to yell at you about. About which to yell. Whatever. I am perfectly in control, and I can guarantee you there will be no yelling."

Drake said nothing as he followed me down the stairs. The silence lasted until my foot hit the tile floor; then I turned around and smashed the tray into his chest. "Your brother, Drake? Your *brother*?"

He sighed, tossed the tray onto a side table, and taking my hands in his, pulled me back up the stairs, into our bedroom. "Yes, he is my brother."

"A real brother?" I asked, pulling my hands from his because we both knew full well that if I maintained any sort of physical contact with him, sooner or later I'd end up flinging myself on him in a wholly shameless fashion. "Not just a brother-in-arms, or a really good friend you think of as a brother, but an actual flesh-and-blood brother?"

"Yes." He stood in front of me, his hands limp at his sides. My heart wrung at the exhaustion that was clearly gripping him despite the few hours of sleep he'd managed to snatch on the plane back to England.

He looked longingly at the bed, sighing. I poured him out a stiff belt of dragon's blood, the spicy wine favored by dragons. He accepted it and sank with rather less grace than normal into one of the two chairs that flanked the fireplace.

"I should go downstairs. There is much to do."

"There's always much to do. Did Gabriel leave?"

He nodded. "He wished to discuss the situation now, but I was finally able to convince him that you needed rest."

"Me?" I made a face. "I slept the whole way back."

"I admit that in this instance, I used your condition as a convenient excuse to get rid of Gabriel," he answered, his eyes haunted. "He will return in the morning."

I glanced at the clock. It was nearing midnight, and despite the sleep I'd had on the airplane, I was feeling as tired as Drake looked. "Yeah, well, he's not the only one who's been put off until then. My uncle was pretty peeved when we dropped him off at the hotel. He muttered something about having a word with me in the morning in regard to my behavior. I don't suppose you'd like to run interference for me?"

Drake cocked a glossy black eyebrow.

I sighed. "I know, you have enough on your plate. I'd just like to point out the same goes for me. At least with Gabriel and Uncle Damian put off until morning it means you and I can have a little chat."

He pursed his lips slightly. "You want to know about Kostya."

"Bingo. Let's start at the beginning, shall we? His mother is Catalina? His dad was your dad?"

"Yes."

"Wait a sec—you told me your dad died right after you were born."

He brushed a hand through his hair, his eyes filled with so much emotion it almost hurt to look at him. "The phrase 'right after' is relative to the life span of a dragon, no pun intended. He died within a year of my birth. Kostya is my older brother."

My resistance failed me, just as I knew it would. Drake sent me a look that evaporated just about all my irritation, leaving me to find myself on his lap, nuzzling his neck and breathing in the wonderfully sexy scent that never failed to make my blood steam.

He turned his head to kiss me. I caught his face in my hands and looked deep into those beautiful eyes of his. "Your *brother.*"

"When you accepted the fact that we were mated, I told you there would be some things I could not share with you."

"Dragon things, I remember," I said, nodding. "And I said I was sure there were some Guardian things I wouldn't be able to spill to you, but this is bigger than just a dragon thing, Drake! This is your family! I thought I was a part of that!"

"You are a part of it," he answered, his hands caressing me as he pulled me down to his mouth. "You are the most important person in my life, *kincsem.* But there are circumstances surrounding Kostya that go beyond family and touch weyr politics. Until you so heedlessly came to rescue us, the world believed Kostya to be dead. Now five others know of his existence. What is worse is that one of their number is Gabriel. It could very well be that this exposure could mean Kostya's destruction."

I let him kiss me, enjoying the taste of him as he invaded my mouth, savoring the sweetness of holding him again in my arms. But my curiosity was stronger than my desire at the moment, and I felt like I had to get a few things straight in my mind before I could concentrate on celebrating his return.

"You keep saying things like that, but I don't understand why. Gabriel didn't try to attack Kostya at all. Far from it, he helped us get him down off that damned mountain. He checked him over for injuries once we got back to town. He did what he could to repair the wounds he had. Those weren't the actions of a man with murder on his mind."

He leaned back, his head cradled by the high back of the chair. "The situation is complicated."

I kissed his chin. "I think that's going to be the understatement of the year. I'm so confused, I don't know where to begin asking questions."

Drake slid another longing glance toward the bed. "I don't suppose you would care to follow the others' lead and put this off until morning? I am very tired, but not so tired I cannot pay homage to you as is your due."

I flinched at the word "homage." It brought up a horribly nagging feeling that I should be focusing on the situation with Bael rather than the more pressing dragon situation. But Bael had given me five days, and I'd only spent two of them. "I think I'm due a few answers first. To be honest, I don't understand why you were so angry with me about rescuing you. You sent me the dream telling me you needed help, after all."

"You mentioned a dream before, but it is untrue. I sent you no dream."

"Then how do you explain the fact that I dreamed about a wind horse?"

He looked startled for a moment, pulling from his pocket

a tattered green scrap of fabric that matched the one I'd woken up with.

"That's it!"

"I was going to bring this home for you, but then we were captured," he said slowly. "I did not send you a dream message, *kincsem.* I would have endangered you by asking you to find me, and as it happens, I am furious with Gabriel for doing just that."

I touched the dirty bit of prayer flag. "I guess your subconscious was less stubborn than your waking mind. Oh, stop looking at me like that—everything turned out OK. Besides, there are more important things to focus on than what might have been."

His hand slid along my thigh. "Such as my desire to make love to you?"

I stopped his hand from climbing any higher, knowing full well that once he bent his mind to seduction, there was nothing short of nuclear war that could stop him. "I would be perfectly happy to let you make wild, passionate, steamy dragon love to me, but first you have to answer a couple of questions."

His chest heaved with resignation, his pupils black slits in a field of green that glittered with speculation and no little amount of passion. "Very well. You may ask me three questions."

"Oh, we're back to three questions, are we?" I asked, smiling against his mouth as I remembered the first wildly erotic dream I shared with him. "All right. First question: was it Kostya you went away to help?"

"Yes."

I waited for more information, but none was forthcoming. "Who was keeping you prisoner?"

"I don't know." His expression turned thoughtful as he

narrowed his gaze on the flames in the fireplace. "I thought at first Chuan Ren had found Kostya, but upon reflection, I decided it could not be her. She would not have let me live if she had me in her power. The one holding us prisoner was very careful not to be seen, and used only mortals to bring us food."

"Hmm. There were two dragons Gabriel found outside, but he said they weren't red dragons. What about that one you knocked out in the hallway?"

He shook his head. "I did not recognize him, nor did I have time to examine him for signs of a sept. I do not know who he was."

"Crap. OK, last question—"

"Your third question was about the dragon in the hallway. Now I demand payment for my amiability." Drake pushed me off his lap just long enough to stand up and scoop me into his arms, marching determinedly to the bed. With moves I didn't even try to follow, he stripped himself, then me, and before I could form a single word of protest, he tossed me onto the bed.

"That question was part of the second one, and you know it," I said, trying to look indignant, but failing miserably when he ran his hand up the bare calf of my leg. I shivered at his touch.

His mouth kissed a path around my belly, heading northwards to my breasts. "Very well. Since I am fond of you, I will this once grant you an additional question. But make it quickly, before I become too busy to attend mere words."

I stopped stroking his back and pinched him hard enough to make him rear back. "Fond of me? You're *fond* of me?"

He grinned, his eyes dancing as wickedly as his fingers, which had found extremely sensitive flesh. As if the touch wasn't enough to drive me senseless, his grin melted me completely. Drake in his usual sober mood was sexy as hell . . . Drake being playful was downright irresistible. His head dipped again as he licked a shape onto my stomach, breaking fire to it to set it alight.

It was a heart.

"Perhaps fond is too mild a word," he conceded as I pulled him down on top of me, my hands and mouth going wild on him. I was suddenly desperate to feel him inside of me, needing the joining to reassure myself that he was safe, and that nothing could take him away from me. He must have sensed that need in me, because he didn't torment me with teasing touches as he normally did; he simply gave me what I wanted, fulfilling the need to hold him deep within me, so deep he was an integral part of my very being.

"If that's fond," I said some time later, pressing a kiss to his damp chest as I scooted upward along his body until I could peer down into his face, "I doubt if I could survive a stronger emotion."

His eyes were closed, his face relaxed, his fingers drawing lazy patterns of fire on my behind. One side of his mouth quirked. I kissed it, decided I liked the taste of the quirk, and kissed it a couple of more times, sucking his lower lip into my mouth until he opened his eyes, a spark of interest in them. "You are a demanding woman, *kincsem*. I will do my best to rise to the challenge you pose, but I fear the events of the last few days will make me a bit slower than normal . . ."

"I have no doubt you'd meet that particular challenge," I answered, squirming when his fingers slid lower. "But that's not actually what I was hinting at. You still owe me a question."

He closed his eyes again, his chest rising and falling more slowly now that we were both recovering from the passion of a few minutes past. "I have never understood how women have the energy or desire to conduct lengthy conversations after lovemaking. I am male. I must rest after I have met your not-insubstantial wanton demands."

"Uh-huh. And if I did this—" My hand slid down his chest, trailed over his belly, and wrapped around interesting scenery southwards. His eyes shot open. "—You wouldn't suddenly be wide awake?"

"What did you wish to know?" he asked, the slow smolder in his eyes gaining brilliance.

"I know Kostya is a black dragon. I know you used to be one before your princess grandmother claimed you as a green dragon, and you were made wyvern. I know that the silver dragons were part of the black sept, but they left because of a horrible wyvern named Baltic."

His fingers stilled, tightening around my butt, his eyes on me but his attention somewhere else.

"But what I don't know is what Kostya has to do with Gabriel. You said yourself the black sept wasn't around anymore—so even assuming there is bad blood between the two septs, why would Gabriel want Kostya dead?"

Drake was silent a few minutes, a pain so profound within him that even I could feel it. "Kostya's coming was foretold by Baltic."

"Oh? In what way?" I spoke slowly, a heavy weight of oppression upon me as if I didn't want to hear the answer.

The fire in his eyes died. "Kostya's existence means the end of the silver dragons."

16

"So, that's it? That's all he said? Just that Kostya means the end of Gabriel and his sept?"

"That's it. Have you seen my pregnancy vitamins?" I opened one of the drawers in the bathroom, poking through an assortment of cosmetics looking for the large bottle of prenatal vitamins.

Jim nodded toward the door leading to the bedroom. "On the nightstand. You do realize those are human vitamins, right? They probably won't work now that you're not mortal."

"The silver dragon doctor said they wouldn't hurt, although it is a bit of a pain taking both dragon and human vitamins. Still, it's nice that I evidently get to forgo all that morning sickness crap."

"Hey, less barf has always equaled good in my book. So, why didn't you ask Drake to explain?"

I took my glass with me into the bedroom, shrugging as I washed down one of the large vitamins with a swig of water. "Can't hurt. And I didn't ask him because he was tired, I was tired, and he promised to explain everything today."

"Uh-huh. You'll notice he managed to leave the house before he did that."

I finished dressing, having more than a bit of a struggle to close the waistband of my pants. "Damn. Now even my fat pants aren't fitting. I guess I'm going to have to go shopping soon."

"What's that, dear?" Paula's head poked through the open doorway as she tapped on the jamb. "Shopping, did you say? I'm so glad to hear you say that. I know you thought that bondage outfit you purchased was lovely, and I agree that the cream skirt is very pretty indeed, but truly, the whole effect of the ensemble is not the sort of memory you want to leave your guests with. Oh." She turned around in the room, obviously looking for someone. "But who were you talking to?"

"Uh . . . just myself. And Jim, of course, ha ha ha."

"You always did have such an odd sense of humor," she said with a tolerant smile as she glanced at her wrist. "Now, we have just enough time to visit one or perhaps two shops before we meet with the new wedding planner."

"What new wedding planner?" I asked, confused. "What happened to Imelda?"

"Oh, my dear, can you seriously ask that after what you put that poor woman through? She quit, of course! I'm not saying that it isn't very inconvenient having to find a new wedding planner at this late date, especially since Drake insists that a wedding be organized in the next few days, but still, you must admit that you drove Imelda to the breaking point with the fiascoes of the last week. I told Drake that this morning, when he asked me to give you a hand with arranging yet another wedding, but you know how men are. They want results and don't care how it's done. Now, as I said, we have two hours before our appointment with the new wedding planner. I would be happy to go shopping with you although I must insist we not be late to the appointment."

Paula gave me a gimlet-eyed look. "They will be quite hard put as it is to deal with the demands of an immediate wedding and a bride who isn't wholly committed to the ceremony."

I was unable to keep from smiling. "I don't think my commitment to Drake is in question, although I'm going to have to beg off the appointment this morning. I've simply got too many things going on, Paula. Can't you do it for me? You know the sort of ceremony we want to have—simple and short, with a reception to follow in an appropriate venue. I'll get my assistant to help you, if you like."

Paula squawked a bit at the idea of attending to the wedding details on her own, but after I pointed out that she was sure to arrange something much nicer than I could possibly do with limited time, she toddled off happily. "Although don't send me that odd man you call an assistant," she said before leaving. "I honestly don't know why you keep him on. He's always telling me about how much more organized his previous employer was . . ."

The door closed on her words. The second it clicked home, I turned to Jim. "Drake left? Where did he go?"

The demon shrugged. "Like I look like a psychic? Dunno where he went, but things are bound to get dicey around here with your stepmom running around."

"On the contrary—bless his heart, Drake obviously thought of that and dumped the wedding onto Paula's lap to keep her from getting underfoot. Well, I guess I'd better get the worst over with until Drake comes back. I assume my uncle is downstairs?"

"Oh, yeah. And how."

Jim's annoyingly cheerful voice followed me downstairs as I braced myself to meet the displeasure of my formidable uncle.

"Morning, Rene. Er . . . have you seen my uncle?"

His lips twisted into a wry smile. "He is in the lounge. Would you like some company?"

"Lord, yes. I'd love a whole battalion of you," I said, mentally girding my loins as I opened the door to the living room. To my surprise, Uncle Damian wasn't the only one occupying it.

"Nora!" I said, rushing forward to hug her.

She hugged me back, her face alight with pleasure. "I've missed you. Hello, Jim."

"Hey, Nora. How's Paco? Still snack-sized?"

"But of course. Chihuahuas don't ever grow past that."

"Not that I'm complaining, but what are you doing here? Aren't I on the verboten list for Guardians?" I asked.

Her gaze slid over my shoulder. "I am here on official Guild business."

I turned to see who she was looking at and froze solid on the spot. Or so it felt for a moment while my body had an intense memory of being squashed by one of the most powerful men in the Otherworld. "Dr. Kostich. Good morning. It's a pleasure to see you," I lied, my palms suddenly going sweaty.

"Aisling Grey," he said, inclining his head. Just the act of him saying my name sent little zings of electrical shocks through me.

"Er . . . I take it you both met my uncle, Damian Carson?"

"Yes, we had that pleasure." Nora's smile was polite, but I sensed a less happy emotion was giving her grief. She glanced at the archimage again, but he stood silent, apparently engrossed in admiring the collection of jade and gold dragon statues that lined the marble mantelpiece. "We are here at the request of Caribbean Battiste. I have been asked

to represent the Guild, while Dr. Kostich is acting on behalf
of the L'au-delà committee. We are here to discuss resolving
the situation concerning your proscription."

"Why don't we sit down and talk about it." I waved Nora
to a chair, one eye on Dr. Kostich. My uncle stood with his
back to the window, his hands clasped behind him, his eyes
watchful. Rene nodded toward the door, clearly asking if I'd
like him to give us some privacy. I shook my head. He sat
next to Nora, giving me a gentle smile that did much to
bolster my spirits. Jim meandered over to the archimage,
clearly intent on conducting a gender check, but stopped
when I hissed a warning under my breath. "As you both
know, I'm very anxious to have the proscription lifted so I
can return to my Guardian duties. And training, naturally."

"You do not believe you are beyond the training given to
apprentices?" Dr. Kostich asked, lifting one of the dragons
to examine it. His voice was mild, but the aura of power surrounding him didn't escape me in the least. I remembered all
too well how easily he'd stopped my heart while we were in
Budapest—I wasn't about to underestimate him now.

"I believe that I have had more practical experience than
most apprentice Guardians, but as I'm sure Nora can attest,
I am far from learned in the art of controlling my abilities.
Or even understanding the full extent of them, although I'm
getting more of a handle on them."

He set down the dragon and turned slowly to face the
room. "Abilities which include the dark power?"

Jim sat next to me and leaned on my leg, a warning look
in its eyes. It didn't have to bother, however. I was fully
aware of the fine line I walked regarding everyone in the
committee. I chose my words carefully. "I have not used
dark power since I was proscribed. It has been with me
daily, tempting me to use it, but I have resisted despite all its

attempts, and I will continue resisting it until the day comes when it can no longer speak to me."

Do you seriously believe you can ever be free of me? That time will not come, Aisling Grey.

"It is not easy for me to ask people for help, especially when those people are strangers to me. But I have asked the Guild for help in lifting the proscription because with each passing day, it becomes more and more difficult to resist the lure of the dark power," I said bluntly.

Nora gasped.

Told you so.

I kept my eyes on Dr. Kostich, knowing it was important that he understand the situation. "I don't want to use it. I have fought against it each day. And god knows, I hate to admit there's something that I can't handle on my own, but I know, deep down I know that if I don't have help in ending the situation, the time will come when I can't resist it any longer."

It is inevitable. Give in to your fate. Be what you were meant to be. Do not prostrate yourself before lesser beings in an attempt to deny what you are.

The room was so silent, I could hear the faint noise of London traffic through the triple-glazed windows. Dr. Kostich watched me silently, his gaze crawling over me in a manner that left me feeling itchy and restless.

"I wonder if you appreciate the full extent of the powers you are so willing to dismiss," he said finally, surprising me into a little jerk.

"The dark power, you mean?" I asked. Was he saying what I thought he was saying?

"Yes. Most people who were granted the ability to use it would not be so eager to lose it. In fact, I cannot think of a single instance where such a thing has happened, which leads me to believe that you do not fully understand exactly what it is you have been offered."

I looked at the others in the room, unable to believe what I was hearing, but didn't find enlightenment on my friends' faces. Nora looked as surprised as I felt. Rene was wearing his inscrutable look, and Uncle Damian just looked downright suspicious.

"I'm . . . are you implying I should use the dark power despite what it is?"

"I am not saying anything of the kind," he answered evenly. "I simply asked if you understand exactly that of which you seek to rid yourself."

A snappy retort was ready on my lips, but I closed my mouth on it as I thought about what he was asking.

How I love it when you turn your full attention to the possibilities. He is right, you know. In the end, no one has ever refused me.

For a second, I let the dark power fill me. The door in my mind swung open, and all the possibilities lay before me in a glorious array. Dr. Kostich was surrounded by a corona of power, but as the warm, thick insidious darkness filled me, I wondered if I could take him on.

There is nothing we can't do together.

I stood slowly and faced Dr. Kostich, smiling to myself as I thought of giving him a taste of his own medicine. I could stop his heart, stop his lungs from breathing, freeze him where he stood and allow his body to start to die, just as he had done to me. It would be so easy, so very easy. All I had to do was will it . . .

Your wish is my command.

I released the images dancing so seductively in my mind, firmly closing the door on the possibilities, and sat back down with a defiant look at the man standing before me. "Did I pass the test?"

Nooooooo!

"Yes," he said, suddenly brusque. "Battiste believes your intentions are honorable. Despite your history, I am inclined to acquiesce to his judgment. Therefore, I will allow you to remain within the protection of the L'au-delà."

"I didn't realize that I was going to be booted out of—"

"For that reason, I will extend to you my help with the matter of the proscription," he continued just as if I hadn't spoken. "There is only one way it may be lifted—the proscripted agent must reject the dark power possessing her, and a forbearance must be granted by the Court of Divine Blood."

"The who?" I asked.

"The Court of Divine Blood is a counterpart to Abaddon," Dr. Kostich answered, his fingers tapping against his legs as he strolled to the window and gazed out of it.

I glanced at Nora but didn't find any help there. "Heaven, you mean?"

"No more so than Abaddon is Hell," he answered. "The mortal concept of Heaven is based in part on the Court, just as their hell is based on Abaddon, but neither concept is truly accurate. Regardless, it is the Court you must convince to grant you a forbearance."

I relaxed slightly, for some reason reassured that I wasn't going to have to do something to convince Bael to let me go in order to end the proscription.

"That is after you have been granted an expulsion from Abaddon, naturally," he added.

Well, *merde!*

"I have to be kicked out of Abaddon first?" I asked, a sick feeling in the pit of my stomach.

"Yes. You will be required to give up your position as a prince, naturally, but I assume you do not object to that?"

My quasi-hysterical laughter was probably all the answer he needed.

"Very well." He glanced at his watch. "I have an appointment I must attend. If you have any further need for assistance from the L'au-delà, I trust you will make it via the appropriate channels."

"Appropriate—uh . . . but I thought you were going to help me?" I asked, getting to my feet quickly as he marched across the room and threw open the door, clearly about to leave. "Aren't you supposed to tell me how to get kicked out of Abaddon and get this Court place to grant a forbearance?"

"It is not the duty of the L'au-delà to hold your hand," he snapped, marching to the front door. Rene leaped ahead to open it for him. Nora stood in the doorway of the living room, my uncle directly behind her. "Miss Charles has volunteered to serve as a liaison between you and the Guardians' Guild. It is unlikely that they will be able to provide you with assistance, but I will leave that to Caribbean. Good day, Aisling Grey."

"But—"

Jim butted its head against my hand. I snapped off my protest, knowing full well it wouldn't do any good.

A car was waiting out front for Dr. Kostich, the driver deferential as she held the car door open. The archimage paused at the car, his gaze piercing mine even across the distance of the sidewalk and entryway. "The answer to your question is no—you would not have been able to 'take me,' as you so quaintly put it."

He got in the car before I could react to him reading my

mind. I closed the door to the house slowly, glancing down at Jim as I did so. "You hear him?"

"Yup," it answered, nodding. "He's wrong. You could have beaten him."

"I know. Scary, huh?"

"You have no idea, sister. You just have no idea."

17

"I'm sorry about all that," I told everyone when I returned to the living room. "Despite what Jim is about to say, I really don't get my jollies from going all evil on people."

Jim snorted. "I wasn't going to say that."

"Oh. My apologies for slurring your good name, then."

"I was going to say that you're a natural at it. Maybe Dr. Kostich was right and you should just dump the whole saving-the-world plan and go with global domination. It'd probably be a lot more fun. Ow! That's demon abuse! I have witnesses!"

"Yeah, I'm really worried. OK, so what's left on the big, big list of things I have to get done before I go insane, or the world comes to an end, whichever comes first?"

Nora smiled. "How I've missed your refreshing attitude. I suppose we should discuss the situation with regards to Abaddon before I leave."

"Right, so that's number one: find a way to get me kicked out of Abaddon. Two—"

The phone rang. I glanced at the ID—it wasn't a familiar number. "I bet that's two right there."

The voice on the phone was abrupt and to the point. "It is arranged. Two o'clock, at the Wyvern's Nest in Soho."

"Huh? Who is this? What's arranged—damn."

The phone clicked off without the caller saying another word.

"What was that?" Uncle Damian asked, suspicion rife in his voice.

"A blue dragon, I think. It sounded like one of Fiat's men . . . but they always deliver his messages in person. Maybe it was one of Bastian's buddies."

"Bastian?" Nora asked, sitting down next to Rene on the couch.

"Bastian is Fiat Blu's uncle and the rightful wyvern of the sept, or he would have been if Fiat hadn't had him declared insane and locked him up last century."

"I see. And you're helping him?"

I summarized the events of the last few days. "Bastian thought a direct challenge against Fiat was the way to go, but he wanted to meet with the few friends he had remaining before he acted. That didn't sound like him on the phone, though." I pinched my lower lip as I thought.

"And Bastian is the second thing on your list?" Nora asked.

"Yup. Number three is currently out of the house, although I hope he'll be back soon, because I have about five million questions to ask him about his brother."

"Oh, dear." Nora's hands folded together. "I feel so out of things. You are speaking of Drake? He has a brother? I've never heard of him having a brother."

"You don't want to go there," Jim said, with an eye on me as I paced back and forth before the now-cold fireplace. "Aisling has her knickers in a twist because Drake has been keeping secrets from her."

"Everyone has secrets," Uncle Damian said unexpectedly.

I was about to tell Jim to pipe down, but looked at my

uncle instead. He wore a cryptic look I could swear he stole from Drake.

To my surprise, Rene nodded. "It is the way of human nature, *hein*?"

"I'm not pissed at Drake because he kept some sept business to himself," I told the two men. "I just don't like it when something as personal as a brother is kept from me because Drake doesn't trust me. It's not like I would have rented a billboard with 'Drake Vireo has a brother, and he's alive and kicking' on it!"

"Broken trust is hard to overcome," Rene answered, his dark eyes sparkling with some inner amusement.

I opened my mouth to refute that statement, recognized my own words (although how on earth did Rene know I had spoken them?), and was about to snap back when a familiar voice in the hallway had me spinning around.

"You are all here? Good," Drake said, entering the room, Pál, István, and Kostya in close formation. "It is a pleasure to see you again, Nora."

She smiled at him as he kissed her hand in that dramatic—but oh, so sexy—way he had. "It's a pleasure I share. You are no doubt wondering what I am doing here—I have been authorized by the Guardians' Guild to assist Aisling with the problem of her proscription."

"Excellent. I am sure she will welcome your help."

My stomach trembled pleasurably as Drake eyed me.

"Stop that," I said softly as he let me feel his fire.

His eyes flashed with wicked intent for a moment before he banked the fire, striding over to stand next to me. "You have not met my brother, I think."

Nora murmured politely as Drake introduced Kostya to her and my uncle.

"You look much better," I told Kostya, looking closely at

him. Although he'd evidently been badly malnourished as well as suffering from a couple of broken ribs, he looked hale and hearty now. I noticed other similarities to Drake— he moved with the same liquid grace, and bore a familiar sinister air of danger that I knew from experience acted like a magnet for women.

He bowed, and I thought again that dragons sure knew how to make simple acts look graceful without being the least bit effeminate or silly. "I am well. Drake has informed me of your situation; you will, I hope, accept my congratulations, and will not be offended if I remove from your house as soon as possible."

"Remove? You're leaving?"

"I must. To stay here would endanger you. It would be unrealistic to expect that word of my presence not spread, and I would not bring trouble to my brother's home."

"Too late for that," Jim muttered.

Kostya glared at the demon.

"Well, it is!" Jim pointed out.

"I agree, it is too late, therefore it doesn't make any sense for you to leave," I said, taking Drake's hand. "This was your mother's home before she gave it to Drake, and you will always be welcome here. As for danger . . . bah. Like we don't have an entire sept trying to bring us down? If we can handle that, we can handle any reaction to your reemergence. Right, sweetie?"

Drake's fingers tightened around mine. I was a bit surprised that he wasn't protesting his brother's decision to leave, but figured he must have a reason. That didn't mean I had to agree with it, though.

"Kostya was never one to allow others to endanger themselves on his behalf," Drake said slowly.

"That's a non-answer if I ever heard one. Look, this is

silly—you're Drake's brother, which means you're my
brother now, and you need protection, so you're going to
stay here. End of story. Now, why don't you guys sit down
and tell us what's going on, because I'm just about bursting
with questions."

Drake resisted my tug on his hand. "We were going to
have a conference about the future, Aisling. I just looked in
to make sure you were all right."

"Overprotection is not a virtue, you know," I told him
with a little pinch. "But that sounds like as good a topic as
any. So, what are going to be the ramifications of Kostya's
reemergence?"

Drake was silent, his thumb stroking the back of my
hand. Kostya frowned at the window. Pál and István shared
a glance, then both turned to Drake.

"Oh," I said, realizing I'd put my foot into it. "I'm sorry.
This is probably sept stuff, huh? Nora, could we get together
a little later today? I want to brainstorm proscription stuff
with you, but this situation is a bit more important."

"Of course," she said, gathering up her things, beaming a
smile to everyone in the room. "You have my number? Call
me when you are free and we will discuss what the Guild
can do to help you."

"Will do."

Rene and Uncle Damian stood up as well, obviously taking the hint. I had started to escort Nora to the door when
Drake's voice made me pause.

"Aisling . . ." He looked uncomfortable for a moment.

"What?"

The silence was almost overwhelming. Jim blew a low
whistle, walking over to nudge me with its head. "Oh, man.
This isn't going to be pretty."

"What isn't going to be pretty? What's wrong, Drake?"

"I'll see you later," Nora said quietly.

"Aisling has time to speak with you now," Drake said, stopping her.

"What on earth has gotten into you?" I asked, giving him a curious glance that was tinged by a bit of anger at his high-handed manner. "You know better than to start ordering me around. The dragon business is more important than the pro-scription . . ."

A horrible thought struck me. A horrible, appalling, un-bearable thought, one that made my stomach twist as I looked from one dragon to the other.

"Oh, my god—you don't want to talk in front of me," I finally said, unable to believe the words even as I spoke them.

I looked at Drake, willing him to deny it.

"It is sept business, *kincsem.*"

"Sept business your brother can hear, but I can't?"

"This concerns how the sept will help Kostya."

The words cut into me like little daggers, the unspoken sentiment quite clear. "And I'm no longer a member of the sept."

He moved so fast he was just a blur until he was directly in front of me, my hands in his. "You are my life, Aisling. You are my mate, regardless of the legalities. Nothing will ever change that."

I searched his face, but the truth was written there— reluctantly, true, but still plain to see. "But I'm not a green dragon anymore."

He said nothing. He didn't need to. The pain in his eyes said it all . . . but it was nothing to the pain I felt.

I'll just whistle a little tune to myself, shall I?

Drake didn't want me.

The sept didn't want me.

The dragons to whom I had sworn my fealty no longer considered me to be a part of them.

And these are people to whom you feel undying loyalty? I do not understand your hesitancy, Aisling Grey. You could be so much, and yet you simply allow others to walk over you as though you did not matter.

Gently I withdrew my hands, my throat tight and aching. "I understand. Rules are rules. Will I see you later?"

"Of course." His thumb brushed my lower lip. "I regret this, *kincsem*. I regret it more than you know."

I nodded and turned away, my being filled with pain, regret, anger, and a whole slew of emotions too twisted together to separate. But I had some pride left, dammit. I wouldn't let them see just how deeply their actions had cut me.

I see it.

"Aisling—"

I paused at the door, taking a moment to push down all the negative emotions threatening to overwhelm me before turning back to face Drake with what I prayed was a serene expression.

"I love you," he said, right there in front of everyone, in a clear, loud voice with no hint of pity.

Any other time, I would have welcomed the declaration with joy, a flock of doves, and a fireworks display that would have lit up half of London. Instead, I just nodded and left the room, too devastated by his actions to speak.

"Oh, my dear, I am so . . ." Nora didn't finish her sentence, just hugged me right there in the hallway. "We can do this another time, if you like."

"I'm OK," I said, giving her a quick hug before stepping out of the embrace. I felt like a cracked piece of glass—any touch would leave me shattered into a thousand little pieces all over the floor.

"You want sympathy or snarkiness?" Jim asked, showing a wisdom I hadn't expected.

"Snarky, please," I answered, my throat sore and tight with the effort to keep from screaming, or crying. Probably both.

"Then I say let's go beat the crap out of Fiat, and you take his place. Then you can boss people around and attend any sept meeting you want."

Pain twisted in my heart.

"That'll be enough of that," Uncle Damian snapped.

"I was just trying to cheer her up," Jim muttered, rubbing its head on my leg.

"She doesn't need cheering," he answered, marching over to a seldom-used room that I was planning on redecorating as soon as the wedding was over. "Aisling, I want to speak to you."

I swallowed down the lump in my throat. "I know you're upset about me warding you and Rene in the car, but could we possibly hold off that conversation for another time?" I rubbed my head, wishing I could just climb into bed and cry away all the pain.

"No," he answered, holding open the door.

"I think perhaps we should come back later," Nora said, glancing at Rene, who nodded.

"Stay where you are. This won't take long," Uncle Damian ordered.

I sighed and donned the mantle of martyrdom as I followed him into a small, dark room. Jim made like it was going to follow me, but Uncle Damian pointed at a spot on the floor and said, "Stay!"

"Hey! I may look like a fabulously handsome Newfie, but I'm no dog! Besides, only Aisling can give me or—"

Uncle Damian slammed the door in its face.

"Well?" I asked, lifting my chin as I braced myself for the onslaught.

"Let it go, Aisling," was all he said.

I stood silent for a moment, the tears I'd fought against so long burning behind my eyes. "It's so hard!" I wailed, wrapping my arms around myself. "Why does everything in my life have to be so damned hard?"

He put his arms around me in an awkward hug, the gentleness of his gesture making the tears well up and over my eyelashes. "I know it's difficult. But you're a fighter."

"They don't want me," I sobbed, giving in to the anguish.

"Do you seriously believe Drake isn't tearing his hair out over this situation? Even I can see he's head over heels in love with you. Don't you imagine he wants you at his side rather than hanging around with that porn star? Don't you think it's ripping him up to know that you're not a part of his clan?"

My tears slowed as I thought about it. "It's not that I think he doesn't love me—I know he does. But he didn't trust me enough to tell me about Kostya, and now he doesn't trust me enough to talk about sept business in front of me."

"Trust has nothing to do with it," he said as I pushed myself back and accepted the handful of tissues he swiped from a nearby table. "What I've seen of these dragons, they're a rowdy bunch. Someone could make no end of trouble if Drake treated you as if you were still his second-in-command."

"Not the green dragons. They're very supportive of him, and aren't like that at all."

"Oh?" His look was level and so pointed, it could skewer cement. "So it wasn't one of the green dragons that tried to overthrow him last month?"

I hesitated. "All right, point taken. But to exclude me now—it hurts!"

"Have you been involved in his business the last month?" he asked.

"I . . . well, not really. I was busy with the wedding, and trying to deal with the situation in Paris, and taking care of the demon lord stuff that my steward kept tossing at me. Then there was shopping and decorating for the holidays, and . . . well, there hasn't been any sept business for me to be excluded from."

"Businesses don't shut down just like that," he said with a dark look. "I can't imagine something so complicated as these dragon septs appear to be would, either."

"Which means he's been excluding me all along," I said, wanting to cry again.

Uncle Damian crossed his arms and gave me a stern, unyielding, wholly unsympathetic look. For some odd reason, it made me feel immensely better. "Buck up, woman! You just took a hard left to the gut, but I trained you better than this."

"I'm pregnant," I said, sniffling as I wiped up the last of my messy tears. "I'm allowed to be emotional."

"You're not allowed to be an idiot, and that's the path you're heading down if you don't stop right now. I trained you to be a smart, savvy woman who could handle herself in any situation. Now let's see the last of this pitiful creature, and more of the Aisling I know you can be."

He was right. I straightened my shoulders, lifting my chin as I sniffled my last sniffle. Drake wasn't excluding me because he wanted to—he'd always been proud of me as his mate, demanding I be at his side for everything. I was just giving in to my hormones, and that wasn't going to help anyone. If I wanted things to change, I'd have to see to it myself. "You're absolutely right. Dammit, I am a Guardian. I am a wyvern's mate—we won't go into whose right now because that's all screwed up—but I am still a wyvern's mate, and that's important."

Righteous indignation filled me, but it was a cleansing, energizing emotion.

"That's better," Uncle Damian nodded as I stormed over to the window and flung back the curtain.

"And I am a demon lord, one of the seven princes of Abaddon!" I yelled, spinning around to face him, shaking my fist to the ceiling. "As god is my witness, I'll never go hungry again!"

"Eh . . ." Uncle Damian pursed his lips.

"Sorry. Got carried away with the moment. Jim, Traci! I summon thee!"

Both demons appeared before me just as Rene cracked open the door and peered in.

"Is everything all right? We heard yelling."

"Come in and join the fun," I said as he slowly came into the room, Nora on his heels. "Everything's crap right now, but it's about to get a whole lot better. I'm tired of the world spitting in my face! If people, dragons, demons, whatever else want to mess with me, if they think they have me cowed, they have another thing coming."

Jim whistled, eyeing my uncle with obvious admiration. "I don't know what you said to her, but you win my uncle-of-the-year vote. Look out, world, Aisling is back!"

"We're going to start at the top and work down the list," I said loudly, slamming my hand flat on the table. "Bastian will get my help when he needs it. Next up is the homage to Bael, and the proscription. I think two birds with one stone will suit us there. Traci, take an e-mail!"

"Take a what?" the demon asked, looking startled.

"E-mail."

"My lord? If you wish to send a message, tradition

dictates it be done via written document, sealed with blood, and sent by hand."

"Yeah, well, I'm the demon lord who owns a software company, remember? We'll use e-mail to contact every single one of my minions, all the demons in every legion. And the other demon lords—Bael excepted."

"But that's . . . that's over a hundred thousand demons in your legions alone," Traci said, gasping slightly.

"You can copy and paste," I said kindly. "Tell my minions to wrap up the business concerns of the software company and to prepare for banishment to the Akasha."

"What?" shrieked Traci.

Jim's eyes widened. Rene looked as surprised as Nora. Uncle Damian almost cracked a smile.

"Then I want you to e-mail the other five demon lord princes—but not Bael—and tell them I want to meet with them to discuss the future of Abaddon."

"The future . . ." Traci's hand clutched its chest, as if it was having trouble breathing. It cleared its throat a couple of times before it continued. "What exactly do you wish me to tell the other lords?"

I smiled at my uncle. He nodded curtly. "Tell them I intend to overthrow Bael and take control of Abaddon myself."

A loud *whump!* echoed around the room as Traci fainted dead away.

18

"This is insane, you know that, right? I think the dark power has warped your sense of what's smart and what's incredibly stupid."

"On the contrary, I'm being proactive and taking charge of things, dammit. You like it when I do that," I told Jim.

"I don't like it when you go stomping off to prove something, and we end up in seriously hot water."

"I always get you out before you actually boil."

"Not always," it answered, looking pointedly at its feet.

"Will you stop with the toes? You have enough of them left."

"I am just surprised that Drake let you go," Nora said as we approached our goal. "He has certainly changed since I have seen him last if he's allowing you to meet with other dragons without him."

"Oh, he hasn't changed. He's worse if anything, because of the baby. But he knows I'm protected."

Her eyes shone brightly behind her glasses.

I grinned at her. "And there's the fact that he is making me check in every half hour, in case something goes wrong."

"A half hour? I'm amazed he let you get away with that long," she answered.

"It started out at five minutes. We negotiated down to half

an hour, but I only got that concession because he knows I won't be alone."

"I just hope you know what you're doing coming here," Jim warned.

"I think we'll be all right. Fiat isn't stupid—he has to know Drake is keeping a close eye on me, and besides, I've got a Guardian extraordinaire with me," I answered, patting it on its head before pointing down the block to where a sign hung announcing a pub named Wyvern's Nest. "There it is."

Nora smiled. "Technically I'm only supposed to be helping you with the proscription situation, but in this case, what the Guild doesn't know won't hurt it. Although . . . Aisling, I have to say, I'm not certain that your plan in regard to Abaddon will go as you hope."

"There's no other option as far as I can see—I've got to make Bael realize that I'm going to be far more trouble than I'm worth without him actually wiping me off the face of the earth. So. What do we think?" I asked, as we stopped outside the pub. I tried to peer into the windows to see what was inside, but the interior was too dark.

"The word 'doomed' comes to mind," Jim said, pouting just a little. "Also 'scary' and 'feed the demon before it ruins this magnificent form.' And lastly, 'what are you thinking walking into such an obvious setup?' but I expect you're going to ignore that last bit."

"Wrong. I'm going to ignore all of it."

Jim sighed heavily as it shuffled forward to the door. "I'm gonna lose more toes, I just know it."

"Gah!" I yelled at it. "One more mention, just *one more mention* of your toes, and I'll see to it you don't have any left to complain about!"

"See?" it asked Nora. "She's all evil and stuff. She never used to be that way. The dark power is warping her brain."

Nora stifled a smile and asked me, "What exactly do you expect will happen here?"

"Despite what Jim thinks, I'm well aware that it's likely to be a trap of some sort," I said cheerfully as I entered the pub, taking a quick look around its interior.

"Ah. A trap. Sounds fun," she said, looking brightly around the room.

Rene sidled up to me from where he'd been sitting at the counter, his furtive manner so pronounced it attracted the attention of everyone sitting nearby. "I have scooped out the pub. It is clean."

I stifled the urge to giggle at his attempts both at subterfuge and idiom, instead nodding gravely and thanking him. "Where's Uncle Damian, by the way?"

"I do not know," Rene answered, a little frown pulling down his brow. "We split up before entering the pub. He asked me to check the rear of the building before we entered. I did that, but by the time I came into the pub, he was nowhere to be seen."

"Hmm. He's probably hiding somewhere, being all stealthy and stuff. He lives for that sort of thing." I allowed my purse to fall, turning around quickly to fuss with it for a minute while covertly surveying the room. It was a typical pub in most respects, with the usual arrangements of small round tables scattered around the bulk of the floor, the walls lined with tables and wooden settles, a jukebox, low timbered ceiling, various glowing neon liquor signs . . . and there wasn't a single visible human in it except for Nora and me. "At least we were right about this having something to do with the blue dragons."

"Yes, but which dragon is it who summoned you? Fiat or Bastian?" Rene asked.

"We're prepared for the worst, and we'll hope for the

best. Jim, I don't suppose it's much good asking you if you sense any danger?"

"Oh, yeah, serious danger," it answered, watching a dragon walk past bearing a couple of glasses and a plate of appetizers. "As in, I'm in serious danger of starving to death unless you order something to eat."

I stepped forward and everyone in the pub turned into statues. "Hello. I expect some of you know who I am."

The publican was a dark-haired dragon with the most startling blue eyes I'd ever seen, framed with thick, lush black lashes. He set down a glass in front of a waiting dragon and inclined his head. "You are the pretender."

I cleared my throat. "The pretender? As in, pretending to be a blue dragon?"

He nodded.

"Ah. Well, that's a bit of a long story, but the upshot is that as nice as you guys are, I'm not Fiat's mate by choice. You are aware of that, aren't you?" I asked, suddenly worried that the blue dragons might think I was slighting them without any due cause.

A woman emerged from a back room, her resemblance to the first dragon marking her as some sort of a relation. A look of dislike swept over her face as she recognized me.

"What are *you* doing here?" she growled, setting a wooden crate on the counter.

"Marta," the man said, putting his hand on her arm as if to stop her from vaulting over the bar. "It is not wise. You do not wish to anger *him.*"

She spat out a word that I had no difficulty translating, although I thought it best to overlook it. "I do not fear Fiat. And I will not treat his whore with respect."

"Whoa now," I said, recoiling from the venom in her voice. "I had a feeling you guys weren't happy about me being in the position of mate to your wyvern, but as you must all know, I am only here because he tricked Drake and me. I dislike Fiat more than I can politely express, and I certainly am not having any sort of illicit relations with him—"

"*Cara!* What a pleasant surprise. You did not tell me you were coming to visit." Fiat's voice cut across mine, the man himself oiling his way out of an all-but-invisible door set into the far wall of the pub.

He tried to take my hands, no doubt to kiss them. I put them on my hips instead, and leveled a glare at him. "I thought it might be you. The next time you want to see me, I'd appreciate it if you could leave your name and the nature of the event, so I know whether to bring Drake, or my uber–protection team."

Fiat's gaze moved from me to Rene and Nora before returning accompanied with a brittle smile. "*Cara,* you abuse me for no purpose. I did not request your presence here today, if that is what you are implying."

"You didn't?" I looked around the room, as if the answer would be found in one of the closed, hostile faces that watched me so closely. "Well, there's obviously been some sort of a mix-up. I'm sorry to bother you."

"As if I could find your so-charming presence a bother," he said, snagging one of my hands and pressing a wet kiss to my wrist.

The woman behind the bar exploded in a fury of Italian. I leaned toward Rene and murmured, "I get the feeling she doesn't like me."

His eyes were round as he watched her evidently chastise Fiat. "This woman, she is most brave. I cannot imagine someone speaking to a wyvern the way she does. It is most hot."

Fiat evidently thought so, too, because he listened to her

for about ten seconds, then slapped her so hard, her head snapped back.

"Hey!" I yelled, leaping forward.

Rene grabbed my arm as I raised it to draw a ward on Fiat. "Aisling, that is not wise, either," he said in a low tone.

Fiat's eyes spat blue anger at me as he spun around to face me. "You dare raise your hand to me, mate?"

"I do not tolerate abuse of women, in any form," I snapped, shaking off Rene to stalk forward. "I don't happen to be horribly fond of this woman, but I will not allow you to smack her around in front of me."

"You *challenge* me in front of my people?" he asked, stepping closer so that we stood toe-to-toe, the threat very evident in his voice and body language.

"No, I do not challenge you," I said, trying to keep a hold on my temper. That was a lie, of course—I wanted nothing more than to smite him where he stood.

Oh, a smiting. I haven't done that in a long, long time. You know, it really is your duty to protect those weaker than you. You owe it to this poor, innocent woman to teach Fiat a lesson.

"I don't want to belittle you in front of your dragons, but I will not stand by while you beat up someone who can't strike back," I said as evenly as possible.

"Do not mistake my tolerance of your past insolence as a given," he answered, leaning forward, his voice low and so mean it raised the hairs on the back of my neck.

I took a step closer. "As long as we're into the warnings, let me remind you who I am and what I control. I may look like a squishy little Guardian, but I assure you I am as badass as they come."

"*Oui,*" Rene said, taking up a position on my left. "As am I."

"I'm not bad . . . er . . . ass, but like Aisling, I will not stand by and watch someone being abused by you," Nora said, moving into a flanking position on my right.

My heart warmed with the show of support.

Oh, give me a break!

"It's a weak man who has to prey on those weaker than himself," Uncle Damian said as he emerged from the shadowed hallway that led to the bathrooms. He took up a position behind me. I flashed him a grateful smile.

"You mess with Team Aisling, you're going to be kissing the pavement," Jim snarled, showing its teeth as it marched over to stand in front of me.

"You dare? No one threatens me!" Fiat yelled, causing me to stumble backwards into my uncle. He righted me, keeping a warning hand on my arm.

He didn't need to hold me back—Fiat's face was suffused with anger, his eyes blazing as he suddenly leaped to the top of the bar. "You will not speak to me in such a manner! I am wyvern here, and you will show respect to me at all times! Kneel before me, Aisling Grey."

"Oh, that is so not happening," I told him, my arms crossed as I tried to decide if I needed to call in Drake or not. On the whole, I thought not. Uncle Damian and Rene were pretty intimidating.

"Still bullying women, eh, Fiat? I see you haven't changed, not that I had any hope you would," a voice said from the door. Fiat's head snapped around, his shock at seeing the man standing there apparent for a fraction of a second before he turned to me and yelled something extremely unflattering.

"*Cazzo!* You did this!" he screamed. "You will pay for such treachery!"

A fireball hot enough to melt steel blasted me. Rene

yelped and leaped to the side. Nora screamed as the fire engulfed her where she stood next to me. I hurled myself on her, throwing her to the ground and covering her with my body in order to protect her from Fiat's fury.

"Stop it!" Bastian bellowed, marching into the room with three dragons in close formation behind him, pulling Fiat's attention to himself. "This will stop now! Aisling is not to blame—it was inevitable that I face you again."

The conflagration eased up on me, but judging by the sound of breaking glass, I suspected Bastian's ploy at invoking Fiat's wrath had worked.

"I am the wyvern here. You do not give me orders!" Fiat shrieked before erupting into violent Italian. The dragons in the bar were apparently frozen at the scene being enacted before them, all of them watching with shocked faces.

Clearly, there wasn't going to be any help from them. "Uncle Damian, call an aid unit," I yelled as I slid off Nora, hurriedly checking her over for injuries.

"I'm all right, I'm not hurt," she said quickly, crawling backwards as the flames burning the floor crept toward us. "Just a little singed around the edges."

"Are you sure?" I asked, helping her up. Uncle Damian, thankfully protected by being behind me, had escaped any injury. He checked Nora over quickly before giving a curt nod.

"No injuries, although that coat won't be the same. Don't these places have fire sprinklers?"

Fiat leaped off the bar and stormed over to Bastian, still blasting him with fire and Italian. He stopped long enough to call for his henchmen, pulling a gun from his jacket, which he leveled at Bastian.

"Most dragon establishments are heavily fireproofed," I told my uncle. "They don't need sprinklers."

"Renaldo and Stephano won't answer your call," Bastian told his nephew. "They have been . . . *detained.*"

Fiat screamed even louder.

"Man, I haven't heard language like that since Amaymon kicked me out of his legion. Fiat's got quite the mouth on him," Jim said, watching the dragons from behind the safety of my legs. "Go, Bastian! I never did like those two."

"Do you think I am afraid of you?" Bastian laughed outright in Fiat's face, causing the latter to turn an interesting shade of crimson.

"Bastian gets points for style, but boy howdy, I don't think I could stand in front of a raving lunatic armed with a deadly weapon and mock him," I said quietly as I helped Nora take off her still-smoking coat.

"And yet that's pretty much just what you're planning on doing," Jim said. "Ash, I know you're immortal and all, but I'm thinking you may want to get out of the line of fire until we see what shakes down."

"I'm in complete agreement," Uncle Damian said, taking me by the arm and pulling me over to a spot behind the bar. "Stay here."

I would have protested being hustled out of the area, but given my present circumstances, I stood half-hidden by the wall and watched as Bastian and Fiat duked it out. The dragons in the bar had finally come to life at the appearance of Fiat waving the gun at Bastian. They formed a loose circle around the men, Bastian and his three buddies facing Fiat alone.

"The sept is mine, old man. Mine!" Fiat snarled. "And I do not allow disrespect in the sept, much less mutiny! You and Aisling may have thought you could get rid of me, but I assure you, I am in full control. And now you both will die for your treachery."

"We are leaving," Uncle Damian said, moving quickly to grab me and haul me toward the back rooms.

"No," I said, grabbing onto the doorjamb and holding tight. "I can't leave, uncle. Not until I see if Bastian is going to take down Fiat."

"It's too dangerous. That idiot dragon just threatened to kill you."

Jim's laughter was more a bark than a laugh. "Death threats are old hat to Ash."

"They really are, you know," I told my uncle, giving his arm a little squeeze. "People have been trying to kill me from day one, and I've survived, so really, a few wild threats from Fiat aren't going to scare—"

The sound of gunfire exploded in the close confines of the pub. Uncle Damian knocked me against a wall, shielding me the way I'd shielded Nora.

"I'm all right, save her," I yelled into his chest, pushing him back in order to make sure my friends weren't being slaughtered.

Nora was crouched down behind the bar, peering over it with Rene.

I squeezed out to see what was happening. Two of Bastian's company were on the floor, one male, rolling in obvious pain as blood stained the floor around him, the other a woman who was sobbing as she tried to rip off the man's shirt to see how badly he'd been injured.

Fiat slammed Bastian up against the wall, holding him off the floor in an impressive display of one-handed strength. Another dragon stooped and picked up the gun from where Bastian had evidently knocked it from Fiat's grasp. He looked unsure of what to do with it, holding it as if it were a toad about to spit warts.

Uncle Damian jetted past me, snatching the gun from the dragon before the latter knew what was happening.

"Uncle, don't—" I started to say as Uncle Damian pointed the gun at Fiat.

"I believe I've seen enough," he said, but before I could stop him, several of the surrounding dragons jumped him. He went down in a flurry of fists.

"Stop this right now!" I bellowed, leaping forward, drawing wards as fast as I could. Nora saw what I was doing and jumped into the fray, her hands flying as she bound the dragons to the floor, leaving them unable to move.

Rene jumped on top of the dragons who had piled onto my uncle, flinging them off until he was down to the Uncle Damian–flavored center.

"I have had enough!" I continued, turning a glare that warned of serious consequences on the couple of remaining unbound dragons. They backed off, with the exception of the woman named Marta. She snarled something and leaped at me with hands curved into claws. Jim broadsided her and knocked her backwards into a table. She went down with a clatter of chairs. I quickly bound her to the floor, then slapped an additional silencing ward on her to stop her stream of abuse.

I turned back to where Fiat was spitting Italian at his uncle, his fingers digging deep into the flesh of Bastian's neck.

"You wanted me as a mate, well, fine, I'm your friggin' mate, and I'm telling you to stop right now!" I yelled at Fiat, marching over to him.

"Aisling, stay away!" my uncle shouted.

Nora hastily drew a protection ward on me, hitting all four sides, the wards shimmering golden in the air for a moment.

I didn't want to pull Fiat's fire at all, didn't want to feel it, didn't want to use it, didn't want to gain strength from it, since it was tantamount to betrayal of Drake's fire, but I didn't have time for the finer points of my feelings. I pulled hard on it and slammed the fire back into Fiat, not causing him any harm, but distracting him enough to release Bastian.

"Maiala," he snarled at me, spinning around to face me.

"Yeah, whatever. Bastian, do it."

Bastian got to his feet with the help of his remaining friend, his face mottled red, his eyes blazing a fury to match Fiat's. It was almost like seeing some sort of a twin act when they were face-to-face—they really were remarkably similar in appearance, but there, thank god, the similarities ended.

"By the laws governing the illustrious sept of the blue dragons, I, Bastiano de Girardin Blu, wyvern by right of tanistry, do hereby issue a formal challenge of transcendence to Sfiatatoio del Fuoco Blu."

Fiat laughed, a scary sort of near-hysterical laugh, the kind that screams straitjacket and lifetime supply of happy drugs. "You have tried to take the sept from me three times, old man, and failed. What makes you think you can do it this time?"

Bastian had challenged Fiat before?

"Oh, man, that doesn't sound good," Jim muttered.

"Yeah. He didn't tell me he'd challenged Fiat before and lost." Doubt entered my mind for the first time since meeting Bastian. I'd been so certain that all he needed was a helping hand to get out of his imprisonment, I'd never considered that perhaps Fiat was just too strong to be overthrown. If the overthrow failed . . . I shuddered at that unthinkable conclusion. "I do not want to think about what evil sort of punishment Fiat will have his sept work up for me if he beats Bastian."

"It ain't gonna be pretty, that's for sure," Jim said in a repulsively cheerful voice.

"I will succeed because I must," Bastian said with much dignity in reply to Fiat's comment, tugging down his shirt and dusting himself off. "It is true that you have managed to manipulate the circumstances of my challenges in the past, but this time, I am prepared for you."

To my intense relief, Fiat's anger had morphed into a wicked sort of amusement, still dangerous, but not explosive . . . at least for the moment. "You put too much faith in the power of my mate. She cannot help you. Do you not know? She is proscribed, banned by her own people, and far too stupid to understand the power she could wield."

"Don't fool yourself," I started to say, but Jim stomped on my foot in warning. I shut up.

"This is not about your mate, although I understand the lady disputes your right to call her that," Bastian said evenly. "This is between you and me. You will leave the others out of it."

Fiat glanced at the three dragons who had accompanied Bastian. The one he'd shot—whether by mistake or intentionally, I wasn't sure—had evidently recovered from the bulk of the trauma and was sitting in a chair while the woman wiped blood off his stomach. The third man stood warily next to Bastian. "I need no others to aid me. But I have a long memory, a very long memory indeed, and I remember equally those who serve me well, and those who do not."

The man next to Bastian edged away a smidgen, licking his lips nervously.

"As do I," Bastian said.

"Name the form the challenge will take." Fiat crossed his

arms and tipped his head to the side, as though he was finding the whole thing highly entertaining.

Bastian smiled.

I fell for that smile just as I was sure Fiat did, for even
though his dragon senses were more heightened than mine,
he didn't react when Bastian suddenly lunged forward, a
black metallic item in his hand. There was a faint sizzling
sound, followed by a crash as Fiat toppled to the floor, his
body jerking violently. Bastian lurched over him, holding
the black thing to his neck for another few seconds before
stepping back.

"Taser," Uncle Damian said as he took up a position behind me. His left eye was swollen almost completely closed,
blood dribbling from both his nose and lip, a nasty-looking
welt seeping more blood from a spot on his forehead. He
stood somewhat crooked, as if he couldn't straighten up.
"Effective but not lethal. Good man."

"This is the challenge," Bastian growled, jumping back
from the still-twitching body on the floor before him. "You
lose."

The silence in the bar was of the stunned quality. I was
just as taken by surprise as everyone else, gawking in obvious confusion as Bastian took a long, slow look at everyone
in the room. "Make it known to one and all members of the
sept that upon this day, I have taken my rightful position as
wyvern by defeating Fiat Blu in challenge."

I opened my mouth to say that that wasn't quite how I understood challenges to take place, but snapped it shut without uttering a word. Who was I to complain if Bastian used
the same sort of dirty tactics that Fiat had used?

"Congratulations," I said.

The dragons in the room looked at one another, those of

them who weren't bound to silence clearly unwilling to say anything.

I took a deep breath and mustered a smile as I faced them. "As mate to the wyvern of the blue dragons, I formally recognize you as wyvern, welcome you to the position, offer my good wishes for a lifetime of peace and prosperity, and am confident the members of the sept will do the same."

The members of the sept turned their disbelieving gazes on me. Fiat twitched one last time, then went still.

Bastian came forward, his face still blotchy from the near throttling. He put a hand on my head and pushed down. Obligingly, I knelt before him. "Aisling Grey, I refute you as mate. You are hereby stripped of all rights and powers as such, and as of this moment, are expulsed from the sept."

"Woohoo!" Jim said, doing a little happy dance. I knew just how it felt, but didn't want to offend any of the blue dragons by celebrating my expulsion from their ranks.

"Thank you," I told Bastian softly.

He nodded as I got to my feet. "It was the least I could do. I will never be able to fully express to you the full depth of my gratitude, but know that I am in your debt."

"What are you going to do about him?" Uncle Damian asked, prodding Fiat's body with the toe of his boot.

Bastian smiled again, a smile at once so similar to Fiat's, and yet so different. "He's had a hard time of it lately, don't you think? He needs a rest. I know just the place where he will have nothing but quiet and peace, and time to contemplate his sins."

"I'm glad you're not going to . . . er . . . destroy him," I said, hesitating to put into words my fear. "I don't have any fondness for Fiat, but I've never been a proponent of the death penalty."

"Liberal," Uncle Damian scoffed.

"Politics has nothing to do with it. I just don't think that a challenge should end in death."

"I have seen too much bloodshed during my lifetime," Bastian said, nodding. "I will not add to it unduly. Besides, there is a certain amount of ironic justice to be had in Fiat's incarceration in the prison he created for me. I am certain that with time, he will appreciate that irony."

"You better just hope no one rescues his butt like we did yours," Jim warned, sniffling Fiat's inert form. It cocked an eyebrow at me.

"No," I told it. "We will be gracious in our triumph. No peeing on the loser."

"Man, you're just no fun anymore. How about the chick with the potty mouth?"

Marta's eyes widened as Jim sauntered over to her.

I smiled.

19

". . . perfect opportunity to pee on someone—which, let me tell you, doesn't happen that often—and you go all 'dignity at all costs' on me. Sheesh. Like that Italian she-witch didn't have it coming to her? A demon's gotta have some fun, you know!"

"Aisling? Is that you?" Paula appeared at the door to Drake's study, her hands on her hips, her lips compressed into a straight line.

"Uh-oh," I said, offering her a weak smile. "Did I miss another appointment?"

"I don't know why you told me to arrange a wedding for you if you refuse to attend any of the planning meetings! Honestly, Aisling, I'm at my wit's end with you, and I'm this close to just washing my hands of the whole situation!"

"Oh, Paula, I'm sorry—"

"Do you know how many wedding planners I've been through in the last week? Five, Aisling. Five!"

I flinched. "I'm really sor—"

She tossed her hands in the air. "Do you have any idea how in demand these people are? Or what it costs to try to have a rush wedding?"

"No, but I'm sure—"

"The situation is intolerable!" she yelled, gesturing

wildly as she paced a circle around me. "It's only for the sake of your father and late mother that I'm still trying."

"And I really appreciate it—"

She took a deep breath and pinned me back with a look that would have stripped paint off a battleship. "Since it's obvious that you are not capable of handling even the tiniest of responsibilities, I have taken it upon myself to arrange a ceremony for you. It will be simple, just immediate family and whatever friends you still have."

I sagged with relief. "That sounds fine, Paula. I know this hasn't been easy on you, but there are mitigating circumstances—"

"There will be no reception. There will be no banquet, no dance band, no decorations."

I tried to summon up a smile. It didn't work. "OK."

"If you had any conscience, any conscience whatsoever, you would return each and every wedding present you received from guests who took the time and effort to attend your first wedding."

"Absolutely," I said meekly, taking a couple of steps toward the stairs, wondering if I dared make a break for it.

She took three steps toward me, literally pressing me against the banister. "The wedding is scheduled for tomorrow at four p.m., in the office of the only individual in the whole of England who was willing to be bribed into making room for you. If you do not make this appointment, your father and I will leave immediately. Do I make myself absolutely clear?"

I nodded frantically. "Perfectly clear."

She snorted as she gave me one last piercing glare, then turned on her heel and stalked back to Drake's study.

As soon as the door closed, the one across the hallway opened. Drake peered out. "Is she gone?"

I nodded weakly and sagged against the banister. "She's in your study."

"I know. It seemed better to let her occupy it. She's in a bit of a mood," he said, coming over to me.

"That's putting it mildly. She scared the crap out of me." I transferred my limp form from the banister to him, wrapping my arms around him as he tilted my head back to examine my face. "I think I need massive kissing to restore my strength. And then if you wouldn't mind mating me again, I'd be very appreciative."

"Jeez, Ash! Just ask him to boink you right in front of me!" Jim tried to look appalled, but failed.

"That's not what I meant, and you know it. I was simply trying to tell this handsome hunk of dragon that I am no longer the mate of the blue wyvern, and if he would be so kind as to offer me a lifetime of undying love, affection, and steamy, sweaty lovemaking, I'd be gracious enough to accept." I nibbled Drake's lower lip as I spoke the last bit, expecting him to sweep me off my feet and make mad, passionate love to me before offering me matedom.

Instead he looked troubled, his eyes more human than dragon. "I'm afraid it's not quite as simple as that."

"Why not? Is there some sort of re-mating ritual we need to do?"

Drake cast a quick glance at the closed door of his study and pulled me into the living room. "We will talk in here."

"Oh, yeah, talk, that's a new name for it. Hey! Don't I get to wa—" Jim started to ask.

Drake shut the door on it.

"I'm getting a little sick and tired of people doing that!" it bellowed, audible even through the door. "Just because I'm a demon doesn't mean I don't have feelings!"

I opened the door and narrowed my eyes at it.

"And I thought your stepmom was scary," it muttered as it took itself off to another part of the house.

"All right," I said, closing the door and leaning against it as I looked at Drake. "What's the problem? Does the sept not want me back?"

"The sept would be delighted to have you back. They accepted you as my mate, and they will not forswear that allegiance."

That warmed the cockles of my heart a bit. I slid my arms around him and bit his chin. "Then what's the problem?"

His hands were warm on my derriere, his eyes shuttered. "The problem is that you are not available to be my mate."

"Ah. I see the confusion is bogging us down. You didn't know that Bastian beat Fiat and took over as wyvern. Well, he did, and his first act was to de-mate me, so I am, actually, available, and if you play your cards right, I can be yours."

He didn't smile at my teasing tone. He didn't even look remotely happy, two things that surprised me.

"I know about the challenge," he said, his hands sweeping up my back. I shivered a little, his touch stirring the desire that was always simmering.

"You do? How? Uncle Damian went off to see some of his friends, and Nora had work to do, so Rene took Jim and me straight here after we left Bastian. Did someone call you?"

He nodded.

"Who? Bastian?"

"No. Fiat."

I stared at him for three seconds before swearing profanely. "Jesus H. tap-dancing Christ! *Fiat* called you?"

"Yes." He pulled me close, nibbling a spot behind my ear that made me turn into a big old blob of goo. "I'm sorry, *kincsem*. Fiat apparently escaped Bastian's custody shortly after you left. He claims he is still the blue wyvern, and you are his mate."

"How can that be?" I wailed. "Dammit, Bastian beat him at a challenge! We were there! We saw it!"

He sighed into my neck, his arms tightening around me. I wanted to cry again, not sure if it was the pregnancy hormones stirring my emotions, or just the frustration of never seeming to catch a break that drove me to the brink. "There is a bit of a situation. Fiat is claiming that the challenge was invalid because Bastian did not present the terms of it before the challenge started."

"You mean he cheated by getting a jump on Fiat? But Fiat did the same thing with Dmitri . . . oh, hell."

"Abaddon," drifted in faintly from the hallway.

"Stop listening at the door!" I bellowed. "And that's an order!"

The sound of toenails ticky-ticking on the tile floor faded away to nothing.

I looked back at Drake. Regret was stark in his face. He nodded, brushing his thumb over my lower lip. I bit him.

"I wondered if you would remember that challenges for a sept always follow the formal challenge, while challenges for a mate are pretty much anything goes."

"So Bastian didn't really win control of the sept?" I asked, my heart breaking into a dozen little pieces.

To my surprise, his frown eased somewhat. "Actually, that isn't quite clear at the moment."

"What do you mean? Either Bastian is wyvern, or Fiat is. They can't both be wyverns . . . can they?"

"Not of the same sept, no," he answered, his hands getting busy.

I grabbed his wrists as they swept along my hips, heading

for higher ground. "Trying to get a straight answer out of you is like trying to ride a greased weasel."

"Would you like to ride me, instead?" he asked, his eyes alight with interest.

"You are utterly shameless. Luckily, that's one of your charms," I told him, pushing myself away from him in order to keep from jumping him right then and there. "Spit it out, Drake. What's the deal with Bastian?"

"I'd rather talk about you riding me," he answered, his dragon fire building inside him.

"You can seduce me after you tell me what I want to know."

He simmered at me. He positively simmered, his eyes molten, his body a temptation that I had to steel myself to ignore. "I can think of other things I'd rather do, naked things, than talking about the blue dragons."

I rubbed my head. My body was demanding I give in to him, but my brain wanted answers.

Sometimes brains are overrated.

"Please, Drake," I said, teetering on the verge of desire. "I hate being kept out of things. Please just tell me, and then I promise I'm all yours."

"You're all mine right now," he growled, pouncing on me with his usual feline grace. His lips burned mine for a moment before he kissed a fiery path to my collarbone, his tongue swirling around the sept brand he'd burnt there. "The situation isn't clear because Bastian is by right wyvern. Fiat never formally challenged him for the sept."

I shivered again and pulled his shirt out of his pants so I could slide my hands under it, my fingers dancing along the long, strong lines of his back. "Which would mean that Bastian wouldn't have to challenge Fiat, because he was already wyvern? Hallelujah! But why is Fiat still claiming to be wyvern then?"

"His claim is that Bastian wasn't formally named wyvern. Aisling . . ." Drake pulled back enough to look me in the eye just as I was nibbling on his delectable earlobe. "Fiat has many followers in the sept. This will likely divide the sept between those members who are loyal to Fiat and those who are loyal to Bastian."

"Oh, no. That would be horrible. Those poor people. Is there anything we can do to help Bastian?"

He shook his head. "No. Intra-sept struggles are beyond my reach. It must be for them to resolve."

"But Fiat has so much power, and he's been around the last hundred or so years, so everyone is more familiar with him than with Bastian. If we don't help Bastian, I'm going to be stuck with Fiat!" My voice rose on the last few words, despair my companion again.

"I will not allow that. *Kincsem* . . . it has not been easy for me, this last month. I have not liked involving myself in sept business without you."

I nuzzled his neck, holding him tight against the pain that stung within me. "I know. It hurts."

His lips were hot on my flesh. "I would not hurt you for all my treasure. And now that I know what the situation is with Fiat, I will take action."

"What sort of action?" I asked, nibbling his jaw, unable to resist the lure of his sexy self. "Are you going to challenge him for me? *Lusus naturae?*"

"No."

The word pierced my heart like a dagger.

"Do not look at me that way," Drake said, pressing his forehead against mine. "I am not betraying you, Aisling. But a challenge with Fiat would not serve the purpose. He would take extreme steps to ensure that he did not lose you, and I am not willing to risk him harming you."

The pain eased as I acknowledged the truth of what he said. Fiat wouldn't hesitate to destroy me utterly if he thought Drake stood a chance of winning me back. "What are you going to do if you can't challenge him?" I asked, ashamed of the pathetic tone of misery in my voice.

Drake smiled. His lips curled up, and his eyes went dragon as the smile grew in a way that made me thankful he was on my side. "I am wyvern of the green dragons."

"Yeah, so?"

"Such a look of confusion in your beautiful face. What do green dragons do best?"

"You're not going to make love to him," I said, scandalized for a moment even though I knew Drake couldn't mean that.

He gave me a long-suffering look. "Hardly."

"Well, good. Because I told you once I don't share, not even with another guy, although I have to admit that . . . um . . . never mind."

One of Drake's eyebrows rose. "Such unplumbed depths to you. I'm afraid that particular fantasy will never be fulfilled. I hold what is mine. No others will have you."

I smiled at the slightly outraged glint in his eyes. "Don't worry, it's not a fantasy. I always kind of wondered what it would be like to have so much attention, but then I met you, and, well, I don't think I could survive more attention than what you give me."

"That was the correct answer," he said, his voice rich with smugness.

"Uh-huh. OK, so back to Fiat . . ." I pulled my mind from the delightful sensations Drake's hands and mouth were giving me, and thought hard. If he couldn't challenge Fiat, what could he do? Drake was a man of many talents, but I couldn't think of one that would help him get me back without some sort of fight between him and Fiat.

And then the penny dropped.

I started laughing, causing Drake to pause as he unbuttoned my shirt. "Figured it out, did you?"

"I'm allowed to be a bit slow. I've had a hell of a day. So, my darling green dragon . . . what treasure of Fiat's are you going to steal?"

20

"Here I am! Sorry I'm late, but I had a bit of trouble locating your secret clubhouse. Did I miss anything good?"

Three of the four male faces in the room turned to me with astonishment. The fourth shook his adorable head resignedly. "We have not yet started. Out of idle curiosity, how did you find this room?"

I donned my most haughty look as I perched myself on the arm of his comfy leather chair. "You expect me to reveal my Guardian secrets? Ha! I think not, plebeian!"

Drake's eyes narrowed in thought. "Ah. The ward at the entrance."

"Dead giveaway," Jim said, plunking itself down in front of a small fireplace that was merrily blazing.

I nodded, patting Drake on the head. "No one binds a perdu ward on a bookcase unless they have something to be concealed. So when I knew you were in the house but couldn't find you, I decided it was time to investigate that bookcase. What's going on?"

"If I told you that we were conducting sept business . . ." Drake's eyebrow rose meaningfully.

I pushed it back down with the tip of my finger. "I wouldn't believe you. For one thing, you don't hide when you have sept business. And for another, you would have just told me if that's what you were doing."

He smiled. "I had a feeling you would see through both the hidden entrance to this room and that objection. As it happens, we are discussing strategy."

"Oh, good. I like strategy. What are we strategizing about?"

Drake pulled me down onto his lap. Before he could answer, Kostya, who had been standing with his hands behind his back, looking out the high, round window that graced Drake's hidden room, turned and said something in what I assumed was Hungarian.

"We will not speak Magyar in front of Aisling," Drake answered, his hands warm on my belly. "And there is no question of not allowing her to remain. What we are discussing is not sept business; if she wishes to participate, then I welcome her input."

I wanted to kiss him for such support, but Drake had rather old-fashioned notions about propriety in front of his sept members, so I contented myself with giving his thigh an unobtrusive squeeze. "I take it we're planning the theft?"

"Yes. I feel certain that Fiat's hoard is in Italy, in a house that is heavily protected. We must find our way through his defenses and into his treasure room."

"Sounds good. When do we leave?"

"We?" Kostya asked, frowning as he paced past me. "You will not be going with us, Aisling."

"Oh, man," Jim said, shaking its head. "He didn't just do that, did he?"

"He did," Pál said, also shaking his head.

I stared at Kostya in disbelief for a few seconds before asking Drake, "Did he just order me around?"

Drake nodded.

"And I thought *you* were the bossiest of all the dragons. He's got some nerve thinking he can tell me what to do."

"He has been isolated for over a century," Drake explained, the very corners of his mouth tilting up. "It is to be expected."

"Expected my Aunt Fanny. It's just another sign of dragon arrogance."

"This is the way you manage your woman?" Kostya asked, stalking across the small room only to turn and pace back to the window. "You allow her to dictate to you, brother?"

My hackles went up at that. "Hey! I am not a wayward sheep to be managed—" I started to say, but Drake interrupted.

"Aisling is my mate in all senses of the word. She has experience in matters that are beyond ours, and I value her insight. There is no question of managing her or allowing her to rule my life. I admit it has taken me a bit of time to realize the value in a partnership, but that is what we have, and it will not change."

"If I wasn't already madly in love with you, that speech would have done it," I told him, giving his ear a quick kiss.

"She carries your child!" Kostya said, his frown almost identical to Drake's, although on him, it wasn't even remotely attractive. "You would allow her to endanger herself and your son?"

"Clear the decks," Jim said, backing up into a corner. "Fire in the hole!"

"Right, now you're getting on my nerves," I said, pushing myself off Drake's lap. He made a grab for me, but I slipped away and marched over to where Kostya had taken up a pose, poking him in the chest as I clued him in to a few points. "I was prepared to like you because you're Drake's brother and part of my family now, but this is way over the line. You're insulting and degrading, and I won't stand for it!"

Kostya looked shocked, shooting Drake outraged looks that demanded he do something. A little puff of smoke escaped from his mouth as he sputtered, "You speak to me thusly?"

"Damn straight I do. This is my house, and you just insulted my husband-to-be."

"I would not insult my brother—"

"You just did, you annoyingly arrogant dragon! Do you seriously think that Drake would allow harm to come to me? He'd die first—not that I'd let him—but you insult him and me both by saying either one of us would endanger our child."

Flames leaped across the floor. Jim yelped and scooted even farther back.

"Control your anger," Drake said, frowning at the fire as István leaped up to stamp it out.

Kostya seethed, turning again to Drake. "You have nothing to say about this abominable treatment by your woman?"

"If you had asked me that two months ago, I would have had much to say on the subject of women who do not know their place," he answered, his eyes lit with amusement. "But I have since learned that there is one woman for whom that place is at my side, and I would not have her anywhere else."

"You"—I pointed at Drake—"are the most adorable man on the face of the earth. You"—I turned to glare at Kostya—"are almost as annoying as he was when I first met him. The sooner you get over yourself, the happier everyone will be."

"I will not be spoken to in that insolent manner!" Kostya all but yelled.

A ring of fire broke out around him. I clenched my fists and struggled to keep from drawing a silencing ward on him.

"Do not yell at Aisling," Drake said, leaping to his feet. He pulled me behind him in his usual dominating way, facing his brother with a dangerous look. "I will not allow you to speak to her in that way any more than I would allow our mother to do so. She is my mate. You will respect her as you do me."

"You take much upon yourself, *little* brother!" Kostya answered, a warning in his voice. "Do not forget who *you* are speaking to!"

Drake's eyes went pure dragon. Pál and István jumped up, immediately taking a position behind Kostya. The fire ring around Kostya grew higher. "I have not forgotten who or what you are," Drake answered in a soft voice that sent shivers down my back. "But you, it seems, have forgotten what you owe to Aisling."

Kostya looked like he wanted to burst, but he managed to rein in his emotions and give Drake a curt nod before spinning around and resuming his abrupt pacing.

The tension in the small room eased. Pál and István sat back down. Jim pursed its lips and whistled a tuneless song.

Drake pulled me back down onto his lap and said somewhat wearily, "Let us stick to less inflammatory subjects. Pál?"

I grumbled under my breath, but listened with interest as Pál pulled up a report on his laptop and read off what information they had about Fiat's house in Italy. It was detailed enough for me to speculate that the green dragons had done a little spying on Fiat, which made me wonder if the other septs were doing the same to us. A half hour later, a basic plan had been agreed upon . . . except for one vital point.

"You cannot be serious!" Kostya stormed, striding past

where I had curled up on a tiny loveseat. "You just got through saying you would not put yourself in danger, and now you expect to come with us? Ridiculous!"

"It won't be dangerous," I answered, my eyes on Drake. He wasn't looking very happy, and had, in fact, offered his opinion that I should stay home lest I come to any harm in Fiat's house.

"There could well be trouble," he said slowly, his brow somewhat furrowed.

"I don't see how. Fiat's in London trying to deal with Bastian. It's not likely that he's suddenly going to jet back to Italy while Bastian is rallying as many blue dragons to his cause as he can. The members of the sept are too busy wondering which of the two wyverns is going to come out on top to be worrying about us."

"There are guards at the house. It will still be dangerous even if Fiat is not present. I do not wish to hurt your feelings, *kincsem,* but it is intolerable to put you at risk."

"Now you are speaking as a man," Kostya said with a sharp nod.

"Oh, pipe down," I snapped at him. "And put out that fire before it reaches the curtain!"

Kostya stomped on a little outbreak of fire next to the curtain, shooting me a seething glance as he did so.

I ignored it, turning to Drake. "There's no risk at all, no more than I run by being at home and possibly being attacked by one of Chuan Ren's hired hit men. I won't get in the way. I'll stay back and let you and Pál and István take down the couple of guys who will be guarding the house. Besides, you can't deny it would be handy having a Guardian and her demon there to help out."

"Especially the demon," Jim said.

"Bah!" Kostya snorted.

Drake hesitated a moment, and I knew I had him. I trailed my finger down his leg and tried to look humble. "Sweetie, I don't want to put myself in danger any more than you do. But even if Fiat's guys did catch us, they aren't going to hurt their boss's mate. I promise I'll do whatever you say. I won't go off and beat up people on my own, OK?"

His lips tightened. "I don't like it."

"I know you don't. You never like it when I want to do things, and you get bonus points for discussing it with me rather than just giving me an order and marching away like *some* people would do."

Kostya muttered something under his breath.

"I would do just that if I thought I could get away with it," Drake answered, his mouth twisting wryly.

Jim made a whipcrack noise. I glared it into silence before giving Drake's knee a pat. "You're learning, sweetie. I'll make a husband out of you yet. When do we leave?"

He sighed, eyeing me unhappily. "I will allow this on one condition—you do not do *anything* without my express consent."

"Deal," I said, batting my eyelashes at him.

István cleared his throat. Pál grinned. Kostya threw glances heavenward and continued muttering.

"And they said Aisling couldn't be subtle," Jim said, shaking its furry head.

"Now that we have that business taken care of, we can turn to the other topic at hand," I said, returning to my loveseat.

"What subject is that?" Drake asked.

"Him." I pointed at Kostya. "No one has yet explained to me why everyone says the black dragons are gone, and yet there's one standing right there. Not to mention why Gabriel was so upset to see him. I know the silver dragons originally came from the black dragons, but they're a sept in their own right now, so what's the big deal? Why has Kostya been hiding for the last couple hundred years? Who was holding you guys prisoner? And why did Gabriel say he didn't like Kostya's hospitality?"

The man in question zipped over to me in super-dragon speed, causing me to jerk backwards in my chair. He leaned over me in a menacing fashion. "You might have my brother twisted around your fingers, but I will not be so facile. My business is none of your concern."

"Except when it concerns my sept or my friends," I answered.

"Kostya, I have told you once that I will not have you threatening Aisling," Drake said, pulling his brother back. "She has a curiosity that is often greater than her common sense, but she has a legitimate interest in the situation."

Kostya's dark eyes glinted dangerously at Drake. "You forget yourself, brother."

"I forget nothing," Drake answered, his muscles tense as if he expected a fight. "You would do well to remember that."

"Would someone open a window? The testosterone in here is stifling," I said lightly, pushing myself between the two men, giving Drake a little kiss on the chin.

He shot me an outraged look at the gesture.

"We're all family here," I answered the look, and gently pushed him back into his chair, seating myself on his lap to keep him down. "Now let's see if we can do this without all the posturing. How many questions do I get?"

"None," Kostya growled, turning his back on us as he stared out the window.

Drake's fire was still running high, but it cooled a little as I stroked his chest. "Three," he finally said.

"You said three the last time. I want six."

"Four," he offered. "But that will be all for the next twenty-four hours."

"You drive a hard bargain. Four it is." I leaned back against the arm of the chair, secretly pleased at getting a bonus question. "OK, first off—why was Kostya hiding from the other dragons?"

"The black sept was destroyed by its wyvern," Drake answered slowly, his fingers making lazy designs on my leg. "Most of the members were killed in the attempt to bring the silver dragons back into the fold. The silver wyvern—this was several centuries before Gabriel was born—swore he would not rest until every last black dragon was destroyed. The few black dragons who survived went into hiding at the death of Baltic. As Kostya was to be the next wyvern, it was decided that he would go into hiding until such time as the black dragons had gathered enough strength to return to the weyr."

"So the black and silver dragons are warring just like we are with Chuan Ren? Wait! Don't answer that! It's not an official question."

"It is not a war," Kostya answered, still staring out the window. "What the silver dragons conducted was nothing less than genocide."

I bit back the comment that it sounded like they had started the whole thing by trying to force the silver dragons back. "That would explain why Gabriel was so hostile when he saw Kostya, but not why he made the reference to not liking the hospitality offered."

"The aerie was Kostya's hiding place," Drake answered.

"That's a heckuva way to hide yourself, in a prison cell," Jim said, rolling over so Pál could scratch its tummy.

Kostya's back twitched.

"The aerie was invaded, and Kostya taken prisoner. When I received word from him that he was no longer safe, I went to rescue him, but we were not prepared for the force that awaited us."

I could tell by the way Kostya muttered that he wasn't happy at all about having to call on Drake for help. Somehow, that made me feel better.

"I know I asked you this before, and you said you didn't know, but you've got to have some idea who the dragons were who infiltrated the aerie."

"I did not know the few I saw," he answered, his eyes troubled. "They were ouroboros."

Jim sucked in its breath.

"Ouroboros?" I poked through the dusty drawers of my memory. "Isn't that a snake eating its own tail?"

"That is a stylized version, yes. In dragon terms, an ouroboros is an outlaw, a dragon who is expelled from or willingly rejects his own sept. They are considered dead by their former sept members . . . it is from that death that they regain life."

"That's why Gabriel said they didn't belong to any sept." Things clicked into place, even though there were still a lot of questions to be answered. "OK, question number three—"

"Four," Drake said. "You asked what an ouroboros was."

"That wasn't—argh! Guys?" I turned to Pál and István. "Am I on three or four?"

"Four," they answered simultaneously.

"Dragons!" I took a deep breath. "Fine. Question number four, not that I'm going to forget this, buster. What is Kostya going to do now?"

Drake's troubled gaze went to his brother, who refused to turn around. "Alas, that question I cannot answer. I believe his first goal is to establish if there are enough members still living to re-form the sept."

Kostya turned at that, a smile curving his lips. "I will have my sept, brother, do not fear. I will retake that which was once ours."

Jim groaned and covered its eyes with its paw.

"That sounded remarkably like a threat," I said slowly, a little chill forming in my heart. "You're not thinking of carrying on where your old wyvern left off, are you?"

"I swore that I would not rest until the black sept was whole once again," he answered, his voice rife with emotion. "And so I will not."

I shook my head and started to get up. "The silver dragons—"

"Aisling, this is nothing to involve us," Drake interrupted, pulling me back against his chest.

I twisted around to look at him. "Yes, it is. Gabriel is our friend—I think—possibly—and I'll be damned if I just sit around while your brother tries to fulfill some madman's plans."

Kostya rounded on me. "I did not support Baltic's actions, but I understood his reasons for taking them. He was not mad . . . just mistaken in his methods."

"You call destroying your own people in an attempt to annex another sept the act of a sane man?" I asked.

"Atta girl, Ash," Jim said.

"They were black dragons once!" Kostya yelled, fire erupting in three different spots in the room. "And with the help of Drake, they will be black dragons again!"

"Cease this!" Drake bellowed, causing me to wince. "We have discussed this enough, Aisling. And you—" He turned his emerald-eyed glare on his brother. "You will remember what I said. The green dragons will not protest your appeal for reinstatement to the weyr . . . provided you do not start a war."

"Well, thank god for someone speaking common sense," I said, relieved that I wasn't going to have to try to make Drake see reason.

"I will not stay here to be so abused!" Kostya sent Drake one last glare before exiting the room.

"If I say I think I liked him better when he was imprisoned, would you think I was crazy?" I asked Drake.

"At this moment? No. István, would you make the travel arrangements? Pál, I will leave security of Aisling's family and the house in your hands."

"Why is Kostya helping us if you're not going to help him take over the silver dragons?"

Drake's jaw tightened. "He foolishly believes he can manipulate me into changing my mind. I do not suffer any compunction at taking his help now, however. He will need our aid later, when it is time for him to rejoin the weyr."

István finished putting out the fires and toddled off, Pál about to follow him. "Will we be gone long?" he asked.

"No. I hope to be back within a few hours. But her family will be vulnerable until we return."

My heart warmed at the thought of him taking such good care that no one was harmed. "Uncle Damian is off with one of his army buddies. He said he'd be around if I needed him for bodyguard duty, but I'm sure he'll be OK puttering around on his own."

Drake nodded. "It is your stepparents I am more concerned about."

"What if we got them out of town?" I said, musing over the situation. "We could send them on an overnight trip to somewhere within day-tripping distance."

"That is what I was thinking. With a suitable guard, of course."

I smiled. "I kind of figured you were having us shadowed when we went out."

"They are your family. They must be protected from harm by any untoward attacks from the red dragons," he answered, turning to Pál. "Aisling will see to it that they are gone for the evening."

"And I will see to their guards," Pál said, giving me a little grin before leaving the room.

"Alone at last," I murmured, pushing Drake back down into a chair.

"Yup. Just you, me, and Drakeykins," Jim said, settling back on the floor. "You guys going to do it in the chair? Where do your legs go? Isn't that hard on the back? Not to mention the upholstery . . . heeeeeeeeeyyy . . ."

Jim's voice trailed off as I banished it to the Akasha.

21

"There's much to be said for wyverns, including their knowledge of people who are willing to portal them at a moment's notice, but one of the best things is their ability to cushion falling objects," I said into Drake's stomach.

He pushed my knee off his face. "You made me bite my tongue."

"Want me to kiss it and make it all better?" I asked, leering at him as I rolled off his body.

"Sheesh, weren't you guys going at it when you so cruelly abandoned me to the torments of the Akasha? And you give *me* a hard time for wanting to call Cecile every day!" Jim grumbled, picking itself up from where it had landed.

"Not that it's in any way your business, but we didn't get to 'go at it,' as you so crudely put it. We didn't have time. Paula felt it vitally necessary to unburden herself of yet another lecture about my apparent lack of interest in the wedding planning."

"Oh. I take back what I said about the Akasha. I'd rather suffer there than have to sit through another one of your stepmom's tirades." Jim indulged in a full body shake, then looked up. "Incoming."

Drake was a blur as he shoved me out of the way just in time. István's body hit the floor with a heavy whump, Pál following almost immediately, cracking his head on István's with an audible thunk.

"Ouchie. You guys OK?" I asked as Drake helped me to my feet.

Pál swore in Hungarian. István rubbed his head and staggered to his feet. "Yes. Maybe not. What was question?"

The two men sidestepped handily when a sixth and final form dropped to the floor.

I was less than happy about having Mr. Bossy Pants along, but Drake insisted that to exclude Kostya would create worse feelings than already existed.

Kostya rose to his feet, muttering.

"Are all portals like that?" I asked Drake as I brushed off a bit of dust from his shirt. Drake preferred raw silk shirts, usually dark green, but tonight he was dressed completely in black. "Hey, how did we get turned around? You were holding me when we went through it."

He shrugged. "Portals are never easy. It is one reason why I wished you would stay home. You could have been harmed."

"Oh, we're not going to go into that again." I straightened my shirt and dusted off the knees to my just-barely-fitting jeans. "You told me yourself that it's a lot harder for me to be hurt, so a little portalling isn't going to do either me or the baby any harm."

"Just remember your promise," he said, leveling a meaningful look at me before opening the door to peer out.

"Like I could forget it? So where first?" I asked, starting to follow him.

István stopped me, pushing me gently back so he could proceed. "Remember your promise," he said in his gravelly voice.

I rolled my eyes and made to follow him.

"You stay behind us," Kostya ordered imperiously, pushing past me.

I stuck out my tongue at his back and turned to consider Pál. "You're a modern man despite your years. You aren't going to pull any of that macho protective crap on me, are you?"

He smiled and slipped ahead of me. "You promised," he reminded me.

My fingers jerked, itching to draw a couple of confinement wards. "Honest to god! As if it's not bad enough having one mother hen . . . now I have three!"

"You love it and you know it. So, this is Fiat's place, huh? Pretty swanky. Drake, I'm thinkin' you're going to have to up the stakes a little if you want to beat the competition," Jim said, snuffling a heavy brocade tablecloth on a glass-topped table.

"Don't be telling him that," I said, swatting Jim on the nose. "Our house is perfectly fine. Besides, this place is . . . too Fiat."

We stood in a room that was bright and sunny, but cold, as if the air-conditioning had been left on high. I shivered a little as I rubbed my arms, examining the room with curiosity. I'd seen Fiat's apartment in Paris, but this was his home in Lake Como, and although it was gorgeous, it was lacking in . . . well, warmth.

Jim wandered over to look out of the window. The room had a high ceiling edged with elaborate moldings. Two crystal chandeliers sparkled in the wintry sunlight shining through tall windows flanked on either side by long, gold drapes. The view revealed a steel gray lake lapping almost to the base of the house. The elegant room was filled with gold and blue furniture.

"You break it, you buy it," I warned Jim as I stood on tip-toe to see what the guys were doing all clustered together.

Pál held a small black electronic box. He directed it around the room, silently pointing in various directions. The others nodded, taking care to touch nothing.

"Looking for bugs?" I asked Pál in my best espionage voice.

He shook his head. "Alarms. We don't want to trigger anything."

Evidently the room was clear of alarms with the exception of the windows. I whispered a command to Jim to not touch anything and silently followed the four men as they opened the door and swept the hallway for signs of a security system. Pál pointed to a small white box perched high on the wall. He pulled out a cell phone–sized gadget, fiddling with it for a minute before setting it on a half-moon table in the hall, nodding to Drake that all was clear.

"What's that?" I asked Pál as we trailed out of the room.

"It interrupts the camera image."

"I see you guys went shopping at the James Bond Emporium o' Spy Stuff," Jim commented. "I can't wait to see the exploding breath mints."

I shushed the demon and gave in to my curiosity by having a good look around. We were upstairs in a pentagon-shaped main hallway, five corridors converging on a sunny spot that had a skylight above. The center was open to the ground floor, flooding the area above and below with light. I had to admit it was very pretty, very elegant . . . and very lifeless.

We made a cursory examination of the upper-floor rooms. There were security cameras at each of the corridors.

"What are we going to do about them?" I whispered to Drake. "Are you going to scramble them, too?"

He shook his head. "We could disable the cameras, but that is not a viable solution."

"Why not?" I asked.

"One might go off-line temporarily without causing concern," he answered. "But more than that would provide a clear signal to anyone watching that someone was in the house. We have another option, although I don't like it."

"Why not?"

He nodded to a couple of discreet small, round disks high on each wall. "Smoke detectors. The smoke bombs I'd planned to use will likely set them off before we wish to alert anyone to our presence."

"Whoever is watching is going to see the smoke anyway—what's the big deal if the alarms go off?"

"The alarms will do more than bring local firemen. They will likely also summon more dragons. I'd rather we just have to deal with the ones here than cope with additional forces as well."

"Yeah, but the dragons here will call for help eventually, won't they?"

He shook his head. "Not if we take care of them quickly enough."

"Ah. Gotcha."

The four men gathered to have a confab while I eyed the smoke detectors.

"You're not thinking what I think you're thinking, are you?" Jim asked, making squinty eyes at me.

"Will it work?" I asked it.

The demon shook its head. "Yeah."

"Then why the Negative Nelly business?"

"I hate it when you call me Nelly! And I'm shaking my head because I know you, and something is bound to go wrong."

"Meh. Don't be such a pessimist. Sweetie? I've got an idea . . ."

Twelve minutes later, the upper hallway was full of dense, black smoke—demon smoke, the stuff generated by the summoning circle. It was nasty and oily and left a pesky residue on walls and furniture, but it had one beneficial quality—it didn't set off smoke detectors.

"I told you that you'd need me," I said smugly as I dusted off my hands and admired my handiwork. I'd drawn five summoning circles, each completed just enough to generate the vile black smoke that billowed out of the floor and filled the corridors.

Kostya snorted, but looked rather surprised at how well the smoke covered our presence. We waited until it obscured us enough to slip past the video cameras, and hurried downstairs before someone could hit the panic button.

Drake caught the two blue dragons who were patrolling their way up the stairs by surprise, handily disabling them. Although he didn't flinch at inflicting violence when he had to, he preferred a bloodless lifestyle. I smiled with approval when Pál whipped out a syringe gun and knocked out the two struggling dragons the other men were holding. Two more men stationed in the lower hall were likewise dealt with, Pál wielding his anesthetic with great aplomb.

"How long will they be out?" I asked Pál as Drake pulled a sleeping dragon to the room where we were storing them.

"Two hours minimum. They'll wake up with a hell of a headache, too," he answered, grinning.

It took a while for us to work through the more populated ground floors, but with István manning the electronics, Drake and Kostya taking down the guards as we found them, and Pál knocking them out, we cleared all the rooms but the most promising one.

The door to the basement was warded and bore an electronic lock.

"Is that going to be a problem?" I asked.

Drake rubbed his chin while examining the lock. "Possibly. It's the same sort of lock I have. They are supposed to be the ultimate in security, although in this case, I have to hope the claim is overly confident."

Jim and I sat down and waited while the boys discussed the situation, pulling out a number of gadgets to try on the lock.

Nothing seemed to work. I was just indulging in a big yawn when Drake growled an oath as he slammed the last electronic gizmo down.

"What about Aisling?" Kostya asked, nodding at me.

I stopped yawning and tried to look perky and attentive. "Hello!"

"She's a Guardian—maybe she can break the lock."

"Hmm." Drake gave me a speculative look and held out his hand for me.

I toddled over and prodded the keypad of the lock a couple of times. "I'm afraid I don't know a ward for unlocking things, not that I'm sure such a thing exists."

"Perhaps there is something else you can do to it," Drake said, frustration evident in his voice.

I knew how important this was to him, so I didn't answer that Guardians were never meant to be housebreakers, and instead, gave the lock a quick once-over. It was housed in stainless steel, but the main components of it were plastic.

"Is it fireproof?" I asked, thinking maybe the combined dragon fire from four dragons might melt the sucker.

"Not the insides, but the outer casing is. We couldn't do enough damage to it to get to the sensitive parts."

"Hmm." I reached out to poke at it again, but the dry, cold

environment caused me to get a static shock when I touched the metal housing. I jumped back, laughing.

"You've thought of something?" Drake asked.

"Oh, yeah. It's a computer at the heart of the lock, right?"

He nodded.

"And what do computers hate?"

The four men just looked at me.

I smiled. "Watch this."

The little door in my mind swung open as I closed my eyes for a moment and used my enhanced vision to see all the possibilities. Static electricity was thick in the room—I simply gathered it together between my hands, shaping it as I would dragon fire.

"Uh . . . Ash?"

"Shh. I'm concentrating."

"Yeah, I can tell. Someone want to put that out before the alarm goes off?"

"Huh?" I opened my eyes and swung around, a glowing blue ball of electricity hovering between my hands. Behind me, the kitchen table that sat in the middle of the room was on fire. "I didn't do that! I can't use Drake's fire anymore, remember? It must be Kostya. He has horrible control over his fire."

"I do not! I am very controlled!" Kostya fumed as Pál and István used dish towels to slap out the fire.

"Uh-huh. Then why were you setting Drake's secret room alight earlier today?"

"That wasn't me! Someone else must have done it."

I shook my head. "Everyone here can control their fire. Well, except me, but like I said, ever since I became Fiat's mate, I haven't been able to use Drake's fire at all." I didn't tell them how profoundly sad I was over that, missing the way we'd share his fire in moments of great intimacy.

Drake looked thoughtful for a moment before walking over to stand in front of me. "Kiss me."

"What?" I glanced at the others. "I thought you didn't like me doing that in front of sept members."

"It's not a matter of like or dislike, it's a matter of respect, but that point is moot at this moment. Kiss me."

He put his hands on my arms and would have pulled me to his body, but I still held the ball of electricity. I dispersed it, shaking my hands to lose the tingling feeling that came from holding energy. "OK, but you asked for it."

Drake stood passive while I nibbled on his lips, my tongue teasing his mouth until it parted for me. I tasted and nipped and squirmed against him in a silent attempt to make him give me what I wanted, but he wouldn't.

"Fire!" I finally said, pulling back just long enough to speak. "Give me your fire."

His lips were as hot as ever as I kissed him again, his fire building within him until it spilled over into me, roaring through me with the velocity of a bullet. It fired my blood, scorched every cell in my body, setting alight not just my physical being, but my soul as well. I flung open the mental doorway and sent the fire back to him.

"Anyone got some hot dogs or marshmallows?"

I ripped my mouth from Drake's, joy welling inside me as I realized that Drake and I stood together, flames licking up our legs. "It's back!" I said, unable to contain myself as I did a little fire dance. "I have your fire again! But . . . how?"

His eyes glittered like backlit emeralds on black velvet. "I do not know, but I can guess. You are my mate again, *kincsem*. That is all that matters."

"Woohoo!" I screamed, and leaped on him. He let me

kiss his adorable face for a few seconds before patting my butt and reminding me of the job at hand.

"Later, we will investigate this miracle in fuller detail," he said, his eyes promising all sorts of wicked acts.

"Boinksville, here we come," Jim said as I stamped out the flames around us.

It took three balls of electricity slammed into it point-blank before the lock gave up the ghost. After that, the subsequent locks on the three inner doors were a piece of cake, and in no time at all, we were deep underground, in a labyrinth of dirt-floored tunnels that stretched out into darkness.

Drake, with the unerring instinct of dragons, led us down one of the tunnels until we arrived at an ancient stone door. We were in a section that was lit by yellow lamps clamped to either side of the passage. I trailed along after the dragons, trying to count the number of doors as we passed them, but lost track by the time we entered a natural cavern with a ceiling a couple of stories high that framed a gigantic stone door.

Just as Drake announced, "This is the entrance to Fiat's lair. It will be heavily protected. Aisling?" I noticed something peculiar.

"Yeah, it looks nasty. Hey, come have a look at this."

He frowned as I indicated a door set into the side wall of the cavern. "We do not have time to explore. I wish for you to look at this door now."

"I'll make a deal with you—I'll look at your door if you look at mine."

His lips thinned. "We do not have much time remaining to us."

"Fine. But you have to look at mine next." I stood in front of the giant stone door and took a good long look at it.

Surprisingly, there were no locks on it. There were a whole
lot of other things, however. "There are three . . . no, four
wards on it. One curse, one prohibition, and something I've
never seen before. It's like words scratched into the surface
of the stone."

"That would be Fiat's bane."

"Bane?"

"A dragon's bane is like a curse. It is unique to each
dragon and used to protect their treasure from thieves. It can
cause grievous injury and most likely death if disturbed. It
will be the most difficult element for us to overcome."

"Lovely. Now come look at my door." I took his hand and
started to pull him toward the door on the side wall.

"Mate, we do not have time—"

"I think you need to make time for this," I answered with
a meaningful look.

Kostya gave an exasperated sigh. "Drake! It will take at
least an hour to break this door, possibly two. We must start
on it now, not give in to your woman's curiosity."

"I'm so glad I met you first," I told Drake. "If I'd known
only Kostya, I probably wouldn't have wanted to meet his
brother."

His expression was grave as I stopped in front of the door.
"I trust you have a very good reason for this."

"Yup. Take a look at that." I gestured toward the small
wooden door. It was made up of planks, bound together with
bands of iron, and looked like something out of a medieval
castle.

He looked. Behind us, Pál and István approached. Jim
squinted at the door, saw what I saw, and raised both brows.

"It is a wall," Drake said. "What's special about it?"

I traced the outline of a simple ward. "It's not just a wall, it's a door, and it's warded. You can't see it because you didn't draw it, but it is warded—with a perdu ward."

That got everyone's attention. I smiled to myself as the men crowded around the door. Perdu wards, as I have mentioned, are only used when someone wishes to obscure the entrance to somewhere. The fact that no one had noticed the door but me was of minor interest. That it was warded to be hidden indicated that something of importance was behind it.

"Can you open it?" Drake asked, fumbling around blindly until his hands closed on the curved door handle. He tried turning it but it was locked.

"No, but there are no other wards on the door. It's wooden, so I think you should be able to break it down."

All four dragons focused on the door. It didn't so much burn as explode, bits of hot, twisted metal flying everywhere, a hail of scorched wood drifting down after it.

I had been ordered to the other side of the cavern, something I was grateful for as I picked my way through the debris. Drake held out a hand for me, following as Kostya led the way into the now-opened room.

"Now this is creepy," I said, looking around the brightly lit room with a sense of something seriously awry. The walls were stuccoed a pale beige. Lights built into the ceiling beamed cheerfully down on a tasteful living room suite of blue tweed. A flat screen TV was attached to one wall, while bookcases lined two other walls. Behind us, a small dining room table sat with four chairs. An entrance led to what I assumed was a small kitchen.

"This is . . . someone's apartment?" I asked, noting the signs of occupancy. A large ashtray on a coffee table bore several cigar stubs. A glass of whisky sat next to an oversized chair, a book resting on the arm of the chair, as if its owner had set it down for a moment.

"That's what it looks like," Drake said, opening a door and flipping on a light. A large bed dominated the inner room. "The question is, who lives here?"

Kostya picked up the book, flipping through it. "Whoever it is, he reads Latin. Not a very pleasant reading choice, either."

I peered over his shoulder to read the title. He handed me the book as he went to scan the bookcase. "Huh. He's reading a grimoire. I haven't seen this one before. It looks like it was just printed. I wonder who the publisher is."

Drake and his men opened the two other doors of the apartment, not finding anything of interest. I flipped the book open to the title page. "Ah. Bookplate. Uh . . . Drake? I think you need to see this."

"Let me have it," Kostya said, taking the book without so much as a "please" slipping past his lips.

He stared at the embossed plate on the inner front of the book, a pallor washing over his face.

Jim put its front legs on the chair and peered over Kostya's arm. "Oh, man."

"Who does it belong to?" Drake asked, shuffling through a stack of papers on a small mahogany desk.

"There's just one name," I said, pulling the book from Kostya's bloodless fingers. His eyes were wide and staring, looking inward at something only he could see.

Jim backed away, its expression wary.

"Yes? What name?"

I held the book out to Drake. "Baltic."

22

"Tell me again why we're doing this if I can share your fire? Doesn't that mean I'm *not* Fiat's mate, and we don't have to worry about him any longer?"

"The circumstances lead me to believe that is so, but until I know for certain that Fiat has no claim over you, we will proceed."

I sighed. "I suppose it wouldn't hurt to have something we can use to ensure his good behavior."

It had been a long two hours. Dealing with the door to Fiat's lair would have been tough enough without having four dragons in denial as we worked to break through the intricate protections Fiat had used to safeguard his hoard.

"Fiat must have come by some of Baltic's library," Drake insisted, pacing behind where I sat as the four demons I had summoned worked on unmaking the last of the wards. Demons can't, as a rule, unmake a ward, unless the wards drawn were of a demonic nature, which surprisingly these were. The prohibition—a weakish sort of curse— had already been lifted, as well as the curse proper; those required a creature of dark being to create them, and thus, assuming you had the capability of summoning and commanding demons, were easily destroyed. "There can be no other rational explanation. Baltic is dead. I saw him die. He was cleaved in two. Not even a dragon can survive that."

"Yeah, well, Gabriel thinks he's alive. Maybe he wasn't cleaved all the way through?" I said, watching the demons as they unmade the last ward.

Drake whirled around to face me, Kostya leaping up from where he'd been sitting on a rock. "What did you say?"

"I said Gabriel thinks Baltic is alive. I told you on the way down from that aerie about the conversation I had with him."

Drake rubbed his eyes for a moment. "I was tired and not listening as well as I ought. Are you sure he said Baltic was alive?"

"Well . . . he didn't say that in so many words, but he spoke of Baltic in the present tense. I got the distinct feeling the guy was still alive and kicking."

Drake and Kostya exchanged glances.

"You both were there when you saw him die?" I asked, momentarily distracted from the puzzle of Fiat's lair door.

"Yes," Drake answered, looking away.

"Oh, like that's not a red flag she's gonna pounce on?" Jim asked from where it lay on my feet. It shook its big furry head.

I crossed my arms. "Go on. You know I'm not going to leave it alone until you tell me about it."

"This is none of your business," Kostya said firmly, marching over to glare at the demons.

Drake pinched his lip.

"Sweetie?" I asked, waiting for him to spill.

"Technically, he's right. It has nothing to do with the green dragons—"

I stopped him. "If it includes you, it's my business."

He was silent.

"Oh, go on and tell us," Jim urged. "You know Princess Nosy isn't going to be happy until you spill, and I gotta admit, I'm a bit curious, too. We never got news of dragon stuff in Abaddon. Except the plagues, of course, which ticked off the lords because they thought you guys were encroaching on demon territory. But other than that—nada."

"You know I hate to agree with Jim on the sheer principle of the thing, and I won't soon forget that Princess Nosy comment, but what did happen to Baltic?"

Drake was silent for a handful of seconds, then said simply, "Kostya killed him."

I thought my eyes were going to bug right out of my head. "*Kostya* killed Baltic? Your brother Kostya, not some strange Kostya I don't know about?"

He nodded.

I looked at the man pacing back and forth behind the demons as they worked. "But . . . he's a black dragon! Baltic was his wyvern! You can kill your own wyverns? Isn't that, like, really bad?"

"Yes. It is not something that is done often, and it's not a subject I am prepared to discuss with you at this time. You wished to possess the facts, and now you do. Explanations will have to wait."

"Do you seriously think you can drop a bombshell like that on me and not answer the hundred or so questions I have about it?" I asked.

"Yes," he said in his most quelling manner.

I opened my mouth to protest, but the glint in his eye was one I didn't particularly wish to mess with.

"Will wonders never cease? You got her to shut up. That's gotta be a first."

I pointed at the large stone door. "Right, Mr. Mouthy. Go work on the bane."

Jim's eyes widened. "Me?" it squeaked. "Those things are dangerous! I could get killed!"

"You can't be kil—"

"My fabulous form could be destroyed!"

"Is the bane really that dangerous?" I asked Drake.

"It could destroy whoever tries to break it if it is not handled properly," he answered grimly.

"Oh, lovely." What constituted handled properly? I wondered.

Was that a little inner monologue? Dare I point out that the answer to all your questions is at your fingertips?

"That is why you will have the demons and your steward break it. I will not risk the chance of harm coming to you," Drake added.

"Uh-huh. We'll get to that in a minute, oh ye of the annoying subject changes. I understand if you don't want to get into a lengthy discussion of dragon politics at this time, but you can answer one question for me. I thought Kostya was a Baltic supporter—he sure sounds like one when he talks about annexing the silver dragons. But if he actually killed Baltic—or tried to—then I'm confused."

"Baltic was . . . difficult," Drake said, looking up when Pál and István entered the cavern.

"They are all still out, although we are running out of time," Pál told him. "The building is secured, and there are no signs that anyone outside it is aware of what's going on."

"And the one in the subterranean apartment?" Drake asked.

István shook his head. "We didn't find him, although there were signs someone had used the bolt-hole recently."

"He must have noted our presence here before we became

aware of the apartment, and left rather than risk meeting us," Drake said.

I raised my eyebrows. "Makes you wonder just who it was."

"It could be that he is amongst the guards we took care of." Drake rubbed his chin in thought. "But I suspect not."

"Would you recognize Baltic if you saw him again?" I asked.

"Yes."

"What about Pál and István?"

"Pál was not born when Baltic was killed," Drake answered. "István saw him at weyr meetings."

Pál gave me a wry smile. "I'm the young one."

"So I gather. Well, it may be as you say then—the person staying in that odd apartment had Baltic's books, and Baltic is dead. Gabriel is either confused, or I misheard him."

Drake said nothing but continued to rub his chin.

It took the better part of the last hour we had there for the demons and Traci to break the bane. But break it they did, with only the loss of three demons (or rather, their forms).

"Love and kisses to Bael," I told the lone surviving demon before I dismissed it.

It looked at me like I had beans sprouting out of my ears.

"If you do not mind my asking, lord, why did you summon Lord Bael's minions and not your own?" Traci asked as the dragons pushed past it to get into Fiat's lair.

"I'm trying to make a point. Did you send out those e-mails like I asked?"

It nodded, looking much put-upon. "I fear you have not thought through your actions thoroughly. They will be sure to anger the other lords and enrage Bael."

"Perfect," I said with a satisfied smile. "What time did you set the meeting for?"

"Tomorrow at noon, as you requested."

"Great. Thanks for your help with the bane."

Traci looked faintly shocked. "I am your servant, Lord Aisling. I am ever at your bidding."

Jim poked its head out of the lair. "Ash? You coming? The guys are having ore-gasms in there, and I think you're going to have to bitch slap a couple to calm them down. Ore, get it? Like gold ore? Heh heh heh. I slay me."

"If only, Jim. I'll see you tomorrow before the meeting, OK, Traci?"

The demon bowed and disappeared. I followed Jim into the lair, which was nothing more than a huge walk-in climate-controlled bank vault. The shelves were filled with priceless objects of art, most of them jewel-encrusted gold, but there were also other items of value—artwork, ewers, statues, boxes of raw gems . . . the list was endless, although thankfully the vault wasn't.

"So, how does it stack up to your lair?" I asked Drake.

He stood in the center of the lair, his body trembling slightly. He took a deep breath, closing his eyes, an expression of bliss on his face, no doubt the effect of being in proximity to so much gold. "It is *nearly* comparable."

"Really? Wow. I can't wait to see yours." I watched him for another second, smiling at the look on his face. "This stuff really is like an aphrodisiac to you guys, isn't it?"

"Oh, yes," he said, a reverential tone in his voice.

I ran my hand down his chest. "So if I was to strip off all my clothes and lie on a pile of gold coins . . . ?"

His eyes popped open, fire leaping in a ring around us. I was startled by that—I wasn't pulling the fire, which meant

Drake had momentarily lost control. "You would just barely survive."

"Oooh," I said, burning even more from the passion in his eyes. "I think we're going to have to try that when we get back home."

He growled at me, a low rumble that was both primal and erotic as hell. I had the worst urge to pull him into a corner and have my way with him, but remembered in time where we were.

"Right, well," I said, clearing my throat. "As Pál said, we're running out of time, so why don't you pick out the biggest and best of Fiat's treasures, and we'll get going while the going is still good."

Pál and István had been opening lockboxes and turning out shelves, making little cooing sounds of pleasure as they touched the treasures. Kostya was in the back of the vault, his eyes glittering onyx as he flung open the lid to a wooden box. It was filled with ancient gold coins.

Drake pulled himself together, shot me one last sultry look, and began scanning the shelves for items.

"Maybe you can answer something for me," I said as I opened a velvet box, admiring the Victorian sapphire necklace and earrings within it. "You told me a while ago that dragons can't summon demons."

"We can't," Kostya answered, running his hands through the gold coins. His voice was rich and thick with pleasure.

I mentally rolled my eyes at the dragons and moved on to another jewelry box. This one contained old Greek-looking gold and silver jewelry. Museum-quality stuff—I wondered how many of the world's treasures were being held by dragons.

"Then how did Fiat come to have all sorts of dark power–based wards on his lair door? And that bane—that was broken by the demons, and they couldn't have done that unless a demon had been used to make it in the first place."

"Fiat obviously engaged the services of someone who could call demons," Drake answered, his voice muffled as he poked around the back of the vault.

"So, why can't you call demons?" High on one of the metal shelves, a small unadorned wooden box sat. I squinted at it. A ward was barely visible on it. I used the small ladder to climb to the top and pull down the box.

"You need to be a part of the Otherworld in order to summon its members. Dragons are bound by the laws of the weyr, not the Otherworld. We are outside of its sphere of influence. However, because of the long-standing treaty the weyr continues to honor, interaction between dragons and non-dragons is tolerated. That courtesy does not, however, extend to the summoning of its denizens."

"Huh. I didn't know you were not part of the Otherworld." I opened the box and pulled aside a bit of blue silk. Inside lay a rough lump of gold, fashioned into a shape that looked vaguely dragonish. A thought struck me. "But . . . I am a part of the Otherworld."

"Yes, you are."

I climbed down the ladder and moved around the tall metal stand that stood in the center of the vault and frowned at Drake as he squatted next to Kostya, the two of them removing the side of a glass case that held what looked like illuminated medieval manuscripts. "Doesn't that mean we have a conflict of interest?"

Drake looked up. "How so?"

"Well, you're in the weyr, governed by its laws. I'm in the Otherworld, bound to uphold it."

"You're my mate. You are a member of the weyr as well.

That takes precedence to your loyalty to the Otherworld. There is no conflict."

I wasn't sure I bought that, but I wasn't willing to argue the point in front of Kostya. "What did you guys find? Anything übervaluable?"

Drake put the manuscript back in its glass case. "Everything in here is valuable."

"But nothing stands out as something he'd move heaven and earth to get back?" I asked.

"Nothing leaps out at me, no. Kostya?"

He shook his head, dusting off his knees as he got to his feet. "There is nothing outstanding. The gold is of a very nice quality, though."

"Why don't you just take some of that?" Jim suggested, nosing around the box of gold coins. "If someone took my big ole herkin' box of gold, I'd want it back. And I'm not even a dragon with a gold fixation."

Drake pinched his lower lip as he looked around. "I would not tolerate anyone taking any treasure from me, but Fiat might not feel it was a sufficiently valuable hostage. I do not see anything that I would value above all others, and yet . . ." His voice trailed off as he looked around the vault. "And yet I feel as if something is here. Something . . . important. István? Pál?"

The two other dragons stopped rummaging and stood with Drake for a moment, the three of them making a slow circuit of the room.

"Yes," István said, nodding. "I feel it, too. Something very old."

"Something gold," Pál said, lifting his chin to scent the air. I sniffed as well. I didn't smell or sense anything different.

"Kostya, do you feel it?"

Kostya paused for a moment, then shook his head. "You green dragons have a better sense of smell than I do."

"What exactly does it smell like?" I asked, wondering if my super–Guardian vision could pick up something that was identifiable only by its scent.

Drake slowly paced the aisle of the vault, his eyes narrowing on me. "Like . . . you."

"Me?"

His eyes focused on the box in my hand. "What are you holding?"

"This?" I held up the battered figurine. "I think it's a kid's dragon toy. An old kid's dragon toy. The details aren't very good."

Drake sucked in his breath, his eyes as brilliant as green crystals. "Aisling, do not drop it."

I looked at the blobby dragon in my hand, trying to see what it was he was getting so worked up about. "Is it valuable?"

The other three dragons descended on me the same time as Drake, all four of them staring with wonder at the thing.

"It is the Lindorm Phylactery." He held out his hand for it, cradling it with both hands when I set the blob on his palm.

" 'K. And that is . . . ?"

"It is a relic of the time before the weyr. It was carried by the first dragon. It has immense importance to dragonkin."

The other men jostled Drake until he reluctantly passed it around.

"Gotcha. So it's the something really important that you felt? Then we take it?"

"I will take it," Kostya said, his hand closing around the blob of gold. "It belongs to the black dragons."

"It belongs to no one," Drake said, rounding on his brother.

"It was held by Baltic before he fell."

"Before you killed him, you mean?" I asked sweetly.

I'm lucky I didn't spontaneously combust. I'm sure that was the intent of the look Kostya fired at me.

"It belonged to him. It passes to me now."

"Kostya—" Drake started to say, and I knew we had a situation on our hands.

"Jim?"

"On it." Before Kostya could move, I had the binding ward on him, and Jim had retrieved the phylactery, dropping it at Drake's feet.

Kostya snarled something that had Drake lunging toward him. I held him back, saying, "Sweetie, it's not really the time or place, remember? Let's get out of here, then we can discuss what to do with this thing."

My words were punctuated by the dim sound of a siren.

Drake swore and grabbed the phylactery, wrapping it back up in its bit of cloth and replacing it in the wooden coffer.

"I assume you have some sort of an escape plan?" I asked.

"Yes. Come."

"What about him?" I asked, nodding toward the still-sputtering Kostya.

"Release him."

I hesitated. "I don't like having to say this, but . . . well . . . he seems to feel this thing is his."

"He is my brother," Drake said with a long look at Kostya. "I trust him."

I erased the ward on Kostya reluctantly. Drake took my arm and hustled me out of the room. I glanced back over my shoulder at where the others were following.

Drake might have faith in his brother's loyalty . . . but I didn't feel nearly so confident.

23

"Drake, I would like you to repeat the following oath: I, Drake, take you, Aisling, to be my wife and companion, my friend in life. Together we will bear the troubles and sorrows life may bring us, and celebrate the good and joyful events with which we are blessed. With these words, and with my heart, I bind my life to yours."

I yawned. I couldn't help myself, I was so tired after a sleepless flight home from Italy, I was having trouble staying awake.

The man performing the ceremony stared in horror at me. To my left, Paula gasped.

I was instantly contrite. How rude is it to yawn at your own wedding? Rummy though I was from lack of sleep, I had enough wits about me to know I had to rectify my apparent gaffe. "Sorry. I'm so tired I'm having a bit of trouble focusing. We had a horrible flight from Italy. It just seemed to go on and on and on. You ever have one of those flights? First we were delayed at the airport because of some weather issue, which was scary enough, because there were dragons after us and they might have found us if I hadn't done a few brain-pushes on some guys to forget they'd seen us, and then there was a mechanical problem, and we had to get off the plane and wait around a couple more hours be-

fore they got that fixed, and you know how impossible it is
to sleep in an airport. You know, sweetie, I think we should
get our own plane. Nothing big like a rock star, but something cute that we can zip around in. One with a bed in the
back," I told the man standing next to me. He was as handsome as sin, with mobile black brows, a lovely nose, and the
most delectable mouth I'd ever seen. And his eyes, oh, his
eyes. I stared at them for a few minutes, wondering if our
child would get his eyes. I sure hoped so. "Your eyes are so
gorgeous, I could just suck them right out of your head."

"Aisling!" Paula gasped again.

"I'm sorry, we were talking about planes, weren't we?" I
felt bad. I had shocked Paula with my lust for Drake, but to
be fair, I couldn't help lusting after him—he was so deli-
ciously lustworthy. "I do love him, you know," I told her,
tugging on her sleeve so she'd know I was being sincere. "I
really, really love him. Honest! I don't just want to suck his
eyeballs, and oil him up and then lick him off, although to
be honest, that sounds pretty good to me right about now. I
can't wait to do it again with his fire, because that makes all
the difference. But we couldn't because there was no time in
Italy, and then when we got home, Paula was there waiting
for us to go get married . . . oh, wait, you are Paula, aren't
you, Drake?"

Tears burnt behind my eyes as I took two steps and
wrapped my arms around him, a horrible presentiment
claiming me at that moment. "My brain doesn't seem to be
working right. I think I may have said something embarrass-
ing."

His voice rumbled above my head as he said, "I'm afraid
this is going to have to wait for another time. Aisling is not
herself at the moment."

The words danced in my brain as I snuggled into him,

sighing with happiness at the feel and scent of him. Then I frowned, what he'd said finally sinking in.

"Wait!" I said, pulling back. I looked around, confused for a moment. Paula and David were standing to my left. Behind them Uncle Damian stood watching me with a frown. On Drake's other side were Pál, István, Kostya, and Jim.

I waved at Jim, giving it a secret wink to let it know that I knew why it wasn't talking. "Good job, Jim. I know it's hard for you because you're such a chatterbox, but you're doing great. Keep it up, 'K?"

Jim blinked at me.

"I'm getting married," I told it, because clearly it was confused about what was happening here. "This is it, the big day. And it's kind of my last chance, so keep up the good work!"

"*Kincsem*, we will do this another time. You are too tired," Drake said, pulling me away from where I was patting Jim on its head.

"Are you kidding me?" I asked, recoiling in horror. "Paula will skin me alive if we don't go through with this wedding. Oh! Hi, Paula. Um . . . I seem to be having momentary lapses of judgment, but I'm fine now, just fine. Better than fine! Let's kick this shindig into high gear."

Paula slapped a hand over her mouth, her eyes huge as I smiled brightly at the guy marrying us.

"Sorry, I interrupted you. Please go on. Is it my turn to say something? Because there are a lot of things I'd like to say to Drake, and no, I know you're thinking I'm going to go on and on about his eyes, but I'm not going to, so there. Ummm . . . where were we?"

"We were leaving," Drake said firmly, taking my hands in his. "You are too tired, Aisling. We will delay this ceremony a day until you are rested."

"Paula's going to be pissed," I told him as he gently pushed me toward the door. "Will you break it to her for me? I hate to make you do that because it really is my problem, but you know, I'm just a skosh tired, and maybe she won't yell if you tell her. Oh, look, a demon. I'm sorry, the wedding is off for another day. Can you come back tomorrow?"

The demon—and it was a demon, even my sleep-deprived brain recognized the fact that the man standing in front of us in a zoot suit that would have been better suited to a 1940s movie was, in fact, a demon—looked confused for a moment before it said, "You are summoned by Lord Bael."

The overhead lights in the small room burst and would have showered tiny little bits of glass down upon us if we'd still been there. But since the demon suited action to words and sucked the entire wedding party off to see Bael, by the time the glass hit the floor, we were gone.

I don't know if it was the act of being yanked through the very fabric of time and space that dropped the euphoric sense of giddiness that lack of sleep had brought upon me, or if it was the look in Bael's eyes as he turned slowly to consider me, but whatever it was, I suddenly found myself as sober as a judge . . . and mad as hell.

"It's only eleven," I told Bael. "Our appointment was for twelve."

"Goodness, what—oh, my!" Paula said, clutching my stepfather. "What just happened? Where are we? David, did you see?"

"Yes," he answered slowly, taking in our situation. We were standing in front of a massive desk, in a wood-paneled room that was filled with books.

"Where are we?" she asked.

"You have yet to keep an appointment. I simply ensured you made this one," Bael answered.

"You interrupted my wedding!" I said, squaring my shoulders as I met the gaze of the demon lord.

"A wedding—how quaint." Bael changed appearances like the rest of us changed clothes. Today he appeared square-jawed and blue-eyed, wearing a navy blue suit and holding a sheaf of papers. He would have been indistinguishable from any other businessman except for the black corona of power that crackled around him. "I assume these people are your parents?"

I moved to stand protectively in front of Paula. "Yes. Please send them back—they have nothing to do with the situation between us."

"On the contrary, I find their presence most refreshing." His eyes moved to Drake. "And a wyvern. It has been many centuries since I have entertained dragons. You are welcome here."

Drake inclined his head politely. "I must insist that my mate's request be granted. The members of the weyr will naturally remain with Aisling, but the mortals must be returned to their world."

"Indeed? But then how will she be able to present me with their sacrifice?" Bael asked, setting down the papers and smiling pleasantly at me.

If I'd been mortal, that smile probably would have taken a good twenty years off my life.

"Mortals? Weyr? Aisling, who is this man? What's going on?" Paula asked.

"Send them back," I said swiftly to Bael. "Now. Please."

"And miss the fun of watching you explain to these good people who and what you are?" Amusement was rife in his eyes. "I think not."

Uncle Damian pulled Paula and David back, murmuring quietly in their ears. I flashed him a grateful look and returned my attention to Bael. I had enough wits left to me to know that what I had planned was going to need every bit of my power to pull off without anyone being destroyed.

"What?" Paula said, her voice rising in a shriek. "Hell? We're in Hell? And that man is the devil? Well! He has some nerve!"

Before I could stop her she marched over to Bael, put her hands on her hips, and glared.

"Oh, my god," I muttered, rushing to her side. "Paula, please—"

"I knew one day I would come face-to-face with the devil, although I didn't think that would be until Judgment Day, but since we're both here, I have a few things I'd like to say to you. Hitler! Terrorists! Chlorine in the water system!"

"I believe it's fluoride you're thinking of, dear, not chlorine," David said thoughtfully.

Bael looked startled for a moment as Paula shook her fist at him. "Does this mother of yours, this mortal, dare to chastise me?"

"Crib deaths! That's you, too, isn't it? And those nasty cult people and their poison Kool-Aid! And drug users! You're probably responsible for all the drug users!"

"Um . . ." I put my hands on Paula's shoulders and pulled her back. "Yeah. She gets a bit overwrought about things."

"Henry the Eighth . . . he was evil, chopping off all his wives' heads. Don't you deny it! Oh! And the Reagan presidency!"

"Now I know where you get your irreverence," he said, looking askance as she poked him in the chest.

"What about cattle mutilations? Don't say you're not

behind those, because I know you are! Just think of all those innocent cows!"

"We're not actually related by blood," I told him, pulling her back again. This time Uncle Damian snagged her and hauled her back to where my stepfather stood.

"I believe cattle mutilations are commonly thought to be caused by aliens," David told her.

"Get thee behind me!" Paula shouted at Bael.

Bael rolled his eyes and waved a languid hand. "I grant your dispensation."

The demon who'd brought us reached up and ripped a tear in the wall and pulled my family through it before Paula could do more than utter, "Mimes! You can't tell me the devil doesn't have anything to do with mimes!"

"Thank you," I told Bael, relieved that at the very least, my family would be safe. "Now, about those six sacrifices you are demanding in homage. Traci, I summon thee."

The steward appeared, wearing a disheveled tuxedo, the bow tie lying open along an unbuttoned, pleated shirt. In one hand it held a champagne flute, its arm wrapped around a blond female who was kissing the demon while stroking a hand down its bare chest. Traci's other hand was holding the right breast of another scantily clad woman, this one nibbling on its ear.

"All in good time, my sweet," Traci said the second the first female demon stopped sucking its face. "I promised your sister I would attend to her needs first."

I coughed and raised my eyebrows.

"Oh, glorious fires of Abaddon. Lord Aisling! You said you would not need me today! I distinctly understood you to say that it was tomorrow that you'd want me. . . ." The anger in Traci's voice trailed away with all sound as it saw Bael. "Most revered Lord Bael! I . . . I was . . ."

"I don't think anyone is confused about what you were doing," I said, leaning against Drake. I was past the point of exhaustion—and thankfully also past the rummy stage of giddiness in which my mouth seemed to operate without any input from my brain—but my body felt slow and unresponsive, as if my limbs were weighted down. "Would you mind getting rid of your . . . thanks."

The two female demons eeped as they saw Bael, and disappeared in puffs of thick, black smoke.

Traci cleared its throat and hurriedly buttoned its shirt before bowing to me. "My lord, you summoned me?"

"Yes. Do you have my sacrifices for Bael?"

Traci's face fell. "Well . . . as to that, my lord . . . er . . ."

Drake leaned toward me. "What sacrifice is this?"

"Bael has demanded I pay homage to him," I answered in a whisper before saying in a louder voice, "I'm sure Bael is a busy man. Go get the sacrifices, and we'll get this over with."

"You are to pay homage to the premiere prince of Hell?" Kostya asked, moving over so he stood directly behind me. Pál and István followed suit, with Jim leaning against my knees. "You cannot do that! Did you not swear fealty to the green dragons?"

Traci bowed a couple of times to Bael as it hurried over and joined the group. I had a horrible suspicion we presented the appearance of a particularly off-kilter football huddle.

"Yeah, yeah, we've been all over that, but it's not a big deal because I'm not really going to do an homage. Traci, where are the sacrifices?"

"I didn't get them," the demon answered miserably.

"What?" I poked my head up and smiled at Bael, who was watching us with an indescribably awful expression of mounting anger. "Sorry. Can we have a quick time-out? Just a few things I need to straighten out about the sacrifices."

Bael's resulting roar of fury shook the house.

"Where the hell are the sacrifices?" I asked Traci, grabbing the demon's sleeves and shaking it.

"Abad—" Jim started to say, but stopped when I let loose with a little frustrated scream.

"I couldn't get them; the people at the farm threw me out after I said I wanted to euthanize them."

I closed my eyes in horror. "Oh, crap."

Drake's voice pierced the miasma of regret that swamped me. "Aisling, tell me you were not planning on making the sacrifice I think you were planning on making."

I nodded, opening my eyes again. "I thought it was a really good plan. Traci got the stuff from a vet and it would have been just perfect if only those stupid chicken-farm people would have cooperated."

"I have had enough of this farce!" Bael bellowed, his hands fisted as he strode toward me.

Instantly, the football huddle turned into a wall of dragons that stood between me and Bael.

"You will present the sacrifices to me now, before I lose my patience and banish you as you deserve!"

"Traci?"

"I'm sorry, lord," it answered, spreading its hands wide.

"Go get the sacrifices," I said in a loud voice, leaning in to add an additional instruction.

Traci looked horrified for a moment before its form disappeared. I smiled over Drake's shoulder. "It'll be just a minute—oh, there it is. You get points for speediness, Traci."

The demon thrust two bags at me. I waved it toward Bael.

"Banish me if you must," Traci said, shoving the bags in my hands. "But I cannot do this."

"Aisling Grey, I have lost all patience with—"

I snatched the bags and ran forward, dumping the contents on the table that sat next to where Bael loomed. "Sorry! Here they are. My sacrifices to pay homage to you."

Bael stared in complete shock at the six items as I arranged them in an attractive presentation.

"There was a slight mix-up in the original sacrifices, but these are just as good," I said, licking one sticky finger. "Better, actually. As you can see, two of the roast chickens are teriyaki, three are some sort of a lemongrass rub, and the last one looks like whisky barbecue."

There was a moment of complete silence before Bael's roar threw me back three feet, luckily straight into Drake.

"You dare!" Bael screamed, his face twisted with fury.

"There's no dare about it," I answered, allowing Drake to wrap his arms around me.

"Mate—" he whispered into my ear.

"I'm OK," I told him quietly. "I know what I'm doing."

"If it gets out of hand, I will have no choice but to take charge," he warned me.

I nodded, my eyes still on Bael. "According to the Doctrine of Unending Conscious, I must present you with six sacrifices. Nothing was said about what form those sacrifices must take. My offering is as you see—six chickens, sacrificed, seasoned, and roasted to perfection in your name."

Bael's face turned bright red. I thought for a moment that he was going to explode right there in front of us. Evidently Drake thought so as well because his arms tightened around me. "Aisling—"

"It's OK," I whispered, raising my voice in what I prayed was a confident tone. "By the laws that govern Abaddon, I have met the terms of your demands."

Bael hissed as he visibly struggled to regain control, but

after a few seconds of a really close call, his color cleared up and he stopped clenching his fists.

"You have mocked everything I represent from the first moment you became a demon lord. Do you think your pathetically transparent attempts to incite an expulsion have fooled me? Do you think I would release one I worked so hard to bring into my power?"

We were on dangerous ground here. I sent up another prayer that Traci's research into the Doctrine was as thorough as it claimed it was. "I will never be what you want me to be, Bael. I will never again use the dark power. You may be able to force me to remain a prince, but I will fight you every step of the way. I will do everything I can to undermine your power and influence over the other demon lords. I will continue to fight the good fight, and I will never, ever, stop trying to get away."

"Aisling." Drake breathed a warning into my ear. "Even I would not speak thusly to Bael."

"Give me one reason, one singular reason why I should not banish you to the Akasha at this very moment," Bael said, walking slowly toward us. The dragons tightened ranks. Jim leaped to its feet and valiantly bared its teeth, even though it knew it wouldn't stand a chance against the premiere prince of Abaddon.

I lifted my chin and tried mightily to meet Bael's gaze, but I couldn't quite do it. I stared at his ear, instead. "Because you can't do that without having a revolution on your hands."

Bael paused in his steady progress toward me.

Drake's arms tightened again. I patted his hand until he loosened his grip somewhat.

"I found the Doctrine very interesting reading. Most of it was just esoteric stuff that went on and on about what form damnations should take, and which torments were allowed, but there was a very interesting albeit short section about the formation of the princes, particularly about the removal thereof."

Bael's face turned to a frozen mask.

"To be specific, it says that you can't banish a fellow demon lord. No prince can—only someone who is not one of the eight princes can banish you guys. Which is why you set me up to banish Ariton, isn't it? You couldn't do it without having the other six princes rise up and overthrow you, so you arranged the situation so I inadvertently took care of a troublesome prince for you." I squared my shoulders. "In other words, you're stuck with me—unless you and the other princes vote me off the island."

Fury flashed in Bael's blue eyes for a moment. I knew he must be feeling cornered at that moment, and a cornered demon lord was a dangerous beast. I picked my next few words carefully.

"I never intended to enact a coup, as you well know. I simply wanted to point out to you what a pain in the ass I will be if you do not convince the others to give me the boot. You can't possibly want me to remain here. I have rejected the dark power time and time again, and with the support and love of my friends and family, I will continue to do so."

A muscle in Bael's jaw twitched, but still he said nothing.

Drake curled one arm protectively around me, his eyes velvety green as he watched the demon lord.

"I am not threatening you, and I am not challenging your authority, but I am saying that I will continue to be a thorn in your side. I will not rest until I have been granted an expulsion from Abaddon, and I am prepared to do whatever it takes—within the bounds of what I consider morally allowable—to see that happen."

Rather than rant and rave, Bael relaxed at what I said, the glint of anger fading as he leaned against the table next to him. "Indeed? You ask much of me, Aisling Grey. I went to great pains to put you into place—granted, you were of use to me in removing the annoying Ariton, but even so, I had come to see the possibilities of your presence in Abaddon. And yet you wish now for me to grant you a great undertaking, for it will not be easy to convince the other lords to expulse you."

I didn't believe that for a second, but I wasn't foolish enough to put my thoughts into speech.

"Your wyvern is no doubt well aware that such a favor as you ask of me will not be granted without a substantial payment . . . and a sacrifice."

I glanced at Drake. His body language read caution. "What price do you demand of my mate?"

"And what sacrifice?" I asked, more worried about that than money.

Bael toyed with a dagger that lay on the table. I refused to think about what it was doing there. "Your wyvern has in his possession three trinkets, I believe. Their return would satisfy the price I demand."

"Trinkets?" I asked suspiciously, casting my mind over the things in Drake's house. "What trinkets?"

Jim stepped on my foot, its eyes trying to tell me something.

"The Tools," Drake said softly, his eyes glittering now as if he was sizing up Bael. "You wish for the return of the three Tools."

"The Tools of Bael?" I asked, my voice rising on the last word. "You're joking! You think I'm going to hand over to you the three Tools? Those things are powerful as all get-out on their own—together, whoever wields them can rule the Otherworld! I don't think so!"

Bael laughed, a horrible sound that made the skin on my back crawl. "Do you think if they had that possibility for me that I would not have done anything to possess them again? The Tools provide the bearer access to my power, something I would point out I already have."

"Oh." I thought about that for a moment or two. It made sense—when I'd handed the three Tools over to Drake for safekeeping, I'd done so to keep them out of harm's way. Drake had enough power and had no need to control the Otherworld, but others were not so trustworthy. I turned to him now, asking, "Is that true?"

He nodded slowly. "The Tools would be of no use to Bael. Which makes me wonder why, then, he is so anxious to have them."

"It is a trivial reason," Bael answered dismissively, his hands gesturing away the question. "They were mine, pretty things, taken from me. Surely a dragon can appreciate the need to possess that which was once his?"

"Yes," Drake answered. "I can also understand the desire to remove a possible conduit to my powers from the reach of others."

Anger flared to life for a fraction of a second in Bael's eyes.

"I think you hit a nerve," I said softly. "What do you think? Are you willing to give up the Tools to him? Would they be safe?"

Drake was silent for a moment. "I would not give them up for anything but you. I do, however, believe that Bael will keep them from being used by members of the Otherworld. Whether or not he does so from his fellow princes is up to him."

"I have not ruled Abaddon as long as I have by being foolish," Bael answered.

"OK, so that takes care of the price. What sacrifice do you want now? I think the local store is fresh out of roast chickens, but I'm willing to spring for a turkey or even a couple of pot roasts if that'll do the trick."

"Oh, no," Bael said, tossing the dagger in the air and catching it by the very tip of its blade. "This sacrifice is demanded of *you*, Aisling Grey. You ask for a sacrifice on my part in going to the trouble of having you removed from Abaddon—you must provide me with a similar sacrifice."

"What, exactly?" I asked, a hollow feeling in my gut.

Bael's hand jerked downward, embedding the point of the dagger a good three inches into the solid wood of the table. I jumped at the violence of the movement, squeezing up tight to Drake as Bael's expression darkened. "Be it known to all that upon payment of the items known as the Tools of Bael, and a formal disavowal of Guardianship, I will grant Aisling Grey, seventh prince of Abaddon, expulsion from our ranks."

24

The dream started as so many others have—with a drowsy sense of presence, Drake's presence, which seeped into the core of my very being and roused my awareness gently, but insistently.

I was disoriented as I always am in Drake's dreamscapes—I was in warm silky water, in a large black pool, ringed with candles whose flames sputtered and danced in the heated air. Shadows stretched behind them in inky infinity, the light dappling only the water of the pool in which I sat.

"Mmm. This is a new one—frankincense and myrrh?" I asked as I cupped my hand and allowed the oiled water to pour from between my fingers. "I like it. It's very dragon. This is awfully sweet of you, to send me a dream just because you had to go to Paris to get those blasted Tools, Drake, but it's not necessary. I could have waited until tomorrow when you got home."

"I, on the other hand, could not wait." His voice slid across my damp skin like velvet, sending little skitters of anticipation rippling down my spine. I turned to look behind me, where his voice had originated, but there was nothing to be seen in the dense shadows.

"Oooh, are you going to be dominant and bossy in this

dream?" I scooped up another handful of water and tilted my head back, letting it pour down my neck to my chest.

"I am always dominant. I am wyvern. You are my mate. It is the natural order of things."

Movement flickered to my left. I peered into the darkness but could make out nothing but the slightest whisper of cloth as it dropped to the floor. I smiled to myself and heaved a mock sigh. "You live in your own little world, don't you?"

"Yes." A little breeze tickled my back. I spun around, but no one was there. "It consists of you and me, and nothing else of importance. Love me, mate."

His lips were warm on the nape of my neck. I arched my back as his hands slid around my oiled skin, cupping my breasts as he nibbled several highly erogenous spots behind my ear.

"Oh-ho, it's going to be an 'all about Drake' night, is it?" I asked, teasing him with more than just my words.

"Yes. Tonight I will take my pleasure of you. And when I am done, if you are worthy, perhaps I will allow you a little enjoyment, as well."

I laughed, pinching the skin of his thigh. "In your dreams, buster. Oh, wait, this is your dream."

"Are you so sure it is only a dream?" he asked, his hands gentle but demanding on my sensitive breasts.

"Oh, yes. If it was *my* dream, you'd be spread-eagled on the bed, and I'd be licking warm chocolate off you."

"We will leave that for an 'all about Aisling' night."

"Deal. Mmm. We've got to stop meeting like this." I leaned back into him, my hands finding the long length of muscles in his thighs. He was warm, and slick, and absolutely wonderful to the touch. "I much prefer you in the flesh, not that these dreams aren't pleasant. But there's something to be said for in-person attendance at these events."

"I agree completely."

I turned on his lap, examining his face, wondering how I could ever have thought I could live without him. He was arrogant, he was bossy, he did what he thought best regardless of my wishes—most of the time, although he was getting better about that—in short, he was the most exasperating man I'd ever met or ever would meet, and yet I loved him with every morsel of my heart and soul. "I used to think that love meant just wanting to be with someone. But it's more than that. It's all the frustrations and irritations and gloriously wondrous times all wrapped together in one magical being that has become so ingrained in me, I don't think we could ever be separated into our original parts."

His lips caressed mine, a familiar heat building within me that was echoed in him. "You are my life, Aisling. I knew that the first moment you strolled into the G&T. I will never forget the way you sauntered across the bar and challenged me without even knowing who or what I was. I did not wish to admit it, but even then you had captured my heart."

I laughed into his mouth even as a tear rolled down my cheek. "You drove me mad then, you know that, right? You were so bossy, so mysterious, never answering any question, but somehow, always there when I needed you."

"You have never needed me," he said, cutting off my objections with a kiss so hot, it set the water ablaze. "You have not needed me to achieve what you wanted, *kincsem*. You were strong even if you did not yet recognize the full extent of your powers. It is a strength that will continue, even in times of darkness."

I closed my eyes for a moment, acknowledging the sad,

dark little corner of my soul. Giving up my Guardianship was the hardest thing I'd ever had to do. It was as much a part of me as Drake had become, and refusing that part of myself, refuting it and denying it, felt like something had been amputated from my life. But I would survive the loss of it, whereas I could not survive the loss of the man I held in my arms, the man who was kissing every last little bit of sadness from me. "We will overcome this, too, mate. You must have faith that all will be well."

"I have faith in you," I whispered.

His tongue twined around mine as I kissed him, opened myself to his fire, accepted it, reveled in it, gloried in the fact that I could share it again, then returned it to him. The muscles of his back bunched under my questing fingers as he lifted me back onto the seat from which I'd slipped. Water lapped at the underside of my breasts as he knelt between my legs, his hands sliding up my thighs, parting them to dance a silky line upward.

"You'll notice I'm losing my waist. I'm getting thick. Jim hid the scale, saying he was afraid of what would happen when I saw my weight." My breath sucked in as his head dipped and he took one aching nipple into the fiery inferno of his mouth. I squirmed on the warm, slick seat of the tub as his fingers danced in my most private of places, the fire he'd started there burning up to where my breast was being laved by his tongue. "Are you one of those men who finds pregnant women sexy?"

He pulled his mouth from my breast, trailing flames as he licked a path to my other nipple. "No."

I pinched his shoulder.

He flashed one of his heart-stopping grins at me, his eyes alight with amused passion. "Unless the woman happens to be you, in which case, yes."

"I'm going to have to deduct five points from your total score for your delay in answering correctly," I told him, presenting my poor, ignored breast for his attention.

He blew a little ring of fire onto it. "I will find you arousing even when these delectable breasts have lost their tone and lie limp along your chest."

"Hey!" I said, indignation filling me. "I'm immortal! Doesn't that mean I won't get saggy boobs and gray hair? Because if it doesn't mean that, I want a refund—"

The rich, deep sound of his laughter filled my heart. He bent down to nuzzle my waiting breast before cupping his hands under my behind, lifting me slightly off the seat. "You give me joy, Aisling. No other woman has ever done that."

He pushed into my body, a hundred little nerve endings suddenly sitting up and paying attention, the burn of his body in mine echoed in the sensation of his fire shared between us. I wrapped my legs around him, welcoming the heat, feeling myself unfurling in the glow of his love, every moment in my life coming to culmination of that moment in time. I clutched the slick skin of his back as my orgasm burst upon me with shattering brilliance, wave after wave of ecstasy causing my muscles to tighten around him even as he cried out hoarsely against my neck. I watched for the exact moment when his body shifted, when the smooth skin of his chest and arms morphed into iridescent green and yellow scales. The back I was clutching changed in form as well, sharp spines bursting to life beneath my fingers. I had a glimpse of familiar emerald eyes smoky with rapture tilting slightly and elongating, long, powerful neck muscles straining upward as Drake flung back his head and roared.

It was the last thing I saw, the last thing I was aware of for a long, long time, until slowly, consciousness returned to me. My heartbeat pounded so loudly in my ears, I could scarcely hear over it. I melted in Drake's arms, allowing him to pull me onto his lap where he had collapsed next to me.

He was back to normal, to all appearances a man, but I knew better. Beneath that gorgeous manflesh lay the heart of a dragon.

And it was all mine.

"I thought this was supposed to be all about you," I murmured into his ear, giving his earlobe a little nibble just to show it I loved it.

"It is. I am well satisfied," he answered, his eyes closed, his head resting against the edge of the tub.

I slid my hand along the wet planes of his chest, smiling to myself at the feeling of his heart beating fast beneath my hand. I was so relaxed, so sated, I felt utterly boneless, drifting along in a world that was made up solely of the wet man beneath me. "We need to have more Drake nights."

"Amen."

The pounding in my heart didn't disappear. In fact, I noted with a frown as I lifted my head from where I'd been resting it against him, it seemed to get louder.

Drake gave a little start as he evidently heard the noise as well. "What?" he said in a loud voice, frowning into the shadows.

A crack of light appeared in the midst of the blackness, growing until it revealed the outline of a door. A hand shoved itself through the opening, the owner thankfully not following. The hand waggled a cell phone at us.

"It is Pál. He wishes to speak with you."

I squinted at the door. "That sounds like István. What's he doing in our dream?"

"What does he want?"

"He is following Kostya, as you asked. He says your brother has taken the phylactery . . . and Pál believes he is on his way to Gabriel."

"No, no, no, no," I said, frowning at the hand with the cell phone. "I am a tolerant woman, but I refuse to have István enter into our lovely erotic dreams. And I especially do not want any of this dragon politics stuff in my dreams. Make it go away, sweetie."

The sight of Drake's naked backside as he jerked open the door wide enough to take the phone made several things clear.

The light from beyond the door lit up the interior of the mysterious dream room. My face, shadowed and startled, stared back at me from a mirror. Familiar counters came into view . . . along with Jim's dog bed (thankfully empty), a heated towel rack, and the negligee I'd worn when I went to bed earlier that night.

"This isn't a dream," I said, realization dawning with full horror in my mind.

"No. We came back early. I did not wish to spend another night without you," Drake said before speaking a Hungarian word into the phone.

"Oh, god. Then Kostya . . ."

Drake snarled a couple of words that I recognized as being not nice at all, slamming shut the phone. He hit the light switch in the bathroom, grabbing the pants he'd laid across a brass bench. "Kostya has gone to confront Gabriel."

"Fires of Abaddon," I said, appropriating Jim's favorite oath as I scrambled out of the now-familiar black marble tub after him.

Drake paused at the door long enough to toss me my bathrobe. I gasped at the look of fury on his face. "He's going to wish he was in Abaddon by the time I get through with him. Brother be damned, he has gone too far this time. This is tantamount to war."

25

"Don't even *think* you're going off without me." I rushed into our bedroom just as István went out the door to the hall. Drake had shifted into high gear, his movements as smooth and graceful as ever as he pulled on shoes, shirt, and jacket, but he was moving so quickly, he was almost a blur.

He did pause at the door to look back at me as I snarled under my breath when I tried to zip up my jeans. "This is dragon business, Aisling."

"And I'm your mate! Dammit, I'll wear a skirt." I yanked open the closet and grabbed the nearest skirt and sweater I could find, grimacing when I wrestled my breasts into a bra that had suddenly become too small.

"The situation is too volatile for you. I would be happier knowing you were home safe."

I yanked the sweater over my head, glaring at Drake as my head popped through the tight neckhole. "Sweetie, you might as well get used to the fact that I'm not going to be left behind. I've got powers, remember. I can be helpful, just like I was at Fiat's—"

He made an exasperated noise, marching over to take my hands, pinning me with a look that was intended to show just how serious he was about the matter. "You are immensely helpful, but this is not a situation where a Guardian will be called for."

"Maybe not," I said grimly, grabbing my jacket. "But Gabriel is my friend—I think—and I'm not going to let Kostya destroy him or the silver dragons."

Pál shouted from the hallway. Drake's face was a study in frustration, irritation, and grudging acknowledgement of what I said. "You will not endanger yourself in any manner," he ordered as he grabbed up his cell phone. "You will do exactly as I say."

"I'm not likely to do anything stupid. Not now when I'm poised on the brink of impending non-proscription. I would just like one last chance to be a Guardian before I have to give it up forever." I ran after him as he bolted down the hallway. I was almost to the staircase when one of the doors opened.

"Aisling? I heard shouting. Is everything all right?"

I stopped at the sight of a sleep-rumpled Paula, consumed by guilt at the look of concern on her face. When we had returned from our little chat with Bael, she was nearly hysterical from the experience, Uncle Damian at his wit's end to try to explain things to her. I'd decided right then and there that she was not going to be the sort of person who could live with the idea of the Otherworld, and had spent half an hour mind-pushing both her and David, ultimately convincing them that I'd taken ill at the wedding and had returned home without event.

And now here she was worried that I was still sick. "I'm fine, Paula. It's . . . it's Jim, my dog. It ate something bad, I think, and we're taking it to an emergency vet hospital. Go back to sleep! We'll call if we're going to be late returning."

Paula grabbed my arm in an iron grip before I could make my escape. "My dear, I absolutely insist that you let

Drake take your dog to the vet. You are too ill to go galli-
vanting around at four in the morning."

"I'm fine now, I'm just—"

"I insist! David? David, wake up and talk some sense into
your girl—"

Oh, lord. That's all I needed. I hated to give Paula another
mind-push so soon after the last one, but Drake was already
at the front door. I fired up my patented Guardian Mind
Meld and beamed its rays straight at her. "It's all right,
Paula. I'm fine. This is nothing to be concerned about. Go
back to bed and go to sleep."

She blinked a couple of times before nodding. "I think
I'll go back to bed if you don't mind."

"Not at all. I'll see you later." I grabbed the banister and
hurried down the stairs even as she asked the now-empty
hallway, "What am I doing out of bed?"

Suzanne was at the front door, holding it open so I could
race straight outside and into the car that was waiting. "You
heard?" I asked her as I grabbed my purse.

"Yes. Take care."

"Will do. Where did Jim go?" I asked Drake as I settled
down next to him. István hit the accelerator, and we zoomed
off into the London night. I averted my eyes from the front
window, feeling it was probably going to be better if I didn't
watch how recklessly he drove.

"It was in the basement watching DVDs of old British
TV shows."

"Not *The Avengers* again? Jim, I summon thee!"

Drake's phone jingled from his jacket pocket. He answered it in Hungarian, his jaw tightening as he listened.

Jim appeared on the seat next to me, wedged between me
and the side. "Jeez, Ash! Give a guy a little room! You're
squashing my magnificent self flat!"

"Keep it down, Drake's on the phone. Get on the floor if you want room," I answered, skewing around in my seat as far as the seat belt would allow. "Oh, for god's sake—you're slobbering like crazy! You and your Mrs. Peel fetish. You're not even the same species!"

"It's not a fetish. I just admire her in a cat suit. Mmrowr!"

"Yeah, right. I notice you don't watch it when you're visiting Cecile, you two-timing rat. Wipe your flews once we get out of the car."

"Boy, you finally get a little, and you're just as cranky as ever," it answered. "Where are we going, or do I want to know?"

I watched Drake. He had spoken few words, but his expression was growing blacker and blacker by the moment as he listened. I touched his arm to get his attention and mouthed, "Kostya?"

He nodded.

"What's Kostya done now?" Jim asked in a whisper.

"Taken the phylactery and gone off to absorb the silver dragons."

Drake erupted into a volley of angry Hungarian.

Jim made a wry face. "I had a feeling this would happen. Kostya was kicking furniture around earlier, muttering about everyone conspiring against him, and that the dragon thingie you found was a sign the time was right for him to take action, yadda yadda yadda."

"Why didn't you tell me that?" I asked, pinching its neck.

"Ow! Demon abuse!"

"Jim!" I said through my teeth.

It affected a hurt expression. "I couldn't tell you, not unless you wanted me to interrupt your journey to boinksville. Drake booted me out of the bathroom and told me to go sleep somewhere else. The only reason I even saw Kostya is because I had to go into the study to get *The Avengers* DVDs."

"Meh."

Drake slammed closed his phone on a curt word, glaring out into the flashing lights of the city as they zoomed by us.

"I take it that Kostya is being unreasonable?"

"Yes." He took my hand, his fingers twining through mine. I cherished the gesture, knowing full well he wasn't happy about having me along. "He insists that the phylactery is a sign that the time is nigh for him to return to the weyr. *Kincsem*, I fear for my brother's sanity. It has not been easy for him to remain hidden for the last few centuries. But now . . ."

I held his hand in both of mine and leaned into him, offering what comfort I could. "Kostya is so prickly about things, I haven't had a chance to ask him about himself. Were you guys close growing up?"

"Close?" Drake looked somewhat pensive. "Not in the sense I believe you mean. I was sent to live with my grandmother when I was young. My mother objected—you know what she is like—but my grandmother was a formidable woman herself. Kostya stayed with the black dragons, and for a while, Mother stayed with him. He was born a wyvern just as I was. Baltic trained him from the very beginning to take his place when his time was over. It nearly destroyed Kostya when he realized the truth about Baltic, and that the only way to save the sept was to eliminate the wyvern . . . but he was too late. By the time we found Baltic, the damage had been done, and most of the sept had been destroyed."

"You were there with him when he . . . er . . . did the cleaving?"

"Yes." Drake's gaze shifted to me for a moment. I

expected it to be stark with emotion, but it was just the opposite—a curiously flat look that boded ill for everyone. "My distant cousin Fodor was still wyvern of the green dragons when Baltic tried to rally the septs in a move that would eliminate the silver dragons, but there was little help to be found. Chuan Ren was still recovering from the Endless War she'd brought about against Baltic. The blue dragons were suffering from infighting, and the sept was in disarray. The green dragons and black had a long history of peace, but Fodor refused to aid Baltic, preferring instead to cast his vote for formal recognition of the silver dragons."

"So you went to help your brother, but not as a representative of the sept?"

"I was one of a number of green dragons who ignored Fodor's decision. We risked going ouroboros, but we honored the agreements we had long held with the black dragons. Fodor was not pleased, regardless." Drake looked back out the window at the lights as they flashed by. "I was fighting at the time to be recognized as his heir, and he threatened to have me removed from the rolls if I lent aid to Kostya. The point was moot—by the time we arrived to help Kostya, the silver dragons had almost destroyed what remained of the sept. I watched sword in hand as my brother slew his wyvern, and was almost killed himself by the man for whom he was named."

I searched my memory of dragon history but came up blank. "Who was that?"

"Constantine Norka. He was the first silver wyvern. It was he whom Baltic cursed."

"Wow." I mulled over the weighty history that Drake had told me, my sympathies divided between Gabriel's people and the hell Kostya must have gone through watching his leader destroy the sept trying to regain what would never be theirs. "If it makes you feel any better, I don't think Kostya is crazy. I think he's probably just frustrated as hell, and he's jumping at any excuse to get back into action."

"Possibly."

I would have pumped him for more information—I wasn't about to let his unusually verbose mood slip away unheeded—but István slammed his foot on the brakes in front of a large, exclusive London hotel. Jim and I scrambled to follow after Drake as the two men bolted out of the car, István pausing long enough to toss the keys at a valet with instructions to keep the car handy. We got a few strange looks from the scattering of people in the lobby at the early hour, but no one stopped us as we ran to the bank of elevators.

Pál emerged from the stairwell and joined us.

"Is Gabriel all right?" I asked him.

"I do not know. Kostya would not let me in. You talked to him?" he asked Drake as we got into the elevator.

"Yes. He says he has not done anything yet, that he wants witnesses from all four septs before he takes action."

"Witnesses?" I asked, scandalized. "Why would he want witnesses to his planned genocide?"

"The witnesses are to ensure he receives votes to allow his sept back into the weyr. He does not wish to exterminate the silver dragons, mate; he wishes to annex them, to bring them back where he believes they belong."

"Uh-huh. Well, I'd say the fact that the silver dragons wiped out the black ones pretty much says what they think of that whole annexing deal."

"I agree, but that is not what concerns me now."

"What does concern you? Oh, that phylactery thing? What exactly is that? I know you said it's old, and some sort of amulet, but does it have super dragon powers or something?"

"It is hard to explain. It holds great significance to dragonkin, although there are no powers directly derived from possessing it. Its value is based more on what it represents: a symbol of the primal forces coming together to create the first dragon. It is widely thought that to hold it is to be at one with those forces. Chuan Ren held it for many centuries, at the height of the red dragons' supremacy, but it was lost sometime around the first millennium. Baltic had it during the Endless War—some say that was why the black dragons came out of that war relatively unscathed. I would dearly like to know just how and when it came into Fiat's possession."

"Yeah, makes you wonder about that mysterious little apartment and who was living there. I wonder—"

A drunken party girl and her equally drunken escort got onto the elevator at that moment. The girl spotted Drake and lurched toward him, an inviting smile on her face as she thrust her barely concealed breasts at him. "Hello, handsome. Would you hold me against you if I told you it was beautiful?"

I pushed myself between her and Drake. "He's very handsome, isn't he? And *very* taken."

"Fat bitch," she snapped, sulking for a moment until she spotted Pál. Her companion slouched against the wall of the elevator, too far gone to care, I guess.

The door opened at our floor and we exited, leaving the drunken woman to pout as Pál avoided her grasp. I stopped just outside the door, pulled on Drake's fire, and set alight a ring at her feet. She shrieked and flapped her arms wildly as the doors started to close. I drew a quick ward on them, and before the outer doors blocked my way, mentally stamped out the fire. I turned to find Drake watching me with crossed arms and a cocked eyebrow.

"What?" I asked, trying unsuccessfully to bat my eyelashes at him.

"You locked them in there with fire?"

"There was a fire extinguisher," I said. "Of course, she's probably too drunk to notice it or know how to use it, but that's hardly my problem."

Drake continued to give me the Eyebrow of Much Displeasure.

"There were sprinklers as well. They're sure to go off at some point . . . oh, for heaven's sake, Drake! What sort of person do you take me for? I put out the fire just before the doors closed, OK? I just wanted to scare her a little. I may be a demon lord, but I'm not a *demon lord*! I wouldn't barbecue a person just because she called me fat."

"Hey, Ash, you know that you're getting fa—"

"*You* are not a person," I told Jim. "If you don't want me to singe off a few whiskers, you'll pipe down."

"Yeesh!" it answered, trailing behind us as we hurried down the corridor to Gabriel's suite.

Part of me, the fanciful part, the part that loved nothing more than a good epic historical novel filled with battles, valiant and incredibly sexy knights, and equally valiant but still retaining a core sense of femininity (not to mention confident and professional) damsels who fight at their side, expected to see some sort of gigantic battle raging within the confines of Gabriel's suite. I imagined blood, and possibly a little gore, with the harsh sound of swords clanging together above the manly rumble of male voices calling abuse to each other.

What I didn't expect to see was Gabriel bound to a chair, Maata and Tipene on the floor beside him, facedown, their arms bound behind their backs. Bastian and Kostya stood next to a window, arguing in hushed voices. Sitting on a couch all by his lonesome was Li, Chuan Ren's mate.

He stood up when we entered the room, smiling and bowing politely. Kostya hurried over as we pulled up short at the sight of the red dragon.

"Where is Chuan Ren?" Drake asked, his eyes flashing.

"She is not here. Her mate is acting as her envoy. You will, naturally, respect the laws governing envoys in times of war and not attack him."

Drake gave his brother a look that made the latter flush slightly. "I have yet to attack any of the red dragons without due cause. The green dragons will defend themselves, but they have not, to date, initiated any hostile moves against the red sept."

"Just so," Kostya said.

"Li Jiaxin," Drake said, bowing in a formal manner to Li. The red dragon bowed first to Drake, then to me.

"Bastian, I'm ashamed of you letting Kostya tie Gabriel up like this," I said, giving him my very best frown.

Bastian held up his hands. "I just arrived a few moments before you. He was like that when I came in. I was trying to reason with Kostya when you arrived."

"Uh-huh. Hello, Li. It's a pleasure to see you again," I said politely, then turned to Gabriel. "I'm so sorry about this, Gabriel. We had no idea he'd go off the deep end and do this to you guys. We'll just untie you so we can talk things over in a civilized manner."

"Thank you," Gabriel said, his voice polite, but the anger in his silver-gray eyes enough to set steel alight.

"Do not touch him, Aisling!" Kostya said in what I was coming to think of as his trademarked bossy voice. "We will hold this conclave with the silver dragons bound."

I ignored him and went around the back of Gabriel's chair to see how best to undo the ropes that held him there. Kostya leaped toward me, grabbing my arm and jerking me backwards. Before I could do so much as gasp, Drake had Kostya pinned against the wall, his face a scant inch away from his brother's.

"Do *not* touch her again," he snarled.

Kostya's eyes narrowed as he shoved Drake, sending him staggering backwards a foot or so. "I told you on the phone to think long before you opposed me, brother. Once our ties are severed, they will not be mended."

"Talk about being a drama queen," Jim muttered softly.

I agreed completely, wanting to tell Kostya to knock off the dramatics, but I was now familiar enough with the dragons to know how they did things, so I kept my thoughts to myself. Besides which, I felt he had a certain cause to be upset. If I'd been through what he'd been through the last few hundred years, I'd probably have a lot of issues to work out, too.

Drake, however, was made of sterner stuff and had no love for the posturing that meant so much to people like Chuan Ren and Fiat. "Don't be any more of a fool than you have already been, Kostya. István, untie Gabriel. Mate, come here."

He waved an imperious hand for me, but I was wholeheartedly behind his efforts to control the situation. I smiled at Gabriel and took my place at Drake's side.

"Now we will discuss the situation," Drake said, but just as István cut the bonds that held Gabriel, the silver dragon was on Kostya, knocking him down, pounding his head against the carpeted floor.

"You'd get a better brain bashing if you pulled back the carpet and did that on the bare floor," Jim offered.

"Oh, for god's sake! Stop it! All of you!" I yelled as Drake and Pál pulled Gabriel off Kostya.

. Bastian helped Kostya up, tsking at the bloody nose Gabriel had given him. "What you need is a Taser. Those things pack a hell of a kick."

"Hey! No taking sides," I told him, making squinty eyes that had him clearing his throat and sidling away. Drake shoved Gabriel in a chair and told him to sit there, before turning a glare on his brother that would have struck down anyone mortal.

"I will have Aisling ward the next person who moves from his chair," Drake threatened, spreading his glare around the room. Pál had cut the ropes on Tipene and Maata, both of whom looked perfectly willing to jump into the fray.

Gabriel, with self-possession that I wanted to laud, told them to sit down.

"This is my conclave," Kostya announced, stomping over to the middle of the room. "I will stand."

Drake ignored him, turning to Gabriel. "What happened?"

Gabriel's dimples were nowhere in evidence, his face unusually somber. "Need you ask? He forced his way in, babbling something about having the means to bring us back to the black sept. I told him what I told you yesterday—the silver dragons will discuss the issue only in the forum of a weyr synod. He struck before we could defend ourselves."

"What's a weyr synod?" I whispered to Pál, who was standing near me.

"It's a formal meeting of the leaders of all the septs. Sort of an elite council."

"Oh. But the black dragons aren't recognized as a sept anymore, are they?"

"No."

"You would hide behind the weyr rather than facing me?" Kostya asked, his voice filled with disdain.

"We are not going to rejoin your sept," Gabriel said, slowly getting to his feet. Instantly Maata and Tipene were at his side, presenting a united front. "There is nothing you can do, nothing you can offer us that will induce us to dissolve our sept and rejoin that which we left so many centuries ago. Too much blood has been spilled over this issue, and although we do not want war with you, we will fight to the death any attempt that is made against our sept."

"Do not mistake me for Baltic," Kostya said, a slight smile on his lips as he withdrew from his inner jacket pocket the small lumpy gold figurine, tossing it in the air. Gabriel's eyes widened as he saw what it was that Kostya held. "I will not be so foolish as he was, to effect a war upon you. I have seen the outcome of such ignorance. I will, however, petition the weyr to restore to the black dragons what was illegally taken from them. Your beloved Constantine was many things, but a man learned in the laws of the weyr was *not* one of them."

I scooted over to Drake, bumping his hand to get his notice. "Is he saying what I think he's saying?"

"I believe so." Drake frowned at his brother. "What is it you are hinting at, Kostya?"

"I hint at nothing, brother. Once formally recognized by the weyr, I will, however, present the evidence that Baltic had ignored for so many centuries—proof that the silver dragons were never formally admitted into the weyr, and thus their sept is not a separate entity in its own right."

Gabriel laughed. "We do not fear you, Kostya Fekete. Your threats are as hollow as your brain."

"Ouch," Jim said softly.

"That was a definite seven-pointer," I said. "Gabriel is well ahead on style points."

"Yeah, but I bet the swimsuit competition is going to be a close call."

I bit my lip to keep from giggling. Jim tipped its head as it looked up at me. "Since when did you become such a staunch Gabriel supporter?"

"Since he helped us get to Drake, got us all back to civilization, and didn't toss Kostya off the side of the mountain on the way down, as he no doubt wanted. And I'm beginning to see why."

Drake overheard the last of our muted comments, giving me a glance that shut up both Jim and me. "Threats and insults are useless. You may present your case to the weyr at the proper time and place, Kostya—neither of which is now."

"Assuming he gets recognition," Gabriel said, his voice as smooth as ever, but there was an undertone in it that had me giving him a second look.

"All I need is a majority vote. Bastian as the new wyvern of the blue dragons has already committed his vote to me."

"And Chuan Ren? Do you think she will be so easily swayed to your side?" Gabriel asked.

Kostya smiled and tossed the phylactery in the air again. Beside me, Drake's body tensed as though he was about to pounce. I took his hand, giving him a little smile as he glanced toward me. I had no desire to see him warring with his brother, and that, I suspected, would be the outcome if Drake retrieved the phylactery.

"She will see the wisdom of recognizing me and my sept if I make it clear to her that I will reward such support with a treasure beyond measure."

Pál gasped at the implication. I watched Drake worriedly,

concerned that he might give in to his brother's arrogance. To my relief, he squeezed my fingers, reassuring me that he wasn't going to do anything stupid.

"That is only two of the three votes needed to allow you readmittance," Drake said slowly.

Kostya drew back, much as a cobra pulls back before striking. "You swore to stand beside me. Do you dishonor that vow?"

"I said I would support your readmittance to the weyr if you did not commit acts of aggression against the silver dragons. Your actions tonight make it clear that our agreement is void."

Fire lit Kostya's eyes as he faced his brother—and it wasn't a friendly little fire. "You will not stand by my side as you did once before?" he asked, his voice harsh with strain.

The room was so silent, I could hear Jim's stomach rumbling.

"We shall see," was all Drake said before nodding at Gabriel. István and Pál opened the door, and without another word being spoken, we left the suite.

"You're the king of exit lines, I'll give you that," I said as we waited at the elevator. "But I hope Kostya doesn't interpret that specimen of exit line superiority as a declaration of war."

He said nothing, but his beautiful eyes were veiled.

I had a bad feeling that things were not going to be so easily settled. A very bad feeling indeed.

I'm not going to say anything. *But I'm going to think it!*

" . . . at which point, we left. It was a hell of a line to leave on, but I just don't know. As much as it pains me to say something negative about a member of Drake's family who isn't his mother, I just don't know what to think of Kostya. Is he going to be content to try to do things on the political level, or is he going to bring about a new war? Is he just an arrogant dragon, or is he bonkers? Will he respect the bounds of brotherhood, or will he try to bring Drake down if the green dragons don't support him? It's very worrisome."

Rene wrinkled his brow as he maneuvered the car off a roundabout and onto a less-traveled road. "Brother against brother . . . that is most tragic. But me, I do not believe Kostya will do this thing. If it was not for Drake and you, he would still be captive. He must owe to you a certain respect, *hein*?"

"You'd think so, but you know dragons. They do things their own way," I answered as we turned onto the drive of the house that was Bael's domain in England, my fingers tightening around the handle of the titanium case bearing the Tools of Bael.

"Drake knows what he's doing," Uncle Damian said from the backseat, where he'd been reading the paper. Jim had its head hanging out the window, thankfully silent for the moment.

"I hope so. Rene, are you sure you want to come with me? Bael said all I have to do is hand over the Tools and do the disavowal, and then he'd give me the expulsion. I'm sure with Uncle Damian and Jim I'll be perfectly safe, if you'd rather pass on another visit to Abaddon."

Rene's chest puffed out as he narrowly missed mowing down a demon clipping a tall yew hedge. "I am not afraid of Bael. I am a member of the Court of Divine Blood. There is nothing he can do to me."

"You're a member of this Court place?" I asked, curious. "I never knew that."

"I am a daimon," he said with his usual expressive shrug. "Daimons are part of the Court. Bael cannot harm me without bringing down the Court upon his head, and that, not even Bael would be stupid enough to do."

Jim had pulled in its head long enough to hear Rene's comment. "Oh yeah, the demon lords don't mess with Court members. Very bad juju."

"What do you know about it?" I asked, turning around in my seat to mop up the long tendrils of drool the wind had pulled from its slobbery flews.

"Boy, you really do have splinters in the windmills of your mind, don't you?" Jim asked, shaking its head.

"No more Carol Burnett DVDs for you, buster. Just answer my question."

"Hello! I was a sprite, remember? That's a member of the Court."

Uncle Damian looked up at Jim in surprise. "Your demon was a what?"

"It's a sort of a lesser angel, I think," I told him as we got out of the car. Two demons emerged from the house to meet us. "Jim got kicked out and sent to Abaddon."

"Why am I not surprised?" my uncle said as he took up a position at my side.

"Like uncle, like niece . . ."

"You have come to pay wer?" the first demon asked, blocking our way into the house.

"Well, I guess I'll pay wherever Bael wants, although I'd like to get this over with quickly."

Jim, the two demons, and Rene all looked at me as if I was suddenly speaking in Serbo-Croatian.

"What have I said now?" I asked them.

"Wer is the name of the payment that Bael has asked. It is not a location, you understand?" Rene explained.

"Oh. Sorry. Um, yes, I've come to pay the wer."

The demons nodded and turned on their heels, clearly expecting us to follow.

"Don't say it," I warned Jim as it opened its mouth. "I'd just like to remind all of you that no one bothered to give me the *Big Demon Lord's Book of Archaic Lingo,* so I'm a little clueless when it comes to unnecessary terms that people use just to impress others."

I could have sworn I heard Jim say, "A *little* clueless?" as we entered the hall, but I had more important things to worry about than a few snipes from my demon.

Bael was waiting for us when we were shown into his room, his eyes lighting on the case I held firmly with both hands. "I see you have brought the Tools. Excellent. And the sacrifice?"

I cleared my throat. I was dreading this moment, hoping against hope that some brilliantly cunning plan would occur to me that would allow me to escape from Bael's hold without the loss of my Guardian abilities. Unfortunately, nothing struck me. Drake was just as much at a loss as I was, and although I badly wanted to call Nora for advice, pride kept me from blubbering all over her about what my own folly had wrought.

You don't have to do this, you know.

"The sacrifice . . . I'm ready," I said, lifting my chin and meeting Bael's eyes even though my soul wept.

Such drama over something for which you have a simple solution.

"Very well. You may proceed," Bael said, leaning back in his chair, his fingertips tapping together.

Uncle Damian gave me an abrupt nod and squeezed my shoulder for a moment. Rene watched me with sad eyes. Jim leaned on my leg and rubbed its head on my knee.

Let's talk this over before you commit yourself to an action you'll later regret.

I set the case down on the table next to Bael, opening the lid and removing the protective layer of foam. "As part of the terms of our agreement, I give to you the three items known collectively as the Tools of Bael: the Anima di Lucifer, the Occio di Lucifer, and the Voce di Lucifer."

You know, if you kept them for yourself, you could defeat Bael and truly reign supreme in Abuddon. Think what changes you could make!

"The blood, eye, and voice of Lucifer," Bael said, satisfaction dripping from his voice as he reached out a long finger and touched the golden aquamanile that was shaped like a dragon. "How nice it is to have them back."

You are foolish, Aisling Grey. So foolish.

I took a deep breath, reminding myself that I was a strong, confident woman even if I was about to relinquish one of the most important things in my life.

Don't make a hasty decision. There are so many other options—

"In accordance with the second term of our agreement, I hereby renounce my Guardian powers, doing so of my free will. From this moment on, I will no longer be a Guardian."

Fame, fortune, happiness—working with me, you can have it all.

My voice cracked midway through my disavowal, but I made it without breaking down and crying. I clung to that fact, and to the knowledge that soon I'd be rid of the dark power forever.

You will never be rid of me. I am part of you. Nothing you can do will change that.

"There now, that didn't hurt so much, did it?" Bael asked, his voice light with mockery.

"There's no need to gloat," Uncle Damian said, his voice a bit rusty. "Aisling's done what you asked. Now you keep your part of the bargain."

Bael didn't even glance at him, but he casually pulled a piece of parchment toward himself, signing below five other signatures.

This is not the last you will hear of me! I will not be—

The voice inside my head suddenly stopped as Bael lifted his pen.

"It is done," he said, pushing the parchment toward me. It bore six signatures on it, Bael's the largest, at the bottom, and no surprise—signed in blood. "It saddens me, but henceforth you will no longer be known as a prince of Abaddon. You are expulsed, Aisling Grey. Now if you don't mind, I have the important job of finding your replacement."

I stood a bit stunned for a moment, watching him for some sign of trickery. It wasn't until my uncle took my arm and forcibly steered me out of the room and down the great hall that I realized I had done it—it had cost me a sum without measure, but I had done it. I was no longer a prince of Abaddon! The dark power could never tempt me again.

I waited a moment for it to say something snarky, but all was silent in my head.

"Are you all right?" Uncle Damian asked as he hustled me out the front door, back to Rene's car.

"I think she's inner monologuing," Jim said, jumping into the backseat. "Dark power's gone, huh?"

"Yes," I said, a strange, light euphoria filling me even as I felt tremendously saddened. "But . . . does anyone else find this whole thing really anticlimactic? Almost as if . . . as if it was planned to end this way?"

"Kinda makes you think, huh?" Jim asked as I took my seat in the car.

"Yes. And I don't like what I'm thinking."

"What is that?" Rene asked, pulling away from the house.

"That Bael was taking me for a ride all along. He had to know I had given the Tools to Drake . . . who's to say he didn't arrange for me to become a prince of Abaddon just so one day, I'd barter the Tools for my freedom?"

Rene looked thoughtful. Uncle Damian grunted something about not worrying over spilt milk, but worry was one of the things I did best.

I looked down at the parchment I held in my hand. "So now what? We take this to the Court?"

"*Oui*. Although your uncle and Jim, they will not be allowed in. Mortals are seldom let in, and as for the demons, eh. You can imagine that they are not welcome."

"Hypocrites," Jim muttered, stepping on the window opener so it could stick its head out.

"Gotcha. You OK with that, Uncle Damian?"

"Drake said I would not be let in, but that you would be safe there. I will read the paper while you're taking care of your business."

"Thanks. So, where are the Pearly Gates?" I asked Rene.

"There are many entrances to the Court," he answered with a particularly vicious yank on the steering wheel to avoid a group of joggers. "But the nearest one is back in London. In the men's restroom in Hyde Park."

"You're kidding," I said, giving him a close look to see if he was pulling my leg.

"Not at all. It is not a very nice restroom, but it serves its purpose."

So it was that two hours later I found myself ducking into a run-down, beat-up wooden building in a little-used section of Hyde Park, half-hidden by trees. "How come they have their entrance here?" I asked, my nose wrinkling as I followed Rene to the last stall. The walls of the bathroom were slightly green tinted, as if mildewed, and the smell was a nasty mixture of cheap toilet cleaner and rotted leaves. "Don't people run into it all the time?"

"See for yourself," he said, opening the stall door with a grand gesture. Although the stall itself was tiny, in the center of it a ward glowed briefly.

"It's warded! Well, that would explain it. So I just go in?"

"Yes. I will follow you."

Pushing through the perdu ward was not difficult, although for a moment everything seemed to spin around, but then I was standing on the cobblestoned street of what appeared to be a small medieval village.

If small medieval villages had latte stands . . . and shops with brightly colored clothing, and people zipping around the cobblestones on Vespas.

"This is Heaven?" I asked, taking in the tall spires, tiled roofs, and half-timbered buildings.

"It is the Court of Divine Blood. The two are not the same thing." Rene pointed toward a grand-looking marble building that sat off to one side. "The library. It is in there that we will find the almoner."

"OK. Is that a McDonald's?" I asked as the door to one of the buildings we were passing opened, and a woman came out with two brown paper bags. "Fast food in Heaven? Isn't that wrong?"

"Shh. One does not look too closely at the little sins of the Court. The office we want is on the ground floor, just there, you see?"

Evidently the almoner was a popular guy, because we had to give our names at a reception desk before taking our places on hard wooden benches with about ten other people.

"What is the almoner going to do, do you know?" I asked Rene in a whisper. "How many hoops am I going to have to jump through to have them lift the proscription? They aren't going to demand another sacrifice, are they? Because really, I don't think I have much left to sacrifice except Drake, and that's so not happening."

"Pfft. You spend too much time in the worrying. The almoner will tell you what he wants of you to grant the removal of the proscription."

That didn't do much to ease my mind. "Given my past history, it'll be my kidney. Or my soul," I muttered darkly.

Rene ignored me to read up on the latest Hollywood gossip, as provided by a glossy magazine. He tutted over a story about a popular actress. "She always did have such a strong will. Just like you—I never could do anything but try to catch up to her."

I gawked at the magazine. "You know J-Lo? You mean you . . . you . . . *fated* her?"

"Perhaps," he said, inscrutable as ever. "I have enjoyed my time with you much more, though. I prefer dragons and demons to the strange beings who inhabit Hollywood."

That thought distracted me for a few minutes. Unfortunately, by the time we were called into the almoner's office, I had worked myself into a swivet and was convinced that I would never have the proscription removed.

It was with much trepidation and no little sense of depression that I entered a small but pleasant office. The almoner sat at a desk, a nondescript man of medium height and build, with brown hair and friendly brown eyes.

"Good afternoon. I am Terrin. And you are?"

"Aisling Grey. This is my friend, Rene."

"Ah, the daimon, yes, I believe we met a few centuries ago. Welcome to the Court, Aisling," Terrin said with a pleasant smile. "Please sit. You are here for . . . let me see . . ." He punched a few keys on the laptop sitting in front of him on the desk. "I'm sorry, I'm not normally the almoner; he's out with a family emergency so I'm filling in for him. If you can just bear with me for a moment or two while I locate your file . . ."

It struck me as a bit odd that someone bearing the name almoner was using a laptop, but I forbore from pointing out the anachronism.

"Ah, yes, there you are. Aisling Grey. My, you are a busy lady. Guardian, wyvern's mate, demon lord, and . . . prince of Abaddon?" Terrin looked up in surprise.

"*Former* prince of Abaddon," I said, passing him the expulsion.

"So I see." He took the form and typed in a few things before looking over the screen at me. "And your status as a demon lord? That is also nil?"

"Um . . . no. I have only one demon, though." I bit my lower lip. "That's . . . that's not going to screw things up, is it? Because my demon isn't a real demon. That is, it was one of you guys, and it got booted out and made a demon, but it's a demon sixth class and is actually not evil at all."

"Ah," he said, enlightenment dawning in his eyes. "Effrijim! Yes, I remember him. He had quite the sense of humor."

"That pretty much sums it up, yes. So, is that going to be a problem?"

Terrin made a little face. "I do not believe we've ever granted a sanction to a demon lord. You would not be willing to give up Effrijim?"

"No," I said, lifting my chin and giving him a firm look. "I wouldn't."

"Brava," Rene said quietly, patting my knee.

"I see." Terrin looked back at his laptop, hit a couple of keys, and asked, "And the other information is current? You are still a Guardian and a wyvern's mate?"

A little shaft of pain threatened to unwind within me, but I stomped down hard on it. "I am still a wyvern's mate. I am . . ." My throat closed for a moment. I cleared it and tried again. "I am no longer a Guardian."

"Really?"

"Bael demanded that I disavow my Guardian status in order to receive the expulsion," I explained, wondering if the day would come when I wouldn't want to burst into tears at the thought of what I'd given up.

"Did he, now? That was very cruel of him, but then, cruel is more or less his middle name, isn't it? Let's see . . . I believe that is everything." He typed in a few more things and gave me a polite smile. "Judy at the front desk will have your statement of sanction. You can pick it up on your way out."

I have a horrible feeling I gawked at him at that point. "Pick it up? You mean . . . that's it? I'm no longer proscribed?" I glanced at Rene, who looked just as surprised as I felt. Could it be that easy? I shook my head at myself. Nothing, not since that first day I stepped into the Orly Airport with the aquamanile in my hands, nothing had been easy.

"Yes. Oh, no, I tell a lie," he said, frowning at the laptop.

I knew it! I braced myself, waiting for the bad news. What was it they wanted . . . to give up Jim? Drake? *Living*?

"I hit shift instead of enter. Silly me." He punched a button, then smiled again. "Now you're set!"

"But . . . you don't want something from me?"

"Er . . . what would I want from you?" he asked, puzzlement wrinkling his brow.

"I don't know! My soul, or for me to hack off a limb with a butter knife, or . . . or . . . I don't know! I just figured this sanction was going to cost me *something*."

"It sounds to me like it has already cost you much pain."

I continued to gawk at him until he gave a little sigh, got up and took me by the hands, gently pulling me to my feet, and with a hand on my back, escorted me down the short hallway to the reception area. "My dear, this is the Court of Divine Blood. I won't say that there are not times when petitioners are asked payment for services rendered, but we do not, on the whole, operate as you are used to with those folks in Abaddon. We like to think of ourselves as the good guys. We like to take care of our people."

A bloom of hope unfurled within me. Could it be this easy after all? "But I'm not a member of the Court."

"No, alas, demon lords are not allowed membership. But we do like to keep tabs on those people we feel are fighting the good fight, and you definitely qualify for that."

I did, until I lost the ability to fight. I pushed away that nagging thought and focused on the miracle that had just been handed me. "Then . . . I'm done? The proscription is over?"

He nodded.

"I don't feel any different. Shouldn't I feel different? Shouldn't there have been—oh, I don't know—some sign like a bolt from above cleansing my soul?"

"That sounds singularly uncomfortable," he answered. "I'm afraid you'll have to settle for understated sanction rather than a splashy Broadway extravaganza of absolution."

I didn't know what to say, so I simply thanked him.

"You're quite welcome. I'm delighted I could help you, and trust you'll find the process wasn't quite as onerous as you believed it would be."

It was over! I wasn't proscribed anymore! No more tears of blood, no more horrible contacts to hide my eyes . . . no more being banned from the Guardians' Guild.

My heart felt like it was made out of lead. "Is there a ladies' room here?"

Terrin blinked in surprise. "Er . . . yes, just there. Second door on the left."

"Thanks." I bolted for the bathroom, intent on ridding myself of the contacts before my tears washed them away.

"Does she always feel the need to run to the restroom to celebrate good news?" I heard Terrin ask Rene.

"Eh. She is a woman, you know?"

I hurried to the mirror in the bathroom, carefully removing one contact. I half braced myself for the sight of a pale gray eye to peer back at me, but the eyeball that watched me so warily was one of a familiar hazel color.

The proscription had really and truly been lifted . . . but too late. I wasn't a Guardian anymore.

I grabbed a box of tissues and ran for a stall to cry.

27

"Out of all the billions of people who inhabit this planet, Drake and Aisling have found each other and committed to share their lives together as husband and wife. They have begun their life journey together and have brought us here to celebrate this beautiful moment in that journey."

I smiled at Drake. He squeezed the fingers of the hand he was holding.

"A good marriage is an entity that is made up of love, understanding, intimacy, and a generosity of spirit that allows you to put aside petty differences and care for each other no matter what the circumstances. Drake and Aisling have vowed to do just that, and have asked us here today to witness those vows."

The voice of the odd little round man Paula had found willing to fit us into his schedule echoed loudly in the small, out-of-the-way chapel. It had taken her two weeks to arrange this wedding, and me almost as long to convince her to stay in England to attend it. Our numbers were a lot fewer than the first one—my cousins had long since returned home, as had David, whose job at an Oregon university demanded his attendance. Most of the green dragons who had gathered in England had also returned to their homes. But a few had shown up, as well as my friends.

So why, then, was a vague sense of alarm starting to prick my awareness?

"Drake and Aisling, before you I have placed three candles, one each to symbolize your separate selves, and one to symbolize your unity. Please light your separate candles and use them together to light the marriage candle, pledging as you do so to keep your union as bright as the flames of your candles."

I wasn't much for the rather dramatic flair the officiating man had, but obediently lit a candle, then used it to light a larger one with a golden heart embossed on it.

Next to me, Paula sniffled happily. "This is so beautiful!" she whispered.

I nodded, and used the opportunity to peek over my shoulder at the audience, wondering if I could pinpoint my sense of unease. Pál was in the front with his arm around Nora (they made such a cute couple). Rene sat next to them with a pretty, petite red-headed woman of indeterminate age whom he had introduced as his wife, Brigitte. István and Suzanne sat on the other front pew, alongside Gabriel and his bodyguards. Gabriel caught me peeking and grinned, his dimples flashing. I winked back, grateful he'd come despite knowing that Kostya would be here.

I was even more grateful that Kostya was on his best behavior. Relations between Drake and him had been strained for ten days, but finally, just before the wedding, the two of them cleared the air with a rip-roaring fight that left Drake with a broken nose, and Kostya with a limp that persisted for forty-eight hours. True, it didn't end in a political reconciliation, but at least the two brothers were talking to each other again. I had confidence that with time, Drake would be able to make his brother see reason.

Jim stepped on my foot.

I returned my attention to the man as he went on about renewing our faith in each other and allowing the marriage to breathe with the air of love and support. I tried to pay attention to him, but the vague something was starting to take on a more alarming state. I ran down a mental checklist of everything I'd had to do and didn't see what it was that would be causing this feeling.

"What token do you, Drake, offer Aisling as a sign of your commitment to her?"

Kostya, standing at Drake's side, handed him a platinum ring. I smiled at the sight of it. Drake had told me that gold on my finger would be too distracting and opted to have our rings made of the less attractive (to dragons, anyway) metal.

"Do you, Drake, take Aisling to be your wife? Do you pledge to honor and respect her, and to live in fidelity and love with her from this day for—"

"Excuse me," I interrupted, turning to Drake. "Something's wrong."

"Aisling!" Paula moaned. "Not again!"

A normal man might point out that what was wrong was a woman interrupting her own long-awaited wedding, but Drake was head and shoulders above normal. Instead of asking silly questions, he simply asked me, "Dangerous?"

"I think so. There's something here that isn't right."

Instantly Pál and István were at his side. "Take Aisling's family and the mortals out the side entrance," he told Pál. "István, check the street. Kostya—"

"I'll have a look around the chapel," he said, suiting action to word.

The sudden breakup of the dragons had Gabriel hurrying up. "What's wrong?" he asked.

Drake filled him in while I turned to the guests and, with an apologetic smile, said in a loud voice, "I seem to have the worst luck with weddings. I'm very sorry to have to do this, but there seems to be a problem with the chapel, and I'm afraid we're going to have to evacuate it. Quickly. We'll regroup outside until we know the problem is fixed."

"Aisling, this is the limit, this is the very limit," Paula said, jerking away from where Pál was trying to move her. "You will go back in front of that minister and you will let him marry you, or so help me, I'll ... I'll ... well, I don't know what I'll do, but it won't be pleasant!"

I hated to do it, I really did, but I didn't have time to reason with her. I swung open the door in my mind and gave her a huge mental push. "Paula, you need to leave the building now. It's nothing but a gas leak, but it's dangerous to stay here. You must help the others get out quickly and stay out until we say it's safe to return."

"Oh, my!" she gasped, looking somewhat stunned. "A gas leak is dangerous! People! Quickly! We must leave immediately!"

She hurried off to herd people out the door.

"I'm going to end up frying her brain one day if I keep doing that," I said under my breath.

Jim heard me. "Think anyone would notice?"

I ignored it as Rene caught my eye. "Can I do anything?"

"No. Just get your wife out and make sure no one comes back in."

He nodded and gave my hand a little squeeze before dashing off to grab his wife and follow the last few people leaving.

"Aisling? What is it?"

Nora's voice was quiet but calming. I turned around to find her, but with my enhanced vision turned on, I wasn't so much seeing people as seeing their elemental parts. "I'm not sure. Do you feel something?"

She was silent a moment, then nodded. "It's very faint, but yes, there is something here that is imbued with evil."

"Jim?" The demon's warm head pushed under my hand. "Where is it, Jim?"

"Can't tell. I wasn't sure there was anything until you started wigging out."

I walked blindly down the center aisle of the chapel, searching in the corners and niches for signs of something that wasn't right.

"Here!" Gabriel emerged from one of the back rooms and shouted out his findings. "I think it's a bomb!"

"Get her out of the building," Drake told his brother, who started toward me at a run, but I knew in a flash that he wasn't going to make it in time.

Everything seemed to slow down, like time itself had telescoped as I flung myself sideways onto Nora, knocking her down onto a wooden pew. An explosion tore through the building with a vengeance, the scream of metal an almost human sound, followed by a concussive blast as the windows shattered. Shards of glass and wood and bits of stone rained down upon us, but to my relief, when I looked up the bulk of the building was still intact, with only the far end having been blown to smithereens.

Drake shouting my name relieved my paramount worry.

"We're here," I yelled, coughing at the dust that resulted from the wall of the nave being destroyed. "Nora, are you all right?"

"I think so. Yes. Dear god, who would bomb a church?"

"Are you hurt?" Drake yelled, pulling a large piece of the baptismal font off of someone.

"No, we're OK."

"Stay back there," he ordered.

I pulled bits of wood and rock off Nora, helping her to sit

up. Her hair was white with dust, her glasses broken and hanging askew.

"I have a pretty good idea that we have some dragons to thank for that. Jim?"

"Right here."

"You OK?"

"No. I don't seem to be able to feel my back legs. And it's . . . it's kinda hard to breathe."

I crawled out of the shelter of the pews to find Jim lying in the aisle, one of the wooden benches that lined the nave broken on top of it.

"Oh, no," I cried, half crawling over to where it lay. "Don't move. We'll get a vet. Oh, dear god, there's so much blood! Drake! Jim's hurt!"

With an effort, Jim lifted its head and turned its eyes toward me, fear stark in their depths. "Ash, I don't feel so good. You think I broke my form?"

"I don't know," I told it, cradling its head and brushing grit from its face. "But if you did, we'll get you another one just as nice."

"I don't think there is another one this nice. I'd like to save it if I could."

"Then that's what we'll do. Nora, can you see my bag anywhere? We need to call the vet's office and let them know we'll be bringing Jim in."

Nora picked her way across the debris to me, blood seeping from a couple of cuts on her arms. She started to search the area, froze, then spun around and faced where the nave used to be. The twisted metal and wood and stone were now reduced to nothing more than a gaping hole that spread from the floor up part of a back wall. Tipene and Gabriel were carrying Maata, smeared with blood and dust, to the nearest pew. Drake shouted orders to Kostya and István, the dragons calling back and forth as they investigated the ruined part of the chapel.

"Ash?" Jim's breathing was raspy and labored. "Don't tell anyone, but I think I'm a little bit scared. You're not going to leave me, are you?"

"No, I won't leave you," I told it, my tears making little wet marks on its filthy coat. "You don't have to be scared. I'm not going to let anything happen to you."

"Aisling, we have a problem," Nora said quietly, still staring toward the nave.

Jim hiccuped a couple of times, its eyes rolling back in its head.

Anguish overwhelmed me as I watched him fight. I knew in my head that it was a demon, not a dog, but my heart told me that my friend was dying before my eyes.

"Noooo!" I wailed, as its body twitched, then went limp. "Goddamn it Jim, I order you to not die!"

"Aisling, you must come with me."

Nora's voice pierced my sobbing as I clutched Jim's head, bawling into its neck.

"Jim's dead," I managed to get out, my body racked with grief so profound, I thought it would consume me.

"Aisling!" A sharp stinging blow to my face brought me out of the grief for a moment. I stared at Nora in stark disbelief. "Jim isn't dead. It can't die. You can summon it again once it picks a new form. Aisling, think! Jim is a demon! They cannot die! Its body is broken, that's all."

I looked down at the furry black form and saw the truth of what she was saying. The body wasn't all of Jim . . . it was the outer shell, nothing more.

"We must go. Drake! Do not go in there! Something terrible has happened," Nora urged.

"Jim is going to be so pissed," I said slowly, allowing

Nora to pull me to my feet. As I spoke the words, rage filled me, rage at whoever would do something so heinous as to arrange for a bomb to go off where innocent people and demons could be harmed.

Fire broke out around me.

"Come," Nora said, taking my hand and urging me down the aisle toward the gaping hole. "We are needed."

Her words penetrated the dense fog of my fury. I stumbled down the aisle after her, mentally squelching the fires I had inadvertently lit. "Needed? How?"

"Can't you feel it?" she asked, skirting where Gabriel was working over Maata.

"Is she going to be OK?" I asked him, cringing at the sight of Maata's injuries.

"Yes. Dragons are strong," he said, giving me a weak smile. "Maata is the strongest of us all."

I nodded and followed after Nora as she skirted a pile of debris and stepped over what remained of a mostly destroyed wall.

"What are you doing here?" Drake asked, crouched at the hole in the floor. He was clearly planning on jumping down into it. "I told you to stay back where it was safe."

"In about thirty seconds, this church is going to be filled with imps, demons, and who knows what else," Nora said, taking off her stained suit jacket.

His eyes widened as his gaze moved to me.

"Jim was crushed by one of the benches," I told him, tears still sticky on my cheeks.

"You will get it back," he said, before turning to Nora. "A portal has opened?"

"Yes. A very old one, by the feel of it. I will need Aisling to help me seal it."

"It's too dangerous. Kostya is down there now. He says there is an old crypt below the chapel."

"I can't do this alone," Nora said, rummaging in her bag. She pulled out a small pink flashlight that she tucked into her shirt pocket before squatting on the edge of the hole.

"But . . . oh, god, Nora, there wasn't time to tell you. I can't help you," I wailed, my heart breaking even more. "I wish to god I could, but I can't!"

"Don't be ridiculous. I know you've not sealed a portal on your own before, but—"

"No, it's not that!" I looked at Drake, his lovely eyes blurred as my own filled with tears again. "I would help you if I could, but I'm not a Guardian anymore!"

"You're what?" she asked, shaking her head abruptly. "We do not have time for this. There are only a few minutes before the seal on that portal is breached, and then all hell will break loose. Literally!"

"I disavowed being a Guardian!" I yelled, clutching her arm and shaking it so she'd understand. "That was the sacrifice that Bael demanded. Don't you see? I'm not a Guardian anymore! I can't help you!"

"Don't be ridiculous! No one can make you stop being a Guardian. It's something you're born to do! Vows have nothing to do with it."

I thought my head would explode with astonishment. "They . . . can't? Then why would Bael—"

"He's a demon lord," she snapped, swinging her legs over the edge.

Drake jumped down into the hole. It was about twelve feet deep, but he called up for her to ease herself down to his grasp.

"But . . ."

"If you aren't a Guardian, how did you know the bomb

was here? You sensed it long before I did, Aisling. You were born a Guardian, and you'll be a Guardian to the end of your days. Now please, I do not have the abilities you have. You *must* help me!"

The truth washed over me in a cold wave, leaving me scrambling after her. Drake stood on a stone tomb, grabbing my legs as I slid myself down into the hole.

"I do not like this," he said, helping me down off the tomb and onto a debris-covered floor.

"I have a torch," Nora said. "This way, Aisling!"

I touched a small cut on his cheek. "I know. But I can't leave Nora alone. I am a Guardian, after all."

His fingers squeezed mine in acknowledgement as we followed the bobbing light. Kostya emerged from a side passage, taking up the rear.

"This is not a good situation," he said.

"We will do the best we can," Drake answered.

A feeling of dread seemed to leach off the walls and into my pores as we passed tomb after tomb, many of them partially broken, bones scattered across the floor. A faint glow of light pierced the darkness ahead, the weak circle from Nora's flashlight jerking before it came to an abrupt stop.

"Oh, dear," I heard her say.

Drake's fingers tightened as he pulled me behind him. Kostya pushed his way past us both, his silhouette blocking most of the soft yellow light that seemed to pour out of a small doorway cut into the stone.

"Chuan Ren," Kostya said, moving aside when Drake gave him a shove.

The name hung on the air for a moment. All my anger, all my frustration, all my sorrow and rage came back to me at the sight of the woman standing across a small room lit with portable camp lights.

She was behind this. She had killed Jim's form. She had blown up a chapel full of innocent people in her attempt to destroy us. And she would not stop until she succeeded.

In the middle of the floor lay a circle created from dusty beige stone, its carvings so obliterated with time that they were almost impossible to make out, but I knew that what I was looking at was a sealed portal. But the seal on this one had been cracked, a piece of a stone lid from one of the tombs lying across it, no doubt knocked there by the force of the explosion above. A greenish black light glowed outward through the cracks, gaining strength with every passing second.

Beyond it, seven people stood. Chuan Ren was flanked on either side by three dragons—none of whom was her mate, I noted absently. I felt oddly relieved—I kind of liked Li, despite the fact that his mate was a homicidal maniac.

"You found us at last," Chuan Ren said, glancing at her watch. "Seven minutes. I had expected you to find me in two."

"I had other things of importance to concern me," Drake said with deceptive mildness. I knew he was mad as hell. Even behind him, I could feel how tense and on edge he was, as if he was poised to attack.

"This portal's seal has been compromised," Nora said, stepping forward to wave at the broken stone circle. "I must seal it immediately or it will be opened permanently."

Chuan Ren smiled at Nora, pulling out two wicked-looking curved swords. "I think not, Guardian. A portal right here will suit me very well."

"Why?" I asked, squeezing between Kostya and Drake so I could see the seal better. Nora was right—the feeling of dread was coming from the portal, and it was increasing greatly with each breath I took. It was clearly about to break, and when it did . . . I refused to think of how many people would die in London alone if dark beings could pass through it at will. "Why do you want a portal opened? It can't harm the green dragons."

Her red lips curved into a cruel smile. "It can harm you, Aisling Grey."

"I'm immortal," I reminded her.

"You *can* be killed."

"All I have to do is seal the portal. If not now, at some later date."

Her smile widened. "I heard you were no longer a Guardian. How will you seal it?"

"Been talking to Bael, have you? Well, you heard wrong," I answered, giving her a cold little smile of my own. "I'm still a Guardian, and I'm very, very angry. And guess who I'm angry at?"

She tossed her head. "You are nothing."

"I have told you before, Chuan Ren—you will address me, and not my mate," Drake said as he moved to my side. "She has nothing to do with what is between us. Threats to her are meaningless."

"Everything is going to be meaningless unless Aisling and I close this portal. You may argue all you want, but I have a job to do." Nora took two steps forward and lifted both hands, clearly about to start the sealing process.

Two of the red dragons jumped forward, their blades flashing. Kostya leaped into action, throwing himself in front of Nora as the dragons descended.

"Seal it," Drake commanded as he, too, ran forward. "Chuan Ren! We will settle this here and now! Meet me body to body!"

She laughed, her eyes glowing with a red light that never

failed to give me the willies. "Do you think I will be so easily beaten as the last time you challenged me, Drake?"

"This ends now," he said, removing his tux jacket.

I didn't have time to do more than draw a ward of protection on him as Chuan Ren laughed again and tossed him one of the blades she was holding. "Yes, I believe it will end now. I will greatly relish destroying you, as well as your mate and your unborn child."

Drake snarled something and lunged toward her, the force of their blades meeting generating a tiny blue spark.

The other four dragons started toward me, but I was ready for them.

"Effrijim, I summon thee in whatever form is handy!" I yelled, my hands drawing lightning-fast binding wards.

The four dragons snarled as, at my feet, a small Scottish terrier appeared.

"Jim?" I asked, momentarily taken aback.

Familiar eyes looked up at me, easing the pain that had held my heart in such a tight grip. "Fires of Abaddon, Ash! I wasn't done picking a form! I was just looking at this one! Oh, man, I'm a *midget*!"

28

"Attack!" I ordered Jim, pointing at the four writhing dragons.

It stared at me in horror. "Are you kidding? Attack with what? My stubby little teeth? I can nip at their ankles, if you think that will help."

Drake spat out an oath as he leaped on top of a tomb, blood spilling out of a cut across his chest. Chuan Ren followed him, screaming something unintelligible.

"Oh, for god's sake, why didn't you pick a Great Dane or something?" I yelled, running over to slap a binding ward on one of the two dragons who were beating the crap out of Kostya. Nora slammed a piece of stone down on the other one's head, causing him to reel backwards.

"We must seal it, Aisling," she cried, closing her eyes and starting to sketch the series of wards of adjournment that were used to seal portals.

"I don't care what you do, just do something!" I ordered Jim, opening the door in my mind as a piece of the stone seal exploded upward. Imps, small, orange in color, and accompanied by a repulsive smell, started to pour out of the broken seal.

Jim bounded over, snarling as it attacked the imps.

Behind me, a man shouted, a dark figure flashing past me

as István leaped over Jim and the imps, tackling the four-
some who I feared were about to break out of the binding
ward. Wards don't last as long on dragons as they do on people, and mine had been hastily drawn.

Pál raced into the room, glanced quickly at Nora and me,
and took in the sight of Drake leaping from tomb to tomb as
he fought Chuan Ren, their blades flashing in the light of the
lamps, and Kostya doing battle with the other two dragons.
He gave a yell and joined the fray with István just as the
ward gave free.

I tried desperately to clear my mind of the chaos around
us, focusing on the acts needed to seal the portal. Another
chunk of the seal exploded, leaving a hole in it about two
feet across.

"Ash, I'm gonna need some help here," Jim yelled, its
body covered in imp blood as it attacked the fresh wave of
tiny orange beings.

I pulled on Drake's fire and blasted the entrance of the
portal with it, incinerating the imps and stopping their flow
for a moment.

Nora drew wards of adjournment, but as soon as they
were drawn, they dissolved into nothing.

"What's wrong?" I yelled across the portal to her.

"This portal is too old. It has too much power. My wards
aren't strong enough. I fear we're going to have to call for
help with it."

"You go get help. I'll try to keep it contained until you get
back," I said grimly.

She nodded, racing past me and out the door.

I closed my eyes for a moment as I gathered up every
negative emotion I'd felt in the last few weeks. The attacks
by the red dragons, Fiat's evil plots, Kostya's stubborn insis-
tence, the pain Bael had deliberately caused me, and the

thankfully brief grief of losing Jim all roiled together in my gut, churning within me until I allowed it to merge with Drake's fire.

"Ash! It's going to blow!" Jim cried, shaking an imp until the little form hung limp in its jaws. "You're gonna have to seal it now!"

The remainder of the seal exploded upward with a tremendous blast, sending me staggering backwards.

"Mate!" Drake bellowed.

"I'm all right!" I yelled back at him as he twisted just in time to avoid a beheading. "Just take care of her!"

The clash of their swords merged into the chaos of noise from the dragons as they fought around us. I stared with horror at the black abyss that lay open at my feet and knew with absolute conviction that Nora would not make it back in time.

I had to seal the damn thing.

Imps leaped out of the portal, singed and blackened by the dragon fire, their teeth needle sharp as they snapped at my legs.

I had to seal the damn thing now!

"Need a little help here," Jim snarled, its teeth clamping shut on another imp.

"István!" Pál shouted, going down under a pile of red dragons that suddenly appeared at the door of the crypt.

I pulled hard on Drake's fire, blasting the portal just as a demon stuck its head out.

"Aisling, close it!" Jim cried.

Behind me, Kostya, István, and Pál flung themselves forward at the incoming red dragons. I didn't wonder at Kostya helping to fight them; I didn't have time to do anything but focus on keeping the wave of incoming horror from escaping the portal.

It wouldn't work. I wasn't strong enough. I couldn't do this without the dark power.

"Like hell I can't," I growled at my doubts, spreading wide my arms and yelling at the top of my lungs, *"Fettered and fastened, I bury you deep!"*

"Oh, man, you've been reading the Merseburg Incantations," Jim said, spitting out a bit of imp. "That's kind of old, Ash."

"This portal is old. It will recognize the power of the binding. *Blood bound to stone, so you will keep!*"

The red dragons swarmed over Pál and István. Kostya was using one of their swords against them, but he was quickly being overwhelmed.

Drake shouted as Chuan Ren knocked him backwards, leaving him vulnerable.

I flung a fireball at her, knowing it wouldn't do her any damage, but it contained enough power to upset her balance. She spun around toward me, screaming at her men.

"The portal!" I yelled above the cacophony to Drake. "Come to the portal! *The red sins of man to my fire be bound!*"

"Arrrrrrgh!" Jim screamed as it went down in a wave of imps. "Not again!"

"Darkness below; life above will resound!"

Three red dragons leaped toward me. I flung a binding ward at them and jumped across the portal to the far side.

"They're going for Aisling!" Kostya shouted as he fell under a wave of dragons.

I hadn't been sure if Drake had heard me or not, but at Kostya's cry, he screamed with rage, a noise that sounded more like the roar of an enraged animal than anything a human could make.

He threw a handful of dirt at Chuan Ren's face, vaulted

to the top of a tomb, and leaped over the heads of the struggling dragons to land a few feet away.

"The portal!" I yelled, pointing at it.

The dragon fire was dying away. Behind it, dark forms writhed, and I knew that I had a matter of seconds before they would burst out.

He nodded and twisted sideways, anticipating Chuan Ren's attack. She leaped off the same tomb he had used, but he was several inches taller than her. He grabbed her in midair, spinning them both sideways as he flung himself to the ground.

Chuan Ren screamed as she fell into the portal.

"Bone to bone, blood to blood, fire to life, so are you sealed!" I shouted, my voice hoarse as I drew one last ward on the portal. The instant the sentence left my lips, a crack of thunder exploded around us, the shock wave knocking everyone backwards.

Echoes of the explosion rang in my ears, leaving me disoriented and confused for several seconds, but at last the various noises resolved themselves into separate sounds, most of them recognizable.

"Kincsem! Aisling!"

I opened my eyes to the glorious sight of Drake's concerned face, bloodied, battered, but whole. "Did it work?"

"The portal is sealed. Do not move. You could be injured. Do you hurt anywhere?"

"Yeah," I said, shifting to the side. "It's my back. There's something . . . I think . . . oh, my god! I landed on an imp!"

Drake didn't even grimace as I wiped my impy hand on his sleeve. "Do not try to sit up. You could have injuries."

I laughed, much to Drake's shock. "Sweetie, I'm a tough cookie. It's going to take more than being knocked onto an imp . . . ew! A pile of imps! Oh, my god, my whole back is covered in imp goo! Argh!"

"Be thankful they were there," he answered, frowning as I got to my feet. "They cushioned the force of your landing. I don't like you moving before a doctor can see you."

"I'm fine. I wouldn't move if something felt wrong, but nothing hurts except the thought of my back being covered in imp guts."

He frowned again at me. I kissed the tip of his nose, my back twitching at the uncomfortable wetness. "I'm not going to look, I'm not going to look," I muttered, then immediately had to look.

I don't know how many imps there were, but they were squashed flat into an Aisling-shaped mound, the sight of which I doubted I'd soon forget.

"I'd demand a shower, but I guess we have a few dragons to take care of," I said as he helped me over a chunk of fallen tomb. To my amazement, the room was empty of red dragons. "Where did they all go?"

Drake understood what I was asking. "They left as soon as they saw Chuan Ren go into the portal."

"You're kidding! They just turned tail and ran?"

He shrugged. "My dragons would not run if I fell, but the red dragons . . . they are different."

"Bunch of weenies," I muttered, taking a quick look around to assess the damage.

Pál sat next to István, whose arm hung at an unnatural angle. Kostya stood at the portal, an odd expression on his face.

"You threw Chuan Ren into Abaddon," he said finally. "You sealed her in there."

"It seemed like too good an opportunity to miss," I said as Drake and I picked our way over to the portal. I looked with no little amount of pride at the stone circle, once again intact, the wards glowing with faint golden auras. "Two birds with one stone, if you'll excuse the unintentional pun. I'd say I'm sorry that it messes up your plans for getting into the weyr, Kostya, but to be perfectly honest, I'm not at all sorry. I don't know if Abaddon can hold Chuan Ren, but assuming it does, I'm thrilled that she's out of our hair."

Gabriel appeared at the door, Tipene at his side. "Are you all right? There was a horrible explosion—half the chapel came down."

"Is Maata all right?" I asked, concerned.

"Yes, we had moved her out before the second wall came down. What has been happening here?"

He and Tipene gawked at the site of destruction.

"I had to close a portal. Chuan Ren kind of got in the way of it and . . . er . . . fell in."

His gawking changed to an outright goggle of astonishment. "She *what*?"

"It's a bit of a long story—"

"One which you will tell later. Sit," Drake ordered, pointing to a convenient piece of stone.

"Sweetie, I'm fine!"

"Sit!"

I sat, smiling to myself as he quickly explained what had happened to Gabriel. I smiled through the quick examination he insisted Gabriel conduct on me, and I was still smiling when, a half hour later, we made our way out of the crypt and up into the relatively fresh air of London.

Nora met us as we skirted the destroyed chapel. Emergency crews had the area cordoned off, but several ambulances were pulled up next to the remains of the building.

"Have you seen Paula and my uncle?" I asked Nora as she rushed toward me. A familiar man was at her side.

Evidently Nora had called in the bigwigs. "Are they all right?"

"Your family is fine," she said, giving me a hug. "Everyone is. Rene got everyone away from the church before the first bomb blew. I had no idea there was a second one, but I can't tell you how worried I was that it had . . . but you're here, and now I'm going to embarrass us both by weeping."

"You're not going to be the only one," I said, tearing up as I hugged. Drake murmured something about being right back and went to help Pál take István to the ambulance.

I smiled at the man next to Nora. "I'm sorry, Mr. Battiste, you're bound to think us a couple of silly women."

"On the contrary, my opinion of both of you holds nothing but admiration. Am I correct in thinking that the bomb has temporarily blocked the portal?"

I shook my head. "That wasn't a second bomb. It was the reverb from the portal sealing."

His brown eyes widened slightly at my words. Nora gasped. "Aisling, you didn't!"

"Yeah. I used a variation on the Merseburg Incantations. I figured if the portal was so old that normal wards and spells wouldn't work on it, then something with a bit more age might. And it worked!"

"Good lord," she said, glancing at the head of the Guild.

He was silent for a moment, his eyes examining me carefully. My happy glow of success faded as I wondered if I had done something horribly wrong.

"I wish to be sure I understand the situation completely. You closed the portal?"

"No. I sealed it. There's a difference, right? Closing means it can be opened again from the Abaddon side, and sealing means it can't?"

They both nodded.

"OK," I said, relieved. "I was worried I had it wrong. The portal is sealed. The big round stone seal that sat on top of it was reforged when I spoke the incantation. I tossed on a couple of wards just to give it a little extra oomph, and they were there when I left."

"You *sealed* the portal," Caribbean Battiste repeated.

"Yes. I have a horrible feeling that you're going to tell me I've done something wrong. Wasn't I supposed to seal it?"

"No," he answered. My heart fell.

He shook his head. "I misspoke. Yes, you should have sealed it, but no, you should not have been *able* to seal it. You were an apprentice when you left the Guild. Am I correct in thinking you've had no formal training in the care of portals?"

"You are correct. There was no time for me to do more than show her the portal I guard," Nora said. There was a glint of laughter in her eyes, and something else, something warm and fuzzy that looked a whole lot like pride.

"I've been through a lot lately," I told him, suddenly wanting to be near Drake. "I guess it all just kind of came together. If you'll excuse me, I've got a wyvern to reassure."

"You have a wyvern to wed," a voice said behind me.

Drake smiled. Like the hand he held out to me, he was bloodied and filthy, his shirt dark red with blood from various slashes across his chest. Next to him stood Gabriel, less damaged but just as dirty.

"I think maybe we're going to have to wait on the wedding idea. I don't think I can mind-push Paula again without driving the poor woman insane, and it's going to take her a long, long time to forgive me for the last attempt."

"We will work that out later. Right now we have a wedding to attend."

I looked at the destroyed mess of a chapel. "Uh . . ."

"I never told you what I did before I was made wyvern, did I?" Gabriel asked, his dimples dimpling like crazy. "I was ordained in several faiths, any one of which would allow me to marry you two."

My laughter startled a nearby pigeon that had settled on a mound of debris. The bird flew into the air, flapped around us a few times, then resettled itself and watched with bright, interested eyes.

Drake raised his eyebrows. "Shall we?"

"Hell, yes! There's no way I'm going to wait for another wedding."

We found a relatively quiet corner, one that was momentarily empty of the emergency crews, police, and bystanders who milled around the remains of the chapel. There, covered in dirt, blood, and imp guts, perched as best we could on a pile of rubble and debris, with only Nora and Caribbean Battiste as witnesses, Drake and I were finally married.

"Congratulations," Nora said a minute later when the quick ceremony was over, a delighted look on her face.

"Mazel tov," said Caribbean Battiste, beaming.

Gabriel's dimples flashed warmly.

It was Drake who wholly held my attention. His eyes were filled with love as he smiled down at me. "Happy now?"

"Yes. But I could be *more* happy," I said, rubbing a smudge of dirt off his cheek, laughing at the surprised look that flashed in the depths of his emerald eyes. "The imp goo is starting to dry and is itching like crazy. Take me home, husband."

"I can't believe you got married without me!"

"I've apologized a dozen times already, Jim. I'm sorry I didn't summon you so you could see us married, although to be honest, it took all of two minutes, and then the police descended on us, and Drake dragged me off to see my doctor."

"I can't believe you sealed the portal without me!"

"Yeah, well, Nora seems to think that means something, but you know, I think it's all part of being a Guardian. And speaking of that, is it wrong, I wonder, to hope Chuan Ren is harassing the hell out of Bael?"

Jim lolled over on its back and presented a hairy belly to be rubbed. "I can't believe you were covered in imp gore, and I missed it. Hey, what do you think of my package? Is it bigger than the old one? I think it is. I gotta remember to tell Cecile I got a new form, in case she notices the difference between this one and the last."

I obligingly scratched Jim's belly and purposely did not look at its nether parts. "I'm just glad you went with another Newfie. I don't think I could have gotten used to you as any other dog."

"Newfies rock," it said, kicking its back legs when I hit a ticklish spot. "Hey, Drake. Hey, Uncle Damian."

My uncle made a face at Jim as he entered the living room on Drake's heels. "Does he . . . it . . . have to call me that?"

"Aww, I think it's cute," I said, grabbing my pillow and down comforter and scooting a few feet down the couch so Drake could sit next to me. He hauled me over his lap, tucking the blanket around my legs.

"How do you feel?" he asked, a familiar glint in his eyes.

"Fine. Better than fine, perfect. Which the doctor confirmed, so you can stop treating me like an invalid."

A little tendril of smoke drifted out of one of his nostrils. I pursed my lips and blew a perfect heart-shaped ring of fire.

"You've been practicing," he said, admiring it.

"That's not the only thing I've been practicing," I answered with a wicked wiggle of my eyebrows.

Passion, love, and interest all came to life in his eyes.

"Oh, yeah, it's gonna be steamy jungle lovin' time," Jim
said, rolling over.

"Out!" I told it, nibbling on Drake's lower lip as I pointed
over his shoulder to the door.

"Oh, man! I missed all the other good stuff—you can't
make me miss this, too!"

"Out!"

Jim grumbled all the way to the door. "Fine. Be that way.
But I'm going to call Amelie and talk to Cecile, and you'd
better not complain at all about the phone charges! When I
think of what I went through for you . . . losing a perfectly
good form, although I gotta admit, having a bigger package
is going to rock . . ."

The door closed on the demon's comments.

"I thought I'd check in before I left, but I see there is
nothing to concern myself about," Uncle Damian said, his
voice gruff, but as near a smile as I've ever seen on his face.
"I take it there is no word on that red wyvern?"

"No." The light in Drake's eyes dimmed a bit. "We don't
know for sure what has happened—the sept has called a
conclave in Beijing. I'm assuming it's to name a new
wyvern, but we won't know for certain until one of them
contacts the weyr."

Uncle Damian nodded. "That porn star—he's gone to
ground, too?"

"Ugh. Fiat," I said, sliding my arms between Drake and
the couch. "No one's heard from him, although he's apparently convinced almost half the blue sept that he is the rightful leader. Bastian is having a real struggle coping, but he
seems confident that he'll be able to pull them back together.

And now that Drake has formally re-mated me, I don't have to worry that Fiat will try to reclaim me."

"Good," Uncle Damian said.

"That leaves only Kostya as the remaining troublesome dragon, and he . . ." I glanced at Drake. "Well, despite everything, he's going to go forward with his plan to gain an official spot at the weyr table."

"Will you support him?" Uncle Damian asked Drake.

His hands were warm under the blanket, stroking my thigh. "I would like to think that our septs will once again support one another, but much of that depends on Kostya."

Uncle Damian was silent for a moment. I knew he wasn't any too fond of Kostya, despite the fact that he'd helped us with the red dragons, and I expected he was just keeping quiet out of respect for Drake's feelings, but he surprised me when he said finally, "Give him time. He's still suffering from being imprisoned. I did a spell as a POW—you never really forget that. He may come around yet."

"That is my hope," Drake agreed.

"Yes. Well." Uncle Damian looked vaguely embarrassed and cleared his throat. "I'll be on my way. I'm glad to see you so happy, Aisling. Drake, if you don't take care of my girl, you'll have me to answer to."

"He'll have *me* to answer to, and that's a whole lot scarier," I told my uncle, kissing the cheek he leaned down to present. "Call me when you get home so I know your flight landed OK."

He nodded. Drake started to move me off his lap in order to see my uncle to the door, but he waved him back. "You stay there and make sure my niece is as well as she says she is."

"You'll come and visit us to see the baby, won't you?" I called after him.

"Wouldn't miss it. Be well, Aisling."

"Love you," I called, covering Drake's ear so I wouldn't deafen him. "Now then, husband mine, I believe you were going to give me a thorough examination to make sure that I was, in fact, just as delectable as you found me before the wedding?"

The fire was back in his eyes. "What form would you prefer this examination to take, *kincsem*?"

"I was thinking a full body exam, perhaps in the tub, with that spicy frankincense oil you used. What do you think of that, dragon of my dreams?"

"I don't think you're going to have the energy to dream tonight," Drake answered, hoisting me up as he got to his feet, the burn of his lips almost as hot as the burn he started within me.

"Is that a threat or a promise?" I asked, licking his lower lip.

"Both."

I smiled to myself as he carried me up the stairs to our bedroom. "Make me burn, baby. Make me burn."

Got Dragon?

Readers who enjoy the dragons are invited to stop by the official dragon Web site at www.dragonsepts.com. There you can read histories of all the septs and become a member of the sept of your choice (or multiple septs, if you so choose), bone up on your Otherworld lore via the Otherworld Encyclopedia, read the dragon FAQs, apply for membership in the prestigious Guardians' Guild, learn how to draw wards, and even join the Minion Corps.

Writing as Kate Marsh, Katie MacAlister has
a dazzling new paranormal mystery series.
Read on for a preview of the first book

Ghost of a Chance

Coming in February 2008

"Busy, honey?" My father walked into the room, carefully stepping over the fallen imp. "What's wrong with him?"

I covered the phone again. "He's having a moment. I'm really going to have to limit their soap opera consumption. They're starting to get out of hand."

"Ah, yes. Ooh, two lattes? Is one for me?"

I nodded. He took the cardboard latte cup in both hands, reaching for the cookie jar, where I kept his favorite ginger cookies.

"People like you ought to be ashamed of yourselves. I've heard all about your type—you prey on people who've lost someone, and give them false hope. I do *not* want you cleaning my house."

A beep on the phone gave me the perfect excuse to end the conversation. "I'm sure it's better if I don't. I have another call, so thanks for venting your spleen on me. Bye-bye."

"Not a client?" my dad asked as I pressed the call-waiting button.

"No, thank god. Hello?"

"Karma Marx, please."

"Speaking." I accepted the latte my father handed me.

"This is Carol Beckett, director at the Home for Innocents. I just wanted to let you know that Pixie O'Hara will be arriving this morning at ten. Please be sure to adhere to the schedule that Pixie will have with her; she's notoriously bad about keeping her counseling sessions, and Dr. Well-bottom feels most strongly that Pixie needs a firm hand in her life."

"Pixie O'Hara? I'm sorry, Ms. Beckett, but I don't have the slightest idea what you're talking about." My father flitted over to the window and began rearranging my collection of ceramic parrots.

"You *are* Karma Marx?"

"Yes." Dad moved on to the dining room, where I could see him moving around, straightening chairs.

The sound of papers shuffling could plainly be heard over the phone. "It says here that you were contacted last week about your offer to help with wayward teens."

"I'm sorry, but I wasn't. I don't know anything about it. And now isn't really a good time—"

"The notes say that the caseworker spoke with . . ." More paper shuffling. "Mr. Marx on Tuesday the seventeenth at ten twenty-three a.m. Arrangements for the custodial care of Pixie were agreed to then."

"Tuesday?" I rubbed my forehead, trying to remember where Spider had been on Tuesday. It didn't make any sense. Spider would never consent to having someone live with us, especially a troubled teen. When he'd found out I had signed up as a foster volunteer with the children's home, we'd had a huge fight, which had ended with him storming out of the house. So for him to be changing his mind without talking to me . . . A thought burst into my brain. I wrapped my hand around the bottom of the phone and leaned into the dining room. "Why the hell did you tell the local children's home that I would take one of their teens?"

"Hmm?" Dad was apparently engrossed in reshelving by height the books in the bookcase. "I have no idea what you're talking about."

"I'm not buying that at all. You're in serious trouble, buster," I said before uncovering the phone and speaking to the woman at the other end. "I'm sorry; there's been a slight mix-up. My . . . er . . . husband forgot that this is a particularly bad week for visitors, so regrettably, we—"

"The arrangements were made last week," the woman said brusquely, shoving aside my excuse. "Pixie will stay with you for a month. During that time you are to see to her general health and well-being, and make sure that she attends her counseling appointments."

"But you don't understand—"

"No, *you* don't understand!" I held the phone a few inches away from my ear at the outburst. "Arrangements were made! You cannot simply wait until the last minute and say it's not convenient! This organization is run on strict rules, and as a volunteer, you have sworn to uphold those rules."

"But—"

"I need not remind you, I'm sure, of the importance of steady, reliable volunteers who fulfill the commitments they make. For them to do otherwise would have grave repercussions."

My jaw dropped open a smidgen. "Are you threatening me?"

"Of course not. I wouldn't dream of doing anything so reprehensible. I'm simply pointing out that someone who holds the position of responsibility and respect that you hold with the Akashic League should think long and hard before she endangers that position. Especially someone who is working off wergeld."

"Son of a—" I bit off the oath, grinding my teeth. She had me by the short and curlies, and I suspected she knew that very well. My job with the League was not one I held by desire, but it was better than the alternative, something that anyone who knew my history, as this woman did, would be aware of. I was trapped, good and proper; I had absolutely no choice but to continue working for the League, but there was going to be hell to pay if Spider discovered we'd taken in a needy teen for a month or more.

I sighed. When it came down to a choice between Spider

and the League, there was only one answer. "Fine. I'll take the girl."

"I knew you'd see reason," she said with smug amusement. "Pixie will be there shortly. At the end of the month, your fitness as a foster parent will be reevaluated. Until then, good luck."

"Problems?" Dad asked as I hung up the phone.

"Just an insurmountable one, thanks to you." A little burble of frothed milk poked out the top of the latte lid. I licked it off, ignoring the patter of little feet as a flash of yellow *eek-eek*ed across the kitchen floor.

"Imp," Dad said helpfully.

"Don't you 'imp' me! How dare you pretend to be Spider on the phone! What on earth were you thinking? Spider is going to have a cow when he finds out I've taken in a teenager for a month."

"I wouldn't be so sure of that," Dad said softly, avoiding my gaze.

I took a deep breath, ignored the headache that threatened to blossom, and chewed my father up one side and down the other. By the time I was done, he was positively dancing with the need to get out of the room.

"Well, the damage is done," I said, slumping against the counter. "The girl is on her way. I have no idea what I'm going to say to Spider, though."

"You're a smart girl; you'll think of something. There's another imp," he pointed out. "You seem to have a problem with them."

I savored a sip of latte. "That's the understatement of the day. They think I'm their mother. They're like a plague. I can't seem to get rid of them. I drop them off in the woods, and they find their way back here. I take them to the beach, and they come back. I even left them in the Hoh Rain Forest . . . and the next day the whole troop of them showed up wet and covered in moss. Who ever heard of homing imps?"

He gave me a sour look. "If you wouldn't mess with powers beyond your abilities, you wouldn't have such strife."

"Not again, please, Dad, not today." I took my latte with me to the tiny dining room, which looked out on a mundane bit of backyard. The headache that had been threatening me since I'd woken up burst into glorious being. I rubbed my forehead and wondered if a handful of ibuprofen would be enough to take care of it or if I'd have to go in for the hard-core migraine meds.

"You wouldn't get those headaches if you left well enough alone," he said, gesturing toward my head. "What you're doing is wrong, Karma. Taking spirits from their natural habitats and banishing them to the Akasha is cruel. I raised you better than that."

"You didn't raise me at all," I pointed out, deciding ibu wasn't going to cut it. I snagged my purse and dug around in it until I found a prescription bottle, then washed down a couple of pills with a swig of latte.

"Now you're being pedantic," he answered, taking a stance at the head of the table, his hands on his hips. "Just because I had the foresight to realize you would be better living with your mother while you grew up is no reason to be snarky. Besides, it has nothing to do with the fact that what you are doing is wrong on many, many levels. As you well know."

"It may be wrong, but someone has to do it. Would you rather it be someone who doesn't rescue as many beings as she can? Someone who doesn't care about them at all?" I rubbed my forehead again, tired even though it was early morning.

"I'd rather no one exterminated beings at all," he said.

"Tell that to the Akashic League; they're the ones who insisted I do this job."

He was silent for a moment, his eyes sad. "How much longer until you've worked off the wergeld?"

"I told you before: I don't know. It's up to the League. And you can stop looking at me like that!"

"Like what?"

"Like I just killed your best friend."

"I'm not—"

I shoved myself to my feet, my head swimming. "You think I don't recognize that look? You're wrong there, Dad, dead wrong. I'm the one who killed her own best friend, remember?"